PHENOMENAL PRAISE FOR
NEW YORK TIMES BESTSELLING AUTHOR
SANDRA HILL
AND HER NOVELS . . .

" . . . wildly inventive and laugh-out-loud fabulous. Once again the talented Sandra Hill proves that a real hero isn't stopped by any obstacle—not even time. Viking Navy SEALs? Time travel will never be the same!"

New York Times bestselling author Christina Skye

"A singular blend of humor and romance, this breezy read will appeal to fans of Viking romances as well as mainstream historicals."

Publishers Weekly

"Fun and fast-paced . . ."

Barnes and Noble Heart to Heart Reviews

"Her books are always fresh, romantic, inventive, and hilarious."

New York Times bestselling author Susan Wiggs

Romances *by* Sandra Hill

SANDRA HILL

KISS OF TEMPTATION

A DEADLY ✖ ANGELS BOOK

AVON

An Imprint of HarperCollinsPublishers

This is a work of fiction. Names, characters, places, and incidents are products of the author's imagination or are used fictitiously and are not to be construed as real. Any resemblance to actual events, locales, organizations, or persons, living or dead, is entirely coincidental.

AVON BOOKS
An Imprint of HarperCollins*Publishers*
10 East 53rd Street
New York, New York 10022-5299

Copyright © 2013 by Sandra Hill
Excerpt from *The Pirate Bride* copyright © 2013 by Sandra Hill
ISBN 978-0-06-206463-9
www.avonromance.com

First Avon Books mass market printing: April 2013

Avon Trademark Reg. U.S. Pat. Off. and in Other Countries, Marca Registrada, Hecho en U.S.A.
HarperCollins® is a registered trademark of HarperCollins Publishers.

Printed in the U.S.A.

10 9 8 7 6 5 4 3 2 1

This book is dedicated to all my fans down on the bayou, and to all those readers everywhere who have fallen in love with my wacky Cajun folk healer, Tante Lulu. The old lady is still bopping along, matchmaking, praying to St. Jude, and generally being her outrageous self. Whoever would have thought she'd show up in a book about Viking vampire angels? On the other hand, why not? Everyone needs a Tante Lulu in their life, right?

Prologue

The Norselands, A.D. 850, where men . . . and
life . . . were always hard . . .

Ivak Sigurdsson was an excessively lustsome man.

Ne'er would he deny that fact, nor bow his head in embarrassment. In truth, he'd well earned his far-renowned
wordfame for virility. On his back. On his front. Standing. Sitting. On the bow and in the bowels of a longship.
Behind the Saxon king's throne. Deep in a cave. High in
a tree. Under a bush. On a bed. In a cow byre. Once even
with . . . well, never mind, that had been when he was
very young and on a dare and another story entirely.

He liked women. Everything about them. Not just the
sex bits. He liked their scent, the feel of their silky skin,
the allure of their secrets, the sound of their sighs and
moans, the taste of them. And women liked him, too. He
wanted them all.

You could say lust was a sixth sense for Ivak. He was
a Viking, after all.

He'd been twelve years old when, swaggering with
overconfidence, he'd tried his dubious charms on his
father's eighth concubine, who'd laughed herself into

a weeping fit afore showing him exactly which hole he should aim for. Now, twenty years and at least two hundred bedmates later—he'd stopped counting after that incident in Hedeby—there was naught he did not know about sex. Men came to him for advice all the time. Women, too.

The cold Norse winds blew outside his keep now, but he and his comrades-in-arms were warm inside as they sat before one of the five hearth fires that ran through the center of his great hall at Thorstead. Their body heat was aided by the mead they were imbibing and the satiety that comes from having tupped more than the ale barrel, and it not yet eventide.

When bored and having no wars to fight, or any other time for that matter, taking an enthusiastic maid to the bed furs was always a worthwhile pastime. Leastways, it was for Ivak. You'd think his jaded appetites would have waned by now. Instead, he found himself wanting more and more. And the things he tried these days pushed even his sensibilities for decency . . . but not enough to stop him.

And, of course, when bored and having no wars to fight, men did what men did throughout time. Drank.

In fact, Esbe, the widow of one of his swordsmen, walked among them now, refilling their horns from a pottery pitcher. When she got to him, she smiled, a small, secretive smile that Ivak understood perfectly. Women told him that he had an aura about him . . . a presence, so to speak. By leaning against a wall just so, or merely staring at them through half-slitted eyes, or gods forbid, winking at them, he sent a silent message. Here was a man who knew things.

He smiled back at Esbe, who shared his bed furs on occasion, and watched appreciatively, along with every one of his men, as she walked away from them, hips swaying from side to side.

Another thing men did when bored and having no wars to fight, and especially when drinking, was talk about women.

"Tell me true, Ivak," demanded Haakon the Horse, a name he'd been given because of a face so long he could lick the bottom of a bucket and still see over the rim, not because of other bodily attributes. Haakon was a master at swordplay if ever there was one, a soldier you'd want at your back in battle, but an irksome oaf when *drukkinn*, and he was halfway there already. "There must have been times when your lance failed to rise to the occasion. It happens to the best of men betimes."

Ivak exchanged a quick glance with his best friend, Serk the Silent, who sat beside him on the bench. Serk, a man of few words, did not need to speak for Ivak to know that he was thinking: *Here it comes!*

Ivak tapped his chin with a forefinger, as if actually giving the query consideration. He could feel Serk shaking with silent laughter. "Nay, it never has, though there have been times I've had to take a vow of celibacy to give it a rest." He cupped himself for emphasis.

"For how long?" scoffed Ingolf, his chief archer. A grin twitched at Ingolf's hugely mustached upper lip, knowing when Ivak was about to pull a jest.

"Oh, a good long time. Two days at most," Ivak admitted.

Everyone except Haakon found amusement in his jest, including Kugge, the young squire he'd been training of late. Gazing at Ivak in wonder, Kugge blurted out, "Did it hurt?"

"The celibacy or the excess?" Ivak asked, trying to keep a straight face.

A blush crept over Kugge's still unwhiskered face as he sensed having made a fool of himself.

Ivak patted Kugge on the shoulder.

Haakon glared at him, his question not gaining the results he'd wanted . . . a fight. Ivak returned Haakon's glare, his with a silent warning that Haakon thankfully heeded. Haakon stood, tossing his horn to the rushes, and stomped off, hopefully to sleep himself sober.

Ingolf took a long draught from his horn of ale, cleared his throat, and proclaimed with a chuckle, "To my mind, a man's cock is like a brass urn."

"Oh good gods!" Ivak muttered.

"How true!" Serk encouraged Ingolf and nudged Ivak with an elbow to share in his mirth.

"Now, hear me out," Ingolf said, stroking his mustache. "Everyone knows that brass needs polishing from time to time, and —"

"Mine is especially shiny these days since I got me a second wife," one of the men contributed.

Ingolf scowled at the interruption and continued, "Of course, a one-handed rub will do to ease the throb, but best it is if the polishing is done in the moist folds of a female sheath's chokehold."

"I don't understand," Kugge said to Ivak.

"'Tis a mystery," Ivak replied with dry humor.

Ingolf, who fancied himself a master storyteller, was on a roll now. 'Twas best to let him finish. "The thing about brass is that too much rubbing and it loses its luster. Even grows pits." Ingolf pretended to shiver.

"Pits? Like a peach?" Kugge whispered.

"Nay. Like warts," Ivak told the boy. "You do not want warts down there, believe you me."

"Even worse," Ingolf told Kugge, "tainted oil in the sheath can spoil all it touches. Remember that dockside whore in Jorvik." The latter Ingolf addressed to the other men. "Now that was a woman with teeth *down there*."

"She had a lot more than teeth," Serk remarked, "as many men soon learned."

"The difference, my friend, is that some cocks are solid gold." Ivak motioned a hand downward.

The other men rolled their eyes and guffawed.

"Mine is solid silver," Bjorn No-Teeth said, his lips twitching as he attempted to hide his gummy smile. "I'm thinking about having it . . . etched. Ha, ha, ha!"

Others offered their own self-assessments:

"Mine is ivory, smooth and sleek, and big as an elephant's tusk betimes. Not that I have e'er seen an elephant."

"Mine is a rock. A rock cock."

"Mine is iron, like a lance. A loooong lance."

"Holy Thor! Do not make me laugh any more lest I piss my braies."

Someone belched.

Someone else farted.

More bragging.

Ivak sighed with contentment. It was the way of men when they were alone with time to spare.

Their merriment was interrupted by the arrival of Ivak's steward announcing Vadim, the slave trader from the Rus lands, who had come from Birka before circling back home. He would probably be the last one to make it through the fjords before they were frozen solid for winter.

Ivak and Serk left the others behind as they went out to the courtyard and beyond that to an outbuilding that usually housed fur pelts. It was empty now, the goods sent to market, and cold as a troll's arse in a blizzard. He waved to a servant who quickly brought him and Serk fur-lined cloaks.

Vadim was a frequent visitor at Thorstead. As often as he dealt in human flesh, Vadim also traded in fine wines, spices, silks, and in Ivak's case, the occasional sexual oddity . . . dried camel testicles, feathers, marble phalluses, and such.

Serk joined the steward, who was examining some of the wares on display in open sacks, while Ivak, at Vadim's urging, walked to the far end of the shed.

"Come, come, see what delights I have for you, Lord Sigurdsson."

Ivak was no lord, and he recognized the obsequiousness of the title dripping from the Russian's lips, but it wasn't worth the bother of correcting him. "So, show me the delights."

Three men were roped together against one wall. Nothing delightful here. An elderly man that Vadim identified as a farmer from the Balkans. With the rocky landscape at Thorstead, Ivak had no need of a farmer and certainly not a graybeard. Next was a boyling with no apparent skills; Ivak passed on him, as well. The third was a young man that Ivak did want . . . a blacksmith's apprentice. He and Vadim agreed on a price, although Ivak did not like the angry exchange of words in an undertone between this last man and Vadim that the trader dismissed as of no importance.

Next came the best part. The delight part. The women. Ivak always enjoyed checking over new female slaves. Serk, who had finished examining the household wares, joined him.

The five women were not restrained, but they were shivering with cold, or mayhap a bit of fear, not knowing that Ivak would be a fair master. They shivered even more when Vadim motioned for them to disrobe. While Ivak pitied them this temporary chill, he was not about to buy a piece of property without full disclosure. Once he'd purchased a prettily clothed slave in Jorvik only to find she had oozing pustules covering her back, from her neck to her thighs.

"I see several you would like," Serk whispered at his side.

Ivak agreed, a certain part of his body already rising in anticipation.

The first was clearly pregnant, normally a condition that would preclude his purchase—there were enough bratlings running about the estate, including some of his own—but he had a comrade-in-arms who had a particular taste for sex with breeding women, so he motioned for her to join the young blacksmith at the other end. With an appreciative nod of thanks at her good fortune, she quickly pulled on her robe and drew a threadbare blanket over her shoulders.

"This one is a Saxon, a little long in the tooth, but an excellent cook," Vadim said.

"I already have a cook," Ivak demurred.

"Ah, but does she make oat cakes light as a feather and mead fit fer the gods?" the heavy woman of middle years, whose sagging breasts reached almost to her waist, asked in Saxon English. The Norse and Saxon languages were similar and could be understood to some extent by either. She'd obviously got the meaning of his remark.

Ivak liked a person with gumption, male or female, and he grinned, ordering her to join the other two. Besides, a Viking could never have enough good mead.

All the thrall bodies were malodorous from lack of bathing . . . for months, no doubt . . . but this next one—an attractive woman of thirty or so years—had a particular odor that Ivak associated with diseased whores. He gave Vadim a disapproving scowl and moved to the fourth woman.

"This one is a virgin," Vadim said. "Pure as new snow. And a skilled weaver."

Ivak arched a brow with skepticism as he circled the shivering female who had seen at least twenty winters. He doubted very much that a female slave could remain intact for that many years. Still, she would be a welcome diversion. New meat for jaded palates. Not to mention, he had lost a weaver this past summer to the childbirth fever. He nodded his acceptance to Vadim.

And then there was the fifth woman . . . a girl, really. No more than sixteen. Red hair, above and below. Ah, he did love a redheaded woman. Fiery, they were when their fires were ignited, as he knew well how to do. He could not wait to lay his head over her crimson fluff and . . .

He smiled at her.

She did not smile back. Instead, tears streamed down her face.

He ran his knuckles over one pink, cold-peaked nipple, then the other.

She actually sobbed now, and stepped back as if in revulsion.

The tears didn't bother him all that much, but the resistance did. Thralldom was not easy for some to accept, but she would settle into her role soon. They usually did. They had no choice. Not that he would engage in rape. Persuasion was his forte.

But wait. She was staring with seeming horror at something over his shoulder.

Ivak heard the growl before he turned and saw the smithy tugging to be free from the restraints being held by both Vadim and his assistant. At the same time, the young man was protesting something vociferously in what sounded to Ivak like the Irish tongue.

"What is amiss?" Ivak demanded of Vadim.

"He's her husband, but you are not to worry—"

Ivak put up a halting hand. "I do not want any more married servants. Too much trouble." He started to walk away.

"You could take one of them," Vadim offered.

Ivak paused. The woman's skin *was* deliciously creamy

and her nether fleece *was* tempting. "I'll take her. You keep him."

The husband didn't understand Ivak's words as he spoke, but Vadim must have explained once Ivak and Serk left the building and headed back to the keep because his roar of outrage would be understood in any language.

"Is that wise, Ivak?" Serk asked. "Separating a man and his mate?"

"It happens all the time, my friend, and do you doubt my wisdom in choosing good bedsport over good metalwork?"

Serk laughed but at the same time shook his head at Ivak with dismay. In some ways Serk had gone soft of late, ever since he'd wed Asta, the daughter of a Danish jarl. Six months and Serk was still besotted with the witch. Little did he know that Asta was spreading her thighs hither and yon. Ivak knew that for a fact because he'd been one of those to whom she'd offered her dubious charms. He would have told his friend, but he figured Serk would grow bored soon enough, and then it would not matter. As long as she did not try to pass off some other man's bratling as his own. When Ivak had mentioned that possibility to Asta, she'd informed him that she was joyfully barren. That was another thing of which Serk was uninformed.

And women claimed men were the ones lacking in morals!

That night he swived the Irish maid, and she was sweet, especially after having been bathed. It was not an entirely satisfying tup, though. The girl was too willing. He kept seeing her husband's face as he was dragged away. No doubt Ivak's distaste would fade eventually, but tonight he had no patience for it, especially as she begged him to be permitted to stay. Instead, he sent her away after just one bout of bedsport, wanting no more of her for now.

He drank way too much mead then, which only increased his foul mood. That was the only excuse he could find for his seeing Asta slinking along one of the hallways and motioning him with a forefinger to come to her bedchamber. Another round-heeled woman with the morals of a feral cat. He knew for a fact that Serk was serving guard duty all night.

Mayhap he should tup Serk's wife and then explain to him in the nicest possible way on the morrow what a poor choice he had made in picking this particular maid for his mate. He would be doing his friend a favor, he rationalized with alehead madness.

Asta was riding him like a bloody stallion a short time later, and while his cock was interested, he found himself oddly regretting his impulsive capitulation. Bored, he glanced toward the door that was opening, and there stood Serk, staring at them with horror. This was not the way he'd wanted his friend to discover his wife's lack of faithfulness.

"Ivak? My friend?" Serk choked out.

"I can explain. It's not what you think." Well, it was, but there was a reason for his madness. Wasn't there?

At the stricken expression on Serk's face, Ivak shoved Asta off him, ignoring her squeal of ill-humor, and jumped off the bed. By the time he was dressed, his good friend was gone. And Asta was more concerned about having her bedplay interrupted than the fact that her husband had witnessed her adultery. To Ivak's amazement, she actually thought they would resume the swiving.

Ivak searched for more than an hour, to no avail. It was already well after midnight and most folks, except for his housecarls, were abed. His apology and explanation to Serk would have to wait until morning. Without a doubt, Serk would forgive him, once he understood that

Asta was just a woman, and a faithless one at that. Oh, Ivak did not doubt that Serk would be angry, and Ivak might even allow him a punch or two, but eventually their friendship would be intact.

Still, he could not sleep with all that had happened, and he decided to walk out to the stables to check on a prize mare that should foal any day now. What Ivak found, though, was so shocking he could scarce breathe. In fact, he fell to his knees and moaned. "Oh nay! Please, gods, let it not be so!"

Hanging from one of the rafters was Serk.

His friend had hanged himself.

What have I done? What have I done? She was not worth it, my friend. Truly, she was not. Oh, what have I done?

Ivak lowered the body to the floor and did not need to put a fingertip to Serk's neck to know that he had already passed to Valhalla. With tears burning his eyes, he stood, about to call for the stable master in an adjoining shed when he heard a noise behind him. Turning, he saw the young Irish blacksmith, husband of the red-haired maid he'd bedded, running toward him with a raised pitchfork. Vadim and his crew were supposed to depart at first light. The man must have escaped his restraints.

Before Ivak had a chance to raise an alarm or fight for himself, the man pierced his chest with the long tines of the pitchfork. Unfortunately, he used the special implement with metal tines that Ivak had purchased this past summer on a whim in the open markets of Miklagard, also known as Byzantium. Why had he not been satisfied with the usual wooden pitchforks for his fine stable? So forceful had the man's surge toward him been that he pinned Ivak into the wall.

"You devil!" the man yelled, tears streaming down his face. "You bloody damn devil! May you rot in Hell!"

He was given a choice: Hell or something like Hell . . .

"Tsk, tsk, tsk!"

Ivak heard the voice through his pain-hazed brain. *I thought I was dead. I must be dead.* Opening his heavy lids, he glanced downward, beyond the sharp tines that still pinned him to the wall, to see his life's blood pooling at his feet. *Definitely dead.* Raising his head, he saw that Serk still lay in the rushes where he'd lowered him. Apparently, neither he nor Serk had been discovered yet. Well, it would be too late for either of them now.

"Tsk, tsk, tsk!" he heard again, and this time realized that the voice came from his right side. "It is never too late, Viking."

If Ivak hadn't been dead, and if he hadn't been immobilized by a pitchfork through his heart, he would have fallen over with shock. Standing there, big as he pleased . . . and he was big, all right . . . was an angel. A big, black-haired man with widespread, snow-white wings and piercing blue eyes.

Ivak knew what angels were since he practiced both the ancient Norse religion and the Christian one, an expedience many Norsemen adopted. Apparently, he would not be off to Valhalla today with its myriad golden shields and virgin Valkyries. "Am I going to Heaven?" he asked the frowning angel.

The angel made a snorting sound of disbelief at his question. "Hardly!"

"Hell, then?" he inquired tentatively.

"Nay, but thou may wish it so."

Enough of this nonsense. Dead was dead. "Who are you?" Ivak demanded. "And how about pulling out this pitchfork?"

"Michael," the angel said, then eyeing the pitchfork, added, "Thou art certain I should do that?"

Before Ivak had a chance to reconsider, the angel . . . Michael . . . yanked it out, causing excruciating pain to envelop Ivak as he fell to the rush-covered floor, facefirst. If he were not in such screaming agony, he would have been impressed at the strength of the angel to have removed, all in one smooth pull, the tines that had not only skewered his body but had been imbedded in the wooden wall behind him, as well. Like one of Ivak's muscle-honed warriors who hefted heavy broadswords with ease, this angel was.

He realized in that instant whose presence he was in. Staggering to his feet, he panted out, "Would that be Michael the Archangel? The warrior angel?"

The angel nodded his head in acknowledgment.

"Am I dead?"

"As a door hinge."

"Is this what happens when everyone dies? An angel shows up? You show up?"

"No."

"I'm someone special? I get special attention?"

"Thee could say that."

Ivak didn't like the sound of that. "Stop speaking in riddles. And enough with the thees and thous!"

The angel shrugged. "Thou art in no position to issue orders, Viking."

He sighed deeply and tried for patience, which had to be strange. A dead person trying to be patient. "What happens now?"

"That depends on you."

More riddles!

"You are a grave sinner, Ivak Sigurdsson. Not just you. Your six brothers are equally guilty. Each of you has

committed one of the Seven Deadly Sins in a most griev-
ous fashion."

"My brothers? Are they dead, too?"

"Some are. The others soon will be."

Ivak was confused. "Which horrible sin is it that I have
committed?"

"Lust."

"Lust is a sin?" He laughed.

The angel continued to glare at him. No sense of
humor at all.

Ivak laughed again.

But not for long.

The angel raised his hand and pointed a finger at him,
causing him to be slammed against the wall and pinned
there, but this time there was no pitchfork involved.
Just some invisible bonds. "Sinner, repent!" Michael
demanded in a steely voice, "lest I send you straight to
Lucifer to become one of his minions. You will like his
pitchfork even less than the mortal one that impaled you."

"I repent, I repent," he said, though he still didn't see
how lust could be such a big sin.

"You do not see how lust can be sinful?" Michael
could obviously read his mind. The angel gaped at him
for a moment before exclaiming, "Vikings! Lackwits, one
and all!" With those words, the angel waved a hand in
front of Ivak's face, creating a cloudy screen in which he
began to see his life unfolding before him, rather the lust
events in his life.

It didn't take Ivak long to realize that not all the girls
and women had been as eager to spread their thighs for
him as he'd always thought, but most of them had. What
surprised him was the number of husbands or betrothed
who'd suffered at his hands . . . rather his cock . . . for his
having defiled their loved ones. Serk hadn't been the only
one. And babes! Who knew he'd bred so many out-of-

wedlock children . . . and how many of them lived in poverty! He would have cared for any of his whelps brought to his keep, but these were in far countries.

And then there was this past night's events . . . the thrall he'd taken to his bed furs knowing she was wed. Worst of all, his betrayal of his best friend.

He shook his head with dismay as shame overcame him. Raising his eyes to the angel, he asked, "What can I do to make amends?"

Michael smiled, and it was not a nice smile. "I thought you would never ask, Viking. From this day forth, you will be a vangel. A Viking vampire angel. One of God's warriors in the fight against Satan's vampire demons, Lucipires by name."

Ivak had no idea what Michael had just said. What was a vampire?

But then, it didn't matter because his pain-ridden body became even more pain-ridden. Even bone in his body seemed to be breaking and reforming, even his jaw and teeth, after which he hurtled through the air, outside his keep, far up into the sky. Then he lost consciousness.

When he awakened, he found himself in another keep of sorts. But it was made of stone, not wood, as Thorstead was. And the weather here was almost unbearably warm, not the frigid cold of the Norselands.

The sign over the entryway read: "Angola Prison."

But then he was whooshed through time and space to his first assignment. Prison would have been better.

One

"Petition denied!"

Gabrielle Sonnier pressed her lips together to avoid saying something she might later regret. Tucking her legal briefs into a massive leather shoulder bag, she nodded at the parole board members, when what she'd like to do was give them the finger. Right in their holier-than-thou hypocritical faces. With a defiant lift to her chin, she walked stoically out of the hearing room. You could have heard a pin drop behind her.

Putting one foot in front of the other, she walked down the hallway. Click, click, click, her high heels marked her path on the worn hardwood of the corridor until she reached the ladies' room, which was thankfully empty. Rushing into one of the far stalls, she dropped her bag to the floor and began to retch, violently. Since she hadn't eaten breakfast before leaving New Orleans this morning just after dawn, not much came up. Still, the urge to upheave went on and on until her throat felt raw with bile and her stomach cramped.

Finally, she sat down on the toilet seat and wept, a weakness she rarely allowed herself. Certainly, never in public. Being vulnerable was not allowed, not when fighting the criminal justice system in Louisiana. The vultures had been circling for years. Give them a chance and they'd peck the resistance out of her.

She'd been so sure that this hearing would be different. With good reason. She'd been promised a different outcome. Be patient, those on the other side had advised her. Lie low. Don't ruffle any feathers. Hah! Look where being a good girl had got her. She should have plucked a few damn feathers and to hell with them all!

How am I ever going to tell Leroy? He'll be devastated. Again. Not that he would show it. No, her brother was more expert than she was at putting on a brave front. She feared the pain would fester in her brother until it erupted in rage, as it did with so many inmates whose hopes were dashed over and over.

With a long sigh, she straightened and swiped at her damp eyes with a wad of toilet paper. Leaving the cubicle, she hefted her leather bag up onto the counter and proceeded to transform her appearance for her trip to Angola, where she would give her brother the news. No way was she walking into that pen of five thousand–plus men wearing a short, fitted black pin-striped suit with a silk blouse that unbuttoned just enough to show off a lace camisole underneath. And definitely no sheer hose and high heels. Once, years ago, when she hadn't been so careful with her attire, she'd seen an inmate in a hallway pull out his wiener—that's what her grandma Sonnier had always called it—and pump energetically as he watched her walk to Warden Pierce Benton's office. And it wouldn't have mattered if she was stump ugly. Being female was enough to whet the deprived appetites of long-incarcerated men.

The local press would want to interview her about the board's decision. But not today. Not when her emotions were so close to the surface.

She used a paper towel and squirt soap to wash off all her makeup before combing her hair tightly off her face and into a knot at her nape that she secured with two tortoiseshell combs. The short-sleeved, white blouse she left on, but buttoned up to the neck, over which she put a red, hip-length, cardigan-style sweater vest, which was too hot for this late August heat, but a necessity, to her mind, to camouflage her "assets," such as they were. Next, she removed her thigh-high hose and replaced her short suit skirt with a pair of loose jeans. Ratty athletic shoes completed the outfit.

She was about to leave the ladies' room when the door opened and she almost ran into Dolly Landeaux, the owner of a wholesale Creole foods business out of Lafayette and a parole board member for the past dozen years. Scanning Gabrielle's appearance, the big woman blocked her exit with her wide hips—*Dolly obviously taste-tests all her products*, Gabrielle noted snidely—and said, "Don't be disheartened, sweetie."

You two-faced bitch! "Disheartened? How about crushed?"

"You can always try again."

"Like I have for the past six years?" Gabrielle couldn't stop herself from asking. "Like Leroy did for six years before that, on his own?"

"It was close this time."

That's what you said last time, Dolly. Have you been playing me? Is this all a game for you? That's what she thought, but making an enemy of people in power wouldn't help Leroy's cause, Gabrielle decided, almost gagging as she said, "Well, thanks for all your help."

Dolly stepped aside to let Gabrielle pass, but then she

said, "Tell that brother of yours that he needs to keep his mouth shut if he ever wants to be free."

Gabrielle bristled, but she knew what Dolly referred to. Her brother was ruthless, and highly effective, in his criticism of prison officials and politicians in Louisiana. The news media loved him and were always willing to give him an outlet for his diatribes. She kept telling him to save his bombs for after he was released, but Leroy was a rage-filled man whose passion for justice was rarely tempered with diplomacy.

Odd that she referred to him as a man. For so long she'd thought of him as the sixteen-year-old boy who'd been tried and convicted as an adult for murdering their abusive bastard of a father fifteen years ago. He would have been out by now, but a boy that age was considered fair game in the prison system and he'd fought against two particularly vicious convicts who wanted him for a "love slave." One of them ended up dead, and the other claimed that Leroy had been the perp with a makeshift shiv or shank. As a result, Leroy was now serving a life sentence. Didn't matter that the convict in question had been a worthless, evil man, or that there was a question as to whether the other convict had been the one who did the crime in a fight over Leroy. In a prison like Angola, where ninety percent of the five thousand inmates would die there, they had nothing to lose.

Leroy was the reason Gabrielle became a lawyer who worked for Second Chances, a Southern version of the Innocence Project. She'd been only thirteen when Leroy had stabbed their father with a kitchen knife, repeatedly, after his usual Friday night beating of their mother and any of the kids, meaning her or Leroy, when they weren't quick enough to run and hide.

Dolly stood in the open doorway watching Gabrielle walk away. The middle-aged lady was no dummy. She knew how Gabrielle felt about her. So it was a surprise when she called out to Gabrielle, "There's someone who might be able to help you."

Gabrielle wanted to keep walking, but she owed Leroy every chance he could get. She paused and glanced back over her shoulder.

"Have you ever heard of Louise Rivard? Tante Lulu, they call her down on the bayou."

"The traiteur?" Gabrielle frowned, having no clue how a folk healer would be able to help her, and a wacky one at that, if rumors were true.

Dolly nodded, the compassionate expression on her face appearing to be genuine. "Tante Lulu knows people. She accomplishes things no one else can." She laughed and added, "Mostly due to her devotion to St. Jude, the patron saint of hopeless cases."

She and Leroy had long ago lost any belief in a Higher Power. But hopeless, they were. With a nod of thanks, the most she was willing to concede to the old bat, she said, "What have we got to lose?"

Even Vikings get the blues . . .

If prison was a microcosm of regular society, as penal authorities purported it to be, then Ivak was living in a village of idiots. And the chief idiot, Warden Pierce Benton, had just made the most outrageous demand of him.

"You want me to put together a talent show on the last night of the rodeo? Why me?"

Twice a year, Angola put on a series of prison rodeos that were open to the public. A more ludicrous, often cruel, event Ivak had never witnessed, except in the days of old Rome when they forced inexperienced slaves to go out into the Colosseum as gladiators.

"Why *not* you?" Benton inquired in a heavy South-ern drawl as he rolled an unlit cigar from one side of his mouth to the other, the whole time staring at him from behind his desk where everyone knew his swivel chair was elevated to give him extra height. The warden, who wore his Christianity on his sleeve, was not a fan of Ivak's less-than-deferential attitude, not to mention his uncon-ventional manner of dress . . . in particular, combining a clerical collar with unclergyman-like attire. But then, Ivak was not a fan of the stocky, gray-haired man who was more autocratic than some kings Ivak had known over the years. King Bork the Boar came to mind, for one. When Benton smiled, as he did now, with that big space between his front teeth, he resembled a shorter, heavier, older David Letterman, but the smile was decep-tive. Behind the amiability was a ruthless autocrat.

No one was exactly sure what or who Ivak was here at the prison. Not an inmate. Nor a clergyman, precisely, although there were chaplains and religious folks aplenty assigned to all the cellblocks and camps. Oh, he had cre-dentials, thanks to St. Michael and his secret sources, proclaiming him a former inmate chaplain from some small European country, now a nondenominational "spir-itual adviser" at Angola, but he didn't fit anyone's idea of a church minister.

Ivak knew better than most the power Benton wielded in this prison. One word from him made the difference between a man being made a trusty with a limited amount of freedom or confinement to a six-by-nine cell for life. One word from him and Ivak's "job" would be toast.

"What do you think I am . . . some kind of Simon Cowell?"

"What a great idea! Y'all can hold an *American Idol*–type competition. Maybe you'll discover a Ruben Stud-dard or Scotty McCreery right here at Angola." Benton smiled at him, but the humor never made it to his beady eyes. "See, I knew you'd be the man for the job."

"Simon Cowell is no longer with *Idol*. He moved on to *X Factor*," he informed the warden. *Or some other friggin' show. It's not as if I follow that crap.*

"Even better."

The Angola rodeos were held in the spring and the fall. That meant in a little over a month—the rodeo would start and continue each Sunday in October—the warden was expecting Ivak to have a talent show to put on.

Ivak did a mental crossing of his eyes. He could just see it now. If he rejected Big Tony Fasano in the tryouts, the convicted Dixie Mafia hit man would cut off his balls while he was sleeping . . . and eat them. Or those thugs in Camp J where the prison troublemakers were housed . . . if they tried to audition as a group and Ivak wasn't impressed, he would find himself someone's girlfriend by morning. Or they could try. Gang rape was not unheard of in this testosterone-oozing jungle, and since most of the inmates would never leave, they didn't fear the consequences. Rape didn't carry a death penalty. Besides that, death would be welcome to many of the hardened souls.

"This is about me trying to get through to Leroy Sonnier, isn't it?"

Sonnier was a model inmate who nevertheless managed to annoy just about everyone in authority at the prison with his attitude. For some reason, maybe because Ivak saw a bit of himself in the man, this particular inmate had become a challenge for Ivak to save.

Benton put a hand over his heart and made a ridiculous moue of innocence around his cigar, as if wounded that Ivak would accuse him of such tactics. "A talent show will bring more people to the rodeo." He put up a halting hand when Ivak was about to speak. "Oh, I know very well how y'all feel about the rodeo, Mistah Sigurdsson.

Dangerous, demeaning, yada, yada, yada. But the more money the rodeo brings in, the more money that can be allocated for prisoner activities. Like your religious mentoring program."

That was a load of bull, and they both knew it. Religious mentoring cost almost nothing. But the warden could single-handedly pull the plug on any of the convict programs without any justification.

"I'll agree to do it, but my way."

Benton raised his brows. "We'll see."

We'll see, all right. I'm a vampire, my good man. How would you like to lose a bucket of blood in a dark corridor one of these nights? Well, actually, he was a vampire angel, and the angel in him curbed his indiscriminate feeding, but he *could* do it. Above all, Ivak was a Viking, and the Norseman in him hated giving in to bullies like Benton. "I need to go home for a few days," he said, suddenly overcome by the oppressive atmosphere in the prison, but especially by the prison warden's presence. "I'll get started on your frickin' talent show when I get back."

Benton arched his eyes with displeasure at his swearword. If he only knew! Vangels never used the Lord's name as an expletive, but every other crude swearword was fair game. "Where exactly is home?"

This was not the first time the warden had asked him that question, which he'd managed to evade so far.

"Did I say home? I meant my fishing camp down the bayou. I don't really have a home." *Next I'll have to buy myself a fishing camp just to prove my lie. And I like fishing even less than I like swamps. Give me a nice five-star hotel in the Caribbean any day. Cool drinks topped with tiny umbrellas and bikini-clad women with no tops.*

That's why you're assigned to a prison, lackwit, he thought he heard a voice in his head say.

And actually it wasn't quite true that he didn't have a home. He and his six brothers, the VIK, considered the run-down castle in Transylvania, Pennsylvania, their headquarters, for now. That's where he teletransported himself as soon as he was outside the prison gates.

Landing in the back courtyard of the castle, he stomped into the kitchen where the cook, Lizzie Borden, was hacking apart a rack of ribs with a meat cleaver. She didn't even look up as he passed her. She must be in a mood, too. Last he'd heard, she went on strike over the vangels' obsessive appetite for pasta. There was usually a minimum of thirty vangels in residence at any one time in the twenty-five-bedroom castle that had been built by an eccentric lumber baron a century ago.

Walking over to the commercial-size fridge, he took out a container of Fake-O, the vangels' makeshift substitute for real blood, and two bottles of beer. He'd just sat down at the counter when his brother Vikar walked in and raised his eyebrows at his presence. Vikar was in charge of renovating this huge pile of stone into a livable residence. Good thing vangels didn't age. Vikar would probably still be working on the project fifty years from now, or a hundred.

"To what do we owe the pleasure of your company?" Vikar took out a bottle of dark ale for himself. If there was anything Vikings appreciated about modern times it was a good beer.

"I'm depressed."

Vikar sat down on a tall stool next to Ivak. "Vikings don't get depressed. We go out and conquer a country, or at the least go a-Viking when an ill-temper comes over us."

Miss Borden mumbled something that sounded like, "Or eat a pigload of ravioli."

"Not having a longship, and being landlocked in a prison, I'm hardly in a position to go off anywhere. The best I could manage there is a small canoe-like boat they call a *pee-row* on a trip down the alligator-infested bayous. A-Viking, it would not be." He hated the whiny tone in his own voice. When had he turned into a whiner?

"Shh!" Vikar put a fingertip to his lips. "You don't want Mike to hear you objecting to an assignment."

Mike was the rude name they'd given St. Michael. And, yes, it was unwise to protest a mission they'd been given by their celestial mentor. They would find themselves given worse. One time his brother Trond had complained about his mission to some misbegotten jungle and found himself slingshotted to ancient Rome where he was a gladiator fighting lions. A lesson learned for all of them: The more you complained, the worse the next job and the longer you lived as a vangel. Of course, the same could be said of sin.

"I know what this is about," Vikar said. "Sex."

"What's that?"

"*You* asking a question like that? The king of sex?"

"Not for a long time. Truth to tell, brother, I've been celibate for more than a hundred years." Ivak could tell that Vikar was astounded. He was, too. His brothers had seen him around women during that time, of course. He'd no doubt been touching them, or flirting. Mayhap even venturing a kiss on occasion, but what his brothers hadn't known was, that was all. No. Sex. "I've been trying to be good in hopes that Mike will give me a 'Get Out of Jail' card."

Vikar grinned.

"It's not funny."

"Oh, I think it's very funny. 'The Sexiest Man Alive . . . Ever.' And he has blue balls? They ought to put you on a magazine cover."

"Easy for you to mock me now that you are wed and have sex on tap."

"I dare you to say that in front of Alex." Alex was Vikar's wife, short for Alexandra.

"What a wench-whipped man you have become!"

"Are you referring to Alex as a wench? She will cut off your blue balls."

"Are you sure you're still a Viking?" Ivak said, basking in the pleasantness of the sunny kitchen. How different it was from the bleak place he called home these days! Even the sun failed to reach many of Angola's dismal corners. It smelled better here, too. Ivak inhaled deeply to appreciate the pleasant aroma of something baking in the oven, something chocolate, and even the bowl of apples and oranges in front of him provided their own scents.

"Have a care, Ivak. I have lopped off the heads of men for lesser insults."

"Whatever!" He took a long draw on his bottle of beer, then added, "Don't you just love that word? Can you imagine how handy such a saying would have been in our time? When King Olaf went on and on about one misdeed after another that we Sigurdsson brothers committed, we could say as one, 'Whatever!' Or better yet, when Mike calls us on the carpet . . . uh, cloud . . . for one teeny-tiny sin or another, we could say, 'Whatever!' "

"You really are going off the deep end, aren't you?"

"Lack of sex does that to a man, makes his sap thicken and clog up his veins."

"Is that a scientific fact?"

"It could be."

They grinned at each other.

"Where are Alex and the bratlings?" he asked. Vangels were unable to breed or bear children, but Vikar and his wife had "adopted" twin toddlers last year, a first in the thousand-plus-year history of the VIK and vangeldom. But then Vikar's being permitted to marry a living soul was a first for vangels, too.

"They went to an Amish market with Armod and Svein. You'll stay until they come back, won't you?"

He nodded.

"Back to sex—" Vikar said.

Ivak snorted his opinion.

"Really, Ivak, I sympathize with you. I don't imagine there are many opportunities for sex . . . I mean, male/female sex . . . in a prison of five thousand men."

"You'd be surprised. There are prison guards, lawyers, Bible-thumping do-gooders who sometimes take do-gooding to a new level. Plus, I go outside the prison on occasion."

"There are women in an all-male prison?"

"Believe me, there are women everywhere."

"And you've managed to resist the temptation. I'm impressed."

"I am, too. I keep thinking that if I can hold out just a little bit longer, Mike will take pity on me."

"Are you demented?" Vikar shook his head at Ivak, as if he were a hopeless case. "Methinks you need to find yourself a life mate and hope, and pray, that Mike will let you have her."

"That is the last thing I want or need. One woman, forever! Pfff!" Ever since Vikar . . . and his brother Trond, too, for that matter . . . had married, they thought there was a soul mate just waiting to catch each and every one of the VIK. As if that was a happenstance Ivak should be anticipating with great glee! It was sickening, really, the way Vikar and Trond and their mates constantly touched and kissed and cooed at each other.

Ivak shivered with distaste.

"Is the alternative any better? No woman?"

"I refuse to believe that I will be forced to go on this way much longer. A man of my appetites should be able to 'eat' once in a while, or lots in a while." He blinked his lashes with mock innocence at his brother.

Vikar laughed. "I cannot wait to meet the woman who will bring you to your knees."

"The only reason I would be on my knees before a woman is because I am about to perform a sexual act on her person."

Vikar laughed some more. "You'll see."

"You seem to forget how angry Mike was after Trond got hooked up with Nicole. He swore that was the end of vangel/mortal relationships."

A shrug was Vikar's only response.

"Actually, the reason I came here is to warn you that there might be Lucies in the vicinity of Angola." Lucies was the nickname for Lucipires, Lucifer's vampire demons. They fed on humans in a state of mortal sin, or fanged a sin taint into those tempted to some great sin. "Their scent is everywhere around the prison perimeter. I'm not sure they've actually infiltrated the complex yet, but it's only a matter of time."

"Well, you know where they're coming from, if they're there," Vikar said, a note of disgust in his voice.

"Dominique," they both said at the same time.

The VIK had recently become aware of Dominique Fontaine's presence in New Orleans where she'd opened a portion of her mansion, Anguish, as a restaurant. Dominique was a powerful haakai demon vampire, one of the top Lucipire Command Council, and a more repulsive woman there never was, especially with her passion for snakes.

"I hadn't heard about her working her evil wiles throughout Louisiana, though," Vikar remarked. "Rather like a dog soiling its own bed."

"We'll soon find out if it's her minions, or some others."

"As for Lucies possibly infiltrating Angola, you have to admit there's a great body of potential victims there. I'm surprised they haven't thought of it before. You've said yourself that many of the inmates are irredeemable."

"Yes, but I've managed to 'save' several dozen these past few years. It's just that for every criminal I save, two others equally in need pop up."

"So, what can we do to help with this new threat?"

"I'll need at least a dozen, maybe even two dozen, vangels incarcerated there, or put on the prison staff, to help me."

"Jarls, karls, ceorls, thralls?" Vikar asked, referring to the various social classes of vangels.

"Some of each."

"Done," Vikar said.

"And I need a quick lesson in talent scouting."

"Huh?"

When he finished explaining, Vikar was bent over with laughter. Even Miss Borden snickered.

"It's not that funny," Ivak contended.

"Ivak! Your idea of talent is a stripper singing 'Let Me Entertain You' while she hangs from a pole."

"Your point?"

Ironically, once he was back at Angola and received a list of potential talent show participants, the first song to be sung by Leo Lister in his cross-dressing role as Linda Lister was "Let Me Entertain You."

Two

It was a hell of a party . . .

Jasper, king of all the Lucipires, one of the fallen angels banished from Heaven ages ago along with his boss, Lucifer, was celebrating in Horror, the name he'd given to his palace hideaway in the coldest northern regions of Norway.

They had much to celebrate. Despite all the roadblocks posed by those blasted VIK, Jasper had harvested more than five hundred lost souls this year, thanks to an increasingly decadent world. *Thank you, Internet. Superhighway to Sin.* And that was just the ones being "turned" into Lucipires. Satan was doing a booming business the regular way . . . bad people dying and riding the quick chute to his fiery pits.

Attending this special party of Jasper's were dozens of haakai demon vampires, including a few haakai lords. Haakais were the upper social strata of demons, just below Seraphims, as Jasper had once been . . . a Seraphim angel, that is. Lucifer had just borrowed the name for the elite demons as well, more to irritate their most hated enemy, Michael the Archangel, than anything else. It was Michael who'd booted them out of Heaven.

Also attending the party were mungs, many of them seven or more feet tall, oozing a poisonous mung or slime from every pore of their red, scaly skin, though most in attendance today were in humanoid forms, but with fangs fully extended. It was easier to dance and move about without a tail obstructing pathways or slipping on the slimy floors. Besides the haakai and mungs, imps and hordlings danced their little hearts away as well, but what a troublesome lot! These foot soldiers of Satan required constant monitoring, lest they created chaos.

Yes, life was good, Jasper thought as he snake-danced his way through the crowd. An imp band was playing "La Vida Loca," and whoo-boy, some of those female backup singers knew how to shake their devilish assets.

Beverages flourished in many formats for those working up a thirst. In an ice sculpture fountain, a well-endowed gargoyle was pissing out fresh blood. At the bar, an array of mixed drinks was offered: Devil's Delight, Demon Semen, Hell, Yeah!, Hot Damn Demon Dew, Hemorrhage, Fangs for the Memories. And his favorite, which featured a large amount of Tabasco mixed in with the blood and vodka: Fire in the Devil's Hole! Of course, there were also bloody Jell-O shots. And Bloody Marys on tap with blood substituting for tomato juice. Some hordlings were gathered around a funnel engaged in a boisterous, wild game of Blood Bong.

The bandleader yelled out: "Anyone in the mood for country?" The band morphed into "The Devil Came Down to Georgia," and the leader added, "C'mon now. Time to line dance, everyone. Hey, you imps over there. Behave yourselves. That's not how we form a line."

Line dancing. Jasper grimaced with distaste. That was his cue to move on to the game room, where one group was playing Pin the Tail on the Newbie's Ass. Screaming, newly turned, naked, no-longer-humans were tied to

randomly placed posts while blindfolded Lucipires tried
to pin their new tails on them. Great fun!

Another group was playing darts. Not with bull's-eye
targets, but instead dead humans who were being difficult in resisting their "turning." They, too, were naked,
but spread-eagled against the wall. Points were given for
eyes, mouth, heart, nipples, and genitals. Jasper was a
champion dart player, if he did say so himself.

Thunk, thunk, thunk went the darts. Scream, scream,
scream went the targets. The sound of human suffering
was music to an aged demon's ears.

Jasper preened as he gazed about at his subjects. "It's
great to be me," he murmured with shameless pride. He
was about to join in a game of eyeball billiards when he
noticed a new arrival coming toward him. What was *she*
doing here?

"Dominique! What a wonderful surprise!" *What are
you up to now, bitch!*

Jasper air kissed each of the woman's cheeks. Any
closer and he would be kissing the huge snake wrapped
around the haakai's neck like a boa. In fact, it *was* a
boa . . . a boa constrictor.

Dominique Fontaine was one of his seven high commanders. She operated out of a New Orleans mansion
named Anguish that housed a five-star restaurant on the
first floor and torture chambers that would impress the
Marquis de Sade on the upper floors. The Creole, six feet
tall and gorgeous by human standards—and she was in
human form at the moment with café au lait skin, rather
than the usual red scales—had no compunction about
kissing him and taking it one step further, snaking her
Gene Simmons–style tongue into his mouth, practically
choking him. Mutual loathing was the name of the game
between the two of them, always had been. She delighted
in goading him.

"To what do I owe this surprise?" he asked, taking her by the elbow and leading her away from the party and down the long gallery displaying the life-size killing jars he used to bring newly dead humans to stasis. Inside the soundproof cylinders, the struggling, naked humans appeared to be screaming, but they would eventually calm down and accept their fate. Next, their bodies would be pinned to display boards with three-foot pins through their hearts. Like butterflies, they were. His special hobby, so to speak. If the humans didn't accept becoming Lucipires by then, they would be moved to the torture chambers in the dungeons below. He wasn't about to take Dominique down there, or he'd never get rid of her. She loved to watch and dispense torture.

Finally, they came to a lounge where he motioned for her to sit on a comfy sofa while he chose a wingback chair, which he felt gave him more authority, being rather throne-like. His French hordling assistant, Beltane, immediately appeared, and Jasper ordered cocktails for them both. Dominique asked for an oyster shooter, a Louisiana favorite that had Tabasco and a raw oyster in one shot glass and bourbon in the chaser, the Lucipire version including a good douse of blood as well.

"I have the most wonderful idea," Dominique told him right off.

It must be big if she had bothered to come all the way here. Whatever it was would require his approval, he assumed. And minions to carry out her orders, more than the thirty or so who resided with her in the Big Easy. He loved that name for the unusual city, by the by, reminding him of how sinfully easy parts of the French Quarter could be.

He waved a hand at her, encouraging her to continue.

"I happened to be near Angola Prison recently. That's several hours away from N'awlins. Consider this, *cher*, there are five thousand men incarcerated there. The dregs of society. Irredeemable sinners of the worst kind, for the most part. Murderers. Rapists. Pedophiles. Armed robbers. Our favorite kind of people!"

"And your point is . . . ?" *I have a party to get back to, and I am not about to let you ruin my day.*

"We should be there."

We? That would be the day when I partner with her on anything. She must have a hundred of those slithering bastards in her parlor alone. Satan only knows how many are in her bed.

The boa raised its head and hissed at him.

Jeesh! A snake that can read minds? Dominique is more dangerous that I thought.

Dominique patted the snake. Its fangs shot out and its flicking tongue caressed the upper swell of her exposed bosoms.

Jasper glanced at his watch and said, "You were saying about Angola Prison?"

"The Lucipire harvest could be monumental in such a setting. Think about it. All those mortal sinners, and they're going nowhere, just waiting for us to pluck them off to our cause."

He hated to admit it, but Dominique might be right. "Wonderful idea! I don't know why we didn't think of it before."

"And it's not just Angola. There are thousands of prisons around the world. We should be in all of them." Dominique smiled at him, her fangs dripping with the saliva of her excitement.

The snake lapped it up.

Eeew! "Let's not get ahead of ourselves. We don't want to call attention to our work. I suggest starting at Angola. See how that goes."

They discussed various details then. A timeline for the initial project. Number of Lucipires she would need to help her. How they would infiltrate the prison grounds.

"We could have a huge harvest at the Angola Rodeo alone. It's coming up in October." Dominique pretended to shiver with delight.

"Whoa, whoa, whoa! Lucipires and horses do not go together. Even worse, riding a bull. Our tails get in the way."

"Tsk, tsk, tsk! I didn't mean that *we* would participate, but the event draws thousands of outside spectators. In the confusion of all the activities, we can hit them hard. Missing inmates will be presumed to have escaped and died in the surrounding swamps or the river."

"Sounds good. Maybe I should send Zebulan to help you. He's in California at the moment. He might relish a vacation from trying to break those special forces sinners. The Navy SEALs have been especially hard nuts to crack."

Dominique made a moue of disapproval with her lush red lips, which looked rather ridiculous with the fangs hanging out. "Zeb doesn't like me."

Here's a news flash, bitch. No one likes you. He shrugged. "It's up to you, but feel free to call on him if the need arises." He would make sure to call on Zebulan. In fact, he might even imply that Zebulan could take over the operation, just to annoy Dominique.

"One more thing. One of my minions swears he saw Ivak Sigurdsson walking into the prison one day."

"A VIK?" Jasper sat up straighter. "Why didn't you say so at the beginning? Maybe I need to visit Louisiana myself."

Dominique smiled. "You can always stay with me."

For the love of Hell! "We'll see," he conceded aloud, but what he thought was, *No frickin' way!*

After Dominique left, Jasper went back to his party, humming that famous Louisiana refrain, just to get in the proper mood, "*Laissez les bon temps rouler!*" Definitely, the good times were going to roll.

Three

She wasn't a desperate housewife, but she was desperate ...

Gabrielle was sweating like a swamp pig by the time she arrived on Bayou Black, which was only an hour's drive from New Orleans in good traffic, but seemed like ten hours today in her fifteen-year-old, un-air-conditioned Buick LeSabre.

Pulling into the driveway, she checked the number on the charming, white-chinked log cottage. Swamps and tropical vegetation overran most properties in this region, but Tante Lulu's place had a neatly trimmed lawn and colorful flowerbeds on all sides. When Gabrielle noticed that there were plaster and plastic statues of St. Jude everywhere, even a St. Jude birdbath, she recalled Dolly's words. The scent of climbing roses and bougainvillea and coffee-colored bayou waters teeming with fish filled the air.

Club Bayou Med.

Yeah, I have time to stop and smell the roses.

Remember why you're here, Gabrielle.

Why am I here?

What can an old Cajun lady do that all my years of legal wrangling hasn't?

Am I really so desperate that I'll try anything?

Yes! The look on Leroy's face when I told him about the parole board's latest decision was scary. He's going to do something. Something impulsive and dangerous. I just know he is. And then there'll really be no hope at all.

Not that my cup is overflowing with hope. Forget about that glass half-full crap. Mine is ninety-nine-and-a-half percent empty.

But right now, the pleasant scenery and her lack of hope were preempted by something else. Shutting her motor down, she barely noticed its embarrassing putt-putt-putt of protest in her need to escape the sauna interior. She swung her door open and staggered onto the crushed shell pathway.

Only to be showered with rain.

Only it wasn't raining.

A tiny woman as old as time was holding a garden hose, spraying her. And smiling, like she was doing her a favor.

Actually, it did feel good.

"What the hell . . . ?" she said, anyway.

"Me, I was jist waterin' mah okra when I noticed how hot you looked. Seemed lak a good idea ta cool you off, right quick. Dint want you havin' a heatstroke or nothin'."

"Well, thanks, I guess." No harm done, she decided, since she was just wearing a Louisiana Second Chances Project T-shirt and shorts with athletic shoes, no socks. She brushed those strands of hair that had come loose from her ponytail off her face and reached inside her car for her briefcase. That's when she turned and really studied the person that she'd hoped would be her salvation.

Good Lord! If anyone should be embarrassed by her appearance, it would be Ms. Bizarro Senior Citizen, whose close-capped head of curls was dyed a brassy blonde. The old biddy wore shorts that hugged her non-existent butt and a little tank top that proclaimed in glittery letters, "Wild Thing," both in hot pink, with pom-pom socks and orthopedic shoes, all of which had to come from the minus-size department of Wal-Mart; she couldn't be more than five foot zero. Hot-pink lip gloss and rouge called attention to every one of the thousand wrinkles on her face. Grandma Moses with a Mary Kay obsession.

Walking forward squishily, Gabrielle extended a hand, "You must be Tante Lulu. I'm Gabrielle Sonnier. We spoke on the phone."

The old lady gave her a surprisingly hard grip with her right hand and continued watering her wire-fenced vegetable garden with the other. For a woman who presumably lived alone, she could feed a large family from the neat plot, where a bumper crop of tomatoes, green peppers, cucumbers, onions, garlic, lettuce, peas, string beans, squash, melons, and lots of okra flourished. Then there were the chickens that free-ranged in her yard, having escaped the chicken coop at one corner of the yard where a gate hung open.

Turning off the hose, Tante Lulu motioned for her to follow around the side to the back of the house that faced the bayou . . . where a large alligator sat sunning itself, watching them, as well as the foolhardy chickens, through beady eyes. Because of the wide expanse of lawn between them and the critter, Gabrielle wasn't alarmed . . . yet. And she had her heavy briefcase for a weapon. The chickens were on their own.

"Um . . . do you know you have a gator in your yard?"

"Thass jist Useless." Tante Lulu waved a hand airily.

"What's useless? The gator or my telling you about the gator?"

Tante Lulu chuckled. "Useless is his name. The critter usta belong to my nephew Remy when he kept a houseboat down the bayou, but Useless moved up thisaway when there was no more Cheez Doodles comin' his way."

"Cheez Doodles?" *Have I entered some alternate universe?*

"Yep. His favorite treat. Doan suppose ya got any in that gas-guzzlin' tank yer drivin'? I vow, that car is noisier than two skeletons makin' love on a tin roof."

Gabrielle would be offended if it weren't a sad fact. Every cent she earned went toward Leroy's defense. "If I did have Cheez Doodles, they'd be baked to a crisp by now." At Tante Lulu's arched brows, she explained, "My air-conditioning broke." *Two years ago.*

"Ah, thass why you look lak the back side of bad times, I reckon. You oughta check out my niece Charmaine's beauty shop," the old lady said with a lack of subtlety she was probably entitled to at her age, which had to be close to ninety, give or take. "I thought lawyers wuz rollin' in cash."

"Like your nephew Luc?" she countered. Gabrielle had done her homework. Lucien LeDeux was a famous lawyer throughout the South, well-known for his sometimes unorthodox tactics.

"I wish! That boy, he could charm the snout off a pig. He needs ta get on one of them court TV shows, if you ask me. But Luc, bless his heart, is stubborn as a cross-eyed mule. Not that I'd want him ta move ta New York or Hollywood, wherever they film them things. Although, if he went ta Hollywood, he might meet up with Richard Simmons. I do declare, I have a hankerin' ta meet up with my fantasy man before I die." She sighed deeply.

Definitely alternate universe. Was she actually saying that Richard Simmons was her fantasy man? Gabrielle wasn't about to ask. This woman's brain bounced around like a Ping-Pong ball. At this rate, Gabrielle would be here all afternoon before she got to the point of her visit. At Tante Lulu's age, that could be risky, time being of the essence.

They stepped onto the narrow back porch that ran about thirty feet, the length of the small cottage, and contained several comfy-looking rockers painted a bright red with thick cushions that had an image on them. St. Jude. Who else?

Inside the cottage, the low ceilings and small rooms contributed to a cozy atmosphere, along with the doily-adorned, upholstered furniture and family pictures everywhere. This was the type of home Gabrielle and her brother would have loved to have when they'd been growing up in a New Orleans slum tenement. They'd never dreamed of luxury, just a homey place, safe from violence and hunger. Like this. Maybe someday if . . . *when* . . . Leroy was free and she could start to save a little cash, she'd buy herself a place like this. Nothing fancy. A haven. As it was now, she had to work at a place like Second Chances because of the flexible hours they offered her to help Leroy. Once her brother was out of Angola, she would join a big-money law firm and make up for all these years of poverty.

"I love your home," Gabrielle said as they entered the kitchen that was a step back in time to maybe the 1940s. The aged cypress cabinets flashed their original polished hardware. An enamel and chrome table with red-Naugahyde-cushioned seats matched the red-and-white checkered curtains on the window above the large farmer's porcelain sink. The air was scented with myriad spices coming from an open pantry off the kitchen where the noted traiteur lady must practice her folk healing craft. Sage, coriander, thyme, lavender, and something pungent she didn't recognize.

"Come, sit yer pretty self down, you," Tante Lulu urged.

First she said I look awful, now pretty. Am I being buttered up for something? Gabrielle had no sooner sat down than Tante Lulu placed a large glass of iced sweet tea in front of her. "Y'all had lunch yet, honey?"

Gabrielle shook her head as she downed half her glass in one large gulp. Before she knew it, she was gobbling up crab gumbo, a fresh lettuce and tomato salad, homemade lazy bread, and sugary beignets, like a soldier just home from the war.

"Now tell me what the problem is," Tante Lulu said as she sat down across from her with two cups of steaming chicory coffee, pushing one of them in front of Gabrielle.

"My brother, Leroy, is serving a life sentence at Angola, and nothing I do as a lawyer through regular legal channels is helping to get him out. I was hoping you might have connections, people who could help me cut through some of the political roadblocks. I shouldn't be bothering you, though. It's hopeless."

"Thass where yer wrong. Nothin' is hopeless when you got St. Jude on yer team. And me, of course." She beamed at her, as if that was all it would take.

Oh God! Gabrielle thought, and could have sworn she heard a voice say, *He's busy. Will I do?*

"How did you do that? I mean, project your voice?"

"I dint perject nothin'. Must be yer hearin' St. Jude in yer head. That happens sometimes when a mission begins."

"A mission?" Gabrielle squeaked out.

"You came here fer help, dint you, girl? Thass what I call a mission." Tante Lulu looked at her as if her brain was a few bricks short of a full load. "Now, tell me everything."

"As I said, Leroy is in Angola, has been for the past

fifteen years. I've tried everything since I graduated from law school four years ago, and years before that, as well, to get him out, but nothing works. I'm ready to give up."

"You ain't tried everything." Tante Lulu tilted her head pointedly at the picture of St. Jude on the wall. "Now, when I say, tell me everything, I mean, start back a piece, at the beginning."

And Gabrielle did. She was twenty-eight years old, but right now she felt as old as the lady facing her with seeming compassion. At this point, she figured she had nothing to lose.

She started back in the early years when she and her older brother by three years had lived in low-income housing in the worst sections of New Orleans with their alcoholic mother, Marie Gaston, and a father, James Sonnier, who was increasingly more and more violent. Their parents had never got around to marrying.

"I can't remember a time when my mother wasn't drunk and my father angry. I don't know if someone warned me, 'Hide when Daddy gets home,' or if I just learned that on my own, the hard way. No, no, I'm not looking for pity," Gabrielle said when she saw the old lady's eyes brim with tears. "This was all before Hurricane Katrina hit the city, of course. I can't imagine how we would have survived that, too."

"Lotsa folks didn't. The hurry-cane smashed that city lower'n a doodle bug."

"The least little thing could set my dad off, like a piece of stale bread. Or it could have been something major, like cat poop on the hall carpet, though I always wondered how he even noticed since the rug was so stained. Leroy had tried to clean it up. Anyhow, Dad's reaction was to toss the cat against the wall and crack its skull open. After that, no more pets."

Tante Lulu tsk-tsked. "Some men are born mean. I

know one jist like that. Valcour LeDeux, the father of
my nephews and Charmaine. I swear, I'd murder the man
myself if it weren't a mortal sin and me bein' so close ta
the Pearly Gates."

Gabrielle raised her eyebrows with disbelief at such an
image . . . a hit man . . . uh, woman . . . in orthopedic
shoes.

"You doan think I could, huh? Girlie, I got me a pistol
I carry in mah purse all the time, and I have a Glock in
mah closet."

Okaaay!

"Dint them government folks ever step in ta help you
little chillen?"

Gabrielle shook her head. "They tried, but you know
how overworked those agencies are."

"Ain't no excuse," Tante Lulu pronounced and got up
to pour them both another cup of coffee. Gabrielle would
be bouncing off the walls with all this caffeine by the
time she got home. Her senior citizen BFF . . . at least
she acted like a good friend already . . . patted her on the
shoulder before sitting down again and saying, "Go on,
honey."

"At first, Mom was the only one who bore the brunt
of Dad's fists, but when Leroy was old enough to protest,
starting at about eight years old, he got as much or more
of the beatings. Until he left home at about age fourteen,
that is, and lived God-only-knows-where on the streets. I
was only eleven then. Oh, he used to drop in fairly often,
when Dad wasn't home. He'd bring me Happy Meals, not
just because I was always hungry but I loved those dumb
little toys, or an item of clothing he'd no doubt shoplifted."
A long-forgotten memory came to her suddenly. "Once he
brought me a stuffed panda, also no doubt bought with
sticky fingers. I loved that panda, kept it under my pillow.
But one day Dad discovered it, guessed where it had come

from, and tossed it in the trash. He just couldn't stand for anyone to be happy when he was so miserable."

"Lak I said, honey. Bad ta the bone, thass what some men are."

"Anyhow, I was fourteen when it happened. And I saw it all."

She didn't have to explain what "it" she referred to. Everyone knew about sixteen-year-old Leroy Sonnier killing his father with a kitchen knife. Twenty-four stab wounds in all. Blood everywhere. Even on the ceiling.

"Leroy had come by, not expecting Dad to be home, but apparently the welfare office had cut him off and said he would be getting no more money, except for food stamps. Told him to get a job. He took his frustration out on Mom and me, of course. The beatings that day weren't even that bad in comparison to some others, but I had a bloody nose which looked worse than it was, and Mom had been practically unconscious from booze before Dad even hit her. Leroy lost it and went after Dad with a knife." She shrugged and was surprised when Tante Lulu shoved a stack of St. Jude paper napkins toward her, and realized she was weeping. Really, it had been so long ago. She never cried anymore. It must be the accumulated tension over the parole board decision.

"Dint yer brother's lawyer tell the jury what a rotten SOB yer father was?"

"Pfff! The public defender assigned to Leroy didn't even call me to testify. Since no one had ever filed charges against Dad, and Mom was no longer there to attest to his brutality—she was run over by a car late one night when she was out on a wine run—well, they chose to consider it a drug crime. Leroy's lawyer told him he had no choice but to plead out with second-degree murder."

"Thass why you decided ta become a lawyer, ain't it?"

Gabrielle nodded. "Lot of good it's done, though."

"God works in mysterious ways."

Gabrielle bristled. If that was the best Tante Lulu could do for her—offer religious platitudes— she'd wasted half a day when she could have been researching another legal angle on Leroy's case.

But just then a car horn beeped outside, and Tante Lulu exclaimed happily, "Company!"

Company? Oh no!

"Yoo hoo! Hallo!" a feminine voice called out.

"It's mah niece Charmaine. Ain't that nice?"

Just swell!

Into the kitchen came the most amazing presence . . . well, two presences . . . because behind Charmaine was a male.

"And Tee-John!" Tante Lulu exclaimed.

If Gabrielle had thought Tante Lulu's appearance was outrageous, it was nothing compared to Charmaine LeDeux Lanier. Gabrielle had never met her before, though she had heard of her. Everyone in Louisiana had. Twenty or so years ago, she had been Miss Louisiana. Now she was the owner of a chain of beauty spas, including one smack-dab in the middle of her husband Raoul "Rusty" Lanier's ranch in northern Louisiana. Even at fortysomething, Charmaine was still beautiful in a trashy sort of way. Today she wore leopard-print jeans that appeared to have been painted on, with gold sandals that exposed her crimson toenails, a perfect match for her really long fingernails and her pouty lips. A stretchy black tank top left about three inches of abdomen exposed and had glittery letters with the provocative words, "Ask About My Vibrator." Tante Lulu and Charmaine must get their clothes from the same place, 1–800–SLUTWEAR.

Noticing the direction of Gabrielle's stare, Tante Lulu giggled and said, "Charmaine jist added a vibrating massage table at her Houma spa. Fer folks with back problems."

"I've got back problems," the male in the room said. He was wearing a Fontaine, Louisiana, police uniform and looked hotter than any man had a right to look. Gabrielle had never met John LeDeux, either, but everyone knew he had been one of the baddest of the Cajun bad boys before his marriage a few years ago. He was only about thirty-two, much younger than his half brothers and sisters. "I wonder if two people with back problems could fit on one of those tables." He blinked innocently at Charmaine.

"In your dreams, bozo," Charmaine replied.

After quick introductions, leaving Gabrielle feeling trapped in her chair, Charmaine placed several glossy pink designer bags on the counter with the stylized logo "Charmaine's" and below that in smaller print, "Where every woman is beautiful." She leaned down and kissed her elderly aunt on both cheeks before telling her, "I brought those new lipsticks and body lotions."

John, known to his family as Tee-John or Little John, long before he'd grown to his current six foot two, winked at Gabrielle, as if he sensed her discomfort, and set several grocery bags on the other counter. "I picked up the boudin sausages you wanted from Beaudreaux's General Store. And rice . . . what you gonna do with twenty pounds of rice, *chère*?"

"Hmpfh! A Cajun cook cain't never have enuf rice."

Just when Gabrielle was about to make her excuses, Tante Lulu pushed her niece and nephew into chairs at the table and placed cups of coffee in front of them with a platter of beignets, and announced, "Gabrielle needs our help. 'Pears we got us a new mission."

"What? No, no, no! No mission. Just advice, that's all I want." *In fact, I don't even want advice now. I just want to escape. Bad idea coming here. Bad idea!*

Charmaine squeezed her hand. "Best you sit back and

let Tante Lulu have her way. There's nothing she likes better than a LeDeux family mission."

"But I'm not a family member," she protested.

"You are now, sweetie," Charmaine said. "An honorary LeDeux."

Tante Lulu quickly brought the other two up to date on what was happening with Gabrielle's brother, leading up to the latest parole board decision.

"His biggest problem is not the murder of our father," Gabrielle added. "He would be released by now on good behavior for that offense, but he was convicted of killing another inmate a few years ago and that got him life, which means twenty more years, minimum. He didn't do it, I swear. I'm afraid he'll go after the witness who testified against him, or maybe even commit suicide. He was morbidly depressed when I saw him yesterday."

"I heard something last week at a criminal justice seminar over at Tulane," John said. "Something like ninety percent of the five thousand inmates at Angola never outlive their sentences. They deserve to be punished, of course. *Mais oui*, they do. Still, it amounts to a living death."

"Thass a cryin' shame," Tante Lulu said, tsking her sympathy.

"You can see why Leroy is feeling so hopeless then," Gabrielle said to John.

John nodded and asked, "Why is the parole board so against him?"

"He earned a college degree the only way possible at Angola, through a theological seminary's prison extension program. Then he antagonized Warden Benton, who fashions himself a savior to the inmates, by refusing to minister. He ended up using his education as a literacy teacher before getting a job on the prison newspaper, the *Angolite*, but that wasn't what Benton had planned for him.

"Most at all, Leroy can't keep his mouth shut. My

brother has become very articulate in expressing his opinion about Louisiana politics in both the *Angolite* and any outside publication that will give him a voice."

"I read that piece where he called the Loo-zee-anna legislature a bunch of corrupt sheep. It was well written. Of course, as a cop, I'm not too fond of his stabs at law enforcement."

"How soon kin we all skedaddle up ta Angola? I aim ta assess the sit-ye-a-shun." Tante Lulu was rubbing her hands together in anticipation.

Gabrielle put her face in her hands. Pistol-Packin' Senior Annie on the grounds of Angola. The image defied description.

"Well, fiddle-dee-dee! Wonder what I should wear?" Charmaine asked.

Good heavens! Charmaine, who must fancy herself a modern-day Scarlett O'Hara, would cause a riot, no matter what she wore in that testosterone-oozing prison. Even Gabrielle, who didn't have Charmaine's wow factor, dressed down for her visits to Leroy.

"There's no way your husband will allow you to go to Angola, *chère*," John said as he licked sugar off his lips from his third beignet.

"Allow? *Allow?* What century y'all livin' in, Tee-John? Besides, Rusty was an inmate himself at one time, as y'all know." She turned to Gabrielle and explained, "Unjustly incarcerated."

"Was that before or after you married and divorced him twice?" Tee-John asked.

"Oh you!" She swatted her half brother on the shoulder. "I only divorced him once."

"Charmaine was a born-again virgin before they got married again. Dontcha remember, Tee-John. She was gonna have her thingamajig sewed back up, but Rusty put a stop ta that."

"Really? I wonder if Celine would have her jig sewed back up, to add a little spice to our love life?" Tee-John pondered, and he looked serious, too.

"Yer wife gives you enough spice, you rascal," Tante Lulu said with a laugh. "I swear, ever' time I see you two t'gether, yer all over her, lak dew on Dixie."

"I wouldn't bring up reattaching Celine's hymen anytime soon, seein' as how Celine just popped out one of your babies last month," Charmaine advised.

Whoa! So, that's the thingamajig they're talking about.

"Good point!" Tee-John agreed. "It might be a *sore* point."

Gabrielle listened to the three wack jobs talk in the charming patois known only here in Cajun country. A bit of country twang, a lazy drawl, an occasional French word thrown in, an exaggerated mispronunciation of words that might trick the outsider into thinking they were illiterate. Gabrielle and Leroy were part Cajun, but they'd never felt that way, having no exposure to the Cajun culture. She was only now realizing how much they might have missed.

She was also enjoying the warm teasing they engaged in, the way only people who loved each other could.

But wait, John was talking to her. "You were saying?" she said.

"What you need is someone from the inside to help while we work from the outside," John told Gabrielle.

We? Damn, how do I get out of this? "Actually, I couldn't possibly ask you folks to get involved. Maybe a little advice. People you know that I might approach, that kind of thing."

It was as if she hadn't even spoken as the three of them tossed around various ideas.

Suddenly, Tante Lulu let out a little whoop. "I know,

I know. I was playin' bingo at Our Lady of the Bayou Church when I heard about this strange bird up at the prison. A sort of minister, I think. A Viking, of all things. Ivan Stevenson, or some such name. No, that doesn't sound right. It's Ivak Sigurdsson. Anyways, this Viking guy is puttin' on some kinda prison talent show. And us LeDeux are famous fer our talent shows."

"Uh-oh!" John said.

"Oh boy!" Charmaine said.

Gabrielle just groaned.

Tante Lulu smiled widely. "We's goin' ta Angola. Yippee!"

Four

The knees will give you away every time . . .

Ivak understood why he, a man guilty of the sin of lust in the worst possible ways, had been assigned to an all-male prison as punishment. Maybe not for this many years, but then the lust still bubbled beneath the surface, even after all these centuries. Temptation was his constant companion.

And he understood the seriousness of his mission to save these dreadful sinners. Truly, five thousand inmates—penned together like animals, knowing that most would never leave their pen—had a need of him and the saving grace he could offer, even if they didn't know it.

What he did not understand was why God or St. Michael, in particular, would lay this latest, ridiculous, doomed-to-fail mission on him. A talent show! He would love to tell Warden Benton he could take this job and shove it, but Ivak's position in the prison was shaky at the best of times. He had to have a legitimate reason for being here, and being a chaplain of sorts was his cover.

Having just finished the morning's latest round of ridiculous auditions, he sighed deeply as he shut and locked the auditorium door behind him . . . inmates stole anything that wasn't nailed down, even the ivory keys on the piano. What he needed was a beer or twenty, not that he would find any here. What he did find, though, was the convict Leroy Sonnier strolling down "The Walk" toward the visitors' center. The Walk was an elevated twelve-foot-wide concrete passageway that connected various places in the Main Prison complex . . . the offices, cellblocks, dorms, dining halls, laundries, and other outbuildings.

Inmates fell into one of three classifications in this maximum security prison: cellblock, Big Stripe, or trusty. Those inmates with good records or trusty status could go about their jobs without a guard for the most part, although they had to account for their whereabouts at every minute. About seven hundred of the five thousand or so inmates were trusties, while another almost three thousand were Big Stripes, working the fields and factories under the close eyes of armed guards. Only fifteen hundred inmates were confined to the kind of cells outsiders usually associated with prisons.

Sonnier had been a Class A trusty the past few years and was thus given certain privileges. That's when he started working on the prison newspaper, the *Angolite*.

Ivak brightened and said with as much pleasantness as he could muster, considering his foul mood, "Hello, Leroy."

"You again?" Leroy shook his head with disgust.

For the past few weeks, Ivak had been trying to approach Leroy to "save" him. It was one of those instinct things where he sensed a man in need of his help. What precisely, he wasn't sure; so he went for a general plea for repentance. Maybe Ivak had been a bit of a nuisance, but for a good cause. "So, how you doing today?"

"Get lost, motherfucker." The young man . . . well, he must be just over thirty years old, like Ivak, give or take a thousand years . . . didn't even stop walking. No deference to authority at all.

Leroy's response was certainly blunt . . . but a lot less graphic than what Ivak was often told to do by the hardened men here in Angola. And so much for Ivak's being pleasant! He tried another tack. "I hear you play a mean trumpet."

"I hear you've been trying to find gold in a shit hole."

Not exactly the way he'd describe his job as a talent scout, but close. He continued to keep pace with Sonnier as they walked down the busy noontime corridor, guards posted at intervals to make sure no one misbehaved. An inmate, even a trusty, couldn't go anywhere in the prison without permission. Every movement from one area of the prison to another required the inmate to stand and wait for the correctional officer to grant him access through one metal door after another. "Leroy . . . that's an odd name for a person in Louisiana, isn't it? Are you named for that famous jazz musician Leroy Jenkins?"

"Pfff! I come from the slums of Loo-zee-anna. I was named after that old Jim Croce song, 'Bad, Bad Leroy Brown.' "

So, I made no inroads with that attempt at conversation. Son of a troll! A Viking trying to make conversation, like a bloody Saxon coxcomb? All right, here goes another try. "I understand you're self-taught on the horn, but good enough to play in a New Orleans jazz club. A young Miles Davis. Could get a job in any French Quarter jazz club if you ever get released, you're that good."

"Kiss my ass."

Ivak had learned that the expression "Kiss my ass" was a perfectly appropriate way to end an argument in Louisiana, but not with him. In fact, the guard arched his brows at Ivak, wondering if he was going to react to the convict's remark. *Where's my broadsword when I need it? There was a time when an insult like that merited a head lopping or at least a fist in the gut.* It took every bit of Ivak's patience to tamp down his temper. "Do I take that for a no? Or a maybe? Yeah, you probably meant that *maybe* you'll do it if you have time to think it over because just maybe I might be able to help a thickheaded lackwit like you." Okay, that wasn't very diplomatic, or angelic, but sometimes subtlety sucked.

"Leave. Me. The. Hell. Alone." Sonnier didn't even look at him now as he spoke, just kept walking.

"Listen, shit-for-brains, I just finished auditioning prison lovebirds Sam Olson and Georgie Dupree, doing a pantomime of Sonny and Cher's 'I Got You, Babe.' Then, river dancing by six lifers, none of whom came close to being a Lord of the Dance, especially wearing heavy work boots. Followed by a former drug dealer who whistled, farted, and wiggled his ears at the same time. And how could I forget the Mississippi triple murderer who can polka standing on his hands?" He saw a smile twitch at Sonnier's lips; so he continued, "And the icing on my personal cake of misery was a three-hundred-pound convict named Bubba doing a tap dance to 'Happy Feet.' So, if you have even a modicum of talent, I'm going to be the personal barnacle on your ass until you agree to help me out."

"No way!"

"I could really use your help, buddy."

Sonnier stopped to stare at him incredulously. "Number one, we are not buddies. Two, I should help you . . . why?"

"It's a nice thing to do," Ivak offered.

"Do I look like a fucking Mother Teresa?" Leroy resumed walking.

And so did Ivak. "No. You look like a man who could use my help."

"Pfff! I thought you were the one in need of help."

"We could help each other."

"Not interested."

"What would it take to get you to participate in the talent show?"

"A busload of hookers parked inside the prison gate for my personal convenience."

"I could do that . . ."

Leroy snorted. "And I could swim the Mississippi and escape to Alabama."

" . . . but my boss would object."

"Tell me about it. Benton has a Puritan streak a mile wide."

"Benton isn't my boss. I answer to a higher authority."

Sonnier rolled his eyes. "You are seriously weird."

"I've been told that before." Suddenly, Ivak noticed something alarming. There were twin marks at the side of Sonnier's neck. Without warning, he leaned close and sniffed. Yep, lemony. Leroy had been bitten by a Lucie. Just a small sin taint at this point, which could account for the inmate's bad attitude. But whoa! The very fact that there was a demon vampire inside the prison compound caused red flags to go up in Ivak's radar. Where there was one there could be more. He'd already told Vikar that he suspected a Lucipire presence outside the prison grounds. Now he knew for sure they were inside, too.

Sonnier shoved him away. "Hey! I don't swing that way."

He must have thought Ivak was trying to kiss him. *Yeech!* "I don't swing that way, either. I was getting a closer look at that . . . um, mosquito . . . bite on your neck."

"That's not a mosquito bite. I was out at Cypress camp

yesterday, and some idiot Striper tried a turning out on me. Not the first time. You know how it is here, there's always some yay-hoo trying to turn you into his bitch."

Ivak was very much aware of the "turning out" ritual that existed at Angola and every other prison in the world. It usually involved the brutal gang rape of a new inmate, or any prisoner deemed to have a weakness. The act was not so much sexual as symbolic of stripping a man of his masculinity and redefining him as a female. Thereafter, the victim could be used, abused, sold, gambled away, whatever, and no one did a damn thing about the "gal boys," "whores," "old ladies," "wives," or whatever names they were given. Sad, it was, and tragic, much like the slavery of the Old South. In fact, Angola had been a slave-breeding plantation at one time. Ironic? Oh yeah! Ivak saved those he could from this life of degradation, but there were so many he was unable to reach.

Sonnier had still been talking while Ivak's mind had wandered.

"Anyhow, we got into a tussle and the douche bag ended up trying to bite me on the face. I turned at the last minute and ended up with a scratch. He ended up with a bloody nose."

"Did you get written up?" Ivak asked with alarm. The boy could lose all his privileges with just one incident.

Sonnier shook his head. "There were no guards nearby at the time."

So many things with that scenario struck a wrong note with Ivak. "What were you doing at Cypress?" It was one of the places where criminals were assigned to hard farm labor. Half of Angola's inmates lived in the Main Prison, while the other half lived in four out-camps among the eighteen thousand acres, some of which were planted in corn, cotton, and soybeans. "Aren't you supposed to be working in the prison newspaper office?"

Sonnier's face reddened and he shrugged. "I was looking for someone."

Ivak knew in that moment who Sonnier had been seeking and why. There was a particular hardened, too-evil-to-redeem inmate—Ivak knew because he'd tried—who had testified against Sonnier over a prison murder a few years back. This was not good. Sonnier was probably seeking revenge, which would have placed him in a state of enough sin that he drew the attention of a Lucie in the area, always sniffing about for the next victim.

Meanwhile, Sonnier just kept walking, trying to get away from him. Ivak couldn't let him go now, even if he wanted to. "Where we going, my man?"

"*We* are not going anywhere, *my man*. I'm going to the visitors' area to divorce my sister, Gabrielle." Surprised at his own revelation, Sonnier glanced over to him. "Why the hell did I tell you that?"

Ivak shrugged. "I have magic powers. So, what unforgivable thing did your sister do to yank your chain?"

"Gabby has given up her life for me. For fifteen years she's done nothing but work for my release. She even became a lawyer to help me, for chrissake."

Ivak cringed at Leroy's taking the Lord's name in vain. "So, you demanded she do all those things for you?"

"Of course not! Sonofabitch! Will you leave me alone?"

"Well, that makes sense then," he said, ignoring Sonnier's rejection of his company. "Divorce her because she loves you. By the way, I've never heard of siblings divorcing each other. Is that some kind of prison law concept?" Prisoners were always researching law books and coming up with crazy new ideas to help their cases.

"Drop dead, asshole!" Leroy snapped and stormed ahead of him.

Been there, done that. "Why don't we sit down and talk about this?"

"Why don't you go fuck yourself?"

Believe me, I would if I could. But wait. Leroy had stopped abruptly in the doorway, almost causing Ivak to walk into his back. "Forget about the hooker bus. God bless Gabby. No divorcing her today."

"Huh?"

"My sister brought me my very own bimbo."

"That *is* love," Ivak agreed, stepping around Leroy to get a better look.

"And she brought one of the Golden Girls, too. The grandma one, but I thought that old bird died. Maybe this senior babe is the pimp . . . or is that pimpess? Nah!" Leroy frowned with confusion. "Something isn't right with this picture."

Ivak wasn't looking at the statuesque beauty with a big mass of black hair wearing a sleeveless red dress with a wide belt and matching stiletto heels, or the blonde midget in a black-and-white polka-dot dress with matching headband. Nope, Ivak's eyes were riveted on the woman in the middle, a dark-haired, dark-eyed woman in baggy shorts and a loose tank top, in deference to the ninety-in-the-shade temperature today, probably a hundred and ten inside with no AC. Unlike the bimbo, she wore no makeup, and her hair was pulled off her face and piled on top of her head with a claw comb. She clearly tried to hide her true appearance, but Ivak was a woman connoisseur from way back. He knew a gem when he saw one.

But it was more than that. Ivak's heart was racing, and his palms had gone clammy. His favorite body part, if it could have talked, would be shouting, *Mine, mine, mine!* He had to concentrate to keep his fangs from emerging, as they were wont to do when he was in high emotion. This was the worst possible thing that could have happened to Ivak, at this time and in this place.

"What the hell's wrong with you?" Leroy asked. "Your face is so white, you look like you might faint."

Without warning, Ivak's loins caught fire, and he sank to his knees, just as Vikar had predicted. "I think I'm going to be sick. Or in love."

Prison creates strange bedfellows . . .

"Ain't this nice?"

Gabrielle looked at Tante Lulu as if she was crazy. They were sitting on folding chairs at metal tables in a prison visiting area that could only be described as bleak, despite the faded mural on one wall that must have been painted by a prisoner. The smell of pine-scented cleaner rose from the newly mopped floors, and institutional cooking wafted from a cafeteria somewhere. Whistles blew periodically to signal that inmates were to be counted before moving on to some new activity or place, like Pavlovian mice. Bars, barbed wire, and armed guards were front and center, everywhere. And it had to be over a hundred and ten degrees inside, without any air-conditioning. "Nice?"

"Well, I was 'spectin' ta see chain gangs outside and jailbirds inside walkin' around, carryin' them homemade knives made from tin foil, and lookin' at us wimmen with hungry eyes lak we was an afternoon delight."

"Oh good Lord!" Gabrielle muttered.

"Remember Paul Newman in *Cool Hand Luke*? Yum! I woulda shared a cell with him anytime."

In all the years Gabrielle had been visiting her brother at Angola, she'd never once seen a Paul Newman look-alike. Not even close. More like the nut cases in *Stir Crazy*. Or bad-ass criminals like *The Sopranos* or that hardened ex-Angola inmate in *Urban Cowboy*. And chain gangs? They'd been outlawed years ago.

"Tante Lulu, you know this isn't regular visiting day," Charmaine said, as if movie celeb convicts would be here on regular visiting days. "They only let us come this afternoon as a special favor to you."

And wasn't that an amazing concession, one Gabrielle had never been able to gain on her own?

"I didn't know you and the warden's mother used to double date with the Jemeaux brothers. I dated Jimmy Joe Jemeaux one time, but he had hands like an octopus."

"So did his grandfather," Tante Lulu said.

Gabrielle did not want to be picturing Tante Lulu engaged in a make-out session, not even a young Tante Lulu.

Charmaine winked at Gabrielle, as if they shared a joke.

Gabrielle felt as if the joke was on her, but then she saw Leroy in the doorway, and she plastered on her positive smile, the one she always wore when visiting Leroy, no matter the news. But he wasn't looking at her. His eyes were riveted on Charmaine. No surprise there. Everyone they'd passed in the past half hour had practically tripped over their hanging tongues.

Gabrielle stood and waved for her brother to come join them.

That's when she noticed the man rising from his knees at Leroy's side. He was the same height as her brother, about six foot four, but his shoulders were broader, his waist and hips narrower, every bit of exposed skin striated with muscle. Long blondish-brown hair was tied at his nape with a leather thong. A designer stubble adorned his classically sculpted face . . . in fact, he resembled that male model with pure, sharp Nordic features in those glossy magazine cologne ads. But no designer clothing on him and no denim prison garb, either. Nope, he wore an odd, little white turtleneck collar under a black muscle shirt that hung loose over tan Bermuda shorts. His big feet were exposed in a pair of rubber flip-flops.

She was staring at the man . . . and couldn't stop herself.

His blue eyes were fixed on her, as well, even when he stood and then leaned against the wall. He shook his head from side to side, as if in disbelief.

"Who is *he*?" she whispered at the same time her brother asked, "Who is *she*?"

She blinked several times to clear her head.

Leroy was gawking at Charmaine.

She reached up to hug her brother and whispered in his ear, "Forget about it. She's married, happily. With children."

"Shit! That figures. Here I thought you brought me some good news, for a change." He sank down to a chair at the table and folded his arms over his chest, his lower lip extended like that of a petulant child denied a treat. In his case, a woman. Jeesh!

"I *have* brought some good news." Quickly, Gabrielle introduced Tante Lulu and Charmaine to Leroy and vice versa, then added, "They're going to help me get you out of here."

"Give me a goddamn break!" He looked pointedly at first Charmaine, the quintessential bimbo, then at Tante Lulu, who had to appear old and weak. He couldn't be more wrong. In the two days she'd come to know these two women, Gabrielle had been given innumerable reasons to admire Charmaine's intelligence, and the old lady was the strongest woman she'd ever met. "What're they gonna do? Hold a friggin' bake sale for my benefit?"

"Watch yer mouth, boy," Tante Lulu warned, whacking him on the arm with her folded Richard Simmons fan. "Yer in no position ta be turnin' down help, wherever it comes from." She took a small St. Jude candle out of her pocket and shoved it into Leroy's hand. "They wouldn't let me bring in any little plastic St. Jude statues 'cause ya might melt it down into a weapon. Talk about!"

Leroy squeezed the candle angrily, probably hoping to break it in half, to no avail. He glared at Gabrielle then, stunning her with the pronouncement, "I want a divorce."

"What?" all three of the women exclaimed.

"I want to divorce you, Gabby. You're no longer my sister. You are no longer my lawyer. I don't want you to visit me anymore. I'm putting you on my official black list. It's over. No more wasting your time and mine on a hopeless cause."

"Bullshit!" Gabrielle said before glancing at Tante Lulu with a shrug of apology. "I'm not going anywhere."

Tante Lulu tapped her fingertips on the candle that Leroy still held in his hand. "Hopeless ain't a word St. Jude recognizes."

"Y'all gotta believe, sweetie," Charmaine added.

"I believe, all right. I believe I've landed in the middle of some senile dingbat circus."

"Are you sayin' I'm a dingbat?" Tante Lulu narrowed her eyes at Leroy.

"Are you sayin' I'm old?" Charmaine narrowed her eyes at Leroy, too.

Both of them wore so much mascara it was a wonder they could hold their eyelids open at all.

"Now wait just a minute," Gabrielle said. "Leroy, Tante Lulu and Charmaine have already done a lot to help you. You should be grateful, not antagonizing them."

He continued to glower at them all, waiting for an explanation. Her brother was not making a good impression, but instead of being mad at him, her heart ached with sadness. He was a good guy caught in a bad place. He had no reason to think that his situation would get any better.

"First of all, don't you think it's odd that I'm here visiting on a nonvisiting day?" She arched her brows at him. When he didn't answer, she went on, "Tante Lulu arranged that, with help from Charmaine's husband, who used to be an inmate here. He's outside right now talking to the head of security about some concessions we want them to allow you."

"Concessions?" he asked, unable to maintain his silence. "Have aliens stole your brain? They don't give concessions to inmates, especially lifers."

Gabrielle waved a hand dismissively. "We can discuss that later. The most important thing is that Tante Lulu, through her connections, has managed to get you another parole board hearing in November."

That news stunned Leroy. "That's impossible. Inmates only get one chance every few years, if that."

"You'd be surprised what you kin do when you rely on the big guy." Tante Lulu pointed to the St. Jude candle now sitting in the center of their table.

"And that's not all," Gabrielle went on. "Tante Lulu thinks there are some folks in the governor's office who might be open to a commutation, if all else fails." Gabrielle took Leroy's hands in hers. They were trembling. Both of them.

"Why . . . why would you be willing to help me . . . a stranger?" Leroy asked Tante Lulu and Charmaine.

"'Cause yer sister asked us to. 'Cause St. Jude is allus lookin' fer hopeless cases ta make hopeful. 'Cause it's the right thing ta do. 'Cause we can." Tante Lulu shrugged. "But you gotta have help from the inside, too. We cain't do all the work."

Leroy straightened, instantly suspicious. "How?"

"Well, you gotta behave yerself. Not get inta trouble."

"And not piss off any more politicians . . . at least for a while," Charmaine contributed.

"And work with us within the prison," Gabrielle said. "Maybe we can influence that guy who was a star witness against you."

"Us? Within? I don't like the sounds of that." Leroy was shaking his head, already rejecting what they wanted to do, even before he knew what that was. "No way are you getting within a mile of Little Eddie Hebert. He's vicious as a rattler in a bucket."

Tante Lulu spoke right over Leroy's objections. "Yep. We's gonna work on that talent show here at the prison. Dontcha be worryin' none. We'll take care of Little Eddie. Betcha I know his mama, or one of his kinfolks. There are Heberts up and down the bayou. He'll be squealin' like a stuck pig before I'm done with him."

Leroy's eyes got wider and wider. He turned to Gabrielle as if for help.

What could she do? She was caught in the path of the same Cajun tornado.

"Does Sigurdsson know you're gonna help with the talent show?" An expression of amusement bloomed on Leroy's face, replacing the usual gloom.

"Sigurdsson? Do you mean Reverend Sigurdsson?" Tante Lulu asked.

"Can you introduce us?" Charmaine wanted to know.

"Oh yeah! The *Rev* is right over there." Leroy turned slightly in his chair and pointed at the man still leaning against the wall, still staring at Gabrielle as if he couldn't believe his eyes.

Gabrielle realized in that instant that the odd little white turtleneck she'd noticed earlier was actually a clerical collar. Under a muscle shirt? And she recalled her physical reaction to him. *Oh my God! I got an instant turn-on over a priest. How pathetic is that?*

"Hallelujah! After all these years my prayers are answered. Thank you, St. Jude!" Tante Lulu had both hands crossed over her chest. The expression on her wrinkled face was one of delighted wonder.

Now what?

"Settle down, Auntie. You look like you're gonna have a heart attack. What's the matter?" Charmaine had her arm around her aunt's shoulders and was squeezing her with concern.

"He's what's the matter," Tante Lulu said, pointing at the man against the wall. "An angel. God has sent me an angel."

Leroy let out a hoot of laughter. "He may be weird for a man of the cloth, but an angel? I don't think so!"

"Did you take your blood pressure pill this morning?" Charmaine asked her aunt.

"She must be hallucinating," Gabrielle told her brother.

"I'm not hallucinatin'. Holy crawfish! Cain't y'all see his wings? They're blue and misty-like."

They all looked at the man, who didn't seem at all discomforted by their joint perusal. And not a wing in sight, as far as Gabrielle could see.

"Armageddon mus' be comin'," Tante Lulu wailed, waving her hands in the air like they were at a revival meeting.

"Yeah, well, let's get a closer look at ol' Armageddie," Leroy said, motioning with a forefinger to the man. "Hey, *Rev*, come on over and meet some folks."

As if he'd been waiting for an invitation, the man shoved away from the wall and began to amble over toward their table. It might have been Leroy who called for him, but the man's eyes were still locked on Gabrielle.

And, *be still my horny heart*, he was even more good-looking up close. In fact, Gabrielle didn't think she'd ever met another man so compellingly attractive. Her heart was racing and her lips parted. She sighed before she had a chance to check herself.

He smiled, knowing perfectly well what effect he was having on her. Without his even speaking a word, Gabrielle knew she was in the presence of a player. The kind of man who could make a woman melt with just an arch of a brow. The kind of man women like her should steer clear of. She had no time for games.

"Rev, these people would like to meet you," Leroy said with a mischievous glint in his eyes. "Charmaine LeDeux Lanier, Louise Rivard, and Gabrielle Sonnier, my sister." He put particular emphasis on that last, as if warning the man off her. Then, "The Rev. Ivak Sigurdsson."

It was an indication of how smart Leroy was that he could recall all those names he'd just been introduced to.

"Rev?" the man replied. "Hardly."

"Aintcha a minister?" Tante Lulu asked, her eyes still filled with wonder.

"Sort of. Just call me Ivak."

"And you kin call me Tante Lulu. Kin I touch yer wings?"

"Sure," he said, while the rest of them asked, "What wings?"

Ivak pulled a chair from a nearby table and shoved it in between Gabrielle and Tante Lulu, forcing Gabrielle to move slightly to his right.

While Tante Lulu was touching his shoulder, Ivak turned to Gabrielle, his eyes smoldering an erotic message at her. "Did Mike send you here?"

"Mike who?"

He licked his upper lip. "My boss."

She felt as if he'd licked *her* upper lip, and she just barely stopped herself from mirroring his action. She shook her head slowly from side to side to clear the odd buzzing in her ears. "No. I went to Tante Lulu for help in getting my brother out of prison. She has a lot of connections, or so I was told. And she heard about some

prison talent show that she thought her family could infiltrate, or something, and I got kind of bulldozed into
coming here today. But holy moly! I'm turning into a
regular Chatty Cathy." She was rambling and couldn't
seem to stop.

He continued to smile at her.

And she felt an erotic thrill pass over her in waves. Just
from a smile. But wait. "Oh my God! You have vampire
teeth," she blurted out. And he did, not that they made
him any less attractive, just different.

"Oops," he said, and wiped a hand across his closed
mouth. Then, he asked, "Better?" He bared his top teeth
at her.

She nodded. The pointed incisors were mostly gone.
He now had perfectly straight, white teeth that would do
an orthodontist proud.

"Sorry about that. I can usually control myself, but
when I'm in high emotion, they come out." He shrugged
helplessly.

"Your teeth elongate and retract at will?" she asked
tentatively.

"Not exactly."

"And why are you in 'high emotion'?"

"Tsk, tsk, tsk!" he chided her. "Surely, you feel it, too."
His voice was husky as he took her hand in his under the
table.

The shock of his touch, palm against palm, was almost
her undoing. In a week that had been filled with one shock
after another, this reaction to a stranger could be her tip-
ping point. As blood drained from her head, she could
feel herself growing faint. The only thing anchoring her
to the chair was Ivak's tighter hold on her hand.

Luckily, Tante Lulu drew his attention from the other
side. "Didja ever meet St. Jude?"

What? Where did that come from? Honestly, the old

lady was a fruitcake, and Gabrielle was beginning to feel like one of the nuts.

"Uh, no, I haven't," Ivak said.

"What seminary did you attend?" Charmaine asked, clearly as puzzled as Gabrielle by his appearance, which was not very clerical.

"Um. St. Michael's."

Tante Lulu leaned up and whispered something in his ear.

He nodded.

Tante Lulu beamed then as she addressed Charmaine and Gabrielle. "Aintcha glad now that we come ta help with the talent show?"

Charmaine and Gabrielle looked at each other, puzzled.

"St. Jude had a hand in our comin' here, sure as shootin'. Speakin' of shootin'," Tante Lulu addressed Leroy now, "dontcha be shootin' anyone 'til we spring you outta this slammer. Thass what they call a prison. The slammer."

"I know what a slammer is. Jesus! Who are you people?" Leroy asked, then speared Gabrielle with a glare.

She shrugged.

Ivak told Leroy not to use the Lord's name in vain.

Charmaine was checking out a chip in her nail enamel.

Leroy swore under his breath, something about his fucked-up life.

Tante Lulu made a hissing noise of disapproval.

Ivak reached across the table and swatted Leroy on the shoulder. "Have a care, lest I show you how fucked up your life can get." He turned to the others then and said, "About your helping with the talent show . . . I appreciate the offer, but I doubt the warden would let any outsiders in here to participate."

"Pooh! I'll take care of the warden," Tante Lulu said, opening her Richard Simmons fan and waving it in front of her face. "It's hotter in here than a goat's butt in a pepper patch."

Noticing the worry on Ivak's face, Charmaine added, "The LeDeux family is noted for its talent shows. We can guarantee you a success."

"I don't know about that, but if you can get this stubborn ass here"—he pointed at Leroy—"to play his horn in the show, it would be a huge help."

Leroy shot him a look of consternation. "Nice try, dickhead."

"Oh, he'll be participatin', all right," Tante Lulu assured Ivak.

"It'll be fun," Charmaine assured Leroy, patting him on the arm.

Leroy stared pointedly at her hand and asked, "Are you sure you're married, honey?"

"I'm married all right, and you best drop the honeys before Rusty gets here. My husband, bless his heart, has a jealous streak wide as Bayou Teche."

Leroy winked at her.

Charmaine laughed. "Tell you what, though. I have a stylist in my Houma salon that looks just like I did twenty years ago. Behave yourself and once you're out, I'll fix you up."

"Deal!" Leroy said, though the expression on his face told another story. He didn't think he'd ever get out.

One of the guard's cell phones rang then and he walked over asking which of them was Charmaine Lanier. When Charmaine stood, his eyes went wide with appreciation before he handed her the phone. After a few "uh-huhs" and "okays" and then a "Love you, too, baby," Charmaine clicked off the phone and handed it back to the guard. Then she told them all, "Rusty has permission for us all . . . including you, Leroy . . . to go over to the area where the rodeo is held and a stage will be erected for the talent show. Let's go check it out."

They all stood to go, except Ivak and Gabrielle. Ivak was holding her hand firmly on his thigh and he told the others, "I have a few things to discuss with Gabrielle. We'll catch up with you."

Gabrielle started to protest, but Ivak whispered close to her ear, "We can settle this in private, or in front of everyone. Your choice."

Seeing that Leroy was about to protest as well, which might very well end in a brawl, Gabrielle said, "Mr. Sigurdsson is right. There are a few details I need to discuss with him."

When the others left, Ivak drawled, "*Mr.* Sigurdsson?" and drew her hand up to kiss her knuckles. She tried to unlace her fingers from Ivak's, but he held tight. Over their entwined fingers, he winked at her.

She was not going to think about how that wink affected her.

"Hardly the way you should address your soul mate, dearling."

Gabrielle just laughed and stood, yanking her hand free.

"You find amusement in me, m'lady?" The Viking actually looked offended as he stood, too, towering over her.

"Well, yeah! C'mon! You have to admit, that is the oldest line in the book. Soul mates went out with bell-bottoms."

"Are you saying that we're not soul mates?" A hopeful expression covered his handsome face and he raised his eyes to the ceiling. "Thank you, God!"

That wasn't very complimentary, not that she cared, of course. "What is it that you wanted to discuss with me? If it's just to put some moves on me, forget about it. I'm immune to womanizers like you."

"Now that's a challenge I can't ignore. Wait here." He went over and spoke rapidly with a nearby guard. The guard in turn spoke into a cell phone, then nodded at Ivak. Ivak returned to the table and said, "I have permission to take you to my office where we can speak in private."

She balked. "Why can't we talk here?"

He shook his head. "The things I have to tell you must not be overheard."

Okaaay. Maybe he has information that would help Leroy's case. "All right, but I have to join the others soon."

He smiled at her as if he'd won some victory.

Five

This kiss! This kiss! And then some, Faith Hill! ...

Ivak had done some bizarre things in his very long life, but dragging a hesitant woman through an all-male prison defied even his admittedly loose boundaries.

Despite her contention that they were not soul mates, Ivak had a nagging suspicion that she was wrong. He had to find out. How he would deal with that calamity, he had no idea, but a warrior had to know what he was up against afore entering battle. And this would be a battle for him, if his suspicions were proved true. He would lose what little freedom he now had.

Actually, he wasn't exactly dragging the woman, and she wasn't exactly protesting. More like leading a stubborn mutt outside on a cold night. Not that he would tell her that. She was already scowling at him like he was a gruesome troll, probably because his office was so far away from the visitors' area.

Finally, he reached the end of the hallway that branched off The Walk. He unlocked his office door with one hand, shoved Gabrielle inside, then locked the door behind him, pocketing the key. Leaning back against the door, he watched as she positioned herself on the other side of his desk, as if she could do anything to withstand his siege.

Not that he was planning a siege.

Unless he had to.

Besides, it was a small room, so there wasn't all that much distance between them, without sieging.

He inhaled deeply and held his breath, hoping to withstand her allure.

She was beautiful.

To me, leastways.

Taller than normal.

We would fit together perfectly.

Thinner than he usually liked.

I could feed her grapes and sweetmeats in bed.

Frown lines bracketed her lush mouth.

Oh, the ways that I could make her smile.

Hair pulled off her face, hard, like a nun.

Not a nun. Definitely not a nun I am picturing with the long silky strands spread over my pillow.

He should be immune to a woman like her, not at all what he usually favored, but he was not immune. Far from it. Every nerve ending in his body was sending him danger signals.

He'd never felt this way before.

There was no explanation.

Unless . . .

She glanced at him, then did a double take. "Why are you looking at me like that?"

"Like what?" he asked, trying to make his face blank.

"Like I'm a tasty praline you'd like to sink your teeth into."

If you only knew, dearling! If you only knew! "I don't know what you're talking about."

Placing both palms on the desk blotter, she told him, "You are in such trouble, buster, if you don't have a very good reason for bringing me back here. I could sue your pants off if you have some ulterior motives. I can do it, too. I'm a lawyer."

"My name is Ivak, not Buster, and, sweetling, methinks you would not have to use legal means to get my pants off. One whiff of your woman scent, and I am ready to surrender all to you." He gave her a slow, lazy smile . . . the one that was a surefire melter of woman throughout time.

She just frowned.

He tried a different smile, the one where his lips were closed and a little pouty. "Or mayhap you would consider surrendering to me."

Nothing.

Am I losing my charm? Oh no! All these years of celibacy must be ruining my woman-luck.

"Are you crazy?"

"A little bit." *It will be a lot if I find out I am now a charmless troll, that is for sure.*

"What the hell is a woman scent?"

"It's the enticing aroma that exudes from the skin drawing a mate. Like roses and musk, yours is."

"Musk! Somewhere in that ridiculous statement is an insult."

He shook his head. "I suspect you are aware of my male scent as well. Scent awareness is apparent only to destined couples."

"That soul mate BS again!" Her face colored.

"'Tis true, I fear."

"Do you mean that odd mixture of cloves and sandalwood? I figured it must be your cologne or deodorant."

He shook his head, then smiled again. He was turning into a regular smiling idiot. "Is that how I smell to you? Cloves and sandalwood? Nice," he decided. "No one has ever remarked on it before, but it is definitely not a manmade substance."

"You're talking about pheromones. Don't give me that destiny bullshit."

He cringed at her crude language, but decided now was not the time to tell her of his preferences. She would soon learn what pleased him *if* she was his soul mate.

Mayhap this is just a trick Mike is tossing my way to trip me up.

Mayhap I got my signals crossed, and she is not my destined mate, after all.

Well, there is one way to find out.

"Come here," he said and wagged his fingertips in a beckoning fashion.

Her eyes went wide. "In your dreams!"

"That, too." Ivak figured he had a limited amount of time before someone came looking for them. So, he shortcut through his usual repertoire of seduction techniques. He held her gaze for a long moment.

She was unable to look away.

There were some gifts a vampire angel had that came in handy.

Almost immediately, she gasped and began to walk woodenly toward him. He was standing against the wall under a security camera. They wouldn't be seen.

When she stood before him, almost touching, he blew softly against her lips. He could not kiss her. Not yet. Lest he lose control. He was on the edge already. *Do not kiss her, Ivak,* he warned himself.

"Ooooh," she moaned softly, and put her hands on his shoulders to keep herself upright. "What are you doing to me?"

"Testing," he said against one side of her mouth. *Do not kiss her, Ivak.*

"Me?"

"Both of us." He pressed his lips to the other side of her mouth. *Do not kiss her, Ivak.*

"I'm very smart. I excel at tests," she said, her breath an erotic feather stroke against his sensitized lips.

"It's not that kind of test," he murmured into her ear. *Do not kiss her, Ivak.*

She shivered. "Have you hypnotized me?"

"Have you hypnotized me?" he countered and nipped at her luscious earlobe. *Holy clouds! When did ear parts become carnal triggers for me?*

The good, saner side of his brain continued to warn, *Do not kiss her, Ivak.*

The bad, or leastways weaker, side of his brain said, *Surely I have enough self-control to withstand one little kiss.*

Guess who won?

Ivak fisted his hands at his side, deluding himself that if he didn't touch her with his hands he could maintain at least a modicum of control, and laid his lips gently on hers. A whisper of a kiss. Nothing, really. And everything.

It felt as if he had a thousand pinpoints of nerve endings on his lips and they were all exploding with the most exquisite pleasure. Even worse, or better, his instantly sword-hard cock felt the same way.

Gabrielle must have been experiencing the same thing because she moaned and parted her lips.

It was all the invitation Ivak needed, or temptation he could withstand.

With a groan of surrender, he gently cupped her face in his hands and angled her head just so. Then he took her mouth voraciously, like a marauding Viking too long at sea. He would have tried harder to slow himself down if Gabrielle weren't so accepting of his "assault." In truth, she was doing a bit of assaulting herself, her arms wrapped tightly around his neck, as if to prevent his retreat. Hah! Retreat was the last thing on his sex-hazed brain.

Some men considered kissing a mere speed bump on the way to intercourse. Not him. A good kiss required a finesse that he had in abundance.

But this kiss was different.

When their lips locked, an odd compulsion overtook them both. He breathed into her mouth, and she breathed back into his. Over and over. They inhaled and exhaled each other's very life sustenance in a most carnal manner. Amazing!

Ivak was a good kisser. He prided himself on all the nuances of the art, the taking and the giving, the coaxing and the demands, the licking and the sucking, all utilizing combinations of the lips, teeth, and tongue.

Gabrielle was a good kisser, too, but Ivak wasn't sure if it came from years of experience, as his skill did, or the unique chemistry betwixt the two of them. As a narcissist from way back—though he had not known the word then—he preferred to think it was the former.

"You taste like mint and woman-lust," he murmured against her mouth during one brief break.

"You really do have wings. Beautiful, misty blue wings," she said against his mouth during a later break. "They are wrapped around me like a million cuddly feathers."

Ivak did not know about that! He'd never actually seen that wispy blue wing phenomenon himself, though he had witnessed it on his brothers. And as for cuddly . . . not quite what he was known for!

They kissed and kissed and kissed, for what felt like hours, but was probably only fifteen minutes or so. He had to stop soon, not just because he was becoming too aroused, but he did not want his first time with this woman—if there was to be a time, at all—to be inside a prison where even the walls had eyes. Though it was other eyes he was more concerned about. Celestial eyes.

With a sigh, he set Gabrielle away from him, hands on her shoulders to steady her shaky frame. Truth to tell, he was shaky himself. "Gabrielle, we must stop," he said. "Much as I would like to hold you for hours"—*and do much more than hold*—"we must catch up with your brother." To Ivak's shame, he'd just realized that Leroy was out and about carrying the Lucie sin taint, not that the demon vampires would attack when he was in a group, or out in the open. No, they would wait until he was alone in a secluded area, if only for a moment.

She blinked several times, as if confused. She had beautiful eyes, brown pools edged in a darker, almost black shade, like caramel with a rim of chocolate. "What . . . what have you done to me?" She shoved away from him and put the back of her hand to her kiss-swollen lips. He loved that he had marked her in that way, and wondered if he was marked by her, as well. He hoped so. "Oh my God! Did you slip me a roofie, or something? No, it can't be that. I haven't drunk anything. I feel so . . . overcome."

He shook his head. "I've done nothing to you. Overcome, that is a good word. It was done to us both."

"By whom?"

He raised his gaze upward.

She looked up at the grimy ceiling, as if the answer lay there. When she understood what he'd meant, she laughed.

He loved her laugh, like a feather tickling his soul, it was.

"That has got to be the all-time lamest-ass excuse for bad behavior. I've heard the expression, 'The devil made me do it,' but 'God made me do it,' that's a new one."

He shrugged. *You have no idea, sweetling.*

"Why would God, assuming there is a God, do such a thing?"

"Ours is not to reason why." *Did I really spout such nonsense?*

She shook her head at him, equally unimpressed with his platitude. "Well, let's get out of here before Tante Lulu and Charmaine do something outrageous, like stage a prison break, or something."

"Uh, there's one thing, sweetling. You must leave Leroy in my hands. Best you stay away from this prison, for the time being, at least. Evil forces are at work here. It is no place for an innocent woman."

"How about an innocent man?"

"That, too," he said.

"He didn't kill that inmate."

Ivak could argue that most inmates claimed they were innocent. "Just leave, and I will take over your mission."

"Is that an order?"

"You could say so."

"I beg your pardon. You don't have the right to give me orders. Do you think a mere kiss gives you some authority over me?"

"There was naught *mere* about our kiss, and you know it. Perhaps I was less than adept in expressing my view; English is not my first language. Let me rephrase. Gabrielle, sweetling, it would be wise if you would step back from your efforts to help your brother, and let me handle things from here on."

"Oh, that was much better."

"Sarcasm ill-suits you, dearling."

"Cut the endearments and unlock that door, Mr. Sigurdsson. I'm going to help my brother, no matter what you say."

Only if I'm glued to your backside, he thought, then grinned at the image. He unlocked the door and they were walking down the hallway when he asked with a casualness that scarce hid his concern, "Where do you live, Gabrielle? Not near the prison, I hope."

"No one lives near the prison, as you well know, or should know, except for a vast number of gators and snakes," she said with more of the sarcasm he misliked. "Not that it's any of your business, but I have a small apartment on Dumaine Street in New Orleans. It's close to the Second Chances legal defense office where I work."

Ivak's heart began to race wildly and a cold sweat broke out on his skin. "Please tell me you are not anywhere near the restaurant Anguish." The haakai demon vampire Dominique used the renowned eating place in the French Quarter as a front for her torture chambers.

Gabrielle glanced at him with surprise. "It's right across the street. I hear they serve the most incredible dish."

What? Grilled humans? Or soul food, literally?

"It's called Blood Gumbo."

Six

Something stinks in Angola . . .

Gabrielle continued to be confused, sitting next to Ivak as they were driven across the prison grounds by a taciturn guard who did little more than grunt yes or no to her questions. Angola covered a massive property, and, although many prisoners were marched double file every morning to the fields by guards on horseback, it was deemed too far for visitors to travel on foot.

Some of the fertile land was planted in various crops, some of it set aside as pasture for cattle or horses, and some was used to house the camp dormitories. It had been the site of a slave-breeding plantation long ago; in many ways the slavery continued. In fact, Angola was the name of the country from which many of those slaves had been taken. There was a sad irony in the fact that most of the inmates were black.

She walked now from the parking lot to the rodeo stands, side by side with Ivak, this strange man who had a strange hold on her. She even liked the way he walked, back straight, eyes ever alert to their surroundings.

Not that she would let him know that. His ego was big enough already.

She was even more confused when they approached the rodeo arena where Tante Lulu, Charmaine, and Rusty Lanier, the handsome husband of Charmaine, were leaning against a corral fence watching some inmates try to ride their resisting horses in tandem for the opening rodeo ceremony. Leroy was off near a shed, talking to another inmate, identifiable by his attire. Inmates wore jeans with either a white T-shirt or a blue work shirt, except for inmates being disciplined; they wore white jumpsuits. Several blue-uniformed prison guards stood nearby keeping an eye on them all, making sure no convicts approached them, or vice versa, she supposed.

That was when Ivak's head shot up, he sniffed the air, shoved her toward the group ahead of them, then literally shot at what seemed to be warp speed off into the wooded area to their right.

"Did you see that?" she shrieked.

"What?" everyone said.

"Ivak . . . I mean, Mr. Sigurdsson . . . seemed to fly off into those woods over there." She pointed to the forested area where not a leaf or blade moved on this breezeless day. Almost immediately, she felt foolish for having voiced such an observation.

"Well, whadja 'spect. He's an angel, ain't he?" Tante Lulu had made the same remark earlier about Ivak being an angel. A ridiculous idea, Gabrielle had thought at the time, but now with an image of those wispy blue things she'd witnessed in his office a short time ago, she wasn't so sure. *Of course he isn't an angel. What am I thinking?*

"There's no such thing as an angel, Auntie," Charmaine said.

My thoughts exactly.

"Next, you'll be tellin' me there ain't no St. Jude, either," Tante Lulu replied huffily.

Rusty rolled his eyes at Gabrielle. She'd gotten to know Charmaine's husband as he drove them to the prison. Although he was a quiet-spoken man, the opposite of his effusive wife whom he obviously adored, he'd told them numerous stories of his wrongful incarceration years ago at Angola.

Leroy came over then and whispered in her ear, "Where did you disappear to?"

"I had some things to discuss with Mr. Sigurdsson." She hoped she wasn't blushing.

It wasn't her cheeks, though, that Leroy's eyes fixed on. It was her lips, which she suspected were bruised from Ivak's kisses. "I'll kill him for laying a hand on you." Leroy scanned the area for Ivak, to no avail.

"Don't even joke about killing someone," Gabrielle chided him. "Besides, Ivak never laid a hand on me." Well, hardly.

"What? You bit your own lips?" Something else seemed to occur to him. "Shit! He bit you."

"Oh, for heaven's sake! The man thinks we're soul mates. Why would he bite me, anyway?" Actually, some of his kisses had been a bit nibbling, but Leroy didn't need to know that.

"Soul . . . soul . . ." Leroy sputtered, then burst out laughing. "Well, I've wanted you to get a life. I just never thought it would be with a weirdo prison chaplain."

Tante Lulu overheard and remarked to Leroy, "Where'd you learn ta whisper? In a sawmill?" But then she let out a hoot of laughter and slapped her one thigh. "I knew it, I knew it. My matchmakin' works, even when I ain't done nothin'. It's a miracle. You got a hope chest yet, girl?"

"Uh . . ."

"Not ta worry. I'll whip one up quicker 'n spit. I gives

'em ta all my family and friends, even the menfolks." She gave Leroy a considering perusal. "You get yerself outta the big house, and I'll make you a hope chest, too."

"That is just great," Leroy muttered. When Gabrielle elbowed him for his rudeness, he added, "Thank you very much, Ms. Rivard."

"Tante Lulu," she corrected him.

They all turned then at the sound of an engine. A pickup truck drove up almost to the fence and out climbed Warden Benton and his assistant Selma Dubois, who was in charge of PR. Both wore business suits, Benton's minus the tie in deference to the heat, Dubois's with a few buttons undone. With wide smiles on their faces, they greeted everyone.

Tante Lulu and her family must have even more clout than Gabrielle had suspected.

Leroy whispered in her ear. "Who *are* these people? Celebrities or something? They must be to merit the top brass Welcome Wagon."

"They may very well be your ticket out of here, so behave," she whispered back.

Leroy nodded.

Just then, Gabrielle felt a warm finger trail down the back of her neck. She jerked around to see that Ivak had returned. His hair was disheveled, strands having escaped their ponytail, and his clerical collar was lopsided inside his muscle shirt. And—

"Sigurdsson! What is that god-awful smell?" Warden Benton asked, frowning at Ivak.

An odor resembling sulfur, or rotten eggs, emanated from Ivak.

"Oops! I must have touched a stinkleberry bush," Ivak said.

Stinkleberry?

He winked at her and went over to a horse trough

where he proceeded to rinse off his hands and arms up to the elbows, not at all flustered by everyone gawking at him. When he returned to Gabrielle's side, the odor was gone. He told the warden then, as if he was in charge, "You can resume now."

The warden looked as if he might like to throttle Ivak on the spot.

Ivak turned to the warden's assistant. "Hi, Ms. Dew-bwah," he drawled out.

The fortyish woman turned beet-red and giggled. She actually giggled. Good Lord, did the man have this effect on all women?

"Do you want Mr. Sigurdsson to return to the Main Prison?" Ms. Dubois asked the warden. "I could drive him back."

She would probably take the long way back, Gabrielle thought meanly.

The warden hesitated for a moment before shaking his head, "We need him here to see how the LeDeuxs might help with the talent show. He's not makin' much headway on his own." He gave Ivak a pointed look, which Ivak chose to ignore.

"Sounds like someone's got a burr under his saddle," Ivak said out of the side of his mouth to Gabrielle. Then he winked at Ms. Dubois. "Thanks anyway, Sel-ma."

Sel-ma? The louse! No, no, no! I have no right to be possessive over him.

Leroy, on her other side, heard Ivak as well. He smiled. "Man, I'm startin' to like this guy. Scary!"

Ms. Dubois was self-consciously fluffing her helmet hair and casting Ivak surreptitious glances.

He just smiled, knowing perfectly well the effect he was having. *The louse!*

"Do you flirt with every woman you meet?"

He seemed to ponder her question, then replied, "Probably." Then, when no one was looking, he pinched her butt and added, "But I only kiss the pretty ones."

There he went with the hokey lines again. "You are so not my type," she avowed, rubbing a hand over her behind.

"That remains to be seen," he countered with annoying self-confidence, as if he would be the one to determine whether they made love or not.

The warden and his assistant proceeded to give them the grand tour of the rodeo arena, stables, and barns. "Our arena seats ten thousand. I figure for the last rodeo in October when the talent show is put on, we can double or triple the admission price. With the LeDeux name attached to the show, it'll be a sellout." Benton preened at relaying that news.

"Where exactly will the show's profits be allocated?" Ivak asked.

Benton bristled and Ms. Dubois flushed with embarrassment at Ivak's blunt question.

"Tsk, tsk, tsk, Mr. Sigurdsson. All of the rodeo funds go to inmate programs, as you well know," Ms. Dubois said, her head-to-toe survey of the Viking "chaplain" a contradiction of her testy words.

"But the talent show funds, the amount charged above the regular admission price, do you have plans for that money? I figure on any one day, at fifteen dollars a ticket, you bring in a hundred and fifty thousand dollars, give or take. If you double or triple the ticket price because of the talent show, we're talking a huge profit, above your regular take."

Ms. Dubois gasped at the word *take*. And Gabrielle could tell that Ivak was really annoying the warden, as well.

Tante Lulu, bless her heart, understood the undercurrents. "Now, dontcha go gettin' all riled up, Pierce. Our preacher friend here is jist askin' the questions we all have."

Charmaine was quick to add, "While we LeDeux don't charge for our talent shows, we like to think they're for a good cause."

"No one is saying you would do otherwise," Rusty tried for the more diplomatic route.

"Where would you like to see the funds go?" Benton asked Tante Lulu.

She turned to Ivak. "Now's yer chance ta speak, boy."

Ivak didn't even blink or hesitate. "Education, for one. Since government grants were cut, the only chance for higher education for inmates is through the ministry program, and while that's a good thing, inmates should have other options."

Since the ministry college program was Benton's pet project, he was not happy with Ivak's suggestion.

"The prisoner legal defense fund is almost laughable," Ivak continued. "Then there's the inmate vet program, hospice, and of course all the prison chaplain expenses, of all religious denominations. And thinking really big . . . how about accommodations for inmate visitors who have traveled a long distance and have no place to stay? Sort of a Ronald McDonald House for convicts, just outside the prison gates. We could call it the Little House. A play on the Big House." He waggled his eyebrows at his own attempt at humor.

The warden was not happy, but he nodded. Ms. Dubois looked interested.

"We kin sit down and discuss all this before the show," the shrewd Tante Lulu offered, not about to wait and leave it all in the warden's hands.

When they were done examining the area where a portable stage would be erected with sound systems, Warden Benton turned on them and asked, "What does Leroy Sonnier and his sister have to do with all this?"

Gabrielle felt Leroy stiffen beside her at the rudeness

of the question. She took his hand in hers, squeezing, as a warning to keep quiet and let her speak. "I went to Tante Lulu for help in my efforts to get my brother a pardon or clemency. She suggested we visit the prison and meet Mr. Sigurdsson. We figured if we could get Leroy involved in a project like the talent show that benefits the prison, it would look good on his record when he comes up for his next parole board hearing." Well, that wasn't exactly a lie, just a little stretch of the truth.

"Whaaat?" Leroy murmured and shot a glare at Ivak.

Ivak shrugged, as if he had nothing to do with this, but was obviously not unhappy. "Better polish up the horn, my friend."

Leroy mouthed something at Ivak that was not friendly.

"And I understand Mr. Sonnier has somehow, miraculously, got another hearing in November," the warden said, his voice reeking with malice. Not a happy camper.

"You got Jude ta thank fer that," Tante Lulu said.

"Who?" both the warden and Ms. Dubois asked.

"St. Jude." Tante Lulu reached into a pocket, pulling out two small St. Jude candles, similar to the one she'd given Leroy back in the visiting area, and gave them to the astonished couple.

They looked down at the candles in their hands with puzzlement.

"What you need here at Angola is more St. Jude. He's the patron saint of hopeless cases, you know. Betcha got lots of hopeless folks here."

"Um," the warden stammered.

"Can we move things along? I have to be back at the ranch by five," Rusty said.

The warden shook his head as if clear it. "I have a penitentiary to run here. While I suggested this talent show to begin with, and I still think it's a good idea, I can't have outside people running around inside the prison willy-nilly."

"Willy-nilly?" Now Tante Lulu was offended.

Charmaine buried her face in her hands, suspecting what was coming next.

"Wait 'til I tell folks how you treated an ol' lady," Tante Lulu warned.

"Now, now, all I'm sayin' is we need ta set some rules. First of all, this is still an inmate talent show. I appreciate you LeDeuxs comin' to entertain, but as for helpin' Sigurdsson with the show, I'm gonna have to insist on only a couple people at one time. Even then, you can't be comin' in here every day."

Ivak raised his hand for attention when everyone started talking at once. "I suggest, respectfully, Warden Benton, that you assign Leroy Sonnier as my assistant for the talent show. You may not be aware, but he's a talented musician."

Leroy started to protest, but Gabrielle dug her fingernails into his forearm.

Ms. Dubois made a gurgling sound that no one noticed except Gabrielle. She had probably been hoping to assist Ivak.

"I'm fine with one or two of the LeDeuxs coming once a week to help me with the talent show. Perhaps closer to the show date, you'll agree to letting the LeDeuxs hold some dress rehearsals on the stage." Ivak looked toward the warden with more deference than Gabrielle suspected that he usually showed.

Warden Benton nodded, tentatively.

"Uh, I want to be involved, too," Gabrielle said.

Ivak shocked her by shaking his head fiercely. "This is no place for a woman like Miss Sonnier. Except for visiting her brother, I do not want her involved with the project."

So much for soul mate! "Hey, just wait a minute here," she said.

But Ivak ignored her and told Warden Benton, "That's a deal breaker for me."

The warden agreed, although he clearly didn't like Ivak dictating terms to him.

"What's that all about?" her brother whispered to her.

"I have no idea," she said, "but I'm going to find out."

As everyone proceeded to leave the arena area, Ivak held her back. "We need to talk."

"Tell me about it, jerk. Besides, I've already had one of your talks, and there wasn't much speaking involved."

He grinned. The man had a death wish. But then when he saw she was about to walk away, he said, "I can explain."

"I doubt it."

"Gabrielle. Dearling."

"Cut the bullshit. What do you hope to accomplish with those hokey endearments? I am not your soul mate. I'm not even your friend. I am not your anything."

His back straightened and he seemed to grit his teeth before saying, "You are mine. Well, probably mine. That is yet to be determined. In the meantime, I protect those under my shield."

"Yeah, well, you know where you can shove your shield." Fuming with anger, she decided she couldn't handle this right now. Swiveling on her heels, she began to stomp away.

She heard Tante Lulu chuckle and advise Ivak, "Honey is sweet, but don't lick it off a briar."

"Not to worry. I have a leathery tongue." Ivak laughed and called out something she never expected the brute to say.

"I can save him."

Gabrielle halted and turned slowly.

Ivak hadn't moved an inch. His arms were folded over his chest. He was angry, too.

"What . . . did . . . you . . . say?"

"I can save your brother."

Abnormal, paranormal, same thing ...

It was hours before Ivak was able to escape to his office and ask that Leroy Sonnier be sent to him for "counseling."

First, he had to submit to one of the warden's lectures. His attire. His attitude. His failure to comply with rules. His familiarity with visitors. His rudeness to visitors. Even his frickin' hair. Blather, blather, blather!

After that, Ivak held more auditions for the talent show. First up was a seventy-year-old lifer who yodeled. Enough said! Things went downhill from there, especially when several of the contestants got into an argument over who had more talent and ended up brawling. Two bloody noses and a goose egg later, Ivak was off to talk with a man in hospice who wanted to repent and discuss the afterlife with Ivak. Even though Ivak didn't feel qualified to do that type of counseling, he could not rebuff the man, and in the end he felt as if the man was more at peace.

Finally, he was back in his office finishing off a Coke and a stale turkey sandwich when Leroy Sonnier arrived. One glance at the inmate's surly expression, and Ivak knew the sin taint was already working in him. Ever since Leroy had been with Ivak and his sister and the LeDeuxs several hours ago, the taint had grown.

He was probably resenting Ivak's calling him to his office. An invitation by any of the prison employees to a convict was tantamount to an order by the powers-that-be, no questions asked. Leroy could not have declined coming if he'd wanted to, which he obviously hadn't.

Ivak motioned for Leroy to sit while he went over and locked the door, closing it on the guard who'd accompanied Leroy. The click of the lock drew arched brows from Leroy.

Then they both spoke at the same time.

"Stay away from my sister."

"You have a problem, Leroy."

"I'm doing hard time, dickhead. Yeah, I have a problem. Don't you think I know that by now?"

"If I were you, I'd shut up and listen. You have problems way bigger than being in prison."

That seemed to get Leroy's attention.

Ivak pulled a folding chair over and sat opposite Leroy. "I'm not really a minister," he started. The security camera could see, but not hear them. A concession given for counselor privilege, rather like a confessional.

"No shit!"

"I'm something else."

"Yeah, I know. You're a Viking. Everyone around here has heard your 'I am a Viking' crap."

Ivak inhaled and exhaled for patience. "I am a sort of angel sent here to help young men like you."

Leroy laughed. "Sort of?"

"I'm a vampire angel. A vangel."

Leroy's eyes, which were very much like Gabrielle's, he realized, went wide before he snorted his disbelief. "Dracula with wings? Give me a break!"

"I prefer to focus on my angel side."

"Sonofabitch! You're serious, aren't you? Man, you're weirder than I thought. I mean it. Stay away from my sister."

First things first. He would discuss Leroy's sister with him later. Before that, the stubborn lout had to be convinced that Ivak was who, or what, he claimed to be.

Ivak stood and hissed. With his back to the camera, he opened his mouth to show his elongating fangs. Then, he concentrated on his back, hoping that the billowy blue wings would emerge but not show on camera.

Leroy jumped out of his chair and backed up against the wall. "Jesus F. Christ!"

"I am not Him, just one of His worker bees. Now sit down and listen to what I have to tell you."

Visibly shaking and watching Ivak guardedly as if a vampire, meaning him, might pounce on him, Leroy sat back down. Ivak did, too, and could feel his teeth and wings retracting.

"Oh my God! You have fuckin' fangs. Holy hell, man! If you're really an angel, that must mean you could pluck me out of this place, just like that"—he snapped his fingers for emphasis—"and land me somewhere far away, like Costa Rica."

"I could," Ivak said, "but I won't."

Leroy's shoulders slumped.

"Oh, I intend to get you out of here, God willing and you keeping your ass out of trouble, but it will be through normal channels. Well, not *normal* normal. The very fact that I'm slightly paranormal means I can cut corners."

Leroy shook his head with disbelief. "Slightly? Wings and fangs are a hell of a lot more than slightly abnormal."

Ivak had said *para*, not *ab*, but he wasn't going to argue semantics right now. "Listen, there's an immediate problem that we have to address before we can do anything else. I have to remove the sin taint from you."

"The what?"

"You have been infected with a demonic sin taint."

At first, Leroy just laughed. When he saw that Ivak was serious, he said, "Uh-oh! I don't like the sound of that."

Ivak explained Lucipires and how the demon vampires preyed on those in a state of sin, compelling them to do some evil, then draining them dry before they had a chance to repent.

"Are you saying one of these creatures bit me, and that I was going to end up dead and on the fast track to some kind of hell if he'd succeeded? Like that very day."

"That's about it in a nutshell. After you'd committed the mortal sin you'd been contemplating."

Leroy recoiled. "No way! No fucking way!"

"Believe me. Way! Because the Lucie only fanged you slightly, the process wasn't completed, but you're already becoming more compelled to sin."

"Just because I refused to be in your stupid show doesn't mean I was bitten by some demon."

"I can smell the sin taint on you. Lemony."

Leroy sniffed his armpit. "No lemons here."

"This is not a joke."

"Okay. I'll play. What will happen if I do nothing?"

"You'll murder someone, and seal your fate inside this hellhole . . ."

"I don't need a demon fanging to do that," Leroy scoffed.

" . . . or you'll kill someone, a Lucie will complete its fanging on you, and you'll end up in a place far, far worse than Angola."

"I'm finding all this impossible to believe. Are there vangels and Lucies all over the prison grounds?"

Ivak shook his head. "I'm the only vangel here. So far. But there are at least a few Lucies inside the fences and probably more in the perimeter. I killed one this afternoon. That was the smell you all noticed when I came back to the rodeo grounds."

"Why are you telling me this? Aren't you afraid I'll squeal to gain points with the warden? Or contact news media."

"First of all, no one would believe you. Second, you have more to gain by getting on my good side. Third, I could erase your memory of what I've just told you if I wanted to."

"If I refuse, will you force me?"

Ivak shook his head. "It must be your choice."

"If I refuse, will you report me to the warden for insubordination or some such shit? That's all I need at this point . . . a write-up."

Ivak shook his head again. "Do you think I would want the warden to know my true identity?"

Leroy still looked skeptical and angry, but he conceded, "What have I got to lose? Okay, what do I have to do?"

"You need to let me bite you and drain some blood. Just a small amount since your sin taint isn't that strong. It won't hurt, and you'll feel better immediately afterward."

Leroy nodded tentatively.

"Arm or neck?" Ivak asked, his fangs already out.

Leroy extended an arm and closed his eyes tightly, like a little kid getting a shot.

Later, after more explanations, the expression of Leroy's face was one of shock at all he'd learned in the past half hour. "I don't feel any different," he said. "I expected to be suddenly holier-than-thou."

"That's not the way it works. Believe me, you *are* different."

"I still don't want you near my sister," Leroy said. "In fact, I especially don't want you and your friggin' fangs near my sister now."

"I have to be near Gabrielle," Ivak insisted. "She is living across the street from a Lucie hangout."

"Whaaat? Oh shit! Oh damn!" He put his face in his hands. When he looked up, he said, "I feel so helpless in here."

"You are not to worry, I will take care of your sister."

"Why would you do that?"

"I am fairly certain"—he shuddered with distaste—"that she is my soul mate."

Seven

Her next-door neighbors are WHAT?...

Gabrielle was back in her small apartment in New Orleans.

She'd showered, conditioned her hair, slathered lotion all over her body, slipped on her favorite sky-blue silk pajamas, and was about to put a frozen Mexican dinner into the microwave. Afterward, she planned to fall into her bed with exhaustion. Some Friday night for a single girl! The usual for her.

She was carrying her dinner and a glass of white wine into the living room where the TV was already set to the local news station. Just then, she glanced at the French doors leading to her second floor balcony, and screamed.

"Shh!" Ivak said, opening the door and stepping inside. He took the glass and dish out of her hand, sniffing at both before setting them on a low table before the couch.

"You can't come in here! How did you get in? That door was locked. It's always locked."

He ignored her questions and remarked, "I love Mexican food. Do you have more?"

"I've got mace, that's what I've got."

"Good. You never know when you might have an intruder."

"*You're* an intruder."

"I am?"

"I could have you arrested for stalking me."

"Me? A stalker?" He appeared offended at her characterization, but then he smiled. "Ah, I see. You are jesting."

She crossed her eyes with frustration.

Just then, his stomach growled.

He shrugged. "I should probably eat before we discuss your willful behavior."

"I . . . I . . ." she stuttered. She should tell him to get lost, but she wasn't really frightened by him, and she did have a few choice things she'd like to say to the lout. A lout who was, incidentally, too good-looking to live. His attire tonight was as odd as it had been earlier today, but in a different way. A black T-shirt was tucked into black jeans that were tucked into ankle-high boots. That was normal enough, but over it he wore a long black cape with epaulets shaped like silver wings. On the sometimes bizarre streets of the French Quarter, he wouldn't stand out. Even with his dark blond hair lying loose to his shoulders, except for the two thin braids on either side of his face intertwined with crystal beads. Still . . .

What kind of man stood in front of a mirror and braided his hair with beads?

One who knew he was a hottie, that's who.

She turned on her fluffy slippers and went back into the kitchen to get more food and wine. When she returned, she noticed he was halfway through her meal, and the glass was drained. Instead of sitting down beside him, or hospitably offering him a refill, she folded herself onto an upholstered chair and placed the second plate on her lap.

He grinned, as if he understood her mood.

"The only reason I'm not calling the police is because you said you can save Leroy."

"I can."

An inexplicable joy overcame her, as if a huge weight had been lifted from her shoulders. Why she should trust his words, she wasn't sure. Maybe because she just wanted to so badly.

"Leroy and I came to an understanding this afternoon," he said.

She chewed on her burrito and washed it down with a sip of the cool wine. She studied him before remarking, "You did?"

He nodded. "You look beautiful tonight, Gabrielle."

"Pfff!" She knew exactly how she looked. Wet hair flat against her head and midway down her back. No makeup to cover the slight sunburn she'd gotten outdoors at the prison today. Fortunately, the swelling had gone down on her mouth. And her loose PJs did nothing to enhance her figure. "Save the BS line. I'm not in the market."

"Of course you are not in the market. You are mine."

"I beg your pardon."

"Well, you are *probably* mine."

"Forget probably. I am not, not, not yours. In any way, shape, or form. Did I make that clear enough?"

"I am not too happy about having a soul mate at this stage of my life, either, but it is what it is. I sensed it the moment I first set eyes on you." He shrugged.

"Oh, that was flattering."

"Surely you need no convincing that there is a fiery attraction between us. Holy clouds! That kiss today about melted my bones and turned my cock into molten metal."

A few of my body parts melted, too. "Flattery will get you nowhere. Jeesh! Hasn't any woman ever told you that crudity is not attractive?"

He bristled. "Women have never complained. You will understand once we have coupled."

Whoa, whoa, whoa!

"If we couple, that is."

That's better. If is a word I can live with.

"I have been celibate for many years now . . ."

Probably not as long as I have.

" . . . and I'm not sure how Mike is going to feel about my breaking that record. Of course, we could always have near-sex. My brother Trond invented that, but I doubt it would be satisfying. We could try." He raised hopeful eyes to her.

"You're an idiot."

"That I am." He winked at her.

"You're talking nonsense."

"It's just that I'm nervous. I never had a soul mate before."

"We are not soul mates."

"How can you tell?" he asked hopefully.

She became more and more puzzled with each of his statements. Oh, not the stuff about the kiss and arousal. That she understood too perfectly. She homed in on the least important thing. "You have a brother?"

"Hah! I have six brothers, and a more bothersome, intrusive, full-of-themselves lot there never was."

Someone else is full of himself, too, if you ask me. But then her eyes widened as she considered everything he'd said. *Six brothers!* She had more than enough to handle with one. "Who is Mike?"

"My . . . uh, boss."

"You have a boss who has authority over your personal life?"

"For my sins, yes." He fluttered ridiculously long lashes at her.

"Is your boss a minister, too?"

A cute blush tinted his cheeks before he confessed, "I'm not really an ordained minister."

Big surprise, there. "Tell me about your meeting with my brother."

"He has agreed to avoid trouble and to work with me on the talent show."

Well, that was good news. "Does he know you're here?"

"Yes. I have his blessing."

For what? No, I'm not going to ask that. I'm afraid what he might answer.

"Come over here." He motioned for her to sit beside him on the couch.

She shook her head. "I'm comfortable right here." Although she probably didn't look comfortable balancing the dish on her knees, with a fork in one hand and a wineglass in the other.

"I can smell you from here."

"You say the most outrageous things. Do you deliberately try to shock me?"

"What is outrageous about remarking on your woman scent? That is one of the nice things about females, how they smell. And each one has her own distinctive scent. Not to mention the mating scent."

She rolled her eyes.

"Come over here. I want to see if you are delicious up close."

The gurgling noise that came from her throat was probably due to wine going down the wrong pipe. "You already told me earlier today that I smell like roses and . . . well, something else. Now you're talking about tasting. Honestly, you go too far."

"Roses and musk, that is what I told you," he said. "No, this is a different scent." He raised his nose and made an exaggerated show of sniffing the air. "Almonds?"

"That's my body lotion."

"Ah," he said, and smiled.

"What does that smile mean?"

"'Tis the way of women throughout time. To anoint their bodies afore the mating."

Mating? First coupling, now mating. What next? "You . . . you . . . you," she sputtered. "It's just body lotion. I got sunburned today."

"If you say so, dearling."

She bared her teeth at him.

"You have very nice teeth."

She crossed her eyes.

"If you're done eating, you should go pack a bag."

"For what?"

"I'm taking you away from here. It is too dangerous."

The audacity of the man turned her speechless for a moment.

Just then, there was a knock on the door. She almost never got company since she had almost no social life. It could be someone from Second Chances, though. She put her plate and glass on the floor, but Ivak had already risen and was peeping through the security hole in her door. "Oh shit!" he said.

Without asking her permission, he opened the door to admit two very large men dressed in black jeans and T-shirts, and what else? Long cloaks with silver winged epaulets, of course.

Her apartment was small at the best of times, but with three six-foot-four men built like tanks, well, a person could get claustrophobic.

"These are my brothers—" Ivak started to say.

"No kidding! Which one invented near-sex?"

The two brothers looked at each other, then at Ivak, then at her, before bursting out with laughter.

"Neither," Ivak said, giving her a telling frown at her

disclosing something private he'd told her. "Gabrielle Sonnier, these are my brothers Harek and Sigurd. Harek is a computer genius, and Sigurd is a physician."

Surprised, Gabrielle reached out and shook both their hands. Too late, she realized that she was still wearing her PJs, and nonrevealing as they were, the situation must look intimate. "We were just having dinner," she stumbled.

"And what's for dessert?" Sigurd mumbled, but she heard him and scowled.

He just winked at her.

Without being asked, the brothers removed their cloaks, and Ivak did, too, belatedly. They hung them carefully on the coatrack near the door. Now Gabrielle understood why they wore them. There was enough weapon power under them to take down the Taliban. Swords, knives, guns, throwing stars, and other things she couldn't identify. She arched her brows at Ivak.

"We like to be prepared," he said with a shrug.

"For what? World War III?"

"Ah, the wench has a bite to her tongue," the one named Harek remarked with a wink of appreciation at Ivak. As if Ivak had done something right.

"Wench? Listen, buster—" But the three men had opened the French doors and were out on her balcony, gazing diagonally across the street at the Anguish restaurant. In fact, one of them, Sigurd, had some fancy kind of binoculars raised.

"Bad! Very bad!" Sigurd concluded.

"I see at least two haakai, a couple mungs, and a bunch of imps and hordlings," Harek said. He was the one looking through the binoculars now. "No sighting of Dominique, though. She's probably in her dungeon. But wait, they don't have basements in New Orleans. Her torture chambers must be above stairs."

"Torture chambers?" Gabrielle gasped out.

"Have there ever been any sightings of snakes loose on your street, Gabrielle?" Ivak turned to ask her.

She was just inside the door. "Actually, yes. There was a cobra out on the sidewalk last week. The police figured it was a pet that got away from its owner." Gabrielle hated snakes, and she shivered with revulsion.

As the three came back in and plopped themselves down, tightly, onto her couch, each elbowing the other to make room, Harek said, "You were right, Ivak. This would make a good place for us to set up a stakeout. From here, we can easily track Dominique's comings and goings. I could have a dozen vangels here by morning."

"Wait just a frickin' minute," Gabrielle said. "This is my apartment, and you aren't moving anyone in here. I have one bed, and I'm going to be the only one in it."

Harek and Sigurd looked to Ivak, who was in the center.

"I didn't get a chance to explain it to her yet. I'd just told her to pack a bag when you knocked."

She put her hands on her hips. "Explain what?"

"It's too dangerous for you to stay here. I'm taking you to Tante Lulu's house as a temporary solution. She's already agreed to take you in. In fact, she said you can help her embroider some pillowcases for your hope chest, whatever that is."

"Aaarrgh! I don't think so!"

"Uh, I think Sig and I will go down to that pizza shop on the corner. We'll be back in an hour," Harek told Ivak.

Now that they were alone, Gabrielle turned on Ivak. "How dare you speak to anyone on my behalf? I've lived here for two years. I'm perfectly capable of taking care of myself."

"You stubborn woman! Can you not be biddable without proof? No? So be it." He stood and grabbed her hand, pulled her out the door and down the steps to the street door, across Dumaine, through an alley that ran beside the Anguish restaurant, then around to a back courtyard. They had moved so fast that Gabrielle could barely comprehend what had happened. One moment they were in her apartment, the next moment she was standing in some bougainvillea bushes behind the Anguish restaurant courtyard in her PJs and fluffy slippers.

She shrugged away Ivak's arm when he attempted to pull her closer. "Have you lost your mind?"

"Just watch," he whispered, "and keep quiet."

She turned to look where Ivak was pointing and gasped. He immediately put a hand over her mouth and held her tightly in front of him, facing forward. Luckily, no one seemed to have heard her.

There were at least a dozen people . . . or creatures—she wasn't sure what they were—moving about the courtyard and entering the building by way of stairs leading up not to the first floor, where the restaurant was located, but to a wide gallery and through big sliding metal doors on the second floor. They seemed to be carrying boxes inside, and bringing large trash bags outside. Some of them were extremely tall and covered with slimy scales, and they had tails. Tails! And red, glowing eyes. And, oh good Lord, fangs? Other smaller creatures were scurrying around creating chaos until one of the larger creatures swatted them into order.

But then she saw the most alarming thing. Several of the creatures, before her very eyes, morphed into regular people. A man and a woman, him dressed in what could be a hand-tailored suit with a red power tie and mirror-shined black wingtips, and her in a little black dress with stiletto heels and enough diamonds to support a small country. They were beautiful.

"I've seen enough," she whispered to Ivak.

Once again, quicker than she could fathom, they were back in her apartment. She blinked several times, wondering if she had imagined the whole thing.

"No, you didn't imagine that scene."

"God! Can you read minds, too?"

"No, I just guessed by the expression on your face. Gabrielle, I swear, what you saw is what goes on behind the scenes at Anguish."

"Who . . . what are they?"

"Lucipires. Demon vampires. Jasper is the leader, and Dominique, who owns Anguish, is one of his top commanders. There are torture chambers there, Gabrielle. Unspeakable things go on. You need to be away from here. It's not safe."

"You mean, I've lived two years with this danger on my doorstep?"

"Mostly you would be safe. Lucies . . . that's our nickname for Lucipires . . . prey on humans who are in a state of mortal sin. They fang them and suck out their blood, causing them to die before their time, before they have a chance to repent. For others who are on the verge of some great sin, they fang them with a sin taint that causes them to grow more and more evil with their deeds; then, they, too, are killed. After that, they either go to Hell, or become Lucies. But that is not to say that you are not in danger. If you get in their way, they would kill you before asking questions. And . . ." He hesitated.

"What could be worse than what you've already told me, or that I've seen with my own eyes?"

Ivak exhaled whooshily. "They might come after you because they were thwarted in getting Leroy."

"Whaaat?" she shrieked.

"Now, don't get upset, but—"

"Don't get upset? I've been nothing but upset ever since I met you."

"—we recently discovered that some Lucies have infiltrated Angola, and one of them tried to fang Leroy."

She started to hyperventilate, panting for breath.

"Wait, wait, wait . . ." he said, "Leroy is fine. I was able to override the sin taint."

"Oh, that makes me feel better."

"As you probably suspected, Leroy had been contemplating something very bad. He probably would have killed the convict who testified against him in the prison murder trial."

She put both hands to her head and pulled at her own hair.

"I'll keep an eye on him from now on."

Gabrielle was reeling with shock. "I thought Angola was hell before, but this takes it to a new level."

"My brothers and I are working to correct that situation."

Which brought her to the most important question, one she was almost afraid to ask. "Who are you? I mean, how can humans fight those paranormal creatures?"

He forced her to sit down on the couch before answering. "Because we are not human. Not precisely."

She felt as if her brain might explode. "What do you mean?"

"I am a vangel. A vampire angel. A Viking vampire angel, to be precise." He smiled at that last addition as if it made what he'd said more palatable.

"I don't believe this. I can't believe this." It was all too much for her to comprehend. Vampires roaming the world? *Twilight* in the French Quarter? Hell at Angola? What next?

He sat down beside her on the couch and pulled her into his embrace. "Trust me, sweetling. I will explain it all to you."

She raised her tear-filled eyes. "Can you really help Leroy?"

"I can."

"Then that's all I need to know. For now."

With those words, she fell into a dead faint.

That was how Gabrielle found herself later that night sleeping in a bed in a small cottage on Bayou Black, the snores of a ninety-plus-year-old woman coming from another bedroom, the sound of a gator growling outside her window, and a St. Jude nightlight providing a dim view of the room. Considering the kind of day she'd had, she was not surprised when she turned over and saw a blue feather lying on her pillow.

Eight

Wet dreams were either gifts from the gods, or else,
just wet . . .

That night, for the first time in ages, literally, Ivak
dreamed. And it was an erotic dream of the most intense
proportions.

Ivak had no home of his own at the present time. He
slept in an isolation prison cell, giving him a limited
amount of privacy. His choice of quarters brought even
more disapproval from the warden; Benton couldn't understand why Ivak wanted to stay with the inmates when
he could have a very nice room in the Ranch House,
the place the warden used as a daytime residence and a
place to entertain visitors; it was near the B-Line village
that housed two hundred or so guard families. Ivak had
souped up his cell accommodation to fit his needs . . . a
better mattress, books on a shelf, a small flat-screen tele-
vision, an mp3 player. Still, it was a cell.

The first years after his turning, his nightly dreams
had been more like nightmares. Over and over and over,
he relived his dastardly deeds that culminated in Serk's

suicide. His best friend's face as he'd hung from the stable rafters featured in all of them.

Centuries and centuries of dreamless nights followed. His pattern thereafter was to sleep lightly and not for many hours at a time. Maybe, subconsciously, he was forestalling the return of the nightmarish retelling of his last human day on earth.

But now, this night, the dreams returned with a vengeance, and they were not nightmares by any definition. Oh, he knew about sleep peakings, what they called wet dreams in this time. Not that he'd experienced them all that much in his human life. Engaging in so much sex as he had then, when he'd fallen into bed, he'd been too sated to succumb to imaginary sleep sex.

It was that kiss with Gabrielle that was to blame, of course. And his suspicion that Gabrielle might be his destined mate.

He was standing in a room full of people. What they called a cocktail party in this country and time.

In walked Gabrielle. She wore the sleeveless red dress that Charmaine had worn this afternoon at the prison, except that it was different. On Gabrielle, it appeared to be a wraparound affair that hugged her abdomen down to a wide belt that cinched her small waist, curving outward over her hips down to her knees. The material molded her behind and her breasts, half exposed by a deep, plunging neckline. It was obvious she wore no undergarments. Sheer silk stockings enhanced her long legs, and her red high heels caused her body to arch seductively. Her lips were painted crimson, matching the dress.

Her dark hair curled from a pile atop her head, leav-

ing bare her nape and the sides of her neck, tempting the vampire blood in him.

Ivak barely stifled a hiss of arousal. He closed his mouth to hide his emerging fangs.

But wait. She was with a man who wore a dark suit with a pristine white shirt and a tie. His face was turned away from Ivak, but then his identity did not matter. He had no business being with Ivak's woman.

Jealousy raged inside Ivak like a green-eyed monster.

He surged forward, but invisible bonds held him back. He could not be angry about the restraints, reminding himself, belatedly, that he was a Viking . . . Ivak the Viking. He shouldn't have to make an effort. Women came to him. He did not pursue them. Leaning back against the wall, Ivak watched. And waited.

The man took two stemmed wineglasses off a tray carried by a waiter and handed one to Gabrielle. To his chagrin, Ivak recalled an old adage the skalds were wont to quote. "Wine makes good women wenches."

It better not, Ivak fumed. Not with another man.

Just then, as she sipped at her drink, Gabrielle raised her thick lashes and looked at him. A little Mona Lisa smile tugged at her lips.

The witch! She knew he was here and was enjoying his jealousy.

He definitely would not go to her now.

The man in the dark suit, his head averted from Ivak, led Gabrielle off to an alcove, directly across the room from Ivak. It was as if there were no other people in the teeming room where at least two dozen people chatted amiably, except for Ivak, Gabrielle, and the mystery man.

Gabrielle's partner stood facing outward in the alcove, his face in shadows. Gabrielle stood in front of him, also facing outward. Framed by the arch, they resembled a picture. A moving picture, Ivak soon realized.

While she sipped at her wine, her dark eyes held Ivak's gaze. And the man leaned down to lick the curve of her neck where it met her shoulder.

Gabrielle shivered and arched outward, which caused her breasts to press against the fabric of her dress. Even from this distance, Ivak could see the clear delineation of her nipples. At the same time, she tilted her head to allow the stranger better access to the delicious curve.

Ivak stiffened and pressed his shoulder blades against the wall behind him. His blood thickened and slowed. His cock swelled.

While he watched, the man set both glasses aside and reached under Gabrielle's arms to lift her breasts, using his thumbs to strum the tips into even harder peaks. Gabrielle's crimson lips opened slightly on a sigh.

She parted her thighs, balancing herself on high heels. Her rump was braced against the man's thighs that were also parted into a widespread stance to cradle her hips.

The man slipped one hand inside the deep neckline of her dress and played with the bare skin of her breast. The other hand tipped her chin so that she was turned sideways for his kiss.

Blood sang in Ivak's ears so he could hear nothing but his racing heartbeat. Fury gurgled up like a volcano about to erupt. But before he could act, Gabrielle was raising the hem of her dress inch by inch, exposing long, long legs that were like a two-lane highway to paradise. The lace tops on her thigh-high hose left a patch of bare skin above leading to the dark curls of her woman-fleece. To his amazement, and, yes, appreciation, she used her own fingertips to pleasure herself.

He saw the moment that her peak arrived because she was undulating her hips forward and backward against the man's thighs.

Ivak's enthusiasm rose and rose until, to his embar-

rassment, though no one seemed to notice, he spilled his seed inside his braies, like an untried youthling.

Only then did Ivak notice something extraordinary. The man behind Gabrielle glanced upward, staring at him.

The man was Ivak.

He awoke in his prison bed, the sheets damp with the evidence of his erotic dream.

Centuries of no dreams, then suddenly he dreamed, and his dreams involved this new woman. What did it mean?

Was Gabrielle intended for him?

Or some other man?

Was he destined to pursue her, to no avail?

Was he being shown what he could have, if only he did something or other?

Was Mike giving him a taste of paradise, just to pull it back in further punishment for his lustsome ways?

Ivak closed his eyes and hoped he would dream again.

Nothing came. Literally.

Where's Simon Cowell when you need him? . . .

The biggest surprise of the day was not the arrival of Tante Lulu to help with the talent show auditions, along with another member of her presumably huge family . . . in this case, her nephew René LeDeux. Nor was it Warden Benton bending over backwards—a difficult task with his excess weight—trying to please these Cajun celebrities.

Ivak really did appreciate the proffered assistance from the LeDeuxs. It was a six-hour round-trip drive for Gabrielle to make her frequent visits to Angola from New

Orleans, and about the same from Bayou Black. Nothing
to be sneezed at. But the old lady had enlisted yet another
nephew, Remy LeDeux, a pilot, to fly them here in a small
plane he owned, then pick them up this afternoon.

No. Ivak's biggest surprise was Leroy Sonnier and how
helpful he was as his assistant now that he'd resigned himself to being in Ivak's, or more precisely God's, hands.
Really, except for being an angel . . . sort of . . . Ivak didn't
consider himself a religious person, but Leroy had taken
his words to heart. He was saved! And that meant he was
sticking to Ivak like celestial glue. And being more than
competent, truth to tell. Prison must have taught Leroy
some skills, or more likely, he'd taught himself.

The only problem . . . well, one of the problems . . . was
that Leroy had the mouth of a sailor . . . or a convict . . .
and every other word was "motherfucking," "goddamn,"
"son of a fucking bitch," "Jesus!" and numerous other
expletives. Ivak had advised him to come up with some
substitute swearwords, as he tried to do. "Holy clouds!"
"Son of a troll!" That kind of thing.

Leroy had gaped at him and said, "Are you nuts? If I
start saying 'golly gee!' or 'good heavens!' or 'son of a
toad!' they're either gonna cart me off to the loony bin, or
some big bruiser of a convict is gonna think I'm gal-boy
bait."

"You could be right. Maybe you should only speak
when spoken to until you can control your tongue, around
outside people, at least."

Using an ancient laptop—at least three years old—
Leroy had compiled a list, peck by peck with his big
fingers on the small keys to the tune of various colorful swearwords, of all the people who had auditioned so
far and those on the list yet to perform, along with background data, like were they prone to shank anyone who
rejected their dubious talents?

"You doan want too many yodelers," Tante Lulu advised Ivak now as they sat side by side in the auditorium.

She must think I am a lackwit.

René, who was a Cajun musician and had masterminded numerous LeDeux talent shows up and down the bayou over the years, made an interesting observation. "You're taking this too seriously, *cher.*"

I have no choice but take it seriously. Do the job or scram (from the warden). Do the job or face unpleasant consequences (from St. Michael).

"You gotta have fun with it. Adopt a *joie de vivre* attitude."

Joy of life. That is just great. Joy to my Angola world.

"You're treating this like finding flea shit in a pile of pepper, my friend," René continued.

Exactly.

"Sorry, Auntie, for my bad language." René turned back to Ivak. "Stop trying to find the best singer or dancer or yodeler."

"What the hell should I be looking for then? The worst singer or dancer or yodeler?"

"Maybe. For example, the Sonny and Cher act you told us about."

"Me 'n Charmaine could create some neat costumes for them," Tante Lulu offered.

Ivak could only imagine what those two would come up with. An inmate in fishnet stockings and a wig, paired with a guy wearing fur and nothing else. Fun times on the tier block that night!

Today Tante Lulu was wearing her talent scout outfit, presumably what she thought the Hollywood crowd wore. A knee-length white dress, belted at her tiny waist, similar to that famous dress of the screen sex goddess Marilyn something-or-other. If she stepped over an air vent, Ivak might have a stroke. And she very well might topple over with those wedge-heeled white sandals she wore. To top it all off, she wore a blond wig that was beyond description. Suffice it to say, there were curls.

But that was beside the point. René was on a roll now. "And combine some of the acts, too. Like Leroy's horn with a soul singer."

"Hey!" Leroy objected. "I never agreed to participate."

Ivak gave him a telling scowl that pretty much said, *Be a team player or I won't help you.*

Leroy muttered under his breath.

"Ooh, ooh, ooh! I have an idea." Tante Lulu was practically jumping up and down in her seat. "We could get about ten hottie convicts to do a Chippendale kinda dance routine. Tee-John was a stripper once fer about a week; he could teach 'em how. They could start out wearing them old-fashioned striped uniforms. And mebbe we could even find a few men that looked like Richard Simmons. Yum!"

There were so many things wrong with what she'd just said that Ivak didn't know where to begin. First, he mouthed to René, "Richard Simmons? The exercise nut?"

René grinned and nodded his head.

"Tante Lulu, I don't think the warden would want that kind of racy act in the show," Ivak tried to explain as politely as he could. *We'd probably have a riot amongst the rest of the prison population wanting the "hotties" for their latest girlfriends. Or boyfriends.* "Besides, I think we'd have trouble finding a large number of 'hotties' willing to dance and bare all for the crowds." Actually, that wasn't quite true. With the right incentive, and it wouldn't have to be much, desperate men at Angola would do just about anything.

As for Warden Benton, he'd probably agree to a beauty pageant with the men in Speedos if he thought it would rake in more cash, some of which would surely fall into his pocket. *Or else, he'd do it just to irritate me.*

Please, God, don't let the idea enter his fool head.

"Betcha I could find a bunch of hot prison Chippies," Tante Lulu insisted. "Leroy here, fer example, he'd make a great Chippie."

"Whaaat? No fuc—no way! Playing the trumpet is one thing. Baring my . . . um, horn is another. No frickin' way!"

Well, at least Tante Lulu had succeeded in getting Leroy's agreement to play his horn.

"You doan hafta swear," Tante Lulu said, a bit offended that no one had jumped on her suggestion.

"Let me explain why I've tried so hard to find real talent here," Ivak said to Tante Lulu and René. "I hate the Angola Rodeo. Untrained inmates 'volunteer' to cripple or kill themselves getting gored by angry bulls. The rodeo makes a joke out of men's desperation. The inmates are expendable entertainment."

"Put a beggar on horseback and he'll ride to Hell," Tante Lulu proclaimed.

"What does that mean?" Ivak couldn't keep up with the old lady's quirky sayings.

"Desperate men do desperate things," she explained.

Ivak couldn't argue with that.

"If you feel so strongly about the rodeo, tell the warden," René advised Ivak.

"Do you think I haven't? That's probably why he assigned me this job. Sorry, Tante Lulu," Ivak said then, glancing her way, "I know Pierce Benton is a friend of yours, but honestly he's a man who enjoys being seen as a kindly dictator, when in actuality he's a bit of a sadist. In my opinion."

"Hah! I trust that man as far as I could sling an alligator by the tail." Tante Lulu waved a hand in dismissal. "Doan be apologizin' ta me. I know Pierce is a toad. Allus was. But sometimes you gotta risk a few warts and pond scum ta get things done."

Don't I know it? In my case, it's slime I've got to risk. Lucie slime.

"Besides, Pierce does a lotta good here, too, I reckon. The prison ain't nearly as bad as it was some years back. They usta call it the Alcatraz of the South." Tante Lulu sighed philosophically. "Sometimes you gotta take the good with the bad."

"Guess you've got more restraint than I have."

"I know how you feel," René said. "Sometimes a good fist in the face holds a lot more appeal than nicey-nice. I used to work as an environmental lobbyist. Believe me, I know all about being polite to people you don't respect."

Ivak was liking Tante Lulu and her family more and more. "Prison dehumanizes men, emasculates them, turns even good men bad. Don't get me wrong, I know how bad the crimes are that these inmates have committed, and I understand the public could not care less about what happens inside these gates, and I know that most of them are irredeemable, but—" Ivak stopped short when he realized that he was sermonizing. Him . . . a world-class sinner . . . sermonizing people? It was a fine turn of events when the fox turned preacher. "Oh shit! I sound like a half-baked, bleeding heart ACLU-er."

Tante Lulu patted his hand. "Yer jist showin' you have heart, honey."

A dead heart.

Time to get back to the business at hand.

Next up was Calvin Corl, a skinny, elderly, black lifer from Alabama who was going to sing the hymn "Amazing Grace." René went over to the out-of-tune upright piano to accompany the singer. He promised to bring his own keyboard next time.

Calvin wasn't a bad singer, and his voice was strong for someone so frail, but he rushed through the song so fast that it was hard to understand the words.

Despite René's admonition that they didn't need perfection, Ivak couldn't stand any more. He jumped up and walked over to the low dais on which the auditions were being held.

"No, no, no! Calvin, that is probably the most beautiful hymn in the word. Each word should be savored. You need to draw out each word, like A-maaa-ziii-ing Graaaa-ce. Do you see what I mean?"

Calvin shook his head slowly, and tears filled his rheumy eyes.

"Now, Calvin," Ivak said, putting an arm around his shoulder. "You have a fine voice. You just need to take your time. Close your eyes and feel the words. Like this."

With that advice, Ivak closed his own eyes, and began to sing. Soon, he was lost in the sweet lyrics. He and his brothers had good voices, they'd discovered. Like angels, some said.

Amazing Grace! How sweet the sound
That saved a wretch like me!
I once was lost, but now am found;
Was blind, but now I see.

The most wonderful thing about this song was that it appealed to almost every person in the world, each making a personal connection with the message. He was especially fond of the stanza that finished some versions of the hymn:

When we've been here ten thousand years,
(or more than a thousand, as I have)
Bright shining as the sun,
(and, yes, vangels were shiny angels-in-training)
We've no less days to sing God's praise
(like forever)

Than when we'd first begun.
(which last count was one thousand, one hundred, and
   sixty-three years ago, give or take)

As Ivak's voice trailed off and he slowly opened his
eyes to tell Calvin that was how he wanted him to sing
the song, he saw that the inmate was staring at him, slack-
jawed, as if he was seeing some glorious apparition. It
was then that Ivak realized how silent the small auditorium was. René must have stopped playing. Turning, he
saw that Tante Lulu was weeping silently, Leroy and René
were staring at him with shock, and spectators had come
in from the corridor . . . prison staff and a few trusties . . .
and were standing at the back, equally stunned.

Ooops! he thought, and immediately admonished
himself. *Do not call attention to yourself, lackwit. Do not
call attention to yourself, lackwit, Do not . . .*

"Uh, that's how I want you to try to sing the song," he
told Calvin.

"You were born on Crazy Creek if you think I could
ever sing like that," Calvin protested.

"I've had years more practice than you have," Ivak assured him. *Many years more! More years than you can
count.* "You'll do fine. Just slow down and think about
the words." And this time, while René accompanied him,
Calvin sounded pretty good.

They were able to accomplish a lot by the time Tante
Lulu and René went off to have lunch at the Ranch House.
Leroy had to report for work at the *Angolite*. Ivak had
a job to do, too. A van full of new inmates was being
brought in, and Ivak liked to be there to help in any way
he could. In particular, he tried to protect those younger,
weaker inmates . . . "fresh fish," who would be pounced
upon by older, jaded, evil-to-the-bone predators to serve
as sexual partners, or even sexual slaves, bought and sold.

To Ivak's surprise, eight of the ten new inmates were vangels sent by his brothers to infiltrate the prison and act as backup for Ivak in routing out Lucies in the area. Ivak had nothing to do with inmate assignments, but he noticed that each of the eight was sent to different living quarters. Mike's doing, he assumed. Two in the Main Prison where the most hardened criminals were housed, and the others to the camps. They made eye contact with Ivak, but did not speak to him directly. The other two inmates were repeat offenders who were familiar with Angola and not in need of Ivak's help.

It was only then that Ivak allowed himself to think about Gabrielle. And not just the kiss, either. There was that wild erotic dream to mull over . . . and over . . . and over.

With a smile, he called Tante Lulu's telephone at her cottage. It was one p.m., so Gabrielle should be up and about by now, even though she had appeared totally exhausted last night when he'd carried her into the tiny bedroom.

Now that he had other vangels in place here at the prison, he might be able to get away for an hour or two to spend some time with his soul mate. Assuming that is what she was. He needed more time with her to make sure. Maybe, if he was lucky, she would still be in bed. Maybe, if he was lucky, he could try some of Trond's near-sex activities. Or they could reenact last night's dream.

Turned out he was not to be lucky that day.

After showering and changing his clothes, he tele-transported himself to the bayou cottage. And found it empty. How could that be? Her car was still back in New Orleans since he'd teletransported them both here. Could she have been taken by Lucies? No, they would have no way of tracing her here to this location; nor would they have reason to pursue an innocent, leastways not until they made a connection with him, or Leroy.

Quickly, he teletransported back to Angola and stomped into the newspaper office. "Where the hell is your sister?"

"Huh?" Leroy said, glancing up from the computer keyboard he had been pecking away at, writing an article, Ivak presumed. "You told me that she wouldn't be visiting me today because she was resting at Tante Lulu's."

"That's where she's supposed to be, but I just came back from there, and the place is empty." He could tell that Leroy was about to ask him how he'd gotten to Bayou Black and returned here in such a short time, but Ivak cut him off. "I left a note for her, ordering her to stay at the cottage today, not to come to the prison. And Tante Lulu left a note telling Gabrielle that she would be back late this afternoon, that she and her nephew would handle things related to the talent show for the time being. I can't imagine why she would leave—"

"Wait a minute." Leroy held up a hand to halt Ivak's next words. "You frickin' *ordered* my sister to stay home?"

Ivak nodded tentatively.

Leroy started laughing hilariously. "You dumb fuck! You don't know my sister at all."

Nine

You can't hold a good woman down . . .

Gabrielle awakened abruptly to bright sunshine and noticed by the St. Jude clock on the bedside table that it was a shocking ten a.m.

Well, no wonder, after that dream last night. It *had* been a dream, hadn't it? Her face burned just thinking about what she had done.

When was the last time she'd had a dream like that?
Never.

When was the last time she'd slept so late?
Not since she was in college, before law school.

Her inner alarm had been a dependable wake-up call at six a.m. as long as she could remember. In fact, her best work was done during those early morning hours before the rise and shine of the rest of the world.

Ah, well, she thought, stretching. She'd been under a lot of stress lately. Forget about six a.m. How about waking up every hour during the night, worrying about Leroy?

Suddenly, she recalled the events of the night before. Not the dream. The *other* events.

Had she really witnessed those horrific creatures in the back courtyard of the Anguish restaurant? Had Ivak Sigurdsson, the Angola chaplain or whatever he was, really told her that fantastic story about demon and angel vampires? Had she willingly agreed to leave her apartment in the city to come stay here at Tante Lulu's cottage? Or had she been under some kind of spell?

Well, she was under no spell now. With belated determination, she jumped off the bed and immediately noticed the blue feather on her pillow. Picking it up, she had the odd impulse to sniff it. The fine hairs stood out all over her body as she recognized the scent of cloves and sandalwood.

Shaking her head to clear it of the creepy sense of unreality that surrounded her, she tossed the feather, chagrined to see it flutter back onto the pillow. Following the aroma of fresh-brewed coffee through a silent house, she made her way to the kitchen.

There was no one in the kitchen, but there was a note. Two notes, actually. The first, on a piece of writing paper with a St. Jude letterhead, was from Tante Lulu, of course. Her small, perfect script read: "Gone with René to Angola to help with the talent show. Make yourself at home and rest today. Tante Lulu."

The other note was from Ivak. For a blip of a second, Gabrielle had a memory of the man placing her in bed last night, tucking her in, and kissing her forehead. Was that a memory, or a dream? And then there was the dream itself! Looking down, she saw the same clothes she'd had on last night . . . the silk PJs . . . and bare feet.

Ivak's note said in big, masculine strokes: "Stay here today, sweetling, and be safe. You are under my shield now. I will take care of everything. Ivak Sigurdsson."

"Stay here today," she repeated aloud. Did the man dare to give her orders? Did he think she would stay home like a meek little lamb, just because he said so? Hah! She hadn't planned to go to Angola today anyhow, having been there yesterday, but she had a job and a two p.m. meeting with all the employees at the Second Chances office in New Orleans to go over the schedule of legal cases for the next month. Leroy was not the only inmate they were working to release from prison. Not by a Louisiana long shot.

Gabrielle drank two cups of the strong coffee that Tante Lulu had left in the pot on the stove, along with a platter of scrambled eggs and sausages and heavenly light, buttered biscuits that had been left warming in the oven. It was only then that Gabrielle recalled that she had no car here. She had no memory of how she'd gotten here, but knew instinctively that it hadn't been in her car. When she looked out the window to the driveway, her suspicions were confirmed. She was trapped here in the middle of bayou nowhere with no vehicle. After a couple of minutes of pondering, she picked up her cell phone and called the number of Charmaine's beauty spa in Houma, which was tacked on a small bulletin board in the kitchen.

"Charmaine LeDeux, please?" she said to the receptionist.

"Who's calling?"

"Gabrielle Sonnier. I'm at her aunt's place on Bayou Black."

"Just a minute. Here she comes."

"Charmaine Lanier here."

Oops. Gabrielle realized that she had asked for Charmaine by her maiden name. "Hi, Charmaine. This is Gabrielle Sonnier. Listen, I'm kind of stuck out here at your aunt's place with no transportation. Is there a taxi service or a bus I can catch to New Orleans? I have a two o'clock appointment."

"How about Lillian?"

"Who?"

Charmaine laughed. "Lillian is Tante Lulu's car."

"She has a car?"

Charmaine laughed again. "Oh yeah! It's parked in the small detached garage on the far side of her cottage."

Gabrielle walked through the house to the other side and glanced out a window. Yep, there was a small building there. "Do you think she'd mind if I borrow the car for the day?"

"She'd thank you for giving it a run. Lillian isn't taken out much these days. The keys are on that pegboard by the pantry."

"Thanks a lot, Charmaine. You're a lifesaver."

"Don't thank me yet. You haven't seen Lillian."

How bad could it be? After tidying the kitchen, Gabrielle showered and dressed, having discovered a packed suitcase in her bedroom. Had Ivak packed it? She shook her head, not wanting to picture him going through her underwear drawer.

Locking the house, she went over and opened the old-fashioned folding wood doors of the garage. She now knew why Charmaine had laughed.

Lillian was a lavender Chevy Impala convertible, circa 1965, with a St. Jude wobbly doll on the dashboard. On the back was a bumper sticker that said, "Not So Close, I'm Not That Kind of Car." It was so big it barely fit in the small garage, and it took Gabrielle a good fifteen minutes before she was able to back out without scraping the sides.

Actually, Gabrielle enjoyed driving the big old relic of a luxurious past, with its white leather interior and all the bells and whistles of an older time, including, thank you, God, blessed air-conditioning, although she wouldn't need that with the top down.

Of course, it took her a half hour to find a parking place big enough for the politically incorrect Purple Princess in the busy Saturday French Quarter, even though the Second Chances storefront offices were on a side street off the usual beaten path. Several of her coworkers who were just arriving stopped to witness her attempts to parallel park the oversize Lillian. She had no idea how the diminutive Tante Lulu managed.

Since she was early, she decided to walk down to her apartment, a mere two blocks away, and check on things. Surely she'd dreamed that a bunch of Viking vampire angels had suggested staying in her place to watch demon vampires across the street. It was too fantastical to be true.

She glanced over at the Anguish restaurant from the other side of the street, and everything looked perfectly normal, with tourists and Quarter residents walking in and out casually. No beasts with tails in sight. It must have been a bad dream.

Enough with the dreams already!

She unlocked the outside, street-level door to her apartment building and walked up the steep steps to the landing. Using a second key, she opened the door . . . and almost had a heart attack as one person yanked her inside the entryway, and five other people crammed into her small living room pointed weapons at her. Everything from rifles to swords. And was that a machine gun over there? Good Lord!

Each of them was yelling at her:

"Drop the briefcase!"

"Hands up!"

"Identify yourself!"

"Frisk her for weapons!"

"Are you carrying a bomb, ma'am?"

She regained her composure once another person entered from the kitchen carrying a mug. With hysterical irrelevance, she presumed the mug must contain her in-

stant coffee. She didn't own a coffeemaker. It was one of
the men she'd met here last night, Ivak's brother Harek.
When he yelled, "Halt!" the others froze. "It's the owner
of this apartment, Ivak's soul mate."

"I am not—" she started to say, then stopped.

"Ms. Sonnier, we were told you wouldn't be coming
back until we gave the safe signal."

"I came in to work today and—"

"You work on a Saturday?" Harek interrupted.

"Yes, some of us need to work," she snapped.

He shrugged an apology, realizing how rude his question had been.

"I needed some papers from my bedroom filing cabi-
net," she prevaricated quickly. Jeesh! Since when did she
need to explain herself to strangers?

"Sorry if we scared you," Harek said, then introduced
her to the other six "vangels" in the room. She knew that's
what they were because that's how Harek identified them.
Welcome to Weirdsville. Again. There were five men and
one woman, besides Harek. All tall, physically fit, and
Norse in appearance. They stared at her with curiosity;
she just stared.

"Come, have some coffee with me in the kitchen,"
Harek suggested.

She was about to protest that she had to be in her
office soon, but he was already walking away from her.
On her kitchen counter now sat a state-of-the-art coffeemaker, the kind that cost as much as her car at stores
like Williams-Sonoma. The kind that used those expen-
sive little individual cardboard cups of specialty gourmet
coffee. When Harek opened her fridge to remove some
cream, she noticed there were about a dozen different
kinds of beer inside, none of which she'd purchased.

"Don't worry," Harek said, motioning for her to sit
at the small table where he placed a cup of coffee along

with packets of sugar and the cream. Most of the table was taken up with a laptop computer and paperwork that Harek must have been working on. "We will leave your apartment like we found it when we finish here."

"I wasn't worried about that. I'm just stunned by all of this." She motioned toward her kitchen-turned-office and the living room that had been turned into a fortress.

Harek shrugged, leaning back against the counter and sipping at his own coffee. "It's the usual reaction of people on first meeting us."

Gabrielle fought for something normal to say in a situation that was far from normal. "Um, how long have you all been around? I find it hard to believe that vampires of any kind exist in real life, let along demon vampires and angel vampires."

"Viking angel vampires," he corrected her. "You can't forget that, at heart, we are still Norsemen . . . and women. As for how long, in the case of me and my brothers, more than one thousand years."

"Impossible!" That would mean Ivak must be . . . no, it was too unbelievable.

"Believe it or not, it is what it is."

"Why are you . . . and Ivak . . . being so open about all this? Aren't you afraid I'll go to the police or the news media?"

"You could try. Before you could do that, though, we could erase your memory, but mainly we do not fear your treachery because you are obviously Ivak's soul mate."

"Aaarrgh! I am not a soul mate."

"Ivak said you were, and I could practically see the sizzle between you two last night."

The dream occurred to her suddenly. "Sizzle does not mean soul mate."

"You could be right about that," he said dubiously, "considering that Ivak is the expert on sizzle."

She shouldn't ask. She really shouldn't. "The expert on sizzle?"

"I suppose Ivak hasn't had time to explain everything to you. My brothers and I were each guilty *in a big way* of one of the Seven Deadly Sins. Mine was greed. Ivak's was—"

"Lust," she guessed.

Harek didn't even bother to answer, just sipped at his own coffee.

"Why am I not surprised? That still doesn't mean I'm some kind of freakin' soul mate. Is this soul mate nonsense a common thing for you . . . um, vangels?"

"Not at all. Until recently, we didn't even know that we vangels, especially the VIK . . . that's what we call us seven brothers as leaders . . . could marry humans. But then my brother Vikar met Alex, a magazine journalist. They live in Transylvania."

"Romania?" Why that shocked her, she wasn't sure.

"No, our headquarters is a run-down castle in Transylvania, Pennsylvania."

When she appeared too confused to ask more, Harek continued, "After that, my brother Trond met his soul mate at Coronado, California where they are both Navy SEALs. Well, he is a SEAL in training. She is a member of WEALS, or female SEALs."

Gabrielle put both hands to her throbbing head. "This is too much for me to comprehend, and I have to get to my meeting ASAP."

As he walked her to the front door, Harek remarked, "It's really not a good idea for you to be in this neighborhood until we clear out the Lucies. I should accompany you, at least part of the way."

She was about to open her door when it burst open and there stood an obviously furious Ivak, hands on hips, legs widespread in a battle stance, glaring at her.

"Wench, you are in such trouble."

Ten

Oh, for the days when women were meek and biddable ...

Ivak was so angry he could scarce hold his fangs in.

The woman stood before him, exactly where he'd told her not to go, and dared to shoot darts of her own anger at him. Was she so stubborn that she would put her life in danger just to prove a point? Did she have any idea what he could do to her?

"There are mules with more sense than you have," he snarled.

"There are asses with more sense than you have," she snarled back.

"What are you doing here?" he demanded.

"What are *you* doing here?" she countered, and stepped around him and proceeded to walk down the stairs.

"Where else would I be?" He followed her to the bottom of the steps, where they both stopped. Deciding he'd had enough of her mulishness, he picked her up by the waist and lifted her against the wall so that her feet dangled above the floor. So shocked was she, and thankfully silent for the moment, that the leather briefcase in her hand dropped to the floor with a thud.

She soon regained her voice, however. "Let me go, you big oaf. I don't appreciate being manhandled by some obnoxious Viking wannabe."

"Obnoxious, am I? A Viking imposter, am I? Have a care, wench, you are pushing the bounds of my temper."

"That's another thing. Are you aware that *wench* is an insulting term to use for a woman?"

"It is?" That surprised him. Somewhat. He shrugged. There were more important issues at hand here. "I do not know if you are truly my soul mate, or not. God knows, I would prefer that you are not. But, on the off chance that you are, that makes you my responsibility, and that means I cannot have you strolling into danger like a willful child."

"You . . . you . . ." she sputtered, and raised a fist.

He kissed her lips quickly, before she had a chance to hit him, and set her back on her feet. "Now, where are you off to that is so important?"

"My office. I have work to do."

"I will go with you."

"You will not!" She turned and leaned down to pick up her briefcase and some papers that had fallen out.

He noticed then that she was wearing braies today, black pleated, linen-like pants that hugged her hips and long legs. On top, she wore a silky white blouse tucked into the waist with a wide silver linked belt. Her black hair was loose, in waves, to her shoulder and held off her face with two pearl combs. "I like your ass," he remarked.

She glanced up at him over her shoulder and then shot up straight. "Are you really so clueless you don't know how obnoxious you are?"

"Huh? I just paid you a compliment. I would not be insulted if you said you liked *my* ass."

She shook her head as if he were a hopeless case, then opened the door and stormed out to the sidewalk.

He followed, of course, checking right and left to make sure there were no Lucies about.

At first, she ignored his presence, but then she made a snide remark. "Don't you ever dress normal?"

"What's wrong with my attire?" He could understand her comment about his apparel at the prison, or his cloak last night, but today he was wearing an open, long-sleeved denim shirt over a white T-shirt with denim braies and lightweight ankle boots. No priestly dog collar.

"It's ninety degrees today. You must be sweltering."

He shrugged. He needed the outer shirt to hide the weapons strapped to his back and tucked into his waistband, and the boots held several knives.

Now that his anger had subsided, he tried to make conversation with her. "Why do you live in New Orleans? Why not somewhere closer to the prison, like Baton Rouge?"

"This is where my work is. I need to be with a firm that understands about my brother and allows me to work flexible hours so I can take care of his business. A big law firm wouldn't be so compassionate."

Maybe he should offer her money to alleviate her hardships. He would save that suggestion for later. If she was so stubborn about his care for her physical safety, she would surely balk about financial help.

"Besides, I love this city with all its history and quaintness. The architecture, like those iron lace railings over there, and the many preserved buildings in the old Quarter. The food. The traditions. Mardi Gras. Jazz. Oh, I know it's seedy in parts, and I certainly grew up in the section that was downright dismal, but it's where I want to be. For now."

He nodded. "I was here before the war, and it was a

grand place, even then. You should have seen opening
night at the Opera House. The men in perfectly tailored
suits with silk shirts adorned with ruffled lace, waistcoats
of brocaded satin, even gloves. And ladies were beautiful
in their hooped dresses and daring décolletages."

"What war?"

He glanced at her. "The Civil War, of course."

She stopped and stared at him.

Belatedly, he realized that she still did not believe his
vangel story. With a sigh, he took her hand as they continued walking. For a moment she resisted his hand holding,
but gave up under his persistence. He continued talking,
"The Vieux Carré, that is what the French Quarter was
called then. It was just as busy as it is now, but instead of
cars and buses, there were horse-drawn wagons . . . the
milk wagon, the water wagon, the kerosene wagon. Then
there was the Waffle Man, and vendors in wagons selling
Roman candy and flavored snowballs."

Her eyes were wide with amazement, but not yet belief.

So, he continued, "It was not uncommon to see black
women carrying baskets or wooden bowls on their heads
as they rhythmically sang out their wares for sale. 'Straw-
berries, fresh and fine!' 'Calas! Calas! Get them while
they're hot!' Shutters would fly open and servants or
housewives would invite vendors over to display their
wares."

"You could have read all that in a book."

"I suppose, but I am not much for reading. I am more
of a doer." He waggled his eyebrows at her.

"You make it sound like a better time than today."

"Not at all. There was also yellow fever, hurricanes,
floods, dueling, unbearable heat and humidity, body odor
like you wouldn't believe, and of course slavery, the biggest abomination."

She still frowned.

He decided that now was not the time to inform her of his having owned slaves himself at one time. "Then, of course, there were the fancy girls in the sporting houses."

"And you know all about them, I'll bet."

"Of course. I saved many a soul about to be taken by the Lucies in the red-light district. Dominique was not established here then, but there were Lucies drawn by the decadent lifestyle."

They had arrived at Gabrielle's offices by then and she put up a halting hand. "You are not coming in with me."

He stiffened. "Are you ashamed to be seen with me?" After all, she had commented on his clothing.

"I don't want to have to explain you."

Just then a woman of forty-some years came up to them. "Are you going in now, Gabby? Hey, who's your friend?"

He could tell that Gabrielle didn't want to introduce him. Tough! He extended a hand and said, "Greetings. My name is Ivak Sigurdsson. I am a chaplain at Angola Prison. And you are . . . ?"

"Estelle Johnson," the woman replied with a warm smile and squeeze of his hand.

"Ah, a good Norse name! Johnsson. I am Viking, too. A friend of Gabrielle's."

He could tell that Gabrielle wanted to refute their connection, but Estelle spoke first, "Are you coming inside to wait for Gabby? I'll put some fresh coffee on."

"Thank you for the invitation," he said, and stepped through the doorway before Gabrielle could object. Tapping a fingertip on her frowning mouth, he whispered, "I do not like the name Gabby. You shall always be Gabrielle to me. Or sweetling. Although you are not looking so sweet at the moment."

She growled. She actually growled.

The sound zapped him with an instant shot of arousal, almost as if she'd grabbed his male parts and given him a little squeeze. He must have been gaping because she said, "What's the matter? Are you sick?"

Truth be told, he feared he *was* getting a little sick. Lovesick. But what he said was, "Hurry up with your meeting, love, and I will show you my side of the Old South. The best side."

So, this is what it's like to date a vampire . . .

Love? Had the man really called her "love"? Not for the first time, she saw Ivak as a player, pure and simple. Did he think he could charm her with such throwaway endearments? Hah!

To Gabrielle's chagrin, however, Ivak did charm every one of the women who entered the offices. He obviously loved women, and he showed it in the complete attention he gave each and every one of them and the way he constantly touched them, the innocent squeeze of a shoulder when Lisa O'Dell, the secretary, told him of her disabled child, or the brush of hair off the face of the newly widowed Georgia Lane, their lead attorney. She also noticed the appreciative scrutiny he gave the good-looking ones, or those with ample curves. A testosterone-oozing horndog, she decided. One she needed to avoid.

But, truthfully, the men were impressed, too. He could discuss the New Orleans Saints or local jazz musicians with equal ease. His size and physique impressed the men, as well as the women. Steve Mason, who managed their office, even asked him if he was a professional athlete.

To her embarrassment and chagrin, in the brief time before her meeting started, he grilled each of the men, clearly staking his claim on her. "Are you married?" "How long have you known Gabrielle?" That kind of thing.

Gabrielle's meeting lasted more than two hours.

She and four other lawyers, as well as aides and other personnel who worked for Second Chances, sat around a conference table discussing several dozen new applications for their services; they agreed to take on five of them. There was only so much manpower to go around, and they had to be selective, not just in terms of deservedness, but winability, too. They were a privately funded nonprofit that had to account for its services, just as any for-profit corporation must.

Two new cases were assigned to her. A young woman incarcerated ten years ago for murdering an abusive husband, and a teenage boy who'd been tried as an adult for robbery with a deadly weapon. Those were on top of the twenty cases she was currently handling. She couldn't complain. Her load was actually comparatively light because of Leroy. Others had as many as fifty cases at one time.

She was shocked when she left the meeting to find that Ivak was still in the waiting room. He was teaching Juan, the seven-year-old son of their young receptionist, Holly Morales, how to engage in swordsmanship using a folded umbrella. Juan was giggling, and Holly along with four other women, who worked in neighboring shops, were clapping their encouragement. Every one of the women was staring at Ivak like he was a sweet praline and they were sugar addicts.

Even while she stood there, transfixed, his smart phone rang. He excused himself to the boy and women and took the call. Rather, a text message, because he sank down onto a folding chair, his long legs crossed at the ankles and propped on another chair while he tapped away on the phone, sending text messages to God only knew who. Maybe God Himself.

"You're still here!" she exclaimed, as he stood and pocketed the phone.

"By the runes! Of course I am here. Did I not say I would wait? My word is my bond, dearling."

She rolled her eyes at the archaic language. "Don't you have work to do? Are you permitted to be away from the prison for so long?"

"I can do whatever I want. I set my own hours. But you are right. Normally I would not want to be absent at such a critical time. However, some of my vangels arrived today, and they will contact me immediately if there is a problem." He must have noticed the concern on her face because he quickly added, "You are not to worry about Leroy. One of my men is watching over him closely."

"Thank you," she said.

"Are you hungry?"

Any denial she might have made was negated by the rumble of her stomach.

He laughed, and she smiled.

"I think that is the first time you've smiled at me," he said. "Do it more often and I would do anything for you."

"Anything? How about feeding me?" she surprised herself by asking. *Where did that come from? I'm supposed to be putting some distance between us. Aren't I?*

He took her hand in his, an action she could no longer evade, or wanted to evade, and said, "Come. I know just the place. I am so hungry myself, I could eat a boar."

"A boar, huh? Do they serve boar at this place you recommend?"

"No, but they do have alligator on the menu. Alligator and mushroom pizza. Yum!"

She didn't know if he was kidding or not, but she liked this playful demeanor of his. *Charm, charm, charm, sex,*

sex, sex, player, player, player. Keep reminding yourself, Gabrielle. I should tell him to get lost right now. This minute.

Maybe later.

Instead, she said, "Did you know Tante Lulu has a pet alligator in her backyard?"

"Do I know it? Hah! I almost stepped on its tail when I carried you in last night."

She didn't want to think about how that image made her feel. Not the alligator, but him carrying her. And the dream. That awful, wonderful dream. So she changed the subject. "Do you want to drive or shall I?" When they got to the car, Gabrielle said, "Meet Lillian. Tante Lulu's Purple Princess."

His eyes went wide before he burst out laughing. "Oh, I will definitely be driving Lillian." When he sat behind the wheel, he turned to her and smiled. "This vehicle is as big as a longboat."

"I like that," she said, smiling back at him. "A longboat of the highways."

"You could say it was a longcar."

"A lavender longcar."

They both laughed as he cruised slowly down the busy streets of the French Quarter. Once outside the city, he stepped on the gas and Gabrielle enjoyed the breeze blowing through her hair and the pure freedom of being out on the road on a beautiful, sunny summer day. Later, she would put up her defenses again, but for now she just wanted to relax and forget all her problems.

When he pulled into the parking lot of what appeared to be a run-down shack with a neon sign proclaiming "Heavenly Eats," she glanced at him with surprise.

"Were you expecting a fancy Garden District restaurant with fou-fou waiters and sterling forks?" His blue eyes sparkled beautifully at her.

She inhaled sharply, feeling like the sparks were actually hitting her skin like carnal caresses. It took all her self-control to get back to the conversation at hand, which had nothing to do with carnality. "No, but this restaurant is a far cry from deluxe dining."

He chucked her under the chin. "Don't judge a book by its cover, or a restaurant by its exterior."

"You're right. Just because a chicken has wings doesn't mean it can fly."

"You've been around Tante Lulu only a short time but already you are picking up her sayings."

She grimaced. "I'm turning into a batty Cajun golden oldie?"

"Hardly," he said, giving her a hot . . . very hot . . . survey.

Laughing, she decided a change of subject was called for. "I've yet to see you in a tie."

"I was wearing a tie in our dream."

"*Our* dream?" she choked out. *No, no, no! I am not thinking about that blasted dream.* "If you did wear a tie, it would probably be something outrageous. Blinking wings, or clouds."

He chuckled, knowing perfectly well how embarrassed she was at his reminder of the dream. Her flushed face, if nothing else, would have given her away. "Anyhow, what any of that has to do with shabby restaurants, I don't know," she grumbled, and exited the car, which was ungracious of her, she realized immediately. It's just that she had been expecting something different. Perhaps a table on an open gallery overlooking a lake or even a bayou stream. After all, he had mentioned showing her the best side of the Old South. If this was it, God help Dixie.

Her opinion changed dramatically, of course, the minute they stepped inside. The exterior might be downright shabby, but inside it was downright chic. Like a Bourbon Street supper club, it was, with soft lighting and intimate tables. There was even mellow jazz playing on an old-fashioned jukebox.

"This is lovely," she said, glancing up at Ivak.

But his attention was directed toward the kitchen where a short, rotund black man in an apron smiled widely and came toward them, arms extended in welcome. "Ivak, Ivak, where you been, boy? It's been months since you've been here. Colette will be so happy to see you. Colette, Colette, come see who's here."

Soon, Gabrielle was introduced to Pierre and Colette Fortenot, father and daughter owners of this small restaurant. Colette, a late-twenty-ish, mocha-skinned blonde in a pretty fuchsia sundress and white high heels, the apparent hostess, was even happier to see Ivak than her father was. That was clear in the way she'd hung on a bit too long when Ivak reached down to hug her and in the way she eyed Gabrielle with question.

They were seated in a booth Ivak requested on the far side and Colette handed them menus, telling them that a girl named Terese would be their waitress. Before she left, she laid a hand on Ivak's arm and said, in a sultry voice, "We'll talk later, *cher*?"

"Definitely," Ivak replied in an equally sultry voice— *the louse!*—and squeezed Colette's hand in return.

Once they were alone, Gabrielle blurted out, "Do you always flirt with other women when you're on a date?"

Ivak's eyes went wide with surprise. Then he laughed. "Are we on a date?"

"No. Of course not. I just meant it's not polite to ignore the woman you're with . . . I mean . . . oh, never mind."

"You're jealous," he accused with a smile of pure male triumph.

"I am not."

"Colette is married to a doctor from Lafayette. They have two children."

That made Gabrielle feel better. Still she said, "That doesn't stop some men."

Instead of going all offended on her, Ivak admitted, "There was a time when that wouldn't have bothered me at all, but I've changed. Leastways, I hope I have."

She was appalled to suddenly realize something. "I never asked . . . are you married?"

"No."

Whew! "Ever?"

"Never."

He deliberately declined to elaborate, but he did ask her, "You?"

She shook her head. Time to change the subject. Gabrielle opened her menu. "What kind of food do they serve here? I assume by their names that the owners are Cajun."

"Creole actually. Do you like Creole food?"

"Love it!" she said, sharing a smile at their having something in common.

They started with a sampler of finger appetizers: oysters Bienville served on the half shell, crawfish boulettes, a fancy name for tiny fish meatballs, stuffed shrimp with a Creole meunière sauce. For entrees, she ordered crevettes saute St. Lucia, which were French Creole–style sautéed prawns, while Ivak preferred a blackened redfish, a Louisiana specialty. There were sides of dirty rice; creamy grits with Creole shrimp; spinach Madeline; petits pois, a mixture of baby peas, pimentos, and other veggies; and fried green tomatoes with a spicy remoulade sauce. Red wine was served from a table decanter. For dessert, they went for the rum-laced bread pudding, which they shared.

The whole time, their conversation flowed freely, without stop. Who knew Gabrielle would have so much to talk about with a man so very different from herself, or the other men she'd occasionally dated? And Ivak constantly reached over with his fork to taste something on her plate, or to offer her something from his.

"I thought vampires didn't eat food."

"I'm a vampire *angel*, and Viking at that. We love food." He'd just popped a cherry tomato stuffed with cheese into his mouth and chewed appreciatively.

"So, how long have you been at Angola?" she asked, buttering a second roll, that's how hungry she was.

"Not long. A couple years. Ummm, try this." He extended his fork with a sliver of redfish on it.

"Ummm," she agreed. The fish was tender and succulent with its coating of the hot lemon pepper sauce that had been poured over it. "How long do you expect to stay at Angola?"

"I'm really not sure. The need for help is great. Never ending, really, but I'm not sure I'll be the one to provide that help on a continuing basis."

She was having a hard time concentrating. She'd rather watch Ivak eat and drink. It was a sensual experience. He chewed slowly, savoring each bite, occasionally closing his eyes in ecstasy. When he drank the wine, he let it sit in his mouth for a second before swallowing. Halfway through the meal, he asked their waitress to bring him a beer. "Do you mind?" he asked Gabrielle. "I'm a Viking. We like our beer."

"I like beer on occasion. Make that two." That seemed to please him.

Back to the subject they'd been discussing. "Would you want to stay at Angola?"

"Do you jest? I hate it there. It is the most dismal, cruel, sad place in the world. The living dead, that is what most of the inmates are. Totally without hope."

Gabrielle gulped, knowing that her brother could very well be one of the living dead if she . . . they . . . didn't help him. "If you feel that strongly, leave."

"It's not up to me. I go where I'm assigned."

"But—"

He shook his head. "I do not get to cherry-pick my missions."

She didn't understand that, at all. He probably referred to that Viking vampire angel nonsense and St. Michael the Archangel. Jeesh!

"What would you do if you had a choice?"

He thought for a long moment, chewing slowly on a bite of his side salad. "Just freedom, I think. Freedom to do whatever I want wherever I want. Maybe in the end, I would choose to be at Angola doing exactly what I am doing, but it would be nice to have the choice."

She nodded. "Even though the reasons are different, lots of people I know are locked into jobs or marriages that they hate but cannot leave because of their particular circumstances." Herself included.

"I shouldn't complain. I was given a second chance to make up for my sins. Without it, I would be in a far, far worse place."

He was referring to Hell, she supposed. "Assuming I believed your story, and I don't, have you ever met God?"

He shook his head slowly. "No, but I have sensed the spirit of Jesus on occasion. Glorious it is. There is a reason why some Christian religions say that Heaven is nothing more than being in the presence of God, and Hell is the absence of God. It is that essential and wondrous to the soul." He glanced at her and could no doubt see her confusion. "I'm not explaining it well, but then there is no good way to explain God."

"I've always wondered exactly how the world was created. The Bible mentions the seven days of creation, but lots of scientist go for the big bang theory."

Ivak laughed. "I'm not going to give you answers to age-old questions, most of which I couldn't answer even if I wanted to. I'm more inclined toward the big bang theory, though, as in God raised His hand, and bang! the world happened."

"You make jokes about your being an angel *of sorts*, and you use a casual nickname for a revered archangel, *Mike*. One could make a case that you don't take any of this seriously."

"Sorry if I've given that impression. It's serious as sin. Mayhap I use humor to cover my nervousness over just how important the work is that I do. I don't know. I do believe that God would not have created humor unless He had a sense of humor Himself."

"I agree. Oh, I'm not religious at all anymore, but I loathe those religions that are all gloom and doom. Nothing about love and hope and faith. My disillusionment with the church probably started when I went to a priest after Leroy's conviction, and all he talked about was my brother's guilt and how we should welcome the pain of prison as a gift from God, a way for long suffering to promote our spiritual growth. Nothing about God's love and forgiveness. Damn! I'm rambling. Obviously, this is a sore point of mine."

He smiled. "You asked me what I would do if I had the freedom to choose? What would you do . . . what *will* you do when Leroy is released?"

"I've been afraid to think about it. It might jinx our chances if I start planning. Really, though, all I want is a normal life. I've never had normal, even before Leroy's conviction. I'm not looking for a grand passion, just a good man who loves me. A house, probably outside the city because I'd love a houseful of children. Three at least. Far away from Angola, from any prisons actually. I can practice law anywhere. Peace and normalcy, that's about it. Pathetic, isn't it, that I dream so small?"

"Not pathetic at all," he said, unexpectedly sad. He

peeled away at the label on his beer bottle before revealing, "I cannot have children."

"Oh. Sorry." She put a hand over his, about to say that he could always adopt.

But he continued, "And I may be assigned to Angola for another week, or another century."

What can I say to that? Better you than me?

"And I will never be normal."

For a blip of a second she wondered if normal was all it was cracked up to be. His cell phone pinged then, cutting off any more of that dangerous line of thinking.

"Sorry, I have to take this," he said, and quickly read whatever text message had arrived. His eyebrows shot up with surprise. After tapping back his own message, he clicked off and stared into space for a moment.

"Bad news?"

He shook his head. "No. It was from Mike. I was just surprised. He's never texted me before. He has other . . . ways . . . of communicating. Harek must be teaching him some electronic skills."

The call seemed to have put a damper on their time together, or maybe it had been the last part of their conversation regarding children and normalcy.

After paying their bill and making polite conversation with Pierre and Colette, they went back to Tante Lulu's car.

"Do you mind if we take a slight detour before I drop you off at Tante Lulu's place?"

"I don't know." She'd already spent more time with this man than was safe. He was too tempting by half.

"Mike wants me to check out a property for sale somewhere in Terrebonne Parish. An old sugar plantation."

She raised her eyebrows in question. "For what purpose?"

"I have no idea. Last month he had me go to Transylvania, Louisiana, to look at an abandoned factory that could be remodeled into an apartment complex, or something."

"There's a Transylvania in Louisiana?"

"Yes. Northern Louisiana. The sign on entering the town reads: 'We Welcome New Blood.'"

She laughed.

"You can laugh. They have ghosts, and bats everywhere. Even its water tower has a bat emblem on it."

"You're kidding."

"I wish!"

"So, are you going to relocate there?"

"By the clouds! I hope not. There are less than a thousand people residing in the town, which would be a plus for us vangels, but, really, one Transylvania in our family is enough. Someday I will tell you about the bizarre Transylvania, Pennsylvania, where my brother Vikar lives. There was so much bat dung in the castle when he first arrived that they had to take the guano out by the truckloads. Of course, Louisiana is just as bad with its abundance of snakes."

A castle? "I read somewhere that there are ten thousand species of snakes, and nine thousand of them live in our state."

He made a cute shivering gesture of distaste.

Gabrielle wasn't too fond of snakes herself.

A companionable silence followed, broken when she remarked, "I notice that you have a nice suntan. I thought vampires couldn't go outside in the daylight."

"That's an old wives' tale. Actually, we vangels cannot spend much time outside if we haven't fed properly or drunk our synthetic beverage, Fake-O. Otherwise, sun is fine."

"I don't understand."

"We save sinners by taking their blood, the amount depends on how tainted by sin they are." He shrugged.

"The blood of a redeemed sinner sustains us for months. Without it, if we go outdoors, our skin gets lighter and lighter, almost translucent."

"Whoa, whoa, whoa. Back up the bus," she said. "Are you saying that you drink blood?"

He looked surprised at her question. "Of course. What did you think the purpose of fangs was?"

"I don't know." She shook her head in confusion and motioned for Ivak to start driving. What kind of crazy had she gotten herself involved in? She glanced over at Ivak, who was concentrating on a right turn he was about to make and didn't notice her scrutiny. He looked entirely normal, but . . .

Once they left Houma and were traveling along Bayou Black, in the opposite direction from Tante Lulu's cottage, Gabrielle observed, "You know, many people think that the bayous are rather spiritual in nature. In fact, with the way that trees arch over the waters from both sides, meeting in the middle, they resemble a cathedral. Sort of."

"Sort of?" Ivak laughed.

"Well, you have to use your imagination." She thought a moment, then made another observation. "You said that you were in Louisiana back in the 1800s. Were you in this section of the bayous then, too?"

He shook his head. "No. Not that I would recognize it, even if I had. As you know, seen from the sky, the network of thousands of bayous resembles an intricate piece of lacework, but it's ever changing. What was here today is gone tomorrow, and new bayous spring up with every storm."

She nodded. The waters were calm today, deceptively peaceful. But the wrong step and a person could land in mud up to her eyeballs, or face-to-face with some deadly animal. Even so, the humidity of the air magnified all

the colors into boldness, like an expressionist landscape.
Pretty.

It took them about an hour to find the remote, *very*
remote plantation house, if it could be called that anymore. "Heaven's End Plantation," the broken-down sign
at the entrance said. How appropriate was that?

The Realtors, or owners, must have cleared a pathway through what had become a tropical jungle, just big
enough for a car to pass through. An allée of live oak trees
dripping moss once graced this lane. Similar paths were
made around both sides of the house and to the outbuildings where ancient trees peeked up through the foliage.
Not just the ancient oaks, but tupelo, chinaberry, willow,
and sycamore, and fruit trees gone wild . . . cherry, fig,
apple, and peach. Flowering bushes, like bougainvillea
and magnolia, resembled small trees. Kudzu was the least
of the problems here.

They both got out of the car and looked up.

"Well!" was the best she could come up with.

"Holy hell!" Ivak said, and he almost never swore.
"The place is about two hundred years old. It's been un-
occupied since the 1970s."

"I believe it," she said, and she referred to both its age
and its neglect.

It was a raised Creole-style mansion, the kind where
the main floor was on the second floor, and the ground
floor was where the kitchen and storage rooms had been
in an age past. There were three-story columns that rose
all the way to the top floor. Once gracious galleries surrounded all sides of the house. Wide steps . . . about
twelve feet wide . . . led from the front drive up to the
second floor entry.

That was the good part.

Parts of the hipped roof had caved in. Many of the tall,
floor-to-ceiling windows were broken. Exterior paint had

long worn off, and moisture had no doubt rotted the wood in many places.

"I love it!" she exclaimed.

"Are you demented? It's a dump. See here," he said, showing her the display screen on his phone. "This is a picture Mike sent of how the place looked at one time. As if I would have recognized this crumbling monstrosity from this photo."

She smacked his arm. "Shh! Don't insult the house."

It was a sepia-toned photo that showed a stately home with manicured flower gardens on the sides and grand oaks framing the road down to a wide bayou stream, where goods and travelers would have arrived here in the pre–Civil War days when the plantation had been built.

"You can't insult a building," he griped.

But she was already walking up the steps when he yelled out, "Come back here. Those steps are rotten. You might . . . oh shit!" He was soon at her side, and they both placed their feet carefully on the wooden boards that were indeed breaking apart in places.

When they got to the top, she tried the double front doors, to no avail; they were probably warped shut, rather than locked. Not to be deterred, she peered through one of the remarkably intact etched glass side windows that bracketed the doors. She sighed.

"Oh look, Ivak. The wood staircase is still there, and the cypress floors are damaged but aren't they beautiful? Look, look, look. There are stained glass French doors leading into one of the parlors or dining room, it's hard to tell which."

Ivak was amused by her enthusiasm, but she didn't care. One thing after another caught her attention. Crystal doorknobs. A tiled fireplace. A kitchen courtyard. A stone pathway leading into a jungle that had once been a rose garden, as evidenced by a lone pink rosebush that had managed to survive its tropical invaders. At her urging, Ivak tore off one of the long stems and handed it to her. She sniffed and smiled.

Without a machete, or a bulldozer, to clear the jungle, it was impossible to investigate any of the outbuildings . . . slave quarters, a sugar refinery, and God only knew what else. Plus, Ivak kept glancing at his watch.

When they were back in the car, Ivak didn't start the ignition right away. He just stared at her.

"Why did Mike . . . uh, your boss . . . want you to look at this place?"

"I don't know, but I have an alarming suspicion."

She cocked her head to the side.

"About a year or more ago, he sent my oldest brother, Vikar, to a run-down castle in Transylvania. I made reference to that earlier. Mike told Vikar to renovate it and make it into a home for vangels. It has twenty-five friggin' bedrooms and will probably take a century to really restore it and by then he'll probably have to start all over again."

"What does that have to do with this?" She waved at the mansion that loomed over them.

"Mike has hinted that he might want each of the VIK to establish command centers in other parts of the world. The VIK is an acronym for me and my six brothers as a leadership group."

"Oh my God! You think he might want you to buy this place and restore it?"

He nodded hesitantly. "I'm pretty sure he has ruled out the warehouse in northern Louisiana."

"Oh, how I envy you!"

"You jest! Gabrielle, I'm not sure what would be worse. Angola or this . . . this place."

"You're wrong," she said.

"Why does this run-down mansion appeal to you so

much? I thought you were all for a little house in the country with a white picket fence and a horde of bratlings."

"I didn't say that exactly. But can't you sense something special about this place, like it has a soul, and it's calling to you for help? It feels like . . . oh, you'll think I'm crazy . . . but it feels like home." Then she burst out crying, big gulping sobs.

He slid over to the middle of the wide bench seat and pulled her onto his lap, embracing her while she wept onto his neck. Finally, she sat up straight and gave an embarrassed laugh. "Some soul mate you picked!"

He pulled her face down to his and kissed her lightly on the lips, then not so lightly. "Not I, sweetling. Mike is responsible for this."

She kissed him then, framing his face with both hands. When she had him panting into her mouth, she leaned back and said, "Tell Mike Gabrielle says thanks."

Eleven

The road to Hell was paved with . . . snakes? . . .

Jasper decided to drop in on Dominique to discuss their latest project: the Angola Prison.

The restaurant that fronted Dominique's activities here in the Crescent City was on the first floor; so, Jasper's tail was dragging by the time he huffed and puffed his way up the steep flight of back stairs to her personal residence. The torture chambers were on the third floor and attics.

He turned to Beltane, his French assistant who'd spent his early human life in the 1700s Vieux Carré, or French Quarter, and had begged to accompany him. "You could have checked ahead, and we would have teletransported directly to the upper floors, instead of the blasted back courtyard," Jasper griped. If he had more energy, he would swat the hordling on his fool behind.

Beltane ducked his head. "Sorry, master. I was so excited about coming home . . . I mean, to Nawleans, not my home now . . . that I forgot."

Jasper's struggle up the stairs wasn't Beltane's fault, Jasper admitted to himself. He needed to stop eating so many human hearts loaded with cholesterol, but, yum, they were like potato chips to him. He couldn't stop at one.

"Jasper, dah-ling, you didn't have to walk up the steps. You could have teletransported."

Well, duh! For some reason, he decided to cover for Beltane. Dominique might very well bite his head off. Literally. He'd lost so many of his close assistants in recent years that he found himself rather protective of the boy, who was not really a boy at nineteen, give or take two hundred years. "I forgot that you weren't in a basement here."

Beltane gave him a look of total adoration.

"There are no cellars in N'awlins," Dominique explained. "You only have to dig a spade into the soil before hitting water."

Hah! He'd like to see the day Dominique ever lifted a spade.

"In any case, welcome, welcome!" She flashed him a big, fangy smile that was not really a smile.

He could tell that the female haakai was surprised, and not a little unhappy, about his sudden appearance, despite her smile. Good. It was always a good idea to keep his Lucipires on their toes, even the high-level commanders.

"Aren't you going to invite me in?"

"Of course." Before he entered, he told Beltane, "Go and visit your old neighborhood. Be back in two hours."

Another look of adoration and Beltane was gone.

As he stepped inside, Jasper instantly wished he'd accompanied his assistant. There were snakes. Everywhere. In glass cases. Loose, on the floor. One was even hanging from the chandelier.

"Holy shit, Dom. Must you have so many of these slimy reptiles? It's disgusting."

"Do I criticize your taste for killing jars, master?" she inquired with an emphasis on "master." The wicked wench no more considered him her master than alligators bowed to fish, even though they swam the same waters, and they both knew it. If he turned his back on her, he'd no doubt have a snake bite on his ass. Or her bite.

There were times when a good bitch slap was the only thing that would do. Unfortunately, Dominique would no doubt reciprocate with what could be called a bastard slap. Leastways, she could try.

"Show me around and then we'll discuss the Angola Project," he said in a tone of voice that put her in her place. He hoped.

Dominique, who was wearing some kind of tight leather outfit, adorned with sharp metal studs, that left her ample breasts almost exposed, led the way up . . . *More stairs*.

He sighed and sucked his stomach in. No way was he going to reveal to Dominique how out of shape he was. The minute he got back to Horror, he was hiring . . . okay, killing and turning . . . a fitness coach.

All the walls had been removed from the upper floor so that it was one massive space. Still, it was not one-hundredth of the size of Jasper's torture chambers. But then, Jasper liked to keep his playthings for long periods, to enjoy their pain, while Dominique was more impatient. She killed, tortured, and turned humans like an assembly line. He'd cautioned her more than once to slow down, she was calling too much attention to herself. Did she listen to him? No.

There were a dozen or more dead humans in various stages of torture and turning, all with ball gags in their mouths to prevent their screams from reaching the restaurant diners below or passersby on the street. All of their eyes were uniformly wide with terror at what they had wrought with their sinful lives. Other than a viper vat, Dominique employed the usual torture techniques and implements: the rack, impalement devices for all body orifices, demons licking, biting, sucking, and gnawing on every inch of skin and bone. That kind of thing. Ho-hum.

They were soon back in Dominique's small salon, which Jasper had insisted be free of all reptiles before he would sit down. Dominique had redone several antique chairs to accommodate Lucipire tails, so Jasper was comfortable when they sat across a small table sipping at tall glasses of Piña Colada Blood cocktails . . . blood drawn from nubile females who'd been permitted to eat only pineapples and coconuts for a week.

It would be an inviting repast if it weren't for all the snake decorations about the place. Carved into the chairs and woodwork. Depicted in paintings, including the famous one in the Garden of Eden. Even woven into the design of the carpet on the floor. He must have grimaced with distaste because Dominique inquired with as much sweetness as she could garner, which wasn't much, "What bit you in the balls, Jasper?"

He hissed his outrage, and, without moving from his seat, hurled her up against the wall, where she dangled like one of her snakes. "How dare you take that tone with me? Commander you may be, high haakai you may be, but always remember you are merely one of my minions."

"I am sorry, master," she said. "I did not mean to give offense."

He released her invisible bonds and she dropped to the floor, just catching herself from falling to her knees. Her red eyes snapped at him, but she deferred to his greater strength.

She had the good sense, belatedly, to bow low at the waist and wait for his permission to return to the table.

Once she was seated again and had composed herself, she announced, "I have news."

It must be good. Her red eyes threw sparks of excite-

ment, and she was shedding scales like a fish about to
become chowder. Saliva pooled at the corners of her lush
mouth.

"I believe one of the VIK is in the area. Ivak Sigurdsson."

With a frown, Jasper remarked, "I thought you told me
before that Ivak might be at Angola."

"There, too," she said with obvious excitement. Obvious, because she was drooling. "And we may have a
weapon against him."

Jasper cocked his head to the side, pretending only
mild interest, when it was his greatest dream to catch . . .
and keep . . . a VIK. He'd had one in his possession a year
or so ago, but the bastard VIK had managed to escape.
Well, not escape exactly. That infernal enemy of his, St.
Michael the Archangel, had rescued him.

"Look at this." Dominique handed him a cell phone.
On it was a picture of one of the VIK . . . Ivak, he believed it was . . . behind the wheel of a big lavender car
with a woman at his side. "They were driving down Bourbon Street when one of my mungs caught this on his cell
phone."

"And . . . ?"

"I believe this woman may be a sister of an inmate at
Angola, one we tried unsuccessfully to turn."

"Unsuccessfully?" He homed in on that word. "You
failed?"

"In that one case. The mung who was fanging the
inmate was interrupted and then later the young man appeared to have lost the sin taint."

"And that is why you think Ivak may be inside
Angola?"

She nodded vigorously.

"Get more information. Do not . . . I repeat, do not rush
in and attack. Take your time. Make sure Ivak is in fact

stationed here in Louisiana, and find out more about the woman. Ivak is attracted to all women with his lustsome nature, but if he has formed a stronger connection to this woman other than with his cock, we might be able to use her as a trap for him."

"Exactly what I thought." Dominique preened.

"We'll need to gather information on this woman. Do you still have that detective?"

Dominique blushed, if a demon could blush. "He is long gone." At Jasper's frown, she went on, "But we have something better."

This ought to be good.

"The Internet," Dominique revealed in a ta-da! fashion.

"Do you know how to use a computer?"

"Bloody hell, no! And I do not want to learn." She glanced down at her two-inch, bloodred fingernails. She would not want to risk breaking them on a keyboard. "But we recently captured a young geek who bilked lots of people out of their money by hacking into their bank accounts. He's almost done turning."

"Put him on it."

Dominique nodded. "Speaking of the Internet . . . I heard a rumor that Michael and Gabriel are setting up an archangel website."

Jasper gaped at her. "For what purpose?"

"To gather more souls for the Lord."

Damn, damn, damn! "Then we will do the same. We will set up a website for Satan."

At first, she frowned, but then she practically jumped up and down in her seat with excitement. "It could be like Dear Abby, except ours would be Dear Satan."

Jasper hated to encourage Dominique but he admitted, "I love it!"

They both raised their glasses in a toast. "To evil!"

When shit hits the fan at Angola, it *really* flies . . .

It was utter chaos back at Angola.

"This facility is on immediate lockdown," a red-faced, furious Warden Benton hollered, spittle flying, to the quickly called meeting of prison personnel. "Is that clear? No one . . . *no one* . . . is entering or leaving these grounds until we've solved this mystery."

How clear could it be? Your voice is two decibels above a screech, my ears are ringing, and thank God I'm not sitting up front, Ivak thought.

An FBI agent and several Justice Department higher-ups stood at Benton's side, stone-faced. They'd brought an army of agents, forensics experts, and other personnel to help in the investigation. A few of them were vangels; Michael's way of getting more aid to Ivak without garnering too much attention. While Benton seemingly welcomed any assistance coming his way, he must resent all the outside "help."

The FBI agent, Jack Laraway, told them, "The administration has learned that at least a dozen day employees, those who live outside the prison gates but drive in to work every morning, have disappeared, and an equal number of terminally ill inmates in the prison hospital or hospice program are gone. No bodies to bury. Just disappeared."

Benton elaborated with names and other details.

Oh damn! The Lucies! Ah, well, this was bound to happen. The demon vampires got greedy and failed to take their evil slowly, covering their evil tracks.

The inmate representative at the meeting, the editor of the *Angolite*, blurted out, "Why has it taken so long to discover these disappearances?"

Benton scowled. The inmate would hear about his intrusion later, for sure.

"Because there are more than fifteen hundred prison staff members, and on any one day, there are always a lot who call in sick, are on vacation, or just decide to quit without notice. That's why. As for the dying, the caretakers assumed the bodies had been taken for burial, and it was only when a routine count was done that we discovered reports of empty beds. Presumed deaths, but there were no bodies to bury."

And, actually, no one really cared enough to keep an accurate count of the dying until this happened, Ivak mused. He knew because of his work in saving some of them.

The general consensus was that there had been one massive prison escape, or a number of individual escapes, that had gone badly awry. The wide Mississippi would have swallowed some of them. The wild predators in the swamps and forests on the other sides would have gobbled up the rest, clothes and all.

It was the large number that had everyone so upset. Could it be a plot of some type? And was there more to come?

For the next few days, as investigators moved about the prison, inmates were permitted no contact with the outside world. And movement inside the prison was severely restricted. Mealtimes were particularly tedious because there were more security guards, and the convicts had to be accounted for every minute. Calls and visits from or to the outside world were forbidden, for the time being. Employees' cell phones had been confiscated for the duration.

The news media were going crazy trying to figure out what was going on at Angola. TV vans with their rooftop dishes were lined up all along Snake Road, leading to the prison gates. To no avail. Anyone who spoke to the press was threatened with imprisonment, and those already imprisoned would have their sentences extended. As a result, rumors and false information were reported as fact, even a headline in the *Star* magazine, "Alien Abductions at Angola."

Ivak was able to move about somewhat and he made sure the second day that he got to visit Leroy's dorm, where one of the newly arrived vangels was keeping an eye on Gabrielle's brother.

"Jesus Christ! What the fuck is going on?" Leroy asked when Ivak sat down on the cot next to him. Ivak cringed at his language, and Leroy corrected himself, "Good grace! What in heaven's name is going on?"

Ivak let out a hoot of laughter. "You don't have to go to that extreme."

"Well?"

"I told you about Lucipires and vangels," Ivak said in a low enough tone that they couldn't be overheard. The bunks in the dorms were only two feet apart, and about sixty to one unit. "Well, apparently the Lucies have gone wild, taking a couple dozen humans already, both inmates and staff."

"Holy hell!" Leroy said, then, "Oops!"

"We have vangels inside now, too. In fact"—he motioned for another man to sit on the next bunk, facing them—"have you met Svein? Svein, this is Leroy Sonnier."

A tall, lean man with light blond hair and pale blue eyes, wearing the T-shirt and jeans "uniform" of an Angola convict, extended a hand to Leroy, "Greetings, Mr. Sonnier." His skin was almost albino-ish white, but would tan up soon enough once he'd fed.

"Uh, hello," Leroy said, gaping, even as he shook hands with the newcomer. He stared at Svein, then Ivak, then back at Svein. "Don't tell me . . ."

Ivak and Svein nodded.

"Holy hell!" he said again.

Svein gave Ivak a telling look about Leroy's language.

"He's learning," Ivak said.

Another inmate, Ed Chesney, tried to sit down next to Svein, figuring it was some kind of casual chat, but at Svein's glower, he backed off, muttering, "Shit! Talk about unsociable! What are you? The 'Mean Boys'?"

"Give it a rest, Chesney. We'll talk later," Ivak said to the departing man, who just waved over his shoulder.

As soon as they were alone again, Svein looked directly at Leroy and dropped a bombshell. "Little Eddie Hebert has third stage colon cancer."

"Fuck!" Leroy exclaimed. "If he dies before recanting, I'm dead in the water here until I die."

"There's more. Hebert has been fanged by a Lucie. That's why he's resisted withdrawing his lie," Svein said.

Leroy stood abruptly. "Oh shit, oh damn, I might as well just give up."

Ivak pushed him back down and warned him, "Don't you dare say it's hopeless, or I'll sic Tante Lulu and her St. Jude brigade on you."

Leroy smiled, halfheartedly.

"The real danger is that Lucies will sense his approaching death and rush in to complete the fanging," Ivak explained.

"You guys are seriously weird," Leroy said, not for the first time.

"Jogeir was in the same prison camp as Hebert, and he's sticking close to the hospital," Svein told Ivak. "He's already trying to save him. No luck so far, but he's keeping an eye on him so that no Lucies can approach."

"Plus, Tante Lulu is going to speak with Hebert's mother to see if she'll intercede on your behalf," Ivak added. "Mrs. Hebert and Tante Lulu play bingo together at Our Lady of the Bayou Church."

"Good Lord!" Leroy muttered. "My fate is in the hands of weirdo angels with fangs and old ladies who bingo."

After Svein left, Leroy asked Ivak, "Have you talked to Gabby lately?"

"Not since Saturday . . . three days ago. Phone lines are shut down for staff, too, except for emergencies, and even then, the calls have to be monitored."

"Can't you use supernatural means to contact her and let her know I'm okay?"

"Best not to draw attention in any way," Ivak said, and told Leroy to hold on until things settled down here.

Actually, Ivak could contact Gabrielle, but he wasn't sure what he would say. That afternoon with her had cemented his certainty that she was his soul mate, despite her protests to the contrary. But he was just as certain that they could have no future together based on their conversation that day.

First and foremost, he was a thousand-year-old vampire angel and she was a human. Didn't matter that exceptions had been made for Vikar and Trond. *I know well and good that Mike shut that gate. He made that announcement after the mess Trond and Nicole created before their marriage.*

Second, Gabrielle wanted children, lots of them. *I can't give her even one.*

Third, *as if I need any more reasons*, she wanted to move far away from Angola and any other prison atmosphere. *I might very well be assigned here for many years to come, even if I managed to live off the premises.*

Fourth, she wanted normal. *Alas, I will never be normal again, if I ever was.*

When he got back to his office, Ivak found two text messages on his hidden second phone. Apparently, some calls . . . those of a celestial nature . . . could get through.

"Buy the plantation."

"Save the girl."

Both were equally alarming.

The plantation, he understood, though not the why of it.

The girl, he understood, too. Mike was referring to Gabrielle.

But why did she need saving? She was not in any state of grave sin, or contemplated sin, that he could detect, requiring his "saving" her with a fanging. It must mean . . .

Oh no! Oh no, no, no! If Mike wanted him to buy that so-called plantation, he must intend Ivak to be in Louisiana and Angola for some time. What did that portend for him and Gabrielle, who wanted nothing to do with either after Leroy's release?

And if Mike wanted him to save Gabrielle, and her heart was not in any state of sin . . . His heart nigh stopped, and his heart was already dead. It must mean that Gabrielle was in some physical danger.

And he was stuck in the Alcatraz of the South.

Twelve

Oh no! The old harem fantasy! . . .

Gabrielle dreamed about Ivak that night. And the night after that. And the night after that. Every one of them had the same theme, one that was erotic and ridiculous at the same time. Sex with a hot stranger.

She was a renowned Saxon beauty being held in an Arab harem for the pleasure of some visiting Norse noblemen.

Imagine that! Her a renowned beauty? And how she, with her short supply of experience, could pleasure some Viking was beyond her. Someone was going to be very disappointed. But it was a dream, and in her dreams anything was possible, she supposed.

"Wake up, miss. Oh, please, wake up. It is time for us to go."

Gabrielle raised her heavy lids slowly, blinked, then opened her eyes wide to the most fantastic scene. She was in some kind of marble palace with fountains and low chaises, such as the one she was lying on. She sat up and saw wispy sheer curtains and low tables with platters of fruit . . . dates, figs, pomegranates, and slices of lush melons . . . and another bowl of green and black olives. And there were women. Lots of women. Scantily clad and chattering like jaybirds in a foreign language, probably Arabic, which she could, amazingly, understand. In fact, in the distance she could hear the haunting adhan, the call to prayer by the muezzin. Much closer, somewhere in this palace—if that's what this was—exotic Arab music filled the air, the kind you heard scantily clad women belly dance to in Middle Eastern restaurants.

With an irrelevance she excused as just being a dream, she remembered a friend in college telling her one time that belly dancers had better orgasms. She'd always intended to take lessons some day but never seemed to find the time. Too late now.

"Come, come," the woman who'd awakened her said, tugging at her hand, pulling her to follow a group of women wearing nothing but scarves. Standing woozily, Gabrielle glanced downward, then did a double take. She was wearing the same kind of outfit. Scarves on the top, which ended just below her breasts, and scarves on the bottom hanging from a waistband of harem-style pants that began at her hips, leaving about eight inches of skin bare, including her belly button, where a red ruby-like stone had been glued. Jeesh! There were tiny bells attached at the ankles. When she walked, she would be like an oversize Tinker Bell.

Just then she noticed something about the other women. She glanced downward at herself. "Oh no!" Lifting the scarves over her breasts, she peeked inside and squealed. "Oh my God!" Her nipples and areolas had been rouged or painted red.

"Good Lord! If the bells don't tell everyone when I'm

coming, these neon sign boobs will do the trick." This breast makeup better be washable, or someone is going to pay. Can anyone say lawsuit?

"Huh?" said the young woman who'd awakened her. She was no more than seventeen and firmer than Gabrielle in strategic places.

A big, heavyset, effeminate-looking man wearing a turban clapped his hands and began to lead the scarf women, herself included, out of the harem and along a corridor. A eunuch? Must be. This is just like a Bertrice Small novel. "Hurry, hurry! The master is anxious to impress his guests."

Oh yeah! All us red-light boobs are going to impress.

"Make sure you lower your eyes when you are dancing," the eunuch reminded them.

Dancing? What dancing?

They were led into a room where several dozen men sat or half reclined on cushions or low divans, some braced on both elbows, some lying on their sides braced on just one elbow, before short tables groaning with food. Barebreasted, nubile girls fanned some of them with peacock feathers or fed them grapes. No kidding! Grapes? What a cliché!

Some male servants moved the food tables aside, leaving a space in the center that was about twenty-bytwenty, just enough room for the ten scarfies who snaked to the center in a hip-shimmying dance. She, the tail end of the dance, wouldn't know how to shimmy if her life depended on it.

And it just might, as evidenced by the sharp-looking swords in evidence.

The men sat in a U-shaped pattern around three sides of the marble-walled room. The floor was covered by an enormous, jewel-colored Persian rug that felt like silk under her bare feet, which, incidentally, sported several toe rings. Most of the men wore Arab attire, long robes of white or black, some with felt caps on their heads and others with the traditional head wraps like turbans held in places with ropes or twisted cloth. Precious jewels in gold-framed pendants hung around their necks or were displayed on numerous fingers.

But then there were the other men. A half-dozen big men wearing brushed leather, thigh-length tunics, cinched in at the waist by gold or silver linked belts, over tight pants, like leggings. Gold and silver arm rings adorned their biceps. Their hair was long, all shades from blond to black, some with single braids down the back, others with thin "war braids" twined with crystals framing their handsome faces. Sharp knives and swords with ornate hilts were close at hand. And in the midst of all these stood the bane of her life . . . or rather her dreams . . . none other than Ivak Sigurdsson in all his Viking glory.

She gave a little wave, causing the eunuch behind her to pinch her butt. She scowled at him, rubbing her sore posterior, and turned back to get Ivak's attention.

But he didn't even notice her. The lout! He was staring at one of the scarfies in the front. A small blonde with breasts that were not so small. They jiggled when she danced, for heaven's sake!

The head Arab guy . . . a sultan, she supposed . . . clapped his hands and said, "Welcome, favored friends and guests." He bowed toward the Vikings. "May Allah shine on you whilst in my country, and may we have good trading tomorrow. Now, let me present my best dancing girls."

Once again, Gabrielle could understand everything that was said, even though it was in Arabic.

"After the dancing, you are free to enjoy any of the girls at your leisure."

Whoa, whoa, whoa! Girls served up like food and drink. I don't think so! *Her fellow scarfies didn't seem to mind, though. They smiled and giggled, some of them batting their heavily kohled eyelashes at particular men. That made Gabrielle wonder with hysterical irrelevance if she was kohled up, too. Probably. A slutted-up Barbie doll, for heaven's sake!*

There was movement among the several musicians, indicating the start of the entertainment. First a flute provided a haunting Arab melody, soon joined by a man with an hourglass-shaped hand drum. And finally, a man began playing a stringed instrument, like a guitar, but it was probably a lute.

The dancers were arranged four across in three rows. Only then did the scarfies begin to move into a circle, adding to the music with cymbals and tambourines, a circle that moved slowly in a walking shimmy. Since Gabrielle couldn't shimmy, or at least had never tried, she just did a little hula-type move, wanting to get as far away from the eunuch as she could. First chance she got, she was going to make a run for it since Ivak was obviously not going to be her knight in shining leather. Her erotic dream was turning into a nightmare.

Several different songs were played, each with corresponding dance moves. Belly rolls, back bends. Holy cow! Gabrielle almost fell over with that one . . . squeezing glutes, a camel walk, hip bumps, and all kinds of shimmies . . . forward, backward, and walking. There was even a solo performance by blondie that ended in her being a whirling dervish that drew much applause from the appreciative crowd. Blondie would undoubtedly be the pleasurer of choice tonight.

Finally, the dance performance seemed to be over and there was much chatter as men began to pick partners. Gabrielle was across the room from Ivak, who was momentarily distracted by a new man who had walked into the room and was whispering in his ear. The man resembled Ivak's brother Harek. The two of them were engrossed in some serious conversation, the expressions on their faces concerned.

Eventually, they stopped talking, and Harek walked off. Turning, Ivak seemed surprised to see that blondie was gone. In fact, all the women, except Gabrielle, had gone off with their partners. A few men had started to approach Gabrielle, but she gave them such dirty looks that they backed away. In fact, one Arab with an especially elaborate turban had motioned with a beckoning finger for her to come to him; she gave him an answer with her middle finger and turned away.

Ivak's gaze locked with hers then, studying her body in the skimpy outfit. Then, to her chagrin, it appeared as if he was going to turn away, rejecting her.

No, no, no! That was not the way it was supposed to happen in dreams. She stomped up to him, put her hands on her hips, and said, "Well?"

A smile twitched at Ivak's lips as he gave her another arrogant head-to-toe survey. "You'll do," he said, and took her by the hand, leading her out of the room.

"I'll do," she shrieked. "Do?" She tried to dig in her heels, but he just dragged her along. She thought she heard him chuckling.

Finally, they came to a small room that was open on one side to a mini-courtyard with a fountain. He shoved her inside and locked the door.

"Well, wench, how do you plan to pleasure me?"

"What?"

"Mayhap you will give me a private dance."

"Dancing is not my strongest talent."

"I noticed."

She made a growling sound that seemed to startle him.

"If not dancing, dost have some special talent in the bedsport to pleasure me?"

"I'm not here to pleasure you."

"No? Why are you here then?" He undid his belt and removed his sheathed sword, laying them both on a low chest. "Am I to pleasure you?" He shrugged. "That works for me. Me first, then your turn." He heeled off first one boot, then the other, and raised his tunic up and over his head, gracing her with a most impressive chest. And shoulders. And arms. Jeesh! Did men really have waists that narrow?

She shook her head to clear her vision. "Hey, hey, hey, stop taking your clothes off."

He arched his brows. "How can I tup you if my cock is covered?"

She had a pretty good idea what a tup was. "No need to be crude. Just keep your pants on. I can't think with all that skin. This is a dream, you know?"

He rolled his eyes. "Why do I always get the barmy ones?"

"We need to talk."

"Ah, sex talk. I can do that." He stretched out on the low bed, his back to the wall. "The scarves are nice, but time to lose them. One at a time, please."

"I am not taking off my clothes."

"Then I am not talking."

"Oh hell. Okay." She took off one of the leg scarves and shot him a glare. "First off, we know each other already."

That surprised him. "Really? It could not have been too memorable a swiving if I do not recall it. Was it in that bawdy house in Jorvik? Or that time in Byzantium when the emperor sent all those women to us Varangian guardsmen? Methinks I was beyond drukkinn at the time." He waved for her to drop another scarf.

Crap! The lech must have screwed women from one end of the world to the other. That's right. He did tell me he was guilty of the sin of lust "in a big way." *She dropped another leg scarf. "Not that kind of knowing. Listen, you've got to help me get out of here."*

"I have no intention of leaving this country for at least a sennight, and if you think I'm going to steal a houri from the sultan's harem, you are barmier than I thought."

"Whore-ee? You son of a . . . I'm no whore."

He rolled his eyes. "Houri, not whore. One of the harem."

"I am not part of the sultan's harem," she said through gritted teeth.

He folded his arms over his chest, waiting.

With a pfff! of disgust, she removed the toe rings and some bracelets.

"You jest!" he snarled, apparently not satisfied with a bit of jewelry.

With another pfff! of disgust, she removed a sheer sleeve.

"Why do you want to leave Baghdad? I would think you lead a pampered life here. Ah, women are always wanting more than they have. Does not matter if they are in the Norselands or in the Arab lands. Where are you from, by the by?"

"America."

"Dost mean that land that Erik the Red has discovered? Nay, do not answer. It does not matter." Without asking for her permission, he raised his hips and shrugged his pants down to his ankles, and then tossed them to the floor.

For a moment, she was speechless. Holy moly! Were men really built like that? Apparently, he wasn't as unmoved by her appearance as he led her to believe, but maybe blondie had primed his pump, so to speak.

"I didn't mean that I want you to help me leave this place . . . Baghdad, or wherever this is. I meant that I want you to help me get out of this dream."

"How would I do that?" he asked, waving peremptorily for another scarf.

She dropped the second sleeve, which didn't leave her with much else to drop. "How? I don't know how! You're the one to blame for this . . . mess." She hadn't meant to shriek.

He pounded the heel of one hand against the side of his head as if to clear his ears. "Mess?"

"Dream."

"I daresay many women dream about me, but you are the only one who ever complained about it." He smiled at her, a slow, lazy smile that was probably intended to be seductive.

It was, actually, especially with the standing sign of his interest, which, unbelievably, seemed to be growing.

"I have no intention of having sex with you," she said.

"Oh? I see. You want to be seduced. I can do that." He stared at her pointedly now, his silent message loud and clear: Lose the rest of the clothing.

Oh hell! She turned her back to him, undid the bra-type scarf garment, and tried to rub off some of the rouge with the fabric, to no avail.

"Are you touching yourself? Wonderful! Turn so that I can watch."

"I can't."

"Why not?"

"Dammit!" she said, spinning on her bare heels. "Because some fool painted my boobs."

His eyes went wide at first. Then he smiled. "It's not so bad."

"Puh-leeze!"

"Your breasts are nice. Lift them for me."

"What? Oh." She lifted them from underneath.

"They look like cherries in small pools of cherry juice. I wonder how they taste. Sweet or tart? Methinks I should lick them to see. Then mayhap I should suck on the cherries themselves. To see if there are pits. Then little nibbling bites."

She couldn't think for a moment, so intense was the pleasure that emanated from her aching breasts and rippled out to every erotic zone in her body, especially between her legs.

"Dost weep for me, wench? Between your legs. Check and see." His compelling eyes held hers, persuading.

As if hypnotized, she dropped the remainder of the harem pants, leaving her bare to his scrutiny. Bare? She glanced downward. Oh my God! She had no hair down below. Someone had plucked out all her pubic hair. She tried to cover herself with both hands.

"That's the way, sweetling. Touch yourself."

"I wasn't touching myself. I was covering myself. This is so embarrassing! I look like a plucked chicken!" She dropped her hands.

His eyes went wide. "Your woman's fleece is gone."

"No shit, Sherlock."

"My name is Ivak. Not Sure-lock. And best you curb your sarcasm and foul tongue, wench, lest you taste the flavor of my wrath."

She rolled her eyes. This was the strangest experience of her life. Had she eaten funny mushrooms, or something?

"A fucked chicken?" Ivak just barely bit back a burst of laughter.

"Plucked, you idiot. Not fucked."

"It has a certain attraction, after the initial shock," he said, but he was grinning.

"If that was an attempt to make me feel better, you failed."

"I must admit, I like a bit of mystery, but betimes a change can be exciting. Is that moisture leaking from your nether folds? A sign of your arousal?"

"Well, it's a not a leaky bladder?" Definitely an idiot! *"It's not polite to remark on things like that."*

"I was ne'er considered very polite. Come closer. I want to tell you something."

"Why can't you tell me from there?"

"Come. Here."

Somehow, she found herself standing by the bed. When had she moved? Why had she moved? Then, before she could blink, Ivak reached over, picking her up by the waist, and lifted her up and over, straddling him.

"Take me," he urged.

And she did.

Holding his massive erection in both hands, she placed him at her opening, then lowered herself inch by inch 'til he filled her. Immediately, her body began convulsing into an intense, never-ending orgasm.

She screamed then.

That's when she heard a female voice say, "Wake up, Gabrielle. Wake up. You mus' be havin' a bad dream."

She sat up and turned on the bedside lamp, realizing dazedly that she was still in modern times, in the bayou cottage.

Tante Lulu looked at her and smiled. "Forget bad dreams. Yer face is all flushed. I may be old as time, but I remember that look. This ol' bed ain't seen that much action since Tee-John was a teenager."

Alone again later, in the dark, Gabrielle could only wonder what real sex would be like if fantasy sex was so hot.

Thirteen

Some days start out bad and go downhill from there . . .

It was a week before Gabrielle was given permission to return to Angola and visit her brother.

In the meantime, she worked on her caseload at Second Chances and returned to Tante Lulu's cottage on Bayou Black every night. Nights that were filled with horrible—or wonderful, depending on the perspective—erotic dreams.

There had been a lockdown at the prison to investigate the disappearance of a number of prison employees and some elderly or terminally ill inmates in the prison hospital. To say that Gabrielle was worried was an understatement, even though there had been no new disappearances, or escapes, or whatever this past week.

She had to wonder if it was related to the story Ivak had told her about demon vampires being around or inside the penitentiary grounds. Investigators had come up with no leads, according to the news media, but visitors were being allowed back in, under tighter security.

The warden was trying to paint this as a picture of

faulty paperwork at the prison, but no one was buying that. People living within fifty miles of Angola were taking extra precautions to lock up their homes, and some were even buying firearms to protect themselves from what they perceived as escaped convicts, including those in the prison medical facility.

Yeah, right, a seventy-year-old convict with congestive heart failure was going to tramp through the swamps outside the prison grounds. Or the one-legged inmate reliant on insulin for his diabetes. Or the AIDS prisoner so thin he resembled a Holocaust survivor.

The news media were going wild with all the conjectures, and not just the tabloids. With the media not being able to enter the prison grounds or contact anyone inside, the reports were wide-ranging, all quoting unnamed sources. The usual alien abduction theory. Government experiments on bodies deemed expendable. Convicts enlisted for covert terrorist operations. A mass prison escape masterminded by a Houdini-type escape artist. Bribery of guards. Hit men within the prison population. Not surprisingly, none of the stories mentioned demon vampires.

Leroy had been permitted to call her collect for the first time yesterday. He'd informed her that Little Eddie Hebert, the only man who stood between his exoneration and a lifetime in prison, had been diagnosed with late stage colon cancer. She was able to tell Leroy that Tante Lulu was working on Little Eddie's mother, trying to get her to persuade her son to tell the truth. And Leroy told Gabrielle that Ivak was working his angel magic on the convict, too.

Oh God! Are we placing all our trust in a magician? A magician who is driving me wild every night in my dreams.

"We don't have a lot of time," Leroy said, "but Ivak says everything will work out in the end."

Gabrielle wouldn't know about that. After the remarkable day she'd spent with Ivak last Saturday, she'd heard not one single word from him. Apparently, the charmer wasn't as charmed with her as he'd claimed to be. Apparently, the dreams weren't having the same impact on him as they were on her.

Well, screw him. Not literally. Except for the dreams. Just no more wasted energy on a womanizer like Ivak. And that's exactly what he was, she decided. A man who could charm a woman silly, then not call . . . well, who needed that? Not her. From now on, she was keeping her distance.

Gabrielle was driving Tante Lulu's car to Angola today with the old lady riding shotgun. René, who had a job up that way, was going to meet them there.

The top was up to preserve the old lady's hair, which had been styled that morning by Charmaine . . . a light brown pageboy that fit perfectly under her cowboy hat that went with rodeo gear: a long-sleeved shirt with snap fasteners and a fringed vest with jeans and tooled leather boots. A dwarf version of Dale Evans. If the old lady thought that anyone was going to let her get on a horse—or God forbid, a bull—she was crazier than she acted sometime.

That was mean, Gabrielle chided herself. Tante Lulu had been nothing but kind to her. Interfering and outrageous, but kind.

In any case, the top was also up because Gabrielle was being cautious in case there were any demons flying around. The only scary thing she'd seen so far, though, was the decrepit truck she'd been tailing for the last five miles with two side-by-side bumper stickers. One read "This Truck Is Insured by Smith & Wesson." And the other: "Keep Honking. I'm Reloading." She had to remind herself at times that she was in the Deep South, which was a law unto itself.

"I still think you shoulda gussied up more. You coulda worn that sundress Charmaine brought for you."

"Tante Lulu! It was pink! And it had sequins!"

"So? You gotta embrace yer inner floozy, hon. Doan mean you gotta go skanky. Nope. Not many gals kin pull off bimbo with a brain lak Charmaine does. In yer case, jist a little bit slut and a little bit librarian would do jist fine."

Good Lord!

As a compromise, Gabrielle had let Charmaine do her hair into a chic French braid, and she wore a knee-length denim skirt with a short-sleeved, scoop-necked, multi-shaded blue silk top. She'd even agreed to a manicure and pedicure so that her stubby fingernails were now a rose color, along with her toenails that peeked out of a pair of bone sandals. She'd adamantly refused sculptured nails.

Tante Lulu slanted Gabrielle a sly look now, from her perch atop two cushions so she could see over the dashboard. "How you gonna land yer fish if you doan throw out any bait?"

"What fish? What bait?" she made the mistake of asking.

"The Viking fish, thass what fish. I cain't be matchmakin' fer you, if you doan cooperate."

Gabrielle rolled her eyes.

"I saw that. If you cain't see that the Good Lord wants you ta light up that boy's life, well, you mus' be blind."

There were so many outrageous things in that statement that Gabrielle didn't know where to start. "I thought you worked with St. Jude, not God."

"Same thing." Tante Lulu waved a hand airily.

"As for lighting up Ivak's life . . . I'm not interested and neither is he."

"Yep. Blind as a bayou bat on a moonless night."

"We spent some time together last Saturday, a late lunch, then a trip out to that old Heaven's End Plantation. He's probably going to be associated with Angola for some time to come, and I want nothing to do with prisons once Leroy is out. Ivak can't have children; I want bunches. Oh, I don't know. We're just too different."

"Pfff! Details! When the thunderbolt strikes, details are like farts on the wind. Soon blown away."

What an image! "What thunderbolt?"

"The thunderbolt of love. I tol' you 'bout that before, dint I?"

She hadn't but Gabrielle wasn't about to give her that opening. "There hasn't been any thunder, lightning, rain, storm, or anything else. Ivak is a man who's hopefully going to help us free Leroy. That's all."

"If you say so!" Tante Lulu said. "Did I ask if you want a tablecloth or place mats fer Ivak's hope chest?"

"Aaarrgh!"

Tante Lulu smiled as if she'd achieved some victory.

They'd just turned onto Snake Road, the only way a person could travel to the prison. There was an old yellow converted school bus ahead of them bringing indigent visitors to the penitentiary. The road was bordered on each side by gullies so deep that the foliage visible above ground level was actually the tops of trees. It was an un-tamed area kept that way to discourage prisoners from ever trying to escape.

"Are you a virgin?" Tante Lulu asked all of a sudden.

Sometimes it was hard to keep up with Tante Lulu's popcorn brain.

"No. Are you?"

"Goodness sakes, no! 'Course it's been a long time fer me. I lost my fiancé in the Big War. Had a few beaus after that, but none that could compare to my Pierre."

"I'm so sorry."

Tante Lulu dabbed at her eyes with a St. Jude hand-kerchief.

"Now, if Richard Simmons had ever come ridin' down the bayou, I woulda jumped on his pirogue any day. What a hunk!"

Gabrielle had to smile at the old lady's fixation on the exercise guru, who was a hunk only in her mind.

"Didja ever find yer G-spot?"

Whaaat? "Uh, maybe."

"I ain't never found mine. Do you s'pose it dried up lak a raisin inside my va-jay-jay? Thass what Oprah calls female parts."

"Uh . . ." was all Gabrielle could come up with.

Didn't matter. Tante Lulu was off on another subject. "Didja say Ivak took you to see that old Heaven's End Plantation? It's a cryin' shame how run down it's become. Thass what happens when there ain't no chillen or gran-chillen to take over a family home. You gots the right idea having a bunch of youngins. If Pierre hadn't died, betcha we woulda had at least five. Mebbe six."

"Uh . . ."

"Why did Ivak take you all the way out there? Is he thinkin' 'bout buyin' it?"

"I'm not sure. Maybe."

Tante Lulu nodded. "I could give him lotsa advice. Some good friends of mine, Angel and Grace Sabato, jist renovated a plantation house not far from my cottage. Betcha they could help you and Ivak."

Angel and Grace? That figures. "Ivak and I are not a couple."

"How many bedrooms they got at Heaven's End?"

"I have no idea. The roof is caving in, and it was unsafe to go inside."

"Mus' be at least eight, not countin' the rooms in the attic where the slaves and servants usta live. Golly, it sure is hot t'day. Gonna have a storm t'night sure as shootin'."

"You can tell that by the heat?"

"Nope. Mah knees and Useless growlin' up a storm
. . . tee hee hee, do you get the joke? The twinges in my
hinges are actin' up t'day. Oh Lordy! Look how the traffic's backed up at the gate?"

There were dozens of news trucks and vans in one lane
alone. After the long lockdown, reporters were anxious
to get inside to investigate on their own. Or as much on
their own as Warden Benton would allow, which wouldn't
be much.

"They're probably friskin' everyone who enters today,
and me wearin' my everyday undies!" Tante Lulu said.
"Didja ever have one of them body cavity searches?"
When Gabrielle just made a gurgling sound, Tante Lulu
went on, "Me neither. Might not be such a bad idea. It
would be the closest I've had ta sex in twenty years. Do
you think a woman could have an orgy-asm with a rubber-
gloved finger up her va-jay-jay? Why're you crossin' yer
eyes? Best be careful. I knew a gal did that all the time,
and her eyeballs got froze sideways."

They passed through security, finally. Without being
frisked. Although Tante Lulu made a big fuss over not
being allowed to bring her big purse inside; nor was she
permitted to carry even one St. Jude statue inside the
prison perimeter. But then, the same thing had happened
last time they were here.

"We can't allow anything inside that could be filed or
melted down into a weapon. Even plastic," the guard declared.

"St. Jude wouldn't allow it," Tante Lulu contended.

"Screw St. Jude."

Tante Lulu gasped and smacked the guard on the head
with her Richard Simmons fan, which she also wasn't
permitted to bring inside this time.

It took a call to the warden's office before the guard
would release them to go inside. As a last shot, Tante Lulu

squinted her eyes at the guard's security badge and exclaimed, "Russell Bouvier! I knew you when you were a snot-nosed brat at Our Lady of the Bayou grade school with mah nephew Tee-John. Jist wait 'til I tell yer mama what you said 'bout St. Jude."

The guard actually looked fearful and said, "Sorry, Ms. Rivard."

"Hmpfh! You oughta be. Make sure you go ta confession. Hear?"

And that was just the beginning of Gabrielle's day!

Gabrielle met Leroy in the visiting shed while a guard led Tante Lulu off to the auditorium where René and Ivak were waiting for her to continue the talent show auditions. Reporters were being hustled off in groups of ten at a time to the warden's office for press conferences. At this rate, the warden would have laryngitis by the end of the day.

"I hafta pee," she heard Tante Lulu tell the guard. Nothing new there. She'd made Gabrielle stop three times on the way here. She used bathroom breaks as an excuse to snoop around, no matter where she was. "You got any clean bathrooms in this joint?"

After hugging Gabrielle, Leroy led her over to a bench on the far side of the crowded room. Normally, on a sunny day, inmates with good records were permitted to go outside to a wooded picnic area to spend time with visitors, but not while the prison was under such tight security. That was the reason for the crowded conditions today.

Leroy gave her a quick recap of the events that led to the lockdown, and the spin Warden Benton was putting on the events: a mix-up in reporting the deaths in the hospital and hospice areas; a botched escape attempt by a half-dozen inmates; and twelve or so prison employees quitting without notice. When you considered that there were more than six thousand inmates and staff at the prison, two dozen bodies was not all that much, or at least that was the story Benton was tossing out there to see if it floated. What other explanation could there be?

"I heard that Mrs. Hebert is here today to visit with that turd bastard son of hers over at the hospital," Leroy told her. "Do you know if she's going to . . . um, try to help me?"

"Not if she hears you refer to her dying son as a turd bastard," Gabrielle remarked. "Whatever she does, it won't be for you. She's a religious woman, honey, like Tante Lulu. Whatever she does, it will be for what she considers her son's good. I don't think she wants him to die with that kind of lie on his soul, assuming she believes that he lied."

Leroy said several foul words, for which she wanted to chastise him, but decided to pick her battles. Instead, she asked him what was new since they'd met last, aside from the prison brouhaha.

Leroy told her that Ivak had assigned one of his men to Leroy's dorm as a protective measure. "This guy has fangs, too."

"Do you really believe all this vampire angel/vampire devil business?" she whispered back. "I must need a reality bypass to even ask this question, but could it really be true? I mean, are we living in a *True Blood* world, and not knowing it?"

"Hell if I know, but wait 'til you hear Ivak sing. You'll believe in angels then, that's for damn sure."

"Huh?" *He sure wasn't angelic in that harem-scarem dream.*

"Your weirdo minister sings like an angel."

"He is not *my* weirdo anything." *Except in my dreams.* "Whatever."

She told Leroy about the work she'd been doing to prepare for another parole board hearing, assuming there was no recantation by Hebert before that time.

"It feels like such chaos here," Leroy said finally. "Even confined to cells or dorms, there's an air of danger or uncertainty making everybody antsy. Nerves are on edge. The least little thing sparks a fight."

Red flags went up for Gabrielle. "Don't you dare get involved in a fight when you have so much riding on your good behavior."

"Yeah, yeah!"

"I was wondering about something, Leroy. Someone asked me recently what I was going to do once you were released . . . what my dreams are. What are yours?"

"I'm afraid to speak them out loud, for fear I'll jinx them."

She nodded her understanding.

"Maybe go to college and get a degree with some skill attached. Maybe some work involved with kids at risk, possibly in those juvie detention centers. Try to catch them before they're prison bait."

She sucked in a breath. "You wouldn't want to get as far away from prisons as possible?"

He cocked his head to the side. "As long as I'm on the outside, I don't see how it matters."

How different he was from her.

"Shit! I've gotta find some way to make all these prison years count for something. Don't you wonder how many families there are, just like ours was? Abusive, alcoholic, drugged-up, negligent parents are more common than anyone realizes." He ducked his head sheepishly. "Hell, I'm starting to sound like a preacher myself."

She smiled. Aside from the bad language, she liked this new side of her brother.

"Maybe we should go inside and help with the auditions," Leroy suggested. "You'll get a laugh or two, at least."

Her face heated up. "I think Ivak barred me from participating."

"Yeah, I remember that. Let me go inside and sic Tante Lulu on him," Leroy said with a wink.

A short time later, a guard walked up to her and said, "Miss Sonnier? I've been directed to take you to the auditorium." They went through several checkpoints on The Walk through the Main Prison complex. Despite the lockdown having been lifted, there were way more precautions being taken, she noticed. Even she was screened more than usual.

Once they got to the auditorium, if the shabby room with a raised platform in front and folding chairs throughout could be called an auditorium, Gabrielle thanked the guard, who'd remained silent on their fifteen-minute walk. She chose a chair at the back, not wanting to call attention to herself.

The room was packed with inmates and staff watching the last of the talent show tryouts, no doubt due to Charmaine's presence. She and René had driven here together, Bayou Black being out of the way for them today.

Leroy gave her a little wave, motioning for her to come up front to join him, but she decided to stay in back, for now. She noticed a large number of guards in the room, including one red-haired one whose eyes seemed to be fixed on Leroy. She would have to warn her brother. Sometimes those in authority developed a dislike for a particular convict and just waited for the smallest infraction to bust him.

Charmaine stood on the low stage teaching a three-man inmate group a dance routine to accompany their pantomimed rendition of that doo-wop standard, "Why Do Fools Fall in Love?" It involved a dip and three steps to the right, a dip and three steps to the left, then bending the knees for a pelvic thrust forward, the whole time wailing out the lyrics. It was the dips and thrusts that had all eyes on the self-proclaimed bimbo with class. Or it might be the tight silver capri pants with a shimmery black T-shirt and silver wedge sandals. Her long black hair was a mass of curls piled on top of her head. A convict's wet dream!

Speaking—rather, thinking—of dreams, Ivak must have sensed her presence because he turned from where he was leaning against the piano talking to René. At first, he looked chagrined that she would disobey his order to stay away, but then he nodded a greeting at her. Their eyes held for a long moment.

And she knew . . . she just knew . . . that he was seeing the same thing she was. The dream. In that instant, she forgot all about her resolve to keep her distance from the lout. He might not think she was his soul mate anymore, as indicated by his silence of the past week, but she was not so sure now.

How could just looking at a man feel so good?

But wait. Had he planted these dreams in her head as a way to seduce her to his way of thinking? Assuming she believed his fantastical story—and she was increasingly leaning in that direction, or else she was finally going crazy—she remembered him telling her that he was guilty "in a big way" of the sin of lust. Add to that some supernatural powers he might have gained when he was turned into a vampire angel. *Did I really say— rather, think—that? Good Lord! I do believe him. Yikes!* And maybe all these feelings that were overwhelming her were not real, or at the least she'd been manipulated.

Oooh, she had a few words to say to the lusty lout.

Fourteen

His dream lover was a pissed-off lover . . .

Ivak felt Gabrielle's presence before he saw her.

At first, an incredible joy suffused him, just from looking at her. But then, he recalled his order for her to stay put at the cottage, and irritation bordering on fury replaced the joy. When God created the world, had He deliberately planted a disobedient gene in women to plague men? They were always doing the opposite of what they were told to do, even when it was for their own good. Just like Eve, who was the model for rebellious women throughout time.

Well, thank God Ivak had thought to assign two vangels to watch over Gabrielle. He would have words for them later. They should have informed him that she'd left Bayou Black and was headed in this direction. Even now, Lucies could be after her, if he was reading Mike's words correctly: "Save the girl."

"Will you take over for me?" he asked René. "I'll be back in a few minutes."

"Sure," René said.

Tante Lulu had joined Charmaine up on the stage and was demonstrating the right way to do a shuffle step. And she was good. In fact, some of the crowd gave her a clapping ovation. To which the old lady gave a little bow and said, "You oughta see me jitterbug."

He walked back and sat down next to Gabrielle. Right away, her scent came up to envelop him in hair-trigger arousal. And it wasn't her perfume, either. It was her woman scent intended to lure a mate.

Seeking a more neutral subject than, oh, let's say, S.E.X., he remarked, "Did you have anything to do with Tante Lulu's outfit today?"

The old lady was wearing cowgirl attire, including a hat and boots.

"She thought you'd be doing a dress rehearsal over at the rodeo arena."

"That won't come for another few weeks."

She crossed one leg over the other and tried to ignore him.

I wonder if she shaved her legs today. They look so smooth and shiny. Dare I touch her knee? Hmmm. Mayhap later.

"What do boots, and chaps, and a hat have to do with a talent show dress rehearsal?"

"It would be at the rodeo arena. I think she was hoping that if she dressed appropriately, someone would let her ride a bull . . . or at least a bronco."

"God forbid!" *Her lips are peach-colored today. I'd wager a fortune that she tastes sweet and juicy.* "The bull would run away at sight of her."

She didn't even smile at that. In fact, she turned her body slightly away from him. What did she have to be annoyed about? She was the one who'd disobeyed orders intended for her own safety. "Spit it out, wench. What has your thong in a twist?" *Oh, that is just great. Now I will*

*be picturing her in one of those wonderfully scandalous
undergarments.*

"I'll tell you what's wrong. If we were somewhere
more private, I would hit you."

"If we were somewhere more private, we would be
doing something, but it would not involve violence," he
countered. Then, "Why would you want to hit me?"

"For planting those horrible dreams in my head."

Just then, the latest dream came to him. In truth, he'd
been dreaming the same fantasy about her for the past
five days.

"So you remember now," she accused him.

He glanced down at her lap, then looked at her frowning face, then back at her lap. After which he flashed her
a wicked, lazy smile. "Cluck, cluck!"

"Oh, that was despicable!" She tried to stand and move
away from him, but he grabbed her hand and made her
stay put. "It's not funny."

"Well, yes, that dream was cause for mirth. And, really,
there is no reason for you to be embarrassed. Women
today deliberately wax themselves there, or so I've been
told." A thought occurred to him. "Do you wax there?"

Her flushed face flushed even more. In fact, the flush
reached down to her collarbone. "No, I do not."

"That's good. I prefer a little cushion for my balls."

Her mouth dropped open, and she seemed stunned into
speechlessness.

"Oops! I did not mean to say that aloud."

"Stop planting those horrible dreams in my head."

"What makes you think I have anything to do with
them?"

"Because you star in them, you idiot."

"Well, it's the most sex I've had in a long, long time. If
I had anything to do with them, they would go on forever
. . . and be the real thing."

"You're incorrigible."

"Is that a good thing?"

She rolled her eyes. He noticed that she did that a lot around him.

"René tells me that his band is playing at that tavern near Bayou Black on Saturday. Would you like to go with me?"

The invitation surprised her. It surprised him, too. He hadn't known he was going to ask her. He hadn't known he had any inclination to go listen to Cajun music in a rowdy bar.

"You're asking me to go on a date? After I just berated you for those lousy dreams?"

He didn't like her describing those sex dreams as lousy, but decided to save his opinion until later. "Our second date, actually, if you count our dinner last week."

"After which you never called or attempted to see me again."

Aha! That is why she is being so schrewish. "Everyone inside the prison was barred from any outside contact."

"Bullshit! You and I both know you could have over-ridden that order."

He felt his face heat at the accuracy of her statement. "I was . . . I am confused by the overwhelming feelings I have toward you. It has never happened to me before."

"Paint us both confused, then," she said. Leastways, her anger seemed to have dissipated.

"Is it a date then?"

She hesitated, but then she nodded.

"I want to touch your knee so bad my fingers ache."

"Aaarrgh!"

"And your lips . . . I am dying to know if they taste like peaches."

"Aaarrgh!" she said again.

"Forget I mentioned those things. It was probably inappropriate to speak of such intimate things in a public place."

"Like you're suddenly concerned about propriety! Like a girl could forget something like that!"

"If you think that's not so bad, dare I mention that I'm having a thickening just smelling your woman scent. My fangs are about to orgasm in my gums."

"Aaarrgh!" she said again.

He was starting to like the sound, choosing to believe it was a groan of arousal.

Just then, Tante Lulu walked up and told Gabrielle, "We's havin' a LeDeux party on Saturday down at Swampy's . . . thass the Swamp Tavern . . . ta raise money fer one of my charities."

Why am I not surprised that Tante Lulu has charities? Before Ivak asked her to elaborate, Tante Lulu turned to him. "Didja ask her yet?"

"I did," he said, grinning at the old lady's obvious matchmaking efforts. He'd love to see this woman encounter Mike some time. He was pretty sure she would be able to hold her own, even with the mighty archangel.

"Are you comin'?" Tante Lulu asked Gabrielle.

"I'm coming," Gabrielle said, then murmured so low that only Ivak could hear, "in more ways than one."

The real Thor had nothing on this guy . . .

Gabrielle was sitting on the porch that evening with Tante Lulu, one of those days out of time where everything seemed peaceful. She could almost believe that the hoped-for better times with Leroy were actually possible.

Faith . . . that's what it boiled down to. She was still worried about Leroy being confined to a prison overrun with some evil influence, more evil than the usual maniacal inmates. The news media accepted, with a dash of skepticism, the warden's explanation that there had been paper errors on the dead inmates, and routine "Take this job and shove it!" type quittings by some staffers who were long gone to parts unknown, despite that being a whole lot of coincidences to swallow. Gabrielle, on the other hand, was going for the "Michael did it!" explanation.

After a huge meal of crawfish etouffée, a side salad, warm biscuits, and banana pudding that Tante Lulu seemed to whip up in no time after they'd returned from Angola, the old lady shooed her out of the kitchen, saying she could clean up herself. Which was a blessing. It gave Gabrielle time to do some paperwork for her caseload at Second Chances. She had appointments with clients all day tomorrow.

Then they'd both retired to the back porch with the requisite sweet tea in hand to watch dusk come over the bayou. The only sounds were of crickets and an occasional growl from Useless, plus the creaking of their rocking chairs. It was such a peaceful place, and yet dangerous at the same time.

Suddenly, Tante Lulu said, "Holy crawfish! Who's that?"

"Huh?" Gabrielle turned to see a tall man in a dark suit with a white shirt and light blue tie making his way around the side of the house.

"Lordy, Lordy, he's almost as good-lookin' as Tee-John."

On closer examination, Gabrielle noticed his short blond hair, light blue eyes, and Nordic features. Another vangel? Yep, that was a white angel wing design against the sky-blue background on his tie.

"Mebbe he's one of yer bodyguards."

"What bodyguards?"

"Ain't you noticed the two men who watch the cottage and follow ever'where you go? Ivak tol' me they's yer guards."

"Why didn't you mention it before?" *Why didn't Ivak mention it?*

"I thought you knew. Blessed Mary! I'm eighty years old and I see 'em jist fine. Mebbe you need eyeglasses."

If she's eighty, I'm ten, and this nightmare I'm living never happened. But guards? That was another bone she had to pick with Ivak. Would the man never stop interfering in her life?

Turns out the answer was no.

"Are you Gabrielle Sonnier?" Mr. Suit said, walking up the back steps.

She nodded dumbly. Tante Lulu was right. This guy was sinfully handsome. Well, if he was in fact a vangel, *sinfully* would not be an appropriate description. Heavenly handsome, then.

"I am," she said, standing. She had to look up at him when she spoke. The guy had to be six foot five, or more.

The man stretched out a hand, the one not holding a briefcase, to Gabrielle. She noticed there was a gold ring on his right middle finger, similar to one Ivak wore with a winged emblem on it. Next he shook hands with Tante Lulu, who had stopped rocking and was staring up at him like he was Richard Simmons . . . or St. Jude. After that, he handed Gabrielle a business card and said, "I'm Thor Robertsson from the law firm of Robertsson, Johnsson, and Olafsson in Baton Rouge."

"And you're here because . . . ?"

"I've come to help you prepare for your brother's legal proceedings," he said. "Didn't you know I was coming?"

She frowned with confusion.

"Jarl Ivak Sigurdsson sent me."

"Whass a jarl?" Tante Lulu asked.

"Something like an earl," he explained, then turned back to Gabrielle. "Did Ivak forget to tell you?"

"Yep. It must have slipped his mind." Yeah, right. He knew what her reaction would be to his interfering once again without informing her first. Not that she wouldn't welcome all the help she could get. She'd just like to be consulted first.

No sooner did Thor arrive than another hottie lawyer came on the scene. This time it was Lucien LeDeux. Didn't matter that he was in his late forties and had silver threads in his black hair, this Cajun attorney was ten kinds of sexy. He wore a suit, too, but his tie was undone, and the top two buttons of his dress shirt were unbuttoned. The end of his workday, Gabrielle presumed. Whether he was there at Ivak's or Tante Lulu's invitation was unclear, and at this point didn't matter.

He shook hands with Thor, leaned down to kiss Tante Lulu, and winked at Gabrielle when his aunt introduced him as her "rascal nephew," as if he were a little boy.

They went inside to the kitchen, where Thor spread out a bunch of papers, and Gabrielle spread out some of her own, on top of which Tante Lulu had prepared a plate for the Viking and Luc, insisting they had to eat. The men, who at first said they weren't hungry, ate two platefuls, and they even finished their banana puddings, which was more than Gabrielle had been able to do.

"First off, I think we should plan on a new trial, instead of a parole board hearing or a plea for clemency," Thor said.

"Why?" Gabrielle asked.

"You've already tried the parole board route, *chère*, and I haven't seen any welcome home parades yet," Luc said, not unkindly. "Getting a parole, or clemency, in Loo-zee-anna is iffy. Too many people to bribe, or threaten."

He grinned at that last statement. Gabrielle would have thought Thor would object, but he grinned, too.

"We likes ta call it lagniappe here in the South," Tante Lulu added as she poured more sweet tea for them all. "Nothin' illegal. Jist a little somethin' extra ta sweeten the pot."

"Definitely nothing illegal," Luc said, and waggled his eyebrows at his aunt.

She smacked him on the arm with a St. Jude dish towel.

"If Hebert recants his testimony, it's the most logical route, anyhow," Thor went on. "You want your brother exonerated, Gabrielle. Not just pardoned or paroled, right?"

"Well, yes, but Hebert hasn't stepped to the plate yet. If he is able to step up, that is. Last word was, he's bedridden at the Angola hospital."

"He will," Thor said with more assurance than she felt. Maybe it was a vangel kind of insight thing. She hoped so.

After two hours of working with Thor and Luc, Gabrielle had to admit she was impressed. They brought up precedents that she hadn't considered, and Luc mentioned a way of them getting a judge who would be more favorable to Leroy.

"A vangel?" she asked.

"No, but there's a rotation in that particular court. If we time our request for retrial just right, we might get the one we want." After taking a sip of his tea, Luc added, "What's a vangel?"

"Never mind," she and Thor said as one, but Tante Lulu piped in with "Ivak Sigurdsson, that preacher over at the prison, he's an angel."

"Okaaaay," Luc said, obviously not surprised that his aunt would come out with such an outlandish statement. After all, she'd been talking to St. Jude for decades. Gabrielle and Thor felt no need to enlighten Luc on the distinction between angel and vangel.

Before Thor and Luc left, they agreed to meet with her again once Hebert recanted . . . something Gabrielle was beginning to think of as a certainty now that Thor had seemed so positive.

So she was in a good mood when she got ready for bed later and her cell phone rang. It was Ivak.

She was no longer upset with him over his "hiring" a lawyer, or lawyers, to help her now that she'd talked with the men. Still . . . "Ivak, you have to stop trying to control my life."

"What have I done now?"

"Thor Robertsson ring any bells? Or Luc 'The Swamp Solicitor' LeDeux?"

"Ah," was all he said. "You can blame me for Thor, but Tante Lulu must have called LeDeux."

"I figured."

"How did it go?"

"Wonderful." She explained everything that she and the other two lawyers had discussed.

"So, my sending Thor was a good thing?"

"Yes, but you should have asked me first."

"I'll try harder," he said.

She rolled her eyes.

"You're rolling your eyes, aren't you?"

"Busted." She laughed.

"I love to hear you laugh. You don't do it often enough."

"I haven't had much cause to . . . until lately." She paused. "Thank you."

"Could you repeat that? I might have misheard."

"You heard all right. I hate to admit it, but I feel much more hopeful about Leroy's prospects since I met you."

"And are you hopeful about anything else?"

"Are you fishing for a compliment?"

"A compliment would not come amiss."

"Why did you call, Ivak?"

"I just wanted to hear your voice. We didn't have much chance to talk after the auditions today."

"Has everything settled down at the prison?"

"Well, the news media is gone . . . for now. Hopefully, unless something major happens, we vangels here should be able to handle the situation, God willing and Mike in a good mood."

"And St. Jude," she reminded him.

"Him too." She could hear the smile in his voice.

"How's the talent show coming?"

"Surprisingly well. Tante Lulu is beyond barmy betimes, but she and her family have helped me so much. We might even be able to pull this crap shoot event off."

"Funny you should say that. Tante Lulu has helped me, too. I can't tell you how much staying here with her has changed my perspective on so many things."

"Such as?"

"Family."

"Ah," he said. "Someday I would like you to meet my family."

"I thought I already had."

"Pfff! Hardly. I have four other brothers you have never met and then there is all my extended family. I am rolling my eyes here, Gabrielle."

"Why?"

"There are more than five hundred of us."

"You mean all the vangels? You consider them family?"

"Definitely. It's hard not to become close to those who share centuries and centuries with you. A secret society we are. Like a family."

She yawned, louder than she intended.

"You are tired."

"It's been a long day."

"I will see you on Saturday," he reminded her. "Wear something sexy."

"I don't own anything sexy."

"You could always borrow something from Charmaine."

"You'd really like me to wear such slutty clothes?"

"Are you serious? I am a man." He laughed. "Just wear something with no undergarments."

She paused for a moment, then said, "You too."

"I like the way you think."

Just before he hung up, she heard his low masculine chuckle and he drawled out, slow and sexy, "Sweet dreams, sweetling."

That's what she was afraid of.

Fifteen

Yes, Virginia, miracles do happen . . .

Ivak was at the bedside of Edward Hebert as he lay dying, and the inmate still had not recanted his lie that had convicted Leroy Sonnier. The lemon scent of a sin taint was heavy in the room. A priest had been called to give him last rites. Whether the holy man would arrive in time was not certain.

Before coming inside, Ivak had killed two Lucies hovering about, waiting for an opportunity to enter the man's room when no one was around. He couldn't worry about the stinksome slime that would be found in a hospital corridor or outside the building. Besides, convicts were always depositing unusual objects and substances about the place, to the chagrin of prison maintenance crews. Luckily, ever since Ivak had first suspected a Lucipire presence inside Angola, he'd taken to carrying specially treated throwing stars and knives in his footwear and under his belt.

Leaning over Hebert now, Ivak whispered, "Edward. Edward, can you hear me?"

Hebert's eyes open slowly. "I know who you are," he said, licking his dry lips. "You're Sonnier's friend."

Ivak put a glass straw to Hebert's mouth so he could drink.

"I am your friend, too," Ivak said. "In fact, I have been sent to you by another *friend*."

Hebert arched his brows, and Ivak could tell that even that movement caused him pain. Death was very close.

Quickly, Ivak showed his fangs to Hebert and concentrated on his back, hoping his hazy blue wing image would be visible. At Hebert's gasp, he assumed he'd succeeded.

"Who . . . are . . . you?" Hebert whispered.

He explained everything and asked if he could remove the sin taint. "I won't touch you without your permission."

"How?" the dying man gasped out, his strength waning by the second.

"I will fang your neck and suck out the bad blood. You will notice a change immediately."

"And then?"

"Remember the Lord's admonition: Thou shalt not bear false witness. I am hoping that when you are in a state of grace, or leastways not in a state of good-be-damned, you will recant your lie against Leroy Sonnier and—"

Hebert was about to say something, but Ivak held up a halting hand so that he could finish.

"—then when you die, you may go to a better place. Presuming that you not only are sorry for your past sins, but that you do not continue with a current sin. You know which one I mean, don't you?"

"Yeah? What if I don't say nuthin'?"

"You will go to Hell." Betimes bluntness was the only way. "Unless the demon vampires get to you first, in which case you will go to a far worse place than Hell."

Hebert still looked skeptical.

"If I cleanse you, and if you repent your sins, you may go to Purgatory. At least there you have a chance for Heaven, sometime."

"What the fuck is Purgatory?"

"You could say it's a holding cell. A very large holding cell that I am told is a pleasant place. Until the Final Judgment."

"Oh, what the hell! Do it," Hebert gasped out. "What . . . have I . . . got . . . to lose?"

And so, Ivak locked the door and did the quickest sin cleansing he'd ever done, fearing the family would want to come back in.

When he was done, Hebert looked up at him. His whole demeanor had changed, of course. "Thank you," he whispered.

"You're not done yet." Ivak unlocked the door and told the guard, "Bring some witnesses in here. Mr. Hebert has a statement to make." Luckily, Thor had sent him legal documents days ago.

The convict died an hour later.

When Ivak left the hospital, he went immediately to the Cypress Dorm, where he killed another Lucie. He asked the guard for entry so that he could speak to Leroy.

"Are you kidding? It's two a.m."

"I need to speak to him. Now."

"Come back tomorrow. With all the new security measures, I'll have a ton of paperwork to do, even if you are staff. What's so important, anyhow?"

"It's personal. Do I really need to call the warden to get his okay? You know how he hates to have his sleep interrupted. If I recall correctly, the last guard who did that got demoted to latrine duty."

The guard said a foul word but he let Ivak in.

Ivak tugged Leroy to the far end of the dorm, motioning for Svein to stand back and watch that no one overheard.

On seeing Ivak, the blood left Leroy's face. "What . . . what's happened? Is it Gabby? Oh God! Was there an . . . accident?"

"No, no, she's fine," Ivak assured him, patting him on the shoulder. "It's Hebert. He died a little while ago."

"Dammit! It's too late then."

"Oh, you of little faith." He smiled at Leroy.

Understanding seemed to dawn on Leroy, slowly. "I hope that shit-eating grin on your face means what I think it does."

"It does. Hebert repented and recanted. More important, he signed an affidavit to that effect with witnesses present."

"It's a miracle." Tears filled Leroy's eyes as his mind worked to assimilate all the implications. "What does it mean?"

"It means you've passed an important hurdle. It doesn't mean you're free . . . yet."

"But there's hope now, right?"

"Oh, Leroy, there was always hope."

Sometimes there is heaven on earth . . .

It was very late when Ivak finally entered his cell room and fell like a rock onto the bed. What a day!

As late as it was, he would have liked to call Gabrielle and give her the good news, but he decided that Leroy should be the one to do that. After all that Leroy and his sister had been through, it would be a memorable moment.

He, on the other hand, wanted to be in the warden's office first thing in the morning to present Hebert's dying affidavit. That, too, would be a memorable moment.

With a long, wide-mouthed yawn, he fell asleep.

And dreamed. *Again!* What would it be this time? Modern times, or the old Norselands?

It was neither of those.

Heaven's End truly was Heaven's End, Ivak thought as he rode his horse up the wide allée of live oak trees to the gleaming white mansion.

A horse? Vikings don't ride horses. Now, longships, that is a different story.

Good fjord! That plantation house looks just like Tara from Gone with the Wind. Does that make me Rhett Butler coming home from the war? Did the Civil War even occur yet? Probably not.

He chuckled. In a dream, no less.

But wait. If he was Rhett, maybe there would be a Scarlett.

Being a vangel meant lots of spare time between saving sinners and catching Lucies. One of the ways they passed the time back at the castle in Transylvania was to watch old movies. While he preferred movies like Saving Private Ryan, or We Were Soldiers, he'd seen that Southern classic at least five times.

But he digressed. In a dream, no less.

He was doing just fine riding his horse, clip-clop, up the road, but then he glanced forward. There was a woman standing on the front gallery. Waiting for him? Yes, she must be Scarlett. At her first sight of him, she let out a shriek of happiness and began to run down the wide center steps leading down to the front driveway. Not an easy task with the hooped skirt of her long gown.

It was Gabrielle, of course. But a Gabrielle that he'd never seen or ever imagined. Her dark hair was a mass of ringlets pulled off her face and cascading down her back. She wore a short-sleeved, pale green gown of some lightweight fabric, embroidered with flowers along the edges that left most of her arms and parts of her shoulders bare.

He'd no sooner dismounted and tied the reins of his

horse to the hitching post than Gabrielle launched herself at him, kissing his face and neck, even his ears, the whole time laughing and weeping. "I missed you so much. Two whole days! Don't go away again."

He smiled. *"I had to go to the mercantile in N'awlins to sell our sugar. You know that, darlin'."* Good heavens, I even have a Southern drawl. He nuzzled her neck and relished the smell of her fresh, clean skin. Like roses and musk, it was. He'd recognize her in a crowd by that scent alone. It was the woman scent that had drawn him to her before their marriage.

Marriage? Whoa! *That was a giant leap he hadn't been expecting. Was he still a vampire angel?*

He ran his tongue inside his upper gums.

Yes, he was.

"Come!" she said then, pushing away from him and lifting her skirts in front so that she could run. Glancing over her shoulder when she was already halfway up the stairs, she laughed and called saucily over her shoulder, *"Catch me if you can."*

Gabrielle being saucy? This had to be a dream. Who cared? Not him. If there was anything a Viking . . . even a Viking Southerner . . . loved, it was a challenge. He took the stairs two at a time.

Oddly, there didn't seem to be anyone else about. A pre–Civil War plantation, as this appeared to be, would be buzzing with house servants and outside workers, not to mention family. Ah, well, privacy was best for what he had in mind.

Unfortunately, or fortunately, they never made it up to the bedroom. Ivak caught up with her in the entryway where the bright midday sunlight was filtered through colorful stained glass windows. Open pocket doors let in more light from a large, elegant salon.

He lifted her by the waist so that her slippered feet

dangled off the marble floor. Twirling her around, they landed against one wall. He took the brunt of the hit, but then turned so that her back was braced against the brocade wallpaper. "Got you," he growled.

She wriggled against him so that her breasts rubbed abrasively against the fine linen of his shirt under his open waistcoat. "Oh, woe is me! What shall I do?" She smiled flirtatiously at him.

It was a game they often played, apparently.

"Show me," he ordered.

Immediately, she lowered both of her sleeves down to her elbows, causing her bodice to come down, too. Now her breasts were exposed to him in a sheer chemise, and her arms were restrained at her sides.

He smiled. Her breasts were among his favorite body parts. They were not too small and not too large. Just big enough. A perfect fit for a man's hand. For his hand. Because she'd never borne a child, the nipples and areolas were a pale pink.

"What shall I do first?" he inquired with mock innocence.

She arched her back so that her breasts pressed forward. A tempting invitation that needed no words. Already the nipples were hard pebbles of arousal.

"You really did miss me, didn't you?" he husked out, tracing each of the peaks with a forefinger.

She inhaled sharply, then demanded, "More."

"Witch!" He leaned down and took one breast into his mouth through the thin cloth, nipple and areola both. Drawing them deep into his mouth, he sucked hard as he drew back until only the nipple was between his lips. Over and over he practiced this exercise until finally he laved the hardened peak with his tongue, then bit it lightly with his teeth. He did the same with the other breast.

She was mewling with excitement by the time he finished.

He kissed her then. Long, hard kisses in which he tilted his head one way, then another, to get the right position so that he would not cut her with his fangs. Only then did he push his tongue inside. She sucked on him, which felt as if she was sucking on his already rock-hard staff that hardened even more.

"I need you, dearling," he husked against her open mouth. Already his balls had risen and swelled, ready to ejaculate. Too soon, too soon!

"Take me, then," she said.

I thought you'd never ask. *Since she was unable to lift her skirts herself, he did that for her, untying the hoops and tossing them to the side. When she was bare from the waist down, except for her slippers, he raised her up so that she could wrap her legs around his hips. With his eyes holding her gaze, he thrust inside her tight, moist folds 'til he was buried to the hilt. For a moment he saw stars and could only press his forehead against hers, inhaling and exhaling in an attempt to tamp down his enthusiasm. It was no good. He had waited too long.*

He began the long strokes, which soon became short and hard, banging her against the wall with an enticing rhythm. She didn't seem to mind. In fact, she looked at him, her heart in her eyes.

He exploded inside her. His fangs were exposed, and he latched on to her neck, taking some of her sweet life sustenance. This was Heaven, he decided. Not Heaven's End.

When he was done . . . or leastways had stopped himself from taking too much . . . he raised his head and licked her blood off his receding fangs. Only then did he say, "You know this is only a dream, Gabrielle. Right?"

She smiled at him, leaned up and kissed one of his fangs. "Frankly, Ivak, I don't give a damn!"

At first, she thought she was still dreaming . . .

Gabrielle was walking into Second Chances that morning when her cell phone rang.

"Gabby?"

Gabrielle stopped just inside the door, frozen with shock. Leroy never called her unless it was at the designated time.

"Leroy? What the matter?"

"You better give Ivak a big kiss next time you see him."

She waved to the receptionist and walked into her office, setting her briefcase down on her desk. "Why?"

"He did it."

"You're scaring me here, Leroy. He did what?"

"Saved my ass."

"Leroy Sonnier! Did you get into a fight?"

"Hell, no. Do you think I'm stupid? Don't answer that."

"Le-roy!"

"Okay, okay," he said, laughing. "Hebert died last night, but before he died, Ivak got him to sign an affidavit recanting his earlier testimony."

Gabrielle sank down into her chair and began to weep.

"Are you crying?"

"What do you think?"

"You should have seen the warden's face when Ivak handed him the documents. I thought he was going to shit a brick."

She was about to criticize Leroy for his bad language but decided to give him a pass this time. "I wish I could have been there."

"Ivak says you need to call some character named Thor and file for a new trial."

"I'll do it as soon as I hang up. Oh, Leroy, we've waited so long for this. Just make sure that you walk the line in the meantime. The folks at Angola aren't going to like admitting a mistake."

"Hah! Ivak has Svein on my tail so close I can't even go in the showers without him. In fact, he asked me last night if I wanted him to soap my back."

"Oh you! I'm glad that you can joke. Even your voice has changed. It's lighter, more cheerful, the way it used to be back when . . . well, just back a long time ago."

"I have a lot to be cheerful about."

"It appears I have a lot to thank Ivak for. Do you happen to know his cell number?"

"He's right here."

"He is?"

"Yeah. Hey, Ivak, my sister wants to talk to you. Will I see you on visiting day this week, Gabby?"

"You couldn't keep me away."

There was a pause before she heard Ivak's voice. "You summoned me, sweetling?"

"Thank you, thank you, thank you."

"Don't thank me. Thank Mike . . . or rather, God. And while you're at it, you might want to thank Tante Lulu and St. Jude, too."

She smiled. "I will. I never thought when I woke up this morning that such a miracle would occur."

"Speaking of waking up," he said, "Have you ever seen the movie *Gone with the Wind*?"

Oh no! He had the same dream as I did. Again. She felt her face heat up. "Uh, I don't think so."

"Liar!" He chuckled. "By the by, you look good in green."

"I'm so happy, I won't even berate you for invading my dreams again."

"I'll see you on Saturday?"

"Definitely."

"I'll practice puckering up to get that kiss Leroy mentioned."

"Hey, I wasn't serious," she heard Leroy say in the background.

"Ivak, you do deserve a kiss."

"Hah! Methinks I deserve more than a kiss," he said in a lower tone of voice so that Leroy couldn't overhear.

"Maybe," she agreed.

"I'll take a maybe. For now," he said. "So," he drawled, and paused for dramatic effect, "I wonder what our dreams will be tonight."

She laughed, too full of joy to contain her happiness. "Frankly, Ivak. I don't give a damn."

Sixteen

A Mission Impossible? . . .

𝔄 summons went out for the VIK to meet at the castle in Transylvania. When Ivak arrived, his six brothers were already there, having been called in from their various assignments around the world.

And, ominously, a hush lay over the castle. Not a bird could be heard. Not a breeze was blowing. Mike was here.

There were workmen's trucks about, but no men in sight. The castle renovations were a never-ending process. A ten-foot-high stone wall surrounding the vast perimeter had been started since he'd been here last, and work continued on reslating the roof. And that was just outside.

He entered from the back courtyard into the kitchen where Lizzie and two helpers went silently about their chores. Moving through the hallway, he noticed that the mural depicting Michael casting Lucifer out of heaven was half completed by one of their vangel artists, then passed the chapel that was overflowing with praying vangels. Everyone wanted to be on best behavior when Mike was in the building.

Ivak and his brothers might refer to their mentor in a

less-than-deferential manner and even make fun of him at times, but there was no question Michael was a powerful entity. Not just an archangel, but an archangel of the highest power. How could he not be? He was God's right-hand man.

That heavenly presence was obvious when Ivak entered the front salon and bowed to the figure sitting on a wingback chair to one side of the massive fireplace, which was unlit in deference to the September heat. His brothers perched nervously on sofas and chairs about the vast room, which, like everything else in the house, was only partially renovated.

Sometimes Michael wore typical angelic attire—white robe with rope belt—but today he wore jeans, a white T-shirt, and athletic shoes, but he looked nothing like a modern-day athlete. Not with that halo-like glow that surrounded his long, silky black hair or the ornate gold cross that hung from a chain around his neck. Unless he was St. Michael Jordan.

Ivak couldn't believe he was making jokes with himself at a time like this.

"Ivak! You're late," Michael pronounced.

Oops! His face heated with embarrassment at being singled out for rebuke. "I had difficulty getting permission to leave the prison. Tight security measures are still in place." At the questioning tilt of Michael's head, Ivak explained, "The unexplained disappearances that we know are due to the Lucies." As if Mike didn't know! After all, he'd been the one to cover all the demon tracks.

"Ah, the Lucipires! Jasper is ever a thorn in the Lord's heart." A sadness came over Michael's face, and Ivak recalled that Jasper had been one of the favored archangels before being cast out of Heaven with Lucifer. In fact, Jasper had once been a friend of Michael's. But then Michael's expression turned resolute. "We must get the Lucipires out of Louisiana. That is why I have come today."

Whoa! Did he say Louisiana? Not Angola. Or New Orleans. All of Louisiana?

"Yes, Ivak, I meant all of Louisiana."

That was the bad thing about Michael. He could read minds. Ivak tried his best to clear his head lest he reveal something he would rather not.

Michael laughed.

His brothers looked at him to see what he'd been thinking that would amuse the archangel.

"Pretty, isn't she?" Michael remarked.

Oh, that is just great! Images of Gabrielle must have flickered through my brain.

"Who is pretty?" his brothers asked as one.

Ivak wasn't about to get involved in that discussion. He sat down on a love seat next to Vikar and asked Michael, "What would you have me do?"

"Not just you. All of the VIK. This is war," Michael said.

That got everyone's attention. He and his brothers leaned forward with interest. There was nothing a Viking liked more than war.

"Men . . . even vangels . . . cannot take down Jasper's operation in one fell swoop. The Heavenly Host learned that long ago. So, thou shalt pick away at his empire one segment at a time."

"Nibbling away like ducks," Harek put in.

"Precisely," Michael said. "Big, deadly nibbles. Thus it has always been, and thus it will always be so. The only way to eat an elephant is one bite at a time."

"Call me dense, but what do all those animal metaphors mean?" Ivak asked. Since Louisiana was his territory, Ivak wanted his instructions to be clear. Besides, being in bayou country, wouldn't an alligator be a better choice than an elephant?

"Idiot!" Mike muttered.

Harek raised a brow and said, "Is anyone else surprised at Ivak's use of the word *metaphor*?" Betimes Ivak would like to stick Harek's virtual Phi Beta Kappa key somewhere that would hurt.

Failing to notice the side play, Michael didn't hesitate to explain in detail. "The Lord wants Dominique gone. Not just relocated to another territory. Not just killed to rise again. She must be annihilated and sent to Satan's domain for eternity. Thus sayeth the Lord."

All right. Ivak got it. Dominique's heart must be speared with either a knife or a sword specially treated with the symbolic blood of Christ or the symbolic slivers of wood from the True Cross. Just "killing" her would not be enough. He nodded his understanding to Michael.

"Also, her building named Anguish in the Sin City must be destroyed. Razed to the ground. Excavated. Set afire. Does not matter how. Thou shalt remove the abomination."

I can do that, Ivak thought, *but it will be difficult when adjacent buildings are so close.*

"I have confidence that you can handle the job," Michael said.

Reading my mind again! Jeesh!

"And of course the Lucipires in and around Angola Prison must be destroyed," Michael went on. "If they succeed there, Jasper will take that as incentive to expand to all other prisons around the world."

Ivak's head was beginning to spin with all that this mission would entail.

"You will not be alone," Michael assured him. "All of the VIK will be there, and, let us say, one hundred vangels? That should be sufficient while not leaving us weak in other places."

There were currently five hundred vangels of various ranks . . . jarls, karls, ceorls, and thralls. Large numbers of new vangels had been created in just the past few months.

"It will be as you wish," Ivak told Michael.

"I am not done," Michael said. "Someone in this room has been contemplating a grave sin." His all-seeing eyes scanned each of them in turn.

Oh no! He knows that I am contemplating sex with Gabrielle. He felt his face heat with guilt.

But then Ivak peeked a glance around the room and saw that each of his brothers had similar blushes on their faces. 'Twould appear they were all guilty of some sin or other.

Michael chuckled in a "gotcha" manner.

That is just great! Now we are a source of amusement for an archangel. What next?

"Did you buy the property yet?"

Ivak's head jerked up and he saw that Michael was addressing him.

Michael referred to Heaven's End, of course.

"Not yet." Ivak flushed some more. Apparently, he was still on the carpet. "I haven't had time yet."

"Make time."

Talk about blunt!

Ivak's brothers did a communal eyebrow arching thing.

"It's a plantation called Heaven's End. A *run-down* plantation," Ivak told them.

Vikar let out a hoot of laughter, understanding perfectly the job that Ivak would face in that regard. "I can give you advice on bat removal."

"Hah! How about snake removal?"

"I like the name. Heaven's End. Very appropriate," Sigurd remarked, tongue firmly planted in his fangy cheek. Sigurd had no doubt cased out the place while in Louisiana and knew what condition it was in.

"Why is the name appropriate?" his brother Mordr wanted to know.

"What is the end of Heaven? Hell. You are a lackwit, Mordr." This from Harek, who considered himself smarter than the rest of them. He was.

Mordr frowned. "Ivak is going to buy a place like Hell?"

"Yes, but he will turn it into Heaven," Michael said. "Or rather a heavenly place."

"I will?" Ivak said dumbly.

Michael nodded. "Just as Vikar has established a headquarters here in the Northeast, and Trond is living in California for the time being . . ."

Trond stiffened into attention at the words "for the time being."

" . . . Ivak will establish another headquarters in Louisiana."

"How in God's name will I be able to do that? I'm not a contractor. Nor am I a particularly good leader."

"And you think I am?" Vikar snorted his opinion of Ivak's lack of self-confidence.

"*In God's name,*" Michael declared, repeating Ivak's words back at him with disapproval, "you will learn the skills needed for the job. Besides, you will have many years to accomplish the task."

Ivak's shoulders slumped. Just as he'd thought, he would be in Louisiana and probably at the prison, as well, for many years to come. There went any chances he had for a future with Gabrielle. Not that there had been any before.

"Do not get ahead of yourself, Ivak. One step at a time," Michael said, shaking his head at Ivak's seeming hopelessness.

What did that mean? He had no chance to ask because the archangel had already moved on to other matters. "Where is my website, Harek?"

Harek looked as if he'd swallowed a mouse . . . the computer kind. "Uh."

"*Uh* is not an answer."

"It's almost ready. I need your approval for a title, though. Dear Archangel is one possibility, like Dear Abby. An advice column. Or The Heavenly Hangout. That would be more appropriate if you are writing columns, with comments from your followers. Or Michael's Home. Or Angels Among Us. I need some direction from you."

Michael tapped a blessed forefinger against his closed lips. "I don't like any of those. You can do better. By the by, have you been playing the stock market again?"

Harek's face went beet red. His Deadly Sin had been avarice or greed, having been a ruthless merchant in their time, garnering wealth upon wealth, often on the backs of slaves. "Just a little," Harek replied, "but 'twould seem I have a talent for predicting trends."

"Do not exalt thyself, Harek. To what good use have you put those profits?"

"They either go back into the VIK treasury to further the Lord's vangel work, or, well, I was thinking about starting a homeless shelter in Transylvania. There is much unemployment in Pennsylvania."

"That is good." In a surprise move, Michael reached over and patted Harek on the head.

The rest of them gaped with envy. Michael had never patted any of them with encouragement. Not that Ivak was looking for pats. Not that Ivak would ever mention the fact that Harek was contemplating the purchase of a condo on the French Riviera. Still . . .

Just then, the momentary silence was broken by a childish shriek, then a giggle, followed by the sound of running feet. Small running feet.

Two little blond-haired creatures hurtled themselves into the parlor. Well, not hurtled so much as toddled fast, chattering toddler nonsense words the whole time. It was Vikar and Alex's "adopted" children, Gunnar and Gunnora.

At first, they ran toward their father, who stood, intending no doubt to grab them up and take them from the room, but Michael smiled and said, "Let them stay."

"I don't want them to bother you," Vikar protested.

Michael held his arms out and the two imps chortled gleefully and walked over to him, climbing up on his knees without hesitation.

Alex came rushing forth, then stood in the doorway exchanging a worried glance with her husband, who shrugged. The children must have gotten away from her.

"This is what you must aim to be," Michael told them all. "Become as little children. Pure, trusting, loving."

Ivak had never been much for children, even when he'd had some of his own. Now Michael wanted him . . . and the others . . . to become like children. That on top of all the directives he'd given him about Lucies in Louisiana. Ivak sighed deeply, wondering how he would ever accomplish it all, or *if* he could accomplish it all.

Michael caught his eye then. "We will talk. Later." With those words, he set the children down gently and he was gone. Before Ivak could ask him what they would talk about.

Does he want to talk with me about the Louisiana mission, in general? About Angola? About Heaven's End? Or—the fine hairs stood out on the back of his neck—*about Gabrielle?*

Alex took the children away, luring them with a promise of puppies about to be born.

Silence reigned, but only for a moment, until his brother Cnut asked with a warped attempt at humor, "So what else is new?" It was easy to make mirth when you were not the one who was subject to Michael's sharp eyes.

Without waiting for Ivak's answer, Trond commented, standing to stretch out the kinks in his big body, which was becoming quite amazing with all his SEAL training, "I could knock back a beer."

"Or five," Sigurd added, "but I need to get back to the hospital to tie things up before heading back to Louisiana."

Once they were ensconced in the kitchen, sitting on stools about the counter where Lizzie had placed platters of nachos for them to munch on with their beers, Ivak asked, "How am I ever going to do everything that Michael ordered?"

"Have you forgotten, Ivak?" Trond inquired after taking a long swig of beer. "We are Vikings. We can do anything."

Ivak drained the last of his beer before replying. "There is that."

"By the by," Trond said, a decided twinkle in his eyes, "is it true that you have found a soul mate?"

Ivak decided it was time to teletransport back to Angola. He could hear his brothers' laughter in his wake.

Men celebrate with booze, women go shopping . . .

Gabrielle celebrated with all her coworkers at Second Chances over coffee and beignets from the Café du Monde. She was so happy that she even sent some out to the two men . . . uh, vangels . . . that she now knew were guarding her at Ivak's direction.

After that, she and Luc met with Thor in his Baton Rouge law office where, together, they drew up the legal documents necessary to request a new trial. The papers would be filed that afternoon, but it could be days or months before a trial date would be set.

On the way back to Houma, where Gabrielle had left her car at Luc's law office, Luc entertained her with stories about Tante Lulu. Like the time the old lady entered a belly dancing contest along with a younger Charmaine, and Tante Lulu won! Or when Tante Lulu held a surprise wedding for René and Valerie, the surprised parties being the bride and groom. "She once gave a state trooper the finger for clocking her at a hundred and ten in her then vehicle du jour, a pink Thunderbird," Luc said, chuckling. "And I'll never forget the time she got hauled in for prostitution, wearing a hooker outfit in a N'awlins red-light district. Said she was looking for a friend. Did I mention she was seventy-five at the time?"

"How do you all put up with her antics?"

"Are you kidding? We adore her, antics and all. She was the saint who saved me and my brothers when we were kids, from an abusive father. She's been there for all of us any time we needed her. No questions asked. Ever. And believe me, Tee-John as a teenager was the wildest Cajun to come down the bayou. 'Tryin' a saint' could have been his motto."

Gabrielle was ashamed of her poorly chosen words. "I am so sorry. I didn't mean to offend. She's been good to me, too. More than good."

"Hey, no need to apologize. She's a dingbat, no doubt about it. But a lovable dingbat."

It was mid-afternoon before Gabrielle returned to Bayou Black. She noticed a BMW sedan in the driveway when she pulled in. She knew who it belonged to once she saw the license plate frame with "Charmaine's Beauty Spa" on it, and a bumper sticker that read: "We Tease 2 Please."

Her guards parked across the road, and sat with the motor running, probably to keep the air-conditioning running. Even though it was technically autumn, the late September weather was still hot in Southern Louisiana.

Gabrielle was carrying a potted African violet and a bag of gifts for Tante Lulu to thank her for all her help with Leroy. The two women were sitting at the kitchen table with index cards spread out before them, trying to figure out the schedule of acts for the talent show.

Tante Lulu stood abruptly when she saw Gabrielle. "Yer home early. Whass wrong, sweetie?'" she asked with alarm.

"Nothing's wrong. Everything's right," she said, then embarrassed herself by bursting into tears. Apparently, the stress of all her worry over Leroy was finally bursting forth.

At her outburst, Tante Lulu and Charmaine, who stood now, too, were clearly starting to worry about her.

In a middle of a three-way hug, she blubbered out, "Little Eddie Hebert died."

"Oh no!" Charmaine exclaimed.

"Son of a gun! I was hopin' his mama woulda got ta him first," Tante Lulu added.

"She did. I mean, Ivak did. Hebert confessed before he died."

"Thank you, St. Jude," Tante Lulu squealed.

"So, those are tears of happiness?" Charmaine asked, smiling, as she handed her a St. Jude napkin to wipe her eyes.

Gabrielle nodded, too overcome with emotion to speak.

Later, Tante Lulu oohed and aahed over her plant and the luxurious silk embroidery threads Gabrielle had bought for her, but declined to take credit for any progress with Leroy's case. "It's St. Jude you gotta be thankin'."

Gabrielle couldn't argue with that. Maybe . . . just maybe . . . she was becoming a believer.

And if she could believe in St. Jude, or the power of prayer, or miracles, what did that say about the concept of vampire angels? Was it possible Ivak was who he said he was?

Speaking of the devil . . . rather the angel . . . her cell phone rang, and she saw by the caller ID that it was Ivak. "I'm going to take this in the other room, if that's okay with you."

Both women nodded.

She went into her small guest bedroom and said into the phone, "Hello, Ivak."

"Sweetling," he said. "Do I detect a happy note in your voice?"

"Very happy. Thank you so much."

"I only played a part."

"An important part. And I *am* thankful."

"Well, if you insist, I can think of certain ways that you can show your appreciation."

"Do you mean sex?"

"What else?"

"Do you always think about sex?"

"Always."

She smiled. "I wish you were here."

"I can hear the smile in your voice."

"I'm happy."

"I wish I was there . . . to share your happiness."

"Yeah, I can tell what kind of sharing you have in mind."

He laughed. "Sounds like someone else is thinking about sex all the time, too."

That was for sure.

"Guess what I'm doing today?" he asked.

"Does it involve sex?"

"No, witch, it does not. I am going to buy a plantation."

"Heaven's End?"

"None other!" He snorted his disgust. "Will you help me with the renovations?"

"Me? I know nothing about restoring a historic building."

"You think I do? In any case, it will be weeks . . . mayhap months . . . before I can think about that."

"I might be able to come up with some names of experts who can help you. For that matter, Tante Lulu would be the first person to start with. I'll talk to her."

"You would do that for me?"

"It would be my pleasure."

"Speaking of pleasure, do we still have a date for Saturday?"

She hesitated. "Why do you ask? Have you changed you mind?"

"No. I just wanted to make sure you wanted to go with me."

"I do." That's all she said, hoping he understood how much she wanted to be with him.

"The warden is calling," he said then. "He probably has another complaint to file against me. If I were an inmate, I'd have been written up so many times, my sentence would be life times three."

"You enjoy needling him."

"That I do."

"You better go."

"I'll pick you up at seven on Saturday. We can have dinner before going to Swampy's, or maybe we could have a late dinner, after."

After what? she wanted to ask, but didn't have the nerve. "Either way is okay with me." She hoped he got the message of exactly what she was okay with.

"One more thing," Ivak said in a voice that was decidedly lower and huskier. "Sweet dreams tonight."

"Is that a threat? As I recall, it's your turn to come up with the . . . fantasy, isn't it?"

"A promise." He just laughed, a low, husky, masculine sound that *promised* something wicked.

She was smiling when she returned to the kitchen.

Tante Lulu glanced up from the table where she and Charmaine had apparently finished their work on the talent show. The cards and charts had been set aside in two neat piles. "Me and Charmaine have a great idea on how we can help you celebrate."

Charmaine winked at Gabrielle.

Uh-oh!

"We're goin' shoppin'," Tante Lulu said, rubbing her hands with anticipation.

Uh-oh!

"Gotta get us some new duds fer the *fais do do* on Saturday night."

At Gabrielle's apparent confusion, Tante Lulu explained, "*Fais do do* is a Cajun party down on the bayou."

"There's this great little boutique in Houma," Charmaine said. "They have everything from killer heels to high-end jewelry."

"Do they have thongs?" Tante Lulu wanted to know.

Gabrielle and Charmaine turned to stare at her.

"Not fer me. I'm too old ta have one of them things ridin' up my crack. I was thinkin' more of you." She was looking at Gabrielle.

"Me?" Gabrielle squeaked out.

"Yeah. Yer butt ain't dropped too much yet. Betcha that Viking would like a back end view of you when you twirl around Swampy's dance floor. Betcha that would get his juices flowin'. Make sure ya get a pair of them high heels, too. The ones what make ya have ta stand with yer rear end arching back. I read in one of the magazines in Charmaine's beauty shop that porno movie stars allus wear 'em, 'specially when they's buck nekkid."

There were so many things alarming with what Tante Lulu said . . . about Gabrielle's butt having dropped, about her twirling, as if she knew how to twirl, about porno high heels. But all Gabrielle said was, "I really don't need any new clothes. I have plenty back at my apartment in the city."

"Bite yer tongue. A gal cain't ever have too many clothes, or too many orgy-asms."

Seventeen

The way that men go to battle, an age-old ritual . . .

Late that night, there were one hundred vangels in and around New Orleans under the command of Ivak and his brothers. They'd waited for the restaurant to close and for those Lucies out on the prowl to return to their evil "nest." By three a.m. this section of the Quarter was finally at rest, residents asleep, businesses closed, including the Anguish restaurant.

Despite his promise of "sweet dreams" to Gabrielle, there would be no sleep for Ivak tonight. Nor dreams.

Not that he wasn't thinking about her. And sex. All the time.

He and his brothers were in Gabrielle's apartment. He could swear he smelled her scent; it enveloped him like an erotic cocoon. Not her perfume, her woman scent. That lure to lust that tugged at him endlessly.

He found himself arguing with himself, often at the most inopportune times . . . like now . . . trying to find ways that justified his having sex with the woman of his dreams *outside his dreams.*

Maybe she needed him in her bed to protect her from Lucies. That would be okay, wouldn't it?

Maybe he should make love to her to show her how it could be done with expertise. That would be a service to her, wouldn't it?

Maybe she had developed some strange ailment that only sexual intercourse could cure. His cock would be like a doctor's instrument.

Sex for medicinal purposes? That would be allowed, wouldn't it?

Maybe he should suck on her breasts so that the nipples wouldn't indent for lack of nurture. Think how bad she would look in a tight shirt. He would be doing her an aesthetic favor, wouldn't he?

He shook his head to clear it and looked around Gabrielle's small home, watching his brothers prepare for battle. More than seventy vangels were stationed outside the city, or hovering above it, waiting for the signal to attack. In addition, another twenty vampire angel warriors were assigned to strategic places between here and Angola, the path it was believed the Lucies would flee on once under siege. When it came to war plans, the VIK were masters, having been at it for more than a thousand years.

They each carried an arsenal of specially treated knives, swords, lances, throwing knives, bullets, and other fighting gear attached to their leather braies and tunics or under the long cloaks with silver epaulet wings. The guns and rifles had silencers on them. The whole operation on Dumaine Street had to take no more than fifteen minutes from beginning to end, lest the city be aware of exactly what was happening. Oh, they would know eventually when there was a pile of rubble where a building once stood, and a lot of missing "persons," like the owner of the famed French Quarter eating establishment.

"Focus, everyone," he said. "Remember, our main goal today is to take down Dominique," Ivak reminded them.

"And a ton of Lucies, as well," Mordr said.

"True, but Dominique is our number one tango," Trond emphasized. *Tango* was a Navy SEAL word for bad guy . . . or bad girl . . . or bad thing, in the case of the Lucies. Terrorists.

"You and your military speak!" Vikar teased Trond.

Trond shrugged. "If I'm forced to walk the walk, I might as well do the talk."

"Bullshit!" Cnut contributed.

"Be careful, or Mike will make you a Navy SEAL, too," Trond warned Cnut. "You do not want to know what Hell Week is."

"Are we good to go?" Harek asked. When everyone turned at his use of modern military speak, too, he just shrugged. "I've been boning up on the Internet."

"I've been boning up, too," Ivak said.

His brothers groaned.

"We all know what kind of boning up you've been doing, Ivak." Sigurd grinned at Ivak, then told the others, "Now that he's found his soul mate, all he does is 'bone up.'"

"That was crude," Ivak pointed out.

"What? You think doctors can't be crude?"

"We're Vikings, Ivak. Didst forget that Vikings are crude?" Trond asked, his blue eyes twinkling with mischief.

They all had blue eyes, for that matter, being vangels. They all twinkled with mischief at one time or another, being Vikings.

"What you are all forgetting is that lust is second nature with Ivak. Remember, lust is his Deadly Sin," Trond went on.

The others nodded.

"Remember the time you told us that you think about tupping every other second of every day," Trond said.

Ivak put his face in his hands.

"And you were shocked to learn that other men thought about their cocks and what it could do, other than piss, much less often," Cnut contributed. "Like every three seconds."

"Actually, scientists have discovered that men everywhere think about sex every seven seconds. I saw it on the Internet." This from Harek, of course.

"That's because they are not as virile as us Vikings," Trond pronounced.

"'Tis true, 'tis true," they all concurred.

This was a ridiculous conversation to be having just before battle, but then it was the way of soldiers everywhere to lighten the mood when they were going to a dark place . . . possibly death. All of their fangs emerged and elongated. As one, they joined hands, bowing their heads.

"May St. Michael lead us in battle. May God be at our backs. May a legion of angels guide our weapon hands," Ivak prayed.

"Death to the Lucies! Hew them down like sheaves of wheat!" Vikar yelled, raising a fist high in the air.

Mordr howled like a wolf.

"Death to the demons!" Sigurd howled, too.

And Trond shouted, "Hoo-yah!" That was SEAL for "Hell, yeah!" or so Trond had told Ivak on numerous occasions.

"Luck in battle!" they all wished one another then, followed by loud war whoops.

Only then did Ivak notice the pounding on the floor, as if someone were hitting the ceiling in the apartment below with a broom handle. Which was proven true when a gruff male voice shouted, "If you don't shut the fuck up, I'm calling the police."

They took that as their signal, and with a whoosh of air, they were outside Anguish, all in preassigned places. Earlier that day, Cnut and Mordr had supervised the discreet planting of explosives in the walls of the historic building that housed the restaurant and Dominique's domicile, but they didn't want the edifice to implode onto itself until after the Lucies were gone. There was no sense in just killing the demon vampires; they would just come back again after healing themselves, a slow or long process depending on the severity of the wounds. No, the vangels would have to eliminate the Lucies one by one using the slivers of the symbolic, specially blessed splinters of the True Cross by He who had hung there. The knives they used had been quenched in the symbolic blood of Christ based on an ancient custom of warfare in which knives and swords were heated by blacksmiths to white hotness, then doused to hardness not in cold water but in the blood of their enemies.

Several of Ivak's ceorls traced a line of holy water around the perimeter of the property, an additional precaution. Holy water would burn the skin of a Lucie, slow them down.

Ivak raised an arm, then chopped it down. The signal to begin. Mordr let loose with a bloodcurdling battle cry Ivak hadn't heard since that last battle with the Saxons.

First, one Lucie peeked out the back door. Then a window upstairs opened. One of the timed explosives went off on the first floor, then one on the roof; these were only noisemakers, intended to alert the Lucies to an attack. The more powerful ones would hit in exactly fourteen minutes.

What followed could only be described as controlled chaos.

The Lucies in full demonoid form came running and flying out of every opening in the building, wood doors and windows crashing. Mungs were especially powerful demons, often seven feet tall with the strength of Goliath.

Ivak and all the vangels were prepared for them. And

no one should discount the strength of a vangel warrior, either, especially those who were more than a thousand years old. Full Lucipire/vangel warfare ensued. Swords swinging, bullets zinging, bodies dissolving into puddles of sulfur. There were at least two dozen destroyed within five minutes before Dominique made an appearance. And what an appearance it was!

Six foot five, give or take, with a long tail and green scales. And breasts! Breasts with huge nipples as red and big as cherries that matched her red eyes. She was one pissed-off Lucie. Hissing, she hurtled out into the yard, swatting with her razor-sharp talons at one vangel after another until she came face-to-face with Ivak, Trond, and Vikar. They all smiled, big fangy smiles.

His other brothers and their vangel soldiers were handling the Lucies coming out of the building like angry bees from a rattled hive. And snakes! For the love of St. Patrick, there were dozens of snakes, some of which erupted into demonoid form, while others just slithered about angrily.

To give Dominique credit, she didn't attempt to escape as many of her Lucie minions were trying to do. She raised herself even taller, a sword suddenly appearing in one hand and a chained mace with pointed studs swinging in the other. She was a powerful opponent, having more than five hundred years on any of them. Ivak wasn't sure any one of them could withstand her force on their own, but the three of them together were formidable. Within minutes, there was a puddle of stinksome slime before them.

He and his brothers, all sporting some serious cuts and abrasions but no mortal wounds, looked at each other and just nodded. No high fives, or hoots of triumphant laughter. This woman . . . this high-ranking Lucipire . . . had been evil at its worst. She had caused so much pain, had turned so many humans into monsters of depravity. It was sad, really.

But Ivak glanced at his watch. "Time to get out of Dodge.

Two minutes to go." He gave the telepathic signal and vangels swooshed out of the immediate area and into the pre-designated hiding places. Some of the Lucies were escaping, but they would chase them down later, if the Lucies were not taken down by vangels along the pathway to Angola.

Just then, there was a massive boom, followed by a series of other explosions, causing the historic brick building to implode on itself. The noise was incredible, waking the entire neighborhood, whose residents came rushing out onto the streets. Police and fire truck sirens could be heard approaching.

Back in Gabrielle's apartment, Ivak and his brothers bowed their heads in thanks for a successful mission. Later, they would assess the number of Lucies annihilated and those sent to Hell, as well as the damage to their own ranks. Ivak suspected there would be many injuries, and he knew of at least two vangel deaths. When vangels were killed before their time, they went to Tranquillity, a place similar to Purgatory or Limbo, to await the Final Judgment. Not a bad place, just not Heaven.

As they were gathering up all their weaponry and belongings—a cleaning service would come in the morning—Ivak talked to his vangels who were patrolling inside and outside the prison, as well as a one-mile swath from New Orleans to Angola.

"We got a swarm of them. Lots of imps and hordlings and a few mungs. No haakai," Mordr told him.

"We didn't get them all, though," Cnut piped in. "I suspect they'll go into hiding for a few days until Jasper is notified of Dominique's demise."

Ivak agreed.

"I'm depressed just being near that prison. I don't know how you stand it." This from his usually dour brother Mordr, a berserker in Viking times, who had seen and done some very bad things.

"Why don't you take off a few days?" Sigurd suggested. "Cnut can watch over things for you."

"Huh? Why me?" Cnut asked.

"Because I have a job to get back to. You're between missions," Sigurd told Cnut.

"I'm not sure if I should be away from the prison right now."

But then Ivak thought of something. Gabrielle and their date for the next evening. They were going to the Swamp Tavern near Houma for some kind of dance to benefit Tante Lulu's charity foundation.

He smiled then and said, "On the other hand . . ."

And he thought of yet another thing. He hadn't thought about sex for a whole half hour. Was that a record or what? Did he qualify for a prize?

By the runes! It was great to be a Viking!

In the end, Ivak did go back to the prison to gather some of his clothing and decided to stay until morning when he would inform the warden that he was going to be gone for a few days. Ivak couldn't remember the last time he had a "vacation." Lots of free time between missions, but somehow this was different.

He hadn't intended to sleep, it being past four a.m. Dawn would soon be rising over the levees and razor wire–topped cyclone fences that enclosed Angola. But he did lie down on his cell cot and folded his hands behind his head, thinking, thinking, thinking. Of Gabrielle, of course. Then his mind drifted toward sleep.

He was on his favorite longship, *Sea Sword*, riding the waves on a fjord near his home. Gabrielle was there, too. And whoa! This was something he hadn't expected . . . or planned. A man couldn't plan something like this. Ivak smiled in his sleep and thought the same thing he had earlier.

By the runes! It was great to be a Viking!

Eighteen

A-Viking she did go . . .

Gabrielle had awakened about four a.m. and turned off the ceiling fan. It had gotten chilly during the night, as it sometimes did on the bayou. Hot as Hades during the day, and blanket weather at night.

She made her way in the dark to the bathroom, and when she returned to crawl back into her bed, she yawned widely and thought, *So much for Ivak's sweet dreams!* Not that she cared. No, the sex dreams were embarrassing, really. Pathetic when you thought about it. So deprived of a love life that she had to conjure one up in her dreams.

She yawned again and fell into another deep sleep.

At first it was the waft of a soft breeze on her bare skin that awakened her. Hadn't she turned off the fan? Oh, maybe she'd just turned it on low.

Then there was the scent of water . . . salt water. How could that be? Here on the bayou?

And the sounds. No chirping, rustling, grunting of swamp animals. No, it was the sound of male voices that

awakened her. And a strange creaking noise. Her eyes
shot open.

To the most amazing sight.

*She was on a longship . . . at least she thought that
was what they called those Viking boats. Beautiful work-
manship on the wood construction. Magnificent red-and-
white checkered sails. Shiny shields arrayed along the
outside of the rails. And men . . . lots of men . . . sitting on
sea chests as they rowed the sleek dragon-shaped vessel.
That's where the creaking sound came from . . . the rubbing of oars in the oarlocks.*

*Standing among the men, hands on hips as he glow-
ered at her, was Ivak Sigurdsson in full Viking attire. A
suede-like, thigh-length tunic, tucked tight at the waist
by a wide leather belt with a luxurious gold buckle in a
writhing beast design. His tight, black, brushed-leather
leggings were tucked into scuffed, calf-high boots. Long,
sun-bleached brownish-blond hair framed a deeply
tanned seaman's face. A Viking stud!*

*That was when she realized that she was tied to the
mast pole, or whatever you called that tall timber thing
that held the main sails. Looking down, she saw that she
was wearing some medieval-type gown of scarlet silk.
Off the shoulders and a wide scooping neckline that exposed the tops of her breasts. Good thing it was a warm
day or she would be freezing her boobs off.*

*Ambling toward her, slowly, Ivak said, "Well, Princess
Gabrielle, have you decided to accept your fate yet?"*

Princess? Me? She giggled.

*"You find humor in your circumstance?" Ivak asked,
walking around her with an arrogance that she didn't find
surprising as he eyed the restraints that held her arms*

behind her around the mast pole, causing her breasts to arch outward.

"Well, yeah. I'm no princess. Unless you consider me Princess of the Bayou. Or Princess of the French Quarter."

He frowned. "French? Nay, you are not from the Franklands. You are a Saxon, daughter of that vicious cur King Edmund."

"Okaaay. And what precisely am I doing here, tied up on a Viking ship?"

"I do not like the games you play, Belle. You know good and well what your fate shall be."

"Belle? My name isn't Belle. See, you've got the wrong person."

"Belle is the short name you were given from birth. Do not deny it."

"Okaaay," *she said again.* "And what is this fate worse than death that you mentioned?"

"Not worse than death. Leastways, many women would disagree with that sentiment." *He gave her a knowing grin.*

Jeesh! "Spell it out, Viking." *Like she didn't know what the macho jerk meant!*

"You were promised as my bride. A peace pact betwixt your father, the self-proclaimed king of the Saxon lands, and my father, the king of Norse holdings in Northumbria. But once our troops withdrew, your father reneged."

"And so you kidnapped me?"

He shrugged. "I prefer to think of it as a wedding journey."

"Except that the wedding is to come at the end of the trip, rather than the beginning?"

"Or anytime in between."

"Doesn't it bother you that I reject your proposal?"

"Not a whit. Besides, you will be willing afore this day is done."

"Oh. What are you going to do? Torture me?"

He nodded. "Sweet torture."

"Oh, puh-leeze! This feels like one of those 1980s romance novels."

"Precisely. Forceful seduction," he said.

"Your language sometimes seems anachronistic."

"Ah. But then, I am a modern Viking."

She would have argued that point, except he was undoing her ties, then securing her wrists again in front of her with a leading rope that he used to tug her toward a doorway. It led to a tiny cabin that was presumably a captain's quarters. It was only big enough for a cot built into the wall, a chair, a large chest, and pegs on the wall holding clothing.

Before she could get a closer look, he picked her up by the waist and tossed her on the bed. She fell back helter-skelter, not able to balance herself with her hands still being tied. "Do you have to be so rough?"

"You consider that rough?" he asked with genuine surprise.

"Untie me."

"You give me orders now, Princess? I think not!" Reaching down, he took the rope between her wrists, yanking it and her arms above her head, looping it over a finial on the headboard.

"How convenient to have a hitching post on your bed. Why not just put hooks in the walls and ceiling?"

He tapped a forefinger to his head in an exaggerated gesture of pondering. "Now there's a thought. Mayhap I could visit the Marquis de Sade on one of my voyages to the Franklands and make a few purchases."

"I thought the Marquis de Sade lived in the 1700s, not Viking times."

He waved a hand airily if that was of little importance.

"I'm not a virgin, you know," she told him.

"And that should matter to me . . . why?"

"I thought men in your time wanted virgins for their brides."

"Virgins are much overvalued, in my opinion."

"Aren't you worried about a wife who might be carrying another man's child?" She'd thought that was one of the reasons for the emphasis on virginity in olden days.

That gave him pause. "Are you breeding?"

"Of course not!"

"Well, then!"

She squirmed up on the small bed, trying to lift her arms and the loop over the finial, to no avail. All she'd accomplished was her bodice riding down dangerously low, and the hem of her gown riding up to her knees. She turned back to flail him with some insult or other, but, whoa!

While she'd been trying to release herself, he'd removed his sword and its belted sheath. It was a really big sword, she noted with irrelevance. He lifted the tunic over his head and tossed it on a chair. Next, he toed off his boots and began to lower his leggings. If he thought to intimidate her, she had news for the idiot. She was enjoying the view.

"There is a priest out on deck awaiting your decision to wed with me," he said, giving her a perfect view of his very fine butt while he walked over and hung both the tunic and leggings on a peg. Then he turned.

"Oh. My. God!"

He smiled, knowing perfectly well that he had a very impressive package . . . an aroused package . . . framed by a body that would put a cover model to shame.

But wait. What did he say? "A priest? I thought Vikings were heathens."

"Another misconception propagated by biased monk

historians. Many Vikings practice both the Norse and Christian religions," he said. Then added with a grin, "For expediency. We would no doubt adopt the Arab religion, as well, if it would be to our benefit."

"Would you mind covering yourself?"

"Why?"

"Because it's hard to carry on a conversation with a man sporting a mondo erection."

At first, his brow furrowed. "Ah, you refer to my enthusiasm." He started to walk toward her, pointing downward at his now bobbing . . . enthusiasm. "Mondo? Does that mean magnificent?"

"Humble, are you, Ivak?"

"Glad I am to hear you call me by my given name. We are making progress, methinks, if you no longer call me Viking all the time, as if it were an insult. I will give you another chance, wench. Will you marry me?"

"With a proposal like that? No way!"

"So be it!"

"You know this is only a dream, right?"

"You can pretend to be dreaming if you wish," he said as if granting her some favor. Before she had a chance to give him a sharp retort, he sat his naked self on the edge of the too-small bed, giving her almost no room to move with the wall on her other side, and ripped her gown from neckline to hem. She was naked underneath, of course. Like . . . come on! Did women really put on luxurious silk gowns like this with no underwear?

Remember, Gabrielle, this is a dream, *she told herself.*

He was staring at her breasts. "They are rather small," he said.

"Huh?"

"I have seen bigger eggs on a hot skillet."

"Are you for real? You expect to win me over with insults like that?"

"I was not trying to win you. When I use charm, you will know it."

She rolled her eyes. "Besides, my breasts only look small because I'm lying down. They're not so small when . . ." Her words trailed off when she saw his lips twitching with a suppressed grin. He'd been deliberately goading her. Well, two could play that game. "You know what they say about men with big dicks, don't you? Premature ejaculation. Wham, bam, I'm done!"

At first, he didn't understand what she meant. Then his face grew flushed. "You dare . . . you dare . . . to suggest . . ." he sputtered. Then, realizing that she had played him at his own game, he gave her a nod of kudos. "Last chance. Will you wed with me, Belle?"

"No. Wait. What's in it for me? If I marry you, where would we live? Would I be free to travel, or, oh, let's say, get a job?"

"Job? Dost mean work? For a lady?" He was truly shocked. At her nod, he said, "You will stay at my home in the Norselands."

"And where will you be?"

"I will be off fighting in my king's wars, or a-Viking. Mayhap trading goods in Birka or Hedeby, even Jorvik. You are not to worry. I will return on occasion long enough to plant another babe in your womb."

"Good grief! You're serious, aren't you? No, I won't marry you. No, no, no!"

He lay down alongside her then, parting her gown even more and tearing the sleeves so that the gown was just like a silk sheet under her. She didn't glance downward, but she could feel his erection pressing against her thigh.

She also didn't have to look downward to know when he was tracing a forefinger over one nipple, then another. She bit her bottom lip to stifle a gasp at the intense plea-

sure that slingshotted to every carnally sensitized spot in her body, especially between her legs.

And he knew, dammit! As evidenced by his smile of satisfaction. "Dost yield yet, Princess?"

"Untie me."

"Then will you yield?"

Not a chance! *"Maybe."*

He chuckled. "You do not lie well, dearling," he said against her mouth. He was leaning over her now, brushing his firm lips against her softer ones, back and forth. Nipping, then laving. Coaxing and demanding. It took all her fast-fading willpower to keep her mouth shut.

"Open for me," he said.

Does he mean my mouth or my legs? *She pressed her lips tighter together and crossed her legs.*

"Stubborn witch," he murmured. But then, while he continued to tempt her with kisses, he pinched a nipple.

She gasped.

And his tongue slipped inside.

The sneaky rogue!

He was the one who gasped then as the unique breath kisses commenced, same as it had the first time they'd kissed weeks ago in his prison office. When his tongue stroked inside her mouth, he breathed life-giving air into her. On the return stroke, when her tongue entered his mouth, she breathed into his mouth. Back and forth, they exchanged tongue kisses and precious air. It was as if they were joined in a most elemental way. Amazing!

The breath kisses went on and on until Ivak raised his head to stare down at her. His lips looked bruised, and he panted slightly. "Please, sweetling, tell me that you yield?"

"Yield?" Gabrielle had forgotten what he wanted her to yield, so aroused was she. Her brain was erotically fuzzy.

"Shall I call for the priest?"

Huh? Oh, he means the wedding nonsense. Aaarrgh! I'm melting with excitement and the brute is calm enough to still persist in his plan to seduce me. We shall see about that! *"Not unless you want him to give you last rites. Because I'm going to kill you once I get up."*

"A challenge. Ah, didst not know, there is naught a Viking enjoys more than a challenge?"

She made a scoffing sound.

But not for long.

Ivak rolled over, and in one slick move, he'd somehow separated her legs, and he lay atop her. Grinning, he said, "Methinks I need to show you the far-famed Viking S-spot."

"Don't you mean G-spot?"

He shook his head and waggled his eyebrows at her mischievously. Before she could question him further, he rose to his knees, grabbed her ankles, and spread her wide. "Look at you," he said then, his voice deliciously husky with arousal.

She was only slightly embarrassed at having him studying her private parts because he was already lowering his head. Just before he was at sex central, he glanced up at her and said, ominously, "Did I mention that the Viking S-spot can only be found with the tongue?"

And he did. Find it.

She screamed when the tip of his tongue touched that special spot she hadn't known she had. Then he fluttered her. The scream went on and on and on . . .

Gabrielle came abruptly awake, realizing that the scream didn't come from her, but from Tante Lulu. "Gabrielle! Hurry!" The old lady's squeal came from somewhere in the house.

Barefooted and wearing just a long sleep shirt, she rushed into the living room where the old lady was sitting with a cup of coffee in her hands, eyes glued to a small TV. She motioned for Gabrielle to come closer.

"What? What is it?" Gabrielle asked with alarm.

"Don't you live on Dumaine Street?"

"Yeeesss," she replied hesitantly, sinking into a nearby chair. "Why?"

"There was an explosion there early this mornin'. The whole buildin' went kaboom! Flattened like batter on a hot griddle."

"My building?"

Tante Lulu shook her head that was covered with pink foam rollers. "Nope. It was that building what had a restaurant with a goofy name. Agony or sumpin'."

"Anguish?"

"*Oui*, thass the one."

"Oh my goodness! That's practically right across the street from my apartment. Was there a fire?"

"Doesn't 'pear ta be."

The New Orleans police chief came on the TV. "At this time, the historic Dumaine mansion is nothing but a pile of rubble. Cause of the explosions heard by the neighbors is undetermined. We have found no evidence of deaths; however, the owner of the building, Dominique Fontaine, appears to be missing, as well as some of her restaurant workers who supposedly lived on the premises."

A reporter, who identified herself as Monica McCall from WDSU-TV, called out a question: "What is that odd smell?"

"Slime," the police replied. "There are piles of it all around the property and inside the remains of the building. We're not sure what it is, or if it could be the cause of the explosions. Samples have been sent to testing labs in Baton Rouge."

Another reporter from the Associated Press asked, "Isn't it odd that only this building was affected by the explosions when structures are so close here in the Quarter?"

"I don't know how odd it is, but it's something to be thankful for."

The AP reporter immediately followed up with "Is it possible this was a result of residual damage to gas lines from Hurricane Katrina eight years ago?"

The police chief shrugged. "I doubt it, but who knows?"

"Justin Comeaux from the *Times-Picayune*. What about all those reports of strange creatures running from the building?" Justin laughed as he added, "Supposedly they were ten feet tall with scaly bodies, red eyes, and long tails. And then there were the vampires chasing them in long black cloaks."

The police chief laughed, too. "Well, if anyone caught an image of them on their cell phones, I would love to see the picture. In fact, the *National Enquirer* would probably pay a bundle for it."

The WDSU reporter said, "It is true that there were a large number of reptiles in evidence. All kinds of snakes. I've seen the photographs."

"That's true. Animal control has been gathering them up, and we believe they've all been recovered. Ms. Fontaine was known to keep snakes as pets. Of course, we had no idea there were so many, which is a clear violation of local animal regulations. In fact, several were endangered species never seen in these parts before."

Ivak, Gabrielle thought suddenly. It must have been Ivak and his brothers and a mission to destroy Dominique. Then, like dominoes flipping inside her head, conclusions hit her with shocking clarity. The creatures being described by residents were exactly what she had witnessed that one night with Ivak. The slime must be what remained of dead demon vampires, according to what Ivak had told her. And the cloaked vampires? It must have been Ivak and the vangels.

When Gabrielle had awakened the first time this morning, she'd been slightly disappointed . . . okay, a lot disappointed . . . by the lack of dreams. Now she knew what Ivak had been doing during the night. And it hadn't been sleeping.

Oh my God! Does that mean I now believe in vangels and Lucipires?

How can I not believe?

"I need to go to New Orleans and check on my apartment," she told Tante Lulu. "I was going to go into the office at one o'clock for a few hours, but I think I'll go early."

"I could go with you. Betcha I could figger out what that slime is. I'm a real good dick."

"Di-dick?"

"Yeah. PI. Whadja think I meant?" She giggled then, letting Gabrielle know that she'd known perfectly well how her word would be misconstrued.

"Thanks for the offer, but I don't know how long I'll be." That's all she needed. Tante Lulu breaching crime scene tape to do her own investigation. Plus, Gabrielle didn't know what condition her apartment would be in, or even if Ivak's brothers were gone. "No, it would be better if I go alone today."

"You are comin' back, aintcha, honey? Doan fergit. We're all goin' ta Swampy's t'night."

How could she forget? For a moment, Gabrielle considered having Ivak pick her up at her apartment, assuming it was empty, but it would be a lot closer to go from here. "I'll come back," she said.

"Mebbe you should stop at Charmaine's on the way back. Remember, she's gonna gussy you up."

That's what she was afraid of. "I'm thinking that I can do my own hair and makeup."

Tante Lulu stood and put her hands on her hips. A five-foot pugilist, about to fight for her cause. In this case, the cause being Gabrielle. "You cain't wear them shoes and that dress without sexing up the rest of you."

Gabrielle groaned inwardly, but it was the truth. What had she been thinking to buy shoes that had a name? Sex on a Silver Hoof! They were open-toed, silver stilettos, with a matching cinch belt that made the waist of the short, silver and teal-blue chiffon, halter-top, no-back dress look amazingly small. A trick of the eye, surely. And she'd even bought, at Charmaine's insistence—although Gabrielle hadn't protested all that much—a pair of skimpy flesh-colored bikini briefs. No bra.

"Thass what we call Sex on a Silver Platter here in the South," Tante Lulu had proclaimed.

"All right, I'll stop at Charmaine's," Gabrielle conceded, "but I draw the line at pouf."

"Jist a little!" Tante Lulu coaxed.

"No pouf!"

"You'll prob'ly change yer mind once she slathers some of that lip plumbin' lipstick on you. Makes the men go wild."

There wasn't a thing in the world Gabrielle could think of to counter that ridiculous statement.

Nineteen

A date with the Bobbsey Twins? . . .

Ivak arrived early for the first real date of his sorry thousand-plus-year-old life, and he was as nervous as an untried youthling about to swive his first maid. Not that Ivak anticipated any swiving taking place tonight. Maybe near-swiving, if he was lucky.

He wore a black T-shirt tucked into denim braies tucked into low-heeled, scuffed-up cowboy boots, that last a suggestion from Mordr, of all people, who claimed that women went apeshit over cowboys. Ivak wasn't sure he wanted Gabrielle going any kind of shit over him. It didn't sound appealing. But Mordr—the dourest of all his brothers, suddenly an expert on women?—said apeshit was definitely a good thing.

Who knew? Who knew that Mordr knew?

Over it all, Ivak wore a dark blue jacket called a blazer, another of Mordr's suggestions. The blazer would hide his weapons. With an irrelevance engendered by nervousness, no doubt, Ivak vowed to check out what Mordr had been up to lately; he was certainly acting out of character.

Ivak was glad he'd gone to so much trouble with his

appearance when he got his first gander at Gabrielle. *Oh. My. Racing. Heart!*

First of all, her hair was long and curly, evoking images of sex-mussed hair after a long bout of lovemaking. Her lips looked poutier than usual and were painted a deep coral color that matched the enamel on the short fingernails and the toenails that peeked out from a pair of silver high-heeled shoes that made her legs look longer with elongated calf muscles.

And that wasn't all. Her dress . . . for the love of a cloud! . . . her dress! It was made of some shimmery fabric that he just knew would feel wonderful in his hands, especially if he were rubbing it against her skin . . . or lifting it off. Tied around her neck, it was demure in front . . . or as demure as a garment could be when it went only to the top of her knees where it billowed out, but in the back . . . well, there was no back. To his erotic appreciation, the fabric moved . . . *it actually moved* . . . when she walked.

"You make my bones melt, sweetling," he said, leaning forward to kiss her cheek. That was all he would permit himself, lest he throw her down and have his way with her right on Tante Lulu's porch where that pet alligator stood nearby staring him down, just waiting to pounce.

Gabrielle blushed. "I think Charmaine went a little too far." She tried to flatten the curls against her head, but they just sprang back out.

"No," he said. "Just far enough." *To bring a man to his knees.*

She smiled, and he could swear his heart swelled to twice its normal size. *What is wrong with me?*

"Is ever'one ready?" Tante Lulu asked, coming out onto the porch. "Gabrielle said I could hitch a ride with you two."

It appeared Ivak was going to have two women on his date.

Then he got a good look at the little woman.

He barely stifled a laugh.

Tante Lulu wore an outfit that matched Gabrielle's. Sort of.

Her hair was red and curly today, though short, capping her head. She wore the same color of lipstick and nail polish as Gabrielle, and silver eye shadow and black kohled lashes framed her eyes, same as Gabrielle's. Her dress was the same, too, though midget-size. And instead of silver stilettos, she wore silver wedge-heeled shoes. Looped over one arm was a silver purse the size of a saddlebag. It probably weighed more than she did.

"What is this? The Bobbsey Twins?" Ivak whispered, having recently learned about that old children's book series because his sister-by-marriage Alex had bought the books on eBay for her "adopted" twins, even though they wouldn't be able to read them for years.

"More like Dumb and Dumber," Gabrielle whispered back.

"Did they have a sale on the same dress?"

It was Tante Lulu who responded now. "How'dja know? Wait 'til you see Charmaine."

His laughter did erupt then, and he noticed that Gabrielle wasn't trying to hide her own mirth, either.

"It wasn't my idea," Gabrielle said. "Honestly, we're going to make fools of ourselves. There's still time to—"

"Complain, complain, complain. Stuff a sock in it," Tante Lulu told Gabrielle. To Ivak, she explained, "The girl needs ta let loose a little."

Ivak was all for that.

As they walked toward his black Lexus SUV with tinted windows, Ivak looped an arm around Gabrielle's shoulder and tugged her close to his side.

Tante Lulu reached inside her purse and grabbed a clear bag of cheese snacks that she proceeded to toss to the alligator in the yard. The beast practically leaped in the air to catch the treats in his big, toothsome mouth.

And people thought vangels were strange!

As first dates went, it was a whopper . . .

Gabrielle was in love.

She couldn't explain how it had happened. She'd only known Ivak for a short time. She didn't really know him that well. It didn't matter.

He claimed to be some otherworldly creature . . . not really a man, but a vampire angel. She was in love with a dead man, really. It didn't matter.

Guilty of the sin of lust, or so he said, he must have been with hundreds of women. A player of the worst sort. It didn't matter.

He worked in a prison. He might always work in a prison, when that was the last thing she wanted to see, ever again, once Leroy was released. It didn't matter.

And children . . . he said he could never have children. That should be a deal breaker for their relationship. It didn't matter.

She was scared and exhilarated at the same time.

As if sensing her thoughts, Ivak reached over to take her hand in his as he continued to drive. When his skin touched hers, there was an electric shock that caused them both to jerk their hands back . . . a shock that started at the palm, then richocheted like warm blood throughout her body. "Did you do that on purpose?" she asked.

"You jest! Why would I deliberately zap myself?"

"It's the lightning bolt," Tante Lulu said from the back-seat.

"Huh?" she and Ivak both said.

"The lightning bolt of love," Tante Lulu explained.

•

"I thought it was the thunderbolt of love," Gabrielle said with an embarrassed laugh.

"Same thing."

Ivak's expression was somber, and Gabrielle knew he was as amazed, and possibly as disturbed, as she was at the intensity of what was hitting them both. This time, when he reached for her hand, he held on tight, right through the zinging.

"Holy moly!" It felt like he was touching her all over.

He said nothing, but he raised her hand and kissed her knuckles.

"Now, no hanky-panky," Tante Lulu ordered.

If she only knew!

With Ivak still holding her hand, Gabrielle turned slightly in her seat to look at Tante Lulu who sat in the middle of the backseat like a little queen. Her eyes twinkled with merriment.

"Tell me about your charity . . . the one tonight's event is about?" Gabrielle asked.

"A few years back, I come across some horrifyin' sit-ye-ations. Even though that Katrina hurry-cane hit Loo-zee-anna a long time ago, there's still families what are sufferin'. I started the Hope Foundation ta help those what are homeless, or hungry, or needin' jist a little boost up. St. Jude gave me the idea."

Not for the first time, Gabrielle realized what a remarkable woman Tante Lulu was. Most women . . . most people . . . at her age would think it's time to rest, having lived a good life, having done enough. But not Tante Lulu. She had so much energy. She just kept going.

"What exactly is planned for this evening?" Ivak asked.

"Well, first off, there's a cover charge ta get inta Swampy's t'night. A hundred dollars a person. Kin you afford it?" That last seemed to occur Tante Lulu suddenly, and her brow furrowed with worry.

Ivak laughed. "Yes, I can afford it, and I'll make a donation, as well."

"How much?" Tante Lulu asked in her usual blunt, outrageous manner.

Ivak laughed again. "Ten thousand?"

"Twenty would be better."

Gabrielle gasped. That really was outrageous. "Tante Lulu! You can't ask someone—"

"Shh!" Ivak said, squeezing her hand. "I really can afford it."

"With your pay as a prison chaplain?"

"Hardly." He told her in an undertone, "Vangels do very well, financially."

"Oh. Is that like battle pay for soldiers?"

"You could say that."

Tante Lulu went off, as if no one had spoken. "Besides the cover charge and René urging folks ta make money pledges, we's havin' a silent auction with goods and services that people and area businesses donate. I even got that boutique we was in yestiddy ta give us a gift certificate, dontcha remember?"

Oh, so that's what she had been discussing with the owner in the back office.

"Ivak gave us one of his swords," Tante Lulu revealed.

"You did?" She turned to Ivak.

He shrugged. "I have lots."

"We put a reserve of fifty thousand on it," Tante Lulu said. "Remy's wife, Rachel, usta be a decorator. She sent a picture of the sword ta some museum fella she knows, and he said it's a thousand years old."

"More than that, actually," Ivak murmured.

Gabrielle digested that bit of information . . . an ancient sword. That only corroborated what she'd already come to believe about Ivak. That he was telling the truth about who and what he was.

Then, another thought occurred to Gabrielle. "Tante Lulu! You had the nerve to ask him for a money donation when he's already given you such a priceless object?"

Tante Lulu exclaimed, "Bull feathers! If you ain't got nerve, you doan never get nothin'."

They'd arrived at Swampy's and the parking lot was jammed. As they dropped Tante Lulu off at the front door, not wanting her to have to walk so far, they could hear René's band belting out a raucous zydeco version of "It's Alright." Zydeco was the hand-clapping, foot-stomping music developed over the years by the French-speaking Creoles of African descent, similar to but different from Cajun music.

Now that they were alone, Gabrielle had questions to ask. "Ivak, I went to my apartment today and saw what happened."

"You went to New Orleans? Tsk, tsk, tsk! Can you not stay put for even a minute?" He paused, then added, "I knew you left the cottage, of course. Your guards notified me. That does not make it right."

She ignored his reprimand and asked, "Was the explosion your doing?"

"Mine. My six brothers. And about ninety vangels, give or take."

"How did you . . . never mind . . . did you accomplish your . . . um, goal?"

"We did. Dominique is gone. For good. She will not come back in some other demon vampire incarnation. And about three dozen Lucies are gone, as well."

"Three dozen! There were three dozen of those beasts in my neighborhood?"

"More than that, probably. At least a dozen escaped. And there were already others working the prison perimeter."

"That means the danger isn't over yet, doesn't it?"

"Gabrielle, I doubt the danger will ever be over totally, but for now your neighborhood should be clean."

"Aren't you worried that law personnel will continue to investigate and find out what happened?"

"How could they? Think about it, sweetling. Who would ever come up with the notion of demon vampires and demon angels? No, they will dig and prod for weeks, mayhap longer, and in the end say it was a mystery. Or a scientist will come up with a quack explanation involving seismic shifts or some such thing."

He was probably right. "Just like the explanation given for the missing people at Angola."

"Right, but we have Mike to thank for that. Somehow he managed to get paperwork in the files showing the inmates actually died and were buried, and the staff members who disappeared just happened to be men who had no family; so the explanation that they just quit their jobs and went off for parts unknown was accepted, if not believed."

"But what if more people disappear?"

"That could be a problem," he agreed. "But we're on it."

Changing the subject, she said, "I was surprised to see my apartment so clean. You'd never know a half-dozen giants had been living there. In fact, it looks better than it did before."

"We sent a cleaning crew in this morning."

"The cleaning crew didn't leave all those roses. The place smells like a funeral parlor." There were vases of different colored roses in every room, and even a potted climbing rose on the balcony. He had to have spent hundreds of dollars on the blasted things.

His expression went crestfallen. "I saw the way you admired those wild roses at Heaven's End, and I thought . . ."

"I love the roses, and your gesture, while overboard,

was sweet. I love them." She put a hand on his arm, making sure to touch the sleeve and not bare skin. "Thank you."

"My pleasure," he said, and placed a hand over hers, then immediately jerked it back at the shock. "Oops."

"I wonder if this is your boss's way of keeping you from doing something you shouldn't," she said.

"Could be. Like a shock collar on a dog. Mike has a warped sense of humor sometimes." When they got out of the car, Ivak remarked, "Have I told you how hot you look tonight?"

"Not half as hot as you, babe," she said, fanning her face. He was clean-shaven, and his dark blond hair was pulled off his face into a long ponytail.

He just grinned, as if he knew how hot he was, but then he redeemed himself by telling her, "I want to look good for you."

It was probably a line he'd practiced with a hundred women, but she didn't care. She liked it! "By the way . . . Viking S-spot? Give me a break!"

"The dream," he said, shaking his head with amazement. "Actually, there is such a thing. The Viking S-spot. And I must say I am a master of the technique. Someday I will demonstrate for you."

Promises, promises, she thought, but what she said was, "And don't think I'm forgetting your remark about my fried egg breasts."

"It was a jest. I like your breasts just fine."

He put a hand to her lower back to guide her, and she got a shock again. This time, emanating from a lower region of her body, it gave sizzle to a part of her body that hadn't gotten any attention in years, except in her dreams.

Her knees almost buckled.

Ivak chuckled and put an arm around her to hold her upright.

"Stop zapping me!" she said.

"I'm getting zapped, too," he defended himself. Then added with a grin, "I like it."

She did, too. Not that she would admit it.

As they walked from the far reaches of a spillover parking lot, deliberately not touching now, the band was already into another zydeco song, "My Woman Is a Salty Dog."

While Ivak paid their admissions and got a number for the silent auction, declining a receipt for tax purposes, Gabrielle got her first view of just how crowded the tavern was as a blast of heat generated by hundreds of bodies hit her. Good thing Tante Lulu had told René to save seats for them and the rest of the family.

Ivak took her hand, despite the little shocks, and led her toward the bar, where Lucien LeDeux was waving for them to join him. The band slowed down for that Cajun classic "Louisiana Man," low enough in volume that she was able to introduce Ivak to Luc.

"Thor called me this afternoon," Luc told her. "We have an appointment with one of the federal judges in the First Circuit Court of Appeals in Baton Rouge on Monday. He wants to discuss Leroy's appeal for a new trial."

She threw her arms around Luc's neck and hugged him. Into his ear, she whispered, "Thanks for all your help."

"Hey, I came into this late. Thor is the one you should thank. And Ivak."

"And your aunt, too."

"Don't I get a hug of thanks, too?" Ivak asked.

"Later," she said.

"I'll hold you to that. Literally," he replied.

"How 'bout trying an oyster shooter to start off the night?" Luc asked.

At Ivak's interest and her puzzlement, Luc gestured to

the bartender, "Hey, Gator! Give us three oyster shooters."

The bartender—a big, bald-headed man with a gold hoop in one ear—placed two shot glasses in front of each of them. One with a raw oyster in it covered with Tabasco sauce. The other with a healthy swig of one hundred proof bourbon. "This is how it's done," Luc said. First he tossed back the oyster, followed immediately by the bourbon, then stamped a foot on the floor. "Whoo-boy! That's good!"

She and Ivak eyed their drinks suspiciously.

"C'mon. You can't be a Cajun—even an honorary one—without having your first oyster shooter. Bok, bok, bok," Luc clucked, daring them to try it.

"Together?" Ivak said to her. "One, two . . ."

They both tossed back their drinks, and while Ivak stamped his appreciation on the floor, Gabrielle practically hyperventilated, the Tabasco was so hot and the booze so strong. But then they settled in her stomach, and she felt a warm buzz. "I like it," she said, and both Ivak and Luc laughed.

Between the erotic sparks and the bourbon, she already felt half drunk.

"Follow me to our table," Luc said then. He was carrying two pitchers of beer. Presumably, the glasses were on the table.

Tables, as in plural, Gabrielle soon realized. Four tables along the dance floor facing the stage had been pushed together to seat the more than twenty LeDeux family and friends present tonight.

Luc quickly made the introductions. They'd already met Rusty Lanier and his wife, Charmaine, who was wearing a dress identical to her and Tante Lulu, but she looked vastly different. She'd put a silver belt around the waist. Her hair was upswept to highlight her big silver chandelier earrings, complemented by a lot of single bangle bracelets. Somehow, Charmaine's dress had more of a décolletage than hers did, creating a deep cleavage. On her feet Charmaine wore silver stilettos, too, but hers were nothing but thin, sexy straps that ended in a little bow at her ankles, the kind of shoes that immediately called a man's attention. Hers had the name Hot Silver.

Next came the four legitimate sons of Valcour LeDeux. Apparently there were lots of illegitimate ones around the country. Tee-John, a police officer, whom she'd already met, with his wife, Celine, a newspaper reporter; Luc and his wife, Sylvie, a chemist; Remy, a pilot—who was a sinfully good-looking man, but on only one side of his face, thanks to burns sustained in an Iraq bombing—and his wife, Rachel, a feng shui decorator, along with the older of their adopted children who were college students; and René, whom they'd also met, with his wife, Valerie, a lawyer, formerly of court TV fame. René was up on the stage at the moment with his band, the Swamp Rats.

Plus, there were close friends of the family. Lena, a gorgeous mocha-skinned girl resembling Halle Berry, and Lionel Duval, her brother; they were among the first families to be rescued by the Hope Foundation. They both attended college, thanks to Tante Lulu's generosity.

They also met Angel and Grace Sabato, who had bought a dilapidated Southern mansion. On being told that Ivak was purchasing Heaven's End, they both laughed, and Angel had asked, "Are you crazy?" Grace had added, "We can give you tips. Lots of tips." She rolled her eyes. "We've been at Sweetland for four years now, and we still have a snake problem."

Samantha Starr, an auburn-haired beauty who helped run the Hope Foundation, was there along with her father, Stanley Starr, founder of the Starr Foods chain. Stanley, a white-haired gentleman dressed like one of those old-time planters in a spiffy white suit, had to be close to ninety years old, and he was sitting with Tante Lulu, very close.

"Does Tante Lulu have a boyfriend?" Ivak whispered in her ear.

"I wouldn't be surprised," she whispered back.

Then there was Daniel LeDeux, a physician, formerly of Alaska, who seemed to have a frowning eye on Samantha, who kept looking at him, too, even as she flirted with his twin brother, Aaron, a pilot.

"Whew!" Luc said when the introductions were done.

They were about to sit down when Tante Lulu said, "Make sure you check out the silent auction items later."

The Swamp Tavern was a small bar with a dim interior, square in shape. A stage for the musicians at the far end, fronted by a postage stamp–size dance floor, a long bar off to one side, and dozens of tables where patrons could drink beer and nibble at finger foods, like hot wings with Cajun hot sauce, crawfish nachos, pretzels, and the like. But off to one side was a large addition with a windowed view of the bayou where the additional crowd could be seated. It was here that the silent auction items were displayed on tables lined in a U-shaped fashion around the edges of three sides of the room.

Tee-John poured a glass of beer for Ivak from one of the pitchers and a glass of wine from a carafe for Gabrielle. The band had been taking an intermission, but were about to begin again.

René, wearing a frottir—a washboard-type instrument that fit over his chest—stepped up to the microphone. "Welcome, everyone, to the fourth annual Hope Foundation fund-raiser."

The loud chatter in the room came to a sudden silence.

The other band members did little riffs on their instruments, a guitar, an accordion, a fiddle, and drums.

"Come up here, Tante Lulu," he urged.

Tee-John helped her up the side steps to the stage and she walked out to resounding applause. Gabrielle would bet that the old lady knew most of the people in this bar, or had touched their lives in some way.

René adjusted the microphone for her and she smiled widely. "Thanks y'all fer comin' out t'night. Spend lots of money on the auction. It's fer a good cause." She started to walk away, but then she turned back and said, "An' doan fergit ta pray ta St. Jude. I left lotsa little statues and prayer cards by the door. Yeah, I know this is a bar, René. Dontcha be tellin' me what ta do. I'm a little older than you."

Everyone laughed at her jab of humor. Most of the audience probably knew how dedicated Tante Lulu was to the patron saint of hopeless cases.

"On a serious note," René said. "I want y'all to know that the Hope Foundation has raised five million dollars in the past four years. That's small potatoes compared to some of the big charities, but believe me, it does a hell of a lot of good right here at home, and ninety percent of the funds go to the families and kids."

Whistles and loud clapping resounded through the rooms.

"Now, folks, bear with me while I introduce a guy most of you already know. John Willie Clayton, or JW, Voice of the Bayou, a deejay on Baton Rouge's WJJJ radio, a man who has single-handedly been trying to preserve Cajun music. JW?"

JW walked out onto the stage and adjusted the mic with an expertise telling of his radio background. "René, thanks for the invitation, and here's back at you, my friend. It's bands like yours that make the young folks remember their Cajun roots."

Turning to the audience, JW got more serious. "I won't

take up too much of your time. I just want to give you a brief 'Hell, yeah!' for Cajun music, which has been around almost two hundred years. Many of the songs popular today are just new spins on the songs that have been handed down for generations, originally in French, by our Acadian ancestors. These songs speak of traditional themes, like love, home, family, loneliness, heartbreak, and joy.

"The one song I like to use as a particular example is 'Jolie Blon' which many music historians believe stemmed from 'La Fille d' la Veuve' or 'The Widow's Daughter,' or even older French ballads. The version made popular today by BeauSoleil and even Bruce Springsteen is said to have stemmed from 'Ma Blonde Est Partie,' or 'My Blonde Went and Left Me.' And isn't that just like country music today?"

Everyone clapped as JW walked off the stage and then René's band exploded into a loud, twangy, poignant-sounding "Jolie Blon" in a heavily accented Cajun French. It was bluesy and syncopated at the same time. Immediately afterward, René belted into the microphone an English version similar to the one made famous by Bruce Springsteen where he refers to "Jole Blon" as his flower. That one had a more optimistic ending than the earlier ones involving a fickle blonde.

Before anyone had a chance to get up and dance or go to the bathroom, René looked down to their table and said, "Lookee, lookee. Do I see someone I know? Could it be one of the Angola Prison chaplains. In a bar? Tsk, tsk, tsk! Hey, if anyone needs a beer and a night on the town, it's someone who works up at the prison. Talk about!"

Ivak just shook his head at being singled out in that way.

"I have the perfect song to introduce this man to Cajun land. It's called, 'Les Barres de la Prison,' or 'Prison

Bars.' Hey, Johnny Cash wasn't the only one who could sing a good prison song."

More laughter. René, who had once been an environmental lobbyist in Washington, D.C., now a local teacher, was a born entertainer, very comfortable on the stage.

When the song was over, René said, "One more thing, folks. Don't forget to attend the Prison Rodeo at Angola on October 27. The LeDeux family will be putting on their famous, or you could say infamous, Village People act to benefit some of the prison programs." He paused for effect, then yelled out, "Now, is everyone ready to dance?"

Loud cheers were the answer.

René segued into a rowdy rendition of "Big Mamou."

Tante Lulu and her beau, Stanley, got up and did an incredibly good Cajun two-step, not quite fast, not quite slow, but a rhythmic mix of the two. They must have danced together before because they seemed to anticipate each other's moves.

All the LeDeux and their spouses and friends soon joined in, except for her and Ivak. She wasn't surprised that the women danced well, but she *was* surprised to see the men obviously enjoying themselves on the dance floor, especially Tee-John, who kept teasing his more demure wife by dancing around her and making suggestive bumps and rolls of his hips to encourage her to loosen up. His wife, Celine, just smiled and continued with her more conservative dancing, shaking her head occasionally at his foolishness. Gabrielle could see why folks said Tee-John had been the wildest of the bad boys of the bayou in the LeDeux family.

Charmaine was . . . well, Charmaine. Every man in the bar appreciated her dance moves. Every woman wished she had the nerve to be so uninhibited. And Rusty . . . well, he was just glad that she went home with him.

"C'mon," Ivak said. "Let's join them."

"Do you dance?"

"Darlin'," he said with an exaggerated Southern drawl, "I invented dancing."

"Humility becomes you." She laughed and got up with him. It was true. Ivak loved to dance, and he was good, too. Nothing energetic. Just slow, sexy moves that brushed her body with a whisper of promise. When he got behind her and held her waist with a hand around her front, she could feel how much he was into this "foreplay." That's what dancing with Ivak felt like to her, anyhow.

When the band morphed into the slower "Colinda," Ivak hesitated about where to put his hands, to avoid the shocks. She placed them on her hips, which earned her a smile. She wrapped her arms around his shoulders and pressed her face against his T-shirt. Chest to breast and groin to belly, they began the swaying, rubbing movement that some mistakenly called dancing, but was really making love. Just enough rhythm. Just enough brushing of skin under their clothing. Just his kiss to her hair, and her kiss to his cotton-covered heart.

While the band moved on to another song, Gabrielle arched her head back and said, "I'm having fun. Thanks for asking me on this date."

"Thank *you*," he said. "I'm the one having fun." And he tugged her even closer with his hands on her bottom now.

"Yep, you're having fun," she agreed, and wiggled her hips a little to emphasize just what fun she referred to.

"Witch!" he said, and pinched her butt.

"I saw that!" Tante Lulu squealed as she danced by.

Ivak winked at the old lady.

And Tante Lulu giggled.

Later, after at least four more dances, mostly with faster beats, like that old Hank Williams classic "Jambalaya," "Don't Mess with My Toot-Toot," "Diggy Diggy Lo," and the required song at any Cajun bar, "Louisiana Saturday Night," to which the crowd sang along, Gabrielle asked Ivak, "Does this mean I can stay at my apartment now?"

He hesitated for only a moment before saying, "Only if you have someone with you."

She didn't hesitate at all before saying, "Let's go."

Twenty

And so the mighty fall ...

Ivak could have teletransported them to New Orleans, but he didn't think Gabrielle would appreciate the favor in light of the seeming normalcy of their "date." Good clouds! A Viking man dating? It was certainly something new for him.

So, he drove as fast as he could without getting the attention of any highway patrol. Eighty on the open roads. He felt as if they were crawling.

Gabrielle had her head back and she remained silent, possibly napping. She'd had the oyster shooter and two glasses of wine, after all, on an empty stomach.

He needed this quiet to think. Her nearness kindled so many long-dead senses to life. In truth, he wasn't sure he'd ever had these kinds of emotions before.

There was one definite truth, though. A bond existed between the two of them, a bond so strong it scared him.

Well, not really scared. Vikings did not scare easily. More like made him wary. Or shocked. Definitely entranced. And tempted. She was the ultimate forbidden fruit.

Or was she?

He'd long ago learned that nothing happened to vangels unless Michael willed it. The question was: Why had Mike placed Gabrielle in his path? As a test? Or as a reward?

After Vikar and then Trond's relationship with mortal women, Michael had sworn it would be the last time. No more love connections, or any other connections—i.e., sex—with women who had limited life spans . . . i.e., heart-beating human beings.

Then there was all that soul mate nonsense. Was that all it was? Nonsense?

Well, that settled it. He wouldn't have sex with Gabrielle. He would just kiss her a little bit. Maybe touch her a little bit. Then he would stop. That would be all right, wouldn't it?

Hah! As if you could stop at "a little bit," the other side of his brain argued, the irksome side best known as a conscience.

He'd gone without "real sex" for one hundred years. For a man with lust running in his blood, he'd proven how much he'd changed, hadn't he?

Only because you haven't been offered a real, heart-racing, I've-got-to-have-you-or-die, bone-hard, continual erection. Easy to be good when Satan hasn't offered you the ultimate temptation.

Oh, that is a low blow. And so untrue. Gabrielle hadn't been sent by Satan. She'd been sent by Michael. Ivak would bet his worthless life on that fact.

Your life will definitely be worthless once Michael finds out what you're up to. "Up to" being the key words. Have you looked down yonder lately?

Down yonder? Someone was hanging around Tante Lulu too much. Okay, new plan. All he was going to do was deliver Gabrielle to her apartment. Maybe have a cup of coffee with her. He would sleep on her couch because he wasn't yet sure how safe she was on her own, even with guards outside. He'd give her a kiss good night, of course. A *good* good-night kiss, to be sure, but just a kiss. Then he'd send her off to bed, alone.

Ha, ha, ha, ha, ha!

They were approaching the outskirts of the Big Easy and he reached over to touch Gabrielle lightly on the knee to see if she was still asleep. No reaction. And surprise, surprise, no shocks. Instead, there was an air of electricity surrounding them with enough sexual energy to power a 747. Like a magnetic field of carnality, it was, or something even scarier . . . love.

His throat went dry.

By some miracle, he found a parking spot on the crowded street in front of Gabrielle's apartment. "Sweetling, we're here," he said softly, touching her on the shoulder.

She awakened immediately and stretched. Then, unlatching her seat belt, she turned and gave him such an open, loving smile his heart swelled almost to bursting. "You let me sleep."

"I wanted you wide awake and eager for what I planned to . . . no, no, no, forget I said that."

She arched her brows.

"You were tired; I let you sleep." *That is so lame. Where is my renowned charm? Gone with the frickin' wind!*

"I liked the first version better."

What? No, no, no! Begone, temptation! Begone! He got out of the car and walked around to open her door. Helping her out, he took her hand and walked, fingers laced, toward her apartment.

"No more sparks," she noticed.

"No more sparks," he agreed. *Worse.*

"It's misty out tonight, isn't it?"

It was the sexual aura that surrounded them, but she didn't need to know that yet. "Yeah, mist."

They walked side by side up the steep stairs to her apartment. He felt as if he were Dead Man Walking.

"Are you staying?" she asked as she inserted a key in the door and started to open it.

He gulped and almost swallowed his tongue. *Is that a loaded question? What exactly does she mean? Maybe she means nothing. Maybe she just wants to offer me a cup of coffee. Yeah, that's probably it.* "Yes, but I'm sleeping on your couch."

She slanted him a glance of surprise, then smiled one of those little smiles that women have been perfecting since Eve.

"I mean it." *Or leastways I am trying to mean it.*

She shook her head with disbelief.

He raised his chin haughtily. "Do you doubt that I can be chivalrous?"

"Sometimes chivalry is overrated," she said with a laugh, and bent over to pick up a small, red, tasseled pillow that must have fallen. The bending over was bad enough because that shimmery dress outlined the double curve of her buttocks, and he was a man partial to female buttocks, but then she leaned over the back of the sofa to replace the pillow. A sucker punch in the form of a backless dress hit him hard.

"Ivak!" she scolded, glancing at him over her shoulder to see him staring at her bottom. Then, as she straightened, she frowned with confusion.

"What?"

"I could swear you just cupped my bottom with your hands, then licked a line down my spine, from nape to waist."

He tried not to look guilty. Then he couldn't resist asking, "Did you like it?"

"Whoo-boy! You have a hot tongue."

Whoo-boy!

"Why are you making those whoofing sounds?"

He realized that he'd been exhaling rapidly in little puffs. A futile attempt to bridle his lust.

She wasn't helping matters, especially when she sealed the deal, so to speak. Heightened color bloomed on her cheeks, and her eyes became luminous pools of arousal as she whispered, "I want you, Ivak."

His blood thickened, his incisors elongated, and his mind went blank. Good intentions be damned. Chivalry? What chivalry?

With a supernatural whoosh of speed, he was in front of her, lifting her in his arms. "Aaah, Gabrielle!" he murmured, forehead to forehead. He did not dare kiss her or nuzzle her neck at the moment with his fangs nigh weeping to take her blood in the ultimate mating.

Her feet were dangling off the floor, but only for a second. With the quick thinking of a woman on a mission, she wrapped her legs around his hips, thus bringing her woman's center smack against his almost painful hardness.

He saw lights behind his eyelids, then released a long sigh of surrender. This must be how Adam felt when he took the first bite of that damn apple.

No, he couldn't blame Gabrielle for tempting him. He'd been in a state of temptation from the first time he'd seen her. It was his destiny.

Without thinking and with the speed only a vangel could engage, Ivak had Gabrielle braced against the wall, her dress up to her waist, her panties ripped off, and his own lower garments puddled at his feet. He was totally out of control, a victim of his own lust.

Worst of all, he was inside her body. Full-blown, to the hilt, in her woman's sheath. How had that happened?

He raised his sorry head to look at Gabrielle.

Her arms were around his neck. So, he hadn't forced her into this position. Thank the heavens for that! Her eyes were huge with wonder, the pupils dilated with arousal. "Wow!" she husked out just before her searing silken folds closed on him and began to convulse, which triggered a like response in him. His balls tightened and rose, his cock flexed and shot forth his male essence in a peaking so powerful it brought him to his knees on the carpet, taking Gabrielle with him.

He blacked out for a moment, something that had never happened to him before. When he came to, he was lying atop her, his male part still half hard and still inside her.

"I am so embarrassed," they both said at the same time.

"You must think I'm pitiful to have climaxed so quickly," she said, her face flushed a lovely shade of pink. "My only excuse is it's been so long since I've had sex."

"You're embarrassed? Hah! I'm a man. A Viking, for the love of a fjord! I'm renowned for my finesse in the bedsport. I didn't even take my jacket off, or remove my weapons."

"I enjoyed it," Gabrielle confessed, her cheeks even rosier.

"So did I, but that is neither here nor there. If my brothers ever heard about this, I would never live it down."

Appalled, she asked, "Do you discuss your sexual activities with others?"

"No! Well, I might have on occasion long, long ago, but mostly 'tis my reputation that I must live up to."

"Pfff!" she said. "Are you aware that you're still inside me, and you're not some squiggly little worm, either?"

To his continuing embarrassment, his cock flexed of its own accord, probably at the mention of squiggles. 'Twas like his appendage had a mind of its own. "Of course I'm aware, but I don't want to tup you again with my braies about my ankles like a lackwit youthling."

She put her hands on his buttocks and he about exploded inside her again.

"We're not going to do it that way again," he asserted through gritted teeth, and carefully withdrew his hardness from her inner folds, which were grasping at him to stay like erotic fingers.

"Good Lord!" she said, gaping at the size of his continuing erection. So hard and big was it now that blue veins stood out like marble. "That's what some people call a blue steeler."

"The Lord has naught to do with this, steel or otherwise, believe you me." He yanked up his pants and underbriefs together, being careful of his extended cock, then lent a hand to help Gabrielle to her feet.

She was smoothing out her dress when she went still and put a hand over her heart with alarm. "You didn't use a condom."

He waved a hand dismissively as he attempted to adjust the fabric at his groin so that he could walk without crippling himself. "I am disease free."

She shook her head. "I'm not worried about that. I don't want to get pregnant."

"That is one good thing"—*or bad thing*—"about vangels. As I told you before, we cannot breed. Our seed is unable to catch."

"You shoot blanks?" At his nod, she asked, "Are you sure?"

"Positive. It is rather like mixed species of animals mating." He could see that she didn't like that comparison. "It is what it is. No changing nature."

"Your fangs are still out. I'm curious. Are they ever used in the sex act?"

He really did not want to talk about this. "Sometimes."

She tilted her head to the side. Clearly, she was not going to drop the subject.

"There is a strong compulsion on the part of vangels to fang their partners. I believe that Vikar and Trond's wives let them take a little of their blood when making love. But you are not to fear. I would not do that to you."

She nodded. "But—"

"Enough talking!" He growled against her neck where the pulse did in fact tempt his fangs mightily. "I have one hundred years to make up for in a short period of time."

"Just one thing," she said, raising a finger. "I thought you weren't allowed to have 'real' sex. What we just did, brief as it was, felt like 'real' sex to me."

"Oh, it was, and you can be sure I will be punished for it. A lot." He shrugged.

"Then maybe we shouldn't do any more."

"Bite your tongue, my teasing wench! If I am going to get many, many years added onto my sentence as a vangel, or whatever punishment will be levied, I'm going to make sure I've enjoyed myself." He waggled his eyebrows at her. "Just wait 'til you see how I live up, or down, to my bad deeds."

He locked the apartment door, then, lifting her into his arms, he carried her to her bedchamber, where he tossed her onto the bed. A click of a bedside table lamp put an ambient light into the small room.

She shimmied her bottom up to a half-sitting position against the pillows.

"Don't move," he ordered.

She arched her brows at his dictatorial tone, but she obeyed. Smart girl!

He took off the blazer and hung it over the back of a chair, being careful to place his weapons . . . a pistol, several knives, and a retractable lance . . . on a high chest. He had no reason to think they were in danger from Lucies at this point, but it was always wise to be prepared. Like the old adage: "Pray to God, but carry a sharp sword."

After heeling off his shoes and pulling off his hose, he began to unbutton his shirt. Slowly. Holding her gaze the entire time. Her breathing accelerated. With his overdeveloped senses, he could smell the musk of her arousal, even from across the room.

"I like your chest," she said as he shrugged the shirt off his shoulders and tossed it onto the floor.

"I used to be bigger, more muscular. Back in Viking times." *I cannot believe I am carrying on a polite conversation about upper body muscles when it is another muscle entirely that has needs attention.* "Wielding a heavy broadsword required great upper body strength."

"Sure it did," she replied, still skeptical of his background. "I prefer the way you are now." Then the impudent wench waggled her fingers for him to continue.

When he began to unbuckle his belt, her lips parted.

When he ran the zipper down, she licked her lips.

When he shrugged out of the pants, her eyes went wide. "Holy cow!"

"No, wholly cock!" he corrected. "But just 'Wow!' will do. I must admit, I am as impressed as you are." *Or embarrassed. Who knew I could be this big? Much bigger and I will need a sling*, he jested with himself.

"Are you saying I'm responsible for *that*?"

"Must be."

"Supposedly, Errol Flynn's penis was so big he had to tuck it under the waistband of his trousers. Tante Lulu read it in some pulp magazine years ago. Did you ever have to do that?"

"No! Holy clouds, no! Who in bloody hell is this Airhole character? Never mind." He crawled up onto the bed and straddled her thighs. "Stop looking at my cock."

"Why?"

Why, why, why! "It likes it too much."

"Your fangs are really big, too."

Tell me something I do not know. Ah. She must be nervous. That is why she has become a chattering. "Sorry. It took me many years to accept them myself."

"They're cute."

Cute? No, no, no, a Viking does not want any of his body parts to be called cute. "I can't control them when I am this aroused."

"I love it. Women can hide their excitement, but men can't hide their erections. But in your case, you have a double whammy. You're like blinking headlights . . . a hard-on and a fang-on."

"Are you enjoying making mock of me?"

"Very much." She grinned up at him.

"Enough talking!" He studied her body. "I can't decide what to do first."

"I can," she said, staring pointedly at the part sticking out of his body like a flagpole.

"Not yet. We did the quick tup already. Now we will take our time. If you only knew! There are so many things I want . . . *intend* . . . to do to you."

"Do me then," she demanded.

"Greedy witch!" And crude, too. He liked it.

The only thing holding up the top of her dress was the tied fabric behind her neck. He made quick work of undoing the knot and unveiling her breasts. "Ah, sweetling, how I am going to feast on you!"

"Like fried eggs?" She grinned with mischief.

"You're never going to let me forget that dream statement of mine, are you?"

"Nope."

"I was goading you. In truth, your breasts are a very nice size. Just right for my hands . . . and mouth." He tasted her then in a special technique he had perfected over the years. It involved bracketing the nipple tightly between a forefinger and middle finger, then licking the distended peak.

She squealed . . . a very nice feminine squeal, one he interpreted as womanspeak for *That feels so damn good I could scream.* There was similar manspeak for men, in Ivak's opinion. When men roared their final peaking, they were actually saying, *Hot damn! That was good!*

But he digressed.

Gabrielle had almost shot off the bed when she squealed. If he hadn't been holding her down with his thighs, she might very well have hit the ceiling.

He did the same to the other breast then. Although he was not a breast man, a term some modern men used, having other body parts he favored more, he did appreciate a fine pair of bosoms. And Gabrielle's were very fine. And extremely sensitive, the way he liked. As a result, he spent an inordinate amount of time playing with them. Fondling, tweaking, caressing, suckling. It was not long before Gabrielle was moaning with her mounting excitement.

Time to move to other territory.

He quickly removed the rest of her dress, then the scant panties, before studying and praising every inch that was visible. Which was not enough, of course. Moving back, he pushed her knees up to her chest and spread them wide.

Another squeal. This time one of protest. "Yikes!"

Now *this* was his favorite body part on a woman.

"Let me," he coaxed. "I like to look."

"I don't know if I like you looking *there* so closely."

"You certainly examined that part of me closely enough."

No longer resisting, she let her knees go wide, but she hid her eyes beneath a raised forearm.

"Coward," he teased, then looked his fill. And he liked what he saw. Dark curls framing a cleft with pretty folds that were moist and plumped with arousal. In the forefront was that distended knot that was the key to many women's pleasure. He leaned down and blew softly on the bud, causing it to further unfurl and her to clutch the bed linen with her free hand. "Methinks I have an idea for our first bed sex. A Blended O. Have you ever heard of that?"

She peeked out from under her arm. "It sounds like a drink."

He let out a little hoot of laughter. "Hardly. You have heard of multiple orgasms, of course. But a talented man such as myself can manage to give a woman double orgasms at the same time. A combination of clitoral and G-spot peakings."

"You have a habit of mixing ancient Viking language with modern terms," she remarked. Probably an attempt to shield her interest in what he was offering. But then she asked, "Is it kinky?"

He almost bit his tongue with his fangy teeth. "Only the first time," he replied, having seen that on a T-shirt one time.

"Okay," she said, surprising him.

If she thought to keep him off kilter, he had news for her. He was a master at this game. "But first I have another idea." He got up off the bed and let her lower and close her legs. He could see that she was confused. Good. Going over to her chest of drawers, he pulled out a pair of fluffy gloves.

"What are you doing with my angora mittens? They were a gift from a client who didn't realize I live in a warmer climate. How did you know they were there anyhow?"

"I saw them when I was here last week."

"You went through my drawers?"

"Yes. I like that lace thong, by the way."

She made a gurgling sound, watching intently as he donned the stretchy gloves, then returned to the bed. "It occurred to me that it might be fun to caress your body, all over, with these gloves. Later you can do the same to me."

"Fun?" She gurgled again, but did not protest when he brushed the light-as-air fur over every part of her body. Front. Back. Under her arms. Between her thighs. He did not dare go further. Not yet.

One continuous moan was coming from her mouth as she tossed her head from side to side. "Oh, oh, oh, please, please, please . . ."

On the other hand, mayhap just a little. He whisked his gloved hand over her woman's fleece.

She screamed.

Surprised, he would have been the one hitting the ceiling then, but she grabbed hold of his cock with both hands, causing such excruciating pain-pleasure that he was frozen, realizing only belatedly that she had stuffed him inside her. He fell forward onto his extended arms.

"Son. Of. A. Bitch!" he gritted out.

Then something happened that stunned them both.

"Did you bring the mist inside with you?" she asked him with wonder in her eyes.

"Huh?" Then, "Oh. No, the mist is not of my doing."

The electrified air that had surrounded them in the car swirled around them now like a blue mist, then settled itself above him, presumably into the blue angel wings. But something even more remarkable was happening. Down below.

The walls of her vagina closed around him and tightened, liked a vise.

"Ivak, what's happening?" Gabrielle asked, a little frightened.

"I have no idea. Can you lighten up your grip on my cock? You're cutting off my blood supply."

"Me? You're the one who keeps growing. A woman can only stretch so far."

He tried to move, but couldn't, not even an inch. "Uh-oh!"

Arching her back in an attempt to undulate against him, she realized that something was wrong. "What?"

"I'm stuck."

Her jaw dropped. Her eyes went wide. Then she burst out laughing. "This has never happened to me before," she said.

"And you think it has for me? I have talents, but this is not one of them."

"What should we do?"

"How would I know? Okay, here's the plan. I'll kiss you and play with your breasts so that you can moisten more and I can slip out?"

"Like a lube job?"

That sounded like a trick question to him. "Um. Sort of."

"Idiot! I'm already slick enough. This isn't a question of oiling up the dick."

He cringed at her blunt language.

Suddenly, he felt a pulling sensation on his shoulder blades. The blue mist rose, swirling around them, and his cock began to move. Tentatively, he began his long strokes. He was able to draw out, even though it seemed as if her inner walls had developed a thousand pulling tentacles trying to hold him in. He didn't think he'd mention that to her, especially since she was staring up at him as if he'd invented chocolate . . . or sex.

"That feels so good," she said.

Good was an understatement. Mind-blowing wonderful would be more accurate.

He experimented with rotating his hips. Amazing! He alternated with thrusts that were deep and slow. More amazing! "Can you corkscrew?" he asked.

"What?" she huffed out.

"Never mind. I'll teach you later." He was huffing, too.

After losing count of the number of times he'd thrust into her spasming folds, he began to worry. Gabrielle had already experienced several small peakings and she was writhing mindlessly, crying out for a final release. Perspiration beaded on his body, and an overwhelming urge for climax roared in his ears. He needed that culmination, too.

"Help me," she pleaded. Then, as if some divine inspiration had occurred to her, she smiled softly, pulled his face down close to her, and whispered, "I love you, Viking."

That was the trigger he needed.

As her body began to convulse wildly, his mounting urgency ended. He slammed into her, reared his head back, and let loose into a swirling mist of ecstasy. Their mutual shattering went on and on.

He, with all his myriad sexual activities over a thousand years, had never experienced anything like this. As his heart slowed to a mere pounding, he rolled over on his side, taking her with him, her face resting on his chest. He kissed the top of her head.

After several long moments, she raised up and asked, "What just happened?"

He knew, and it was something he'd never expected to say. "Love."

Twenty-One

Love hurts, for sure . . .

Gabrielle was in a state of wonder and disbelief.

It was a cliché to say that Ivak Sigurdsson had rocked her world, but he had. Literally. Gabrielle had never had sex like that before. She didn't believe any woman had.

"You love me?" she asked, raising her head from his chest, which was damp with sweat from their energetic bout of lovemaking. She had been perspiring, too. They would take a shower soon.

"Yes," he replied with a tone of surprise in his voice that should have offended her, but she understood what it implied. This thing between them was too remarkable. He reached over and laid his lips against hers, being careful that his fangs did not cut her. He looked sad, though, and that did offend her.

"Why are you so unhappy?"

"Not unhappy. Never that. What we just shared is a memory I shall cherish forever."

She sat up and pulled the sheet up over breasts, staring down at him. "That sounds rather ominous."

He rolled over to his back and ran his fingertips along

her arms and up to cup her face. "I have nothing to offer you, Gabrielle. Oh, I don't mean monetary things; cash or worldly goods are easily accessed. But I can't give you a future."

"Oh please! The commitment phobia already!"

He shook his head. "That's not what I mean."

"I hope this isn't about the sterility issue. Love is the most important thing. If children become important, they can be adopted."

"Heartling, you warm this long-dead heart. I hope to be with you as long as possible, but I know without a doubt that Mike will be calling me on the angelic carpet any minute or day or week now. It will end, no matter what I may want. Do not doubt that."

Gabrielle's heart ached at that prospect, but at the moment she cared more about how sad Ivak was. It took every ounce of courage Gabrielle had to say, "Well, then, let's enjoy every moment we can have together.

He smiled up at her. "Do you have anything in mind?"

"Well, how about a shower?"

"I have a better idea. Do you have any bubble bath?"

She laughed. "You? A big macho Viking wants a bubble bath?"

His cheeks heightened with color. "I'm fairly certain my brother Vikar takes bubble baths with his wife. The idea always intrigued me."

"A bubble bath it is, then." Before she got of bed, though, she leaned down and kissed first one of his fangs, then the other. "I love you, darling."

For the next day and night, until Monday morning, they made love in every way and place conceivable in her small apartment. They slept only in short spurts and ate takeout or whatever she had in her cupboard. It was as if a time clock was ticking away, and they had to grab every chance they had to be together.

Toward dawn on Monday, they made love for what might be the last time. She had that appointment with Thor and Luc in the Baton Rouge Federal Court's office at ten a.m. And Ivak had to get back to Angola.

Ivak awakened her by walking his fingers up her leg to her belly button. He was lying on his side, braced on an elbow, staring down at her. His long hair was loose but tucked behind his ears. She loved his hair. She loved running her fingers through his hair. She loved him.

"You were snoring," he said, smiling.

"I do not snore."

"It was a cute snore."

"I do not snore."

"Whate'er you say, dearling." He waggled his eyebrows at her.

"Again? Haven't you depleted your chest of sexual tricks yet?"

He had in fact shown her the Blended O, the G-spot Tickle, the Corkscrew, and many other amazing feats. "Hah! We've scarcely tapped the chest. But this time, I think I would like to try something different."

"Uh-oh!"

"I just want to make love to my beloved."

She put her fingers to her mouth to stifle a sob.

"You are not to move. Just let me adore you."

And he did.

He was beside her, at first, then over her. He turned her, this way and that. Every inch of her body was ministered to by his hands, and lips, and teeth, even his fangs that were starting to emerge. With each touch, he murmured compliments or made naughty suggestions, and melted her farther and farther 'til she feared she would dissolve and he would not be there to put her back together. Over and over he drove her to the point of madness, then withdrew. Each time the wave of arousal rose higher and higher. His hands created magic, and she was powerless to resist.

"You're torturing me," she said.

"Shall I stop?"

"Don't you dare."

He chuckled and continued his sweet torment.

Oh, she was not as passive as he'd suggested. Her hands ran over the supple muscles of his back, including the bumps on his shoulder blades that seemed to be particularly sensitive. She rubbed her calves over his furred legs. She kissed him everywhere that she could reach.

A dreamy intimacy surrounded them. No sign of the blue mist, but she felt like they were in some unworldly cocoon nonetheless.

When he eased inside her and began his long strokes, their eyes held. "I love you," he said.

"I love you, too," she whispered, then arched upward and turned her head to the side. "Do it."

"No, no," he said.

"I want you to." She drew his face down to her.

And while he continued to thrust inside her, his fangs sank into her neck. It didn't hurt, or not much. No worse than a shot. But then it felt wonderful as she felt the draw on her blood.

He was murmuring his pleasure against her skin as his thrusts were short and hard into her vagina, which was rippling with the most incredible, endless orgasm. Then he withdrew his fangs and arched his back as his own climax overtook him. She imagined she could feel his sperm hitting her womb.

Later, as they lay side by side, sated, they murmured softly.

"Call me after your meeting," he said.

"I will. I'm afraid to be hopeful."

"Don't let Tante Lulu hear you say that."

She smiled. "Will I see you again?"

"Of course. As much or as long as I'm able."

She nodded.

"Don't be sad, heartling. You are the best thing that ever happened to me. I can only be thankful for that."

Sometimes the wheels of justice move faster than others . . .

Gabrielle arrived fifteen minutes early at Judge Thibault's chambers in the Baton Rouge Federal Court Building. Luc was already there in the waiting room.

He took one look at her and burst out laughing.

"What?" she asked.

"You look different. Did you have work done? Maybe a shot of Botox in your lips? Since Saturday night?"

She knew what he was referring to. Her lips were kiss-swollen. That's why she hadn't applied any lipstick when she'd got ready this morning. She looked like Angelina Jolie, and not in a good way.

Before she had a chance to reply, he spoke again. "Or maybe it's the chemical peel on your face. I know about those because Charmaine talked my wife, Sylvie, into one a few years back. She looked like a boiled crawfish. Talk about!"

He was referring to the whisker burns. If he only knew where else she had them. Actually, he probably did know.

"Oh my God! I better go to the ladies' room and put on more makeup."

"Not to worry, *chère*. I'm the only one who'll notice. Besides, I was just teasing."

Thor came in then and the three of them discussed various things about Leroy's case and how it would be affected by Hebert's recant of court testimony, the only evidence against him in the murder of another inmate. Just before the secretary told them to go into the judge's chambers, Gabrielle couldn't resist asking Thor, "Aren't you going to make a remark about my appearance?"

He chuckled. "I'm a Norseman. I don't need to ask."

"What does that mean?"

"You've been with a Viking, obviously. Enough said."

Gabrielle rolled her eyes.

"Hey, we say the same thing about Cajuns," Luc said to Thor.

"What? You wanna have a pissing contest over which men are more virile?" Thor countered.

"Not a pissing contest. A fucking contest." Luc laughed then and clapped Thor on the shoulder.

At her tsking sounds and a remark of "Men!" the two idiots ducked their heads and apologized for their crudity in front of her.

They went into the chamber then where Judge Thibault, a middle-aged man with a receding hairline, waited for them on one side of a conference table. There was a court stenographer there, too, to take notes.

Right off, the judge looked at Luc and said, "Luc! Good to see you again? How's your aunt?"

"Tante Lulu is great. I swear she'll outlive us all." Turning to Gabrielle, he explained, "Tante Lulu and Judge Thibault's grandmother used to go to USO dances together during World War II."

Was there anyone that Tante Lulu didn't have a connection to?

The judge looked at Thor then and asked, "Roberts-son, good to see you again. You still have that boat out on Lake Pontchartrain?"

"Yes, sir, although I haven't had much time to go out this year."

"Time!" The judge sighed. "A problem we all have."

She was introduced to the judge then, and the three of them sat down on the opposite side of the table.

The judge opened a folder . . . presumably Leroy's case file . . . and studied it for a few moments. "The other judges on this court, and myself, have studied the request for an appeal. It's granted. I'll turn this back to district court in East Feliciana Parish where Mr. Sonnier was convicted of the prison murder."

What? Just like that they had been granted an appeal? Stunned, Gabrielle turned to the lawyers on either side of her. She realized then that it truly did help to know the right people.

"I'll send this material to the prosecutor there and alert him to the fact that you'll be contacting him for a court date," the judge concluded, closing the folder. "I doubt it will ever go to trial."

And just like that, they were done. Leroy was going to get his day in court . . . his new day in court.

"By the way, Dolly Landeaux from down Lafayette way gave me a call last week and told me to work my ass off to move this case off my desk," the judge told them just before he left. "If you know Dolly, you know she'd come here and give me a shove, if she had to." They could hear his continuing chuckles in his wake.

So, Gabrielle would have to add Dolly, the parole board member whom she'd thought had been so unhelpful, to the list of people she would never be able to thank enough.

When they were walking outside to their respective cars, Gabrielle asked, "What next?"

"We meet with the DA in East Feliciana."

"When? I mean, how long will it take?"

"As long as he wants," Thor said. "Honestly, Gabrielle, it could be tomorrow or months from now."

Her shoulders slumped.

"Hey, *chère*, look at where you are today compared to several weeks ago," Luc reminded her.

Thor added, " I work in Baton Rouge. This is record time for a appeal decision."

When she got to the car, though, Gabrielle didn't leave right away. Instead, she sat there, dazed, and started to weep, then sobbed into a wad of tissues. Mostly, they were tears of relief.

Finally under control, she called Ivak's cell number. He picked up immediately.

"Gabrielle? What happened?"

"They've granted the appeal."

"So soon?"

"Well, I think Tante Lulu being a buddy of the judge's grandmother might have helped."

"Good old Tante Lulu!" Ivak said. She could hear the smile in his voice.

"Will you tell Leroy for me? And ask him to call me first chance he gets?"

"Of course."

"You might want to alert the warden about today's events, too."

"With pleasure. I wish I could take a photograph of his face for you when I do."

She found herself smiling, too. "I miss you already," she said softly.

"Same here, sweetling."

"When will I see you again?" She shouldn't have asked that question, shouldn't be pressuring him, but she couldn't help herself.

"As soon as possible. We're still under tight security here at Angola, and there's a strong presence of Lucies in and around the prison."

Now she would be worried about his safety. "Are your brothers and the additional . . . uh . . . vangels still around?"

"Mordr and Harek are, and about thirty vangel warriors. Don't worry. We'll take care of the problem shortly."

"I love you," she said then.

"Ah, Gabrielle! It warms my heart to hear you say that. I love you, too."

After she hung up with Ivak, Gabrielle wanted to make one more call. It rang quite a while before an out-of-breath voice said, "Hello!"

"Tante Lulu?"

"Yep. Is that you, Gabrielle?"

"Yes. You sound like you're having trouble breathing. Are you okay?"

"Good as rain. I was outside pickin' okra in my garden when I heard the phone ring. I forgot to bring the cell phone out with me."

"I have good news, Tante Lulu. They're granting Leroy a new trial."

"Thank you, Jesus! We'll have to celebrate. Why dontcha come back here and I'll call the fam'ly ta come over? I already got one of my Peachy Praline Cobbler Cakes in the oven."

"Not today. I have too much work to do back at my office, and, really, we're still a long way from getting Leroy out. Still, it was a good day, and I want to thank you for all your help."

"I dint do nuthin'. You know who you gotta thank, dontcha, girl?"

She did. When Gabrielle clicked off her cell phone, she bowed her head and said, "Thank you, St. Jude."

She could swear the bobble-head St. Jude doll on her dashboard, a gift from Tante Lulu, winked at her.

Silence can be golden . . . or not . . .

For the next few weeks, Ivak talked to Gabrielle every day, but he was unable to be with her. Everything was happening all at once, keeping him confined to the prison.

First, he and his brothers Mordr and Harek were planning a sweeping campaign against the Lucies to be held the day before the rodeo. It was their belief that the Lucies, under Jasper's direction now, were planning a grand finale here at Angola to coincide with the last rodeo of the month and all the distractions that would be occupying the prison staff.

Second, with everything that had been happening in Leroy's case, Ivak was keeping an especially vigilant eye on him. Ofttimes when a prisoner was up for release, other inmates tried to get him in trouble. A case of jealousy, mostly, but sometimes they provoked trouble just because they were downright mean. The same was true of some prison staff. There was one red-haired guard in particular that concerned Ivak. He was always there whenever Ivak saw Leroy, and he always seemed to find something wrong.

Then, there was the talent show that was coming along nicely, thanks to Tante Lulu and her family. In fact, so much attention were they getting that a number of TV stations had asked if they could film it. Benton, smart as he was, decided to have it filmed himself and sell the rights to whoever wanted to use it. Benton and René were arguing over that issue, whether Benton had the right to profit off the LeDeux family.

Finally, Gabrielle was extremely busy with two new court cases. A thirty-four-year-old woman who was put in a women's prison ten years ago for killing a husband who had beaten her mercilessly . . . Gabrielle was trying to get a lesser sentence for her. And then she was also working with a young boy who had robbed a gas station using a pistol. Apparently having a weapon, even with a minor robbery, was enough to get a youthling tried as an adult. Gabrielle had a soft heart, and her job at Second Chances allowed her to use her sympathies for good causes.

If that wasn't enough, Ivak's purchase of Heaven's End was going ahead full-throttle. Faster than he was ready to handle. He had a closing scheduled for next Friday, with Thor handling the legal details. And Tante Lulu had already made arrangements on his behalf to have a landscape firm come in and make a preliminary effort to clear out the jungle. It would be no small feat because apparently there were at least a hundred acres with the place. Just in case he wanted to raise sugar sometime, Thor had pointed out. In jest, Ivak hoped.

But Ivak's biggest worry was Michael's silence.

Twenty-Two

There's a bimbo in every woman just waiting to
come out . . .

Finally, the day of the rodeo arrived, and Gabrielle kept checking her compact mirror to see if she looked all right. She would be seeing Ivak today.

"Settle down, honey. Yer as nervous as a long-tailed cat in a room full of rockin' chairs," Tante Lulu said from the other side of the backseat. Rusty and Charmaine were in the front seat of the smooth-riding BMW.

The rest of the family was following them in a caravan of cars and vans. Apparently, they needed a lot of equipment and costumes for their Cajun Village People act, which had been transformed for this occasion into the Cajun *fais do do*, loosely interpreted Cajun party. Plus, a few of René's band members would be there, too.

"How was the dress rehearsal yesterday?" Gabrielle asked.

"Wonderful," Charmaine answered. "But I knew it would be. Any production I've been in . . . seems like chaos 'til the last minute, but it always comes together at the last minute."

"They sold out weeks ago," Rusty told them. "The warden is already planning to expand the arena for next year."

"Hah! He better not think we're gonna do this fer him every year," Tante Lulu said.

When they got to Angola, it took them more than an hour to go through heightened security. In fact, two of the earlier rodeos this month had been canceled. They needed today's event to be successful to bring in funds for special programs. As a result, every single guard was on duty today. And any person entering the penitentiary grounds went through screening devices brought in especially for the occasion. Women had to check their purses. Men had to empty their pockets. Prison officials were taking no chances of hidden weapons.

Finally, they were inside, and the first thing she saw was Ivak. He was wearing his clerical collar under a short-sleeved button-down shirt tucked into blue jeans. Very respectable. The gleam of knowing in his eyes was not.

He smiled and walked straight to her, squeezing both her hands in his as he kissed her cheek. It was the discreet thing to do in front of everyone, especially in his minister attire.

Tante Lulu just chuckled and said something about a hope chest being almost ready.

Ivak took her hand and laced his fingers with hers. No one noticed because the rest of the LeDeux clan and friends were trailing in, chattering and laughing.

"Where's Leroy?" she whispered to Ivak.

"In the auditorium with the other talent show contestants. I'll have to go back in a minute. I've missed you, sweetling."

She nodded, her eyes telling him more than words could.

Just then, she heard Tante Lulu ask Luc, "Whass that stuff yer carryin'?"

"Sylvie's outfit for the show." It was a scrap of red cloth and red high heels. "She tripped over a loose carpet last night and sprained her ankle. The doctor told her to keep it elevated today."

"Ah, thass too bad. I'll call her later," Tante Lulu said. "I have some gator spit ointment that'll fix her up jist fine."

"Who's going to take Sylvie's place in the act?" Charmaine asked.

There was a pause, then everyone turned to Gabrielle.

"What? No, no, no! I don't sing."

"All you gotta do is move yer lips and shake yer booty," Tante Lulu said.

Shake my booty? In front of ten thousand people? Are you nuts?

Remy's wife, Rachel, spoke up then. "I know how you're feeling, Gabrielle. I felt the same way the first year they tricked me into participating. But, honestly, all you have to do is sing a few doo-wops and watch our dance steps."

"Dancing, too?" She was horrified and her voice must have said so.

Tante Lulu narrowed her eyes at Gabrielle. "Are you sayin' yer not willin' ta make a sacrifice fer the cause?"

That's how Gabrielle got conned into being part of a loony-bird Cajun musical act.

"A velvet bulldozer, that's what we call Tante Lulu," Tee-John's wife, Celine, told Gabrielle.

Luc shoved the red outfit and shoes into Gabrielle's reluctant hands.

When she turned back to Ivak, she saw that he was grinning.

"It's not funny. I'm tone deaf."

"Forget about your singing. I can't wait to see you in

that." He pointed to the spandex dress that looked as if it would fit a pencil.

She had even more misgivings when they did a little practice run in the auditorium. Honestly, these LeDeux were born entertainers. Sexy and funny and talented theatrically, all of which she was not. But she was being a sport. And turned out, she *could* doo-wop. A little.

Leroy pumped a fist in the air when he saw her, and after seeking permission from a scowling red-haired guard to leave his seat with the other contestants in the talent show, he came over to sit beside her. "I didn't know you could sing."

"Please!"

"It wasn't too bad."

"Talk about faint compliments!"

He grinned at her.

"It's good to see you so happy."

"I have hope now. Thanks to you." He squeezed her hand, knowing a hug would probably have the guards pouncing on him.

"Don't thank me. Thank Ivak and Tante Lulu and her family."

He chuckled. "You know who Tante Lulu would tell me to thank, don't you?"

"St. Jude," they both said at the same time.

"Hey, if . . . *when* . . . I get out of here, I'm gonna put his statue smack-dab in the middle of my home."

She wanted to ask him where that home would be, but now was not the time.

"I better get back to my group," he said, squeezing her forearm before standing to leave.

After watching several of the contestants practice one last time, some of whom were really good, she decided to go over and watch the rodeo, which she'd never attended before. When she went up to tell Tante Lulu her intentions, the old lady said she'd stay there, having no interest in watching the rodeo again. Apparently, she'd attended several times.

"Make sure you're at the dressing room by four p.m.," Charmaine interjected. "The rodeo should be winding down by then, and the talent show starting. I'll bring your outfit."

Thanks a bunch. I was hoping it could get lost. "There's a dressing room?"

"An office in the stable," Charmaine informed her with a laugh. "Don't worry. I brought my makeup case."

That is just great! Like lipstick and eye shadow are my biggest concerns!

"An' I got air freshener in my purse, if they let me bring it over there. Doan wanna faint from smellin' horse poop."

She carries air freshener in her purse. Good Lord! Between the pistol she mentioned once before, all the St. Jude statues, air freshener, and God only knew what else, the thing must weigh a ton.

"I'll go with you to the rodeo," Rachel offered. "I've never seen it before, either."

Ivak muttered something about it being no great loss. Gabrielle already knew how he felt about the prison rodeo.

Remy, Rachel's husband, came up to her, a worried frown on his brow, both the good and damaged sides. "Are you sure it's safe, honey?"

"I'll be fine." She leaned up and kissed his cheek. On his scarred side.

When they went to the door and told the guard they wanted to go to the rodeo grounds, he told them they'd have to have an escort. He motioned for someone behind them to come forward, and of all people it was the red-haired guard. The surly man remained silent the whole way through the dreary corridors and checkpoints and out to a prison vehicle.

Rachel crawled in the backseat first and the guard asked Gabrielle before she followed, "Are you Sigurdsson's whore?"

"I beg your pardon."

"Word is that you're sleeping with the . . . chaplain."

"If I were you, I'd stop right there. Do you really want me to report you to the warden?" She glanced pointedly at his name tag, which read "Roland O'Malley."

"Go right ahead. No skin off my ass." He went to the driver's door, not even waiting for her to get in and close the back door.

"What did he say?" Rachel whispered to her.

"Later," Gabrielle whispered back, but she knew her heated face must be a clue that she was angry.

The man didn't say a word the whole way, and neither did she and Rachel. When they got to the crowded rodeo grounds, he just sat there, letting them get out themselves. When she glared at him, he smirked. She couldn't let him get away with such behavior. Walking over to his open driver's window, she said, "You could lose your job over this."

He shrugged and drove away.

"That was weird," Rachel said once Gabrielle told her what the guard had said to her. "You really should report him."

"I will. Later. Oh my goodness! Look at this!" There was a sign that said, "Rodeo Sold Out, Hobbycraft Tickets Only." That's not what amazed her. What did was the fact that not only would the rodeo arena hold ten thousand people, but there was a prison craft fair already drawing at least a thousand more people.

She and Rachel bought their tickets and bypassed the prison museum, neither of them having an inclination

to see old electric chairs, sample prison cells, an array
of homemade prison weapons, and such. Instead, they
strolled through what could only be described as a giant
flea market, all run by and benefiting the individual convicts.

The men, clearly identified as inmates by their white
T-shirts and denim pants, some with name tags, sold all
kinds of food. The usual hot dogs, hamburgers, French
fries, onion rings, nachos, pizza, funnel cakes, snow
cones, cotton candy, and candy apples, but also po' boys,
barbecued ribs, tacos, grilled chicken, fried catfish,
gumbo and jambalaya, baked potatoes and rice, crack-
lin's, and salads. Numerous signs warned that no food or
drinks could be taken into the arena. So, all about, people
were enjoying the food. Never mind that it had been made
by inmate hands, maybe even a murderer's.

She got a cheeseburger and soda, while Rachel bought
a grilled chicken sandwich with a lemonade. Delicious!

Despite all the criticism of Warden Benton, she had to
give him credit for allowing the inmates to make items
with the freedom to sell their products on rodeo days.
And he'd taken Angola from one of the bloodiest prisons
in the world to one in which prison violence was drasti-
cally cut. The only other money the inmates could earn
was two cents an hour for prison labor by the majority of
inmates and twenty cents an hour for trusties. Yes, Benton
did some good, despite some of his methods.

Gabrielle had heard a story one time about the earli-
est days of Angola Prison when one of the disciplinary
actions was to place an inmate in an iron casket buried
in the ground for a period of time. Gabrielle shouldn't be
surprised by man's inhumanity to man, but she was, even
if it was convicts. What if something like that had ever
happened to her brother? She stiffened at the thought.

Aside from souvenir T-shirts and caps—like Gabrielle

would ever want to wear an Angola Prison shirt!—there was everything from jewelry to wooden lawn furniture. All kinds of things tooled from leather, not the least of which were belts. Woodcarving had been taken to an art form; it was obvious these men must have worked year-long on these projects. Several paintings were displayed on handmade easels, including a beautiful one of Angola that eerily depicted the coldness of the buildings contrasted with the bucolic setting. Ordinarily, Leroy would be required to man the table selling subscriptions to the prison newspaper.

Wanting to support the inmates, she bought a carved angel and figured she could always give it to Ivak. But, no, she had the perfect spot on the top of her bookcase. Rachel bought two wooden bowls and a carved alligator for one of her children.

While all this was going on, an inmate band was playing raucous versions of popular songs.

It was time for them to enter the arena. Given complimentary tickets, they found themselves on the fifth row of the bleachers, center field. To her surprise, Ivak soon slipped into the space next to her. At her raised eyebrows, he said, "I was able to get away for a little while. Tante Lulu and the others are having lunch with Selma."

"Selma?"

"Selma Dubois, the warden's assistant. You met her, remember."

"Oh, I remember." The woman who had flirted with him. "You didn't want to do lunch with Sell-mah?" she inquired sweetly.

He winked at her, recognizing her spurt of jealousy.

She hated when he winked at her because she liked it so much.

A trumpet blared then, causing the crowd to quiet down and look to the other end of the arena.

"Wait until you see this," Ivak warned.

Out came three inmates on black horses wearing white robes and gold rope belts. And fake feathered angel wings.

"A lot of chickens gave their lives for those props," Ivak remarked with dry humor.

"Are you kidding me? Angels?" Rachel said.

Gabrielle was staring, mouth agape. She soon understood the significance of the angels when Warden Benton, wearing a cowboy hat and boots, rode out on a white horse, carrying a banner that read: "JESUS SAVES!"

The crowd cheered as the warden and his three angels galloped in tandem around the arena. Thus began the official rodeo opening.

The Angola Rough Riders came out then. All the convicts participating in the rodeo were required to wear black and white striped shirts reminiscent of old-time convict uniforms. Each of these riders carried flags, all the flags that had flown over Louisiana through the years, according to the voice on the loudspeaker. The most surprising was an elderly black man holding up a Confederate flag. The ACLU would have a field day!

"Are y'all ready for Bust Out?" the announcer yelled.

About ten thousand people minus three answered, "YES!"

Eight bucking horses carrying convicts burst out of chutes at the same time. It was pitiful to see how quickly the men hit the dirt. A few limped off the field, waving to the crowd.

With the bull riding, an inmate had to stay on the snorting animal at least eight seconds to score points. Only two of the twelve managed that feat.

"Have you noticed how young the participants are?" Ivak asked. When neither she nor Rachel answered, he said, "It's because young bones heal faster."

Next came Convict Poker. Four convicts sat at a table

in the middle of the arena, pretending to be unconcerned about the thousand-pound, foam-flying bull that came barreling toward them. The last person sitting was the winner. And the way the man . . . no more than nineteen . . . was raising his fist jubilantly, you'd have thought he'd won an Olympic gold medal.

If the Convict Poker wasn't pathetic enough, next came Guts and Glory. A red chip worth one hundred dollars was strung between an angry bull's horns, and thirty convicts ran around the arena trying to grab the prize.

This rodeo reminded Gabrielle of the Roman Colosseum events where inexperienced people were pitted against gladiator warriors or wild lions. Especially the way the crowd cheered, as if wanting to see blood.

"Does anyone ever get hurt?" she asked.

"Of course," he said, "but the warden would tell you that they all volunteered to participate."

"I can only imagine how I'd feel if it was Leroy out there."

They left before the end of the rodeo. Ivak went back to the prison to gather his talent show contestants. René's band was already setting up on the stage.

A short time later, Gabrielle was in a prison stable being turned into a Cajun bimbo. The red spandex dress did, in fact, fit . . . if being molded skin-tight to every bump and curve on her body counted as fitting. The other women wore the same dress and high heels, but in different colors. Tante Lulu's was bright yellow, and with her blond wig, she looked like either a daffodil or a canary. With a tease comb and a can of hair spray, Charmaine had given the rest of them big hair, too. They'd applied their own makeup. Celine, Tee-John's wife, leaned over and whispered to Gabrielle, "Every year I swear it's the last time I'll do this act, but I get conned into it every time."

"Same here. Except in my case it's my husband who manipulates me into coming." This from Valerie LeDeux, normally a very dignified lawyer, now sexed up into a bluebell tart. Gabrielle had seen her on TV in her conservative suits and skinned back hair. She was married to René LeDeux.

"I can only guess how René manipulates you, Val," Charmaine said with a laugh. "God bless *man*-ipulation."

"Well, it's definitely my one and only time," Gabrielle avowed.

"We'll see," said Grace Sabato, a friend of Tante Lulu's. Apparently, she'd been a nun at one time. Hard to imagine when seeing the redhead in the sexy green dress.

None of them had any way of knowing how they looked, except through each other's eyes, since there was no full-length mirror. Gabrielle was afraid to find out.

But then, Gabrielle was the first one out of the stable. And boy-howdy! did she find out!

Ivak had been walking up some steps when he saw her. He tripped and almost fell on his face, especially when she turned and wiggled her butt a little to show him the full effect of the dress. All he said was: "Oh my God!"

Since Ivak never swore, Gabrielle figured he must be praying.

She took that for a good sign.

His new favorite color was red . . .

Once Ivak was able to stand without keeling over, he grabbed Gabrielle by the arm and pulled her to the side. Already, she was drawing attention to herself. No surprise there! She would make a perfect poster for SEX.

Make sure you save that dress, sweetling, and definitely those shoes. I have plans! "Are you out of your friggin' mind? You can't come out here like that!" he snarled.

"Like what?"

Does she really not know how she looks? "Like sex in an ice cream cone with five thousand sex-starved men just wanting a lick. Forget lick. They'd want to do a lot more than that." *I certainly do.*

"Don't you think you're overreacting?"

He counted silently to ten in Old Norse. "Gabrielle! I can see your nipples."

She glanced downward. "Oh. I should have put Band-Aids on them like Charmaine suggested."

I am not picturing that. Not, not, not! "Or you could wear a *brynja* over your dress."

"What's that?"

"Chain mail."

"You had no problem with the dress when you saw Luc hand it to me earlier."

"I had no idea just how revealing it would be." *Medieval men had the right idea when they put chastity belts on their women and locked them in towers.*

Ivak's eyes went wide as he saw something even more alarming over Gabrielle's shoulder.

It was Charmaine in a hot pink outfit.

She could pose for Playboy *in that thing and not even have to be naked to have two million men jerking off.* "You women are going to cause a riot."

He shoved them all back into the stable and told them to wait until he brought a van. Soon he drove them around the arena to the back of the stage where the Swamp Rats were already warming up the crowd. He raised his brows when he saw Luc, Remy, Rusty, Angel, and Tee-John wearing cowboy outfits, minus shirts. Well, Remy and Rusty wore vests with no shirts, but Luc and Tee-John wore Western shirts fully unsnapped, exposing their bare chests. "Don't ask," Remy said. Both Remy and Rusty were scowling, obviously *reluctant* cowboy performers.

This whole family is barmy.

But he had no more time to think about what they were up to. He had a talent show to put on. René gave the signal for his band to stop playing and for Ivak to come up onto the stage. Turns out Warden Benton came out, too, from the other side.

Before Ivak had a chance to speak, Benton took the microphone and said, "Welcome to the first annual Angola Prisoner Talent Show. I can't tell you how hard we've worked to pull this together."

We? Benton hadn't lifted one finger to help with the talent show auditions or practices.

"We hope to make this an annual event, and we think you'll agree after you see the entertainment we have provided for you. After all the contestants have performed, a panel of trusty judges will pick the winner. A prize of one hundred dollars has been donated by Jerry's Ford Dealership over St. Francis way."

Wow! Talk about generosity!

"Now for a word from my assistant on this project." Benton smiled at Ivak and slapped a hand on his shoulder as if they were best buds.

Whatever.

Ivak was pleased to see most of the crowd stick around and be enthusiastic about his twenty contestants, although it was approaching the dinner hour. They were probably waiting for the LeDeux musical extravaganza, but, hey, he'd take his perks however he could get them.

The most amazing thing happened to Ivak then as each of the individuals or groups came up to the stage. He was proud. Not of himself, but of them.

Leroy was amazing on the trumpet, especially when

one of the inmates joined in near the end singing a bluesy rendition of "Stormy Weather."

When Calvin Corl, the skinny black lifer from Alabama, sang "Amazing Grace," the crowd grew silent, then burst into a standing ovation at the end.

Ivak might have got a tear in his eyes.

Calvin was so happy. Whether he won or not didn't matter.

"Sonny and Cher" were hilarious. The tap dancing wasn't half bad. The gymnast did an impossible double back flip and almost landed off the stage. Some of the other singers were more than okay. An inmate had come to Ivak at the last minute asking if he could play the piano, and his rendition of Mozart's Fifth Piano Sonata had the house . . . rather arena . . . stunned.

In no time, all the contestants had performed. The convict judges would deliberate while the LeDeuxs performed, with a winner announced at the end. Ivak had already had to have one of the judges excluded when he learned that the man had been trying to sell his vote among the contestants. What the idiot had been asking for in exchange didn't bear mentioning. Think blow-job times three.

René and his band were coming up the steps while he went down. René shook his hand and said, "Man, that was incredible!"

And Tante Lulu, who looked like she'd swallowed a can of yellow paint, said, "Mebbe next year when we do a charity event at Swampy's, you could run a talent show."

I don't think so! "We can talk about it later."

Gabrielle's eyes were misty with emotion as she hugged him warmly and said, "Do you have any idea what you did for those men? You really are an angel." Tante Lulu was yanking on her to come with the other women; so Gabrielle gave him a quick kiss and said, "Wait for me."

As if he would leave her here alone!

Rene's band, without any introduction, immediately launched into that famous Johnny Cash song "Folsom Prison Blues," but whenever they came to the lyrics involving Folsom, they changed it to Angola. The spectators loved it, especially the convicts, who went wild with applause, singing along.

Folding chairs had been moved into the arena to supplement the regular bleachers. Ivak sat in the front row, not far from Benton and his pals, some legislators and businessmen he'd invited.

The band played several Cajun songs that would appeal to inmates: "Les Barres de la Prison," or "Prison Bars." "It's Lonesome in Prison." And "Convict Waltz." Then they blasted out a lighter song, a lively rendition of "Diggy Diggy Lo."

When they were done with that song, René took the microphone and said, "Has anyone noticed what's missing up on this stage?"

A whole lot of men yelled out, "Women!"

René smiled and said, "I don't know why you say that. Hey, look at me. Me, I'm so pretty!" He paused for effect and raised his arms, doing a slow turn with a little shake of his butt before crooning, "I'm sexy and I know it."

The crowd knew what was coming and burst out laughing. It was the lead-in to that popular song of the same name by the musical group with the ridiculous name, LMFAO. In other words Laughing My Fucking Ass Off. Some modern people had a warped sense of humor.

At René's cue, the band began playing the up-tempo song, and out snake-danced the five men and seven women, all singing the suggestive lyrics. They were good. All of them. But the spectators' eyes were on the women in their sexy, skin-tight dresses and sex-on-the-hoof high heels as they shimmied and rolled their hips and shook their bottoms, laughing the whole time. Even Gabrielle. Especially Gabrielle.

Warden Benton's eyes went wide when he first saw what the women were wearing. He never would have allowed it, if he'd known ahead of time. Soon he relaxed, however, and enjoyed the show.

The band played several more numbers, both country and popular, with René doing a running commentary to amuse the crowd. He especially enjoyed teasing his backup singers and dancers whom he joked were going to try out for some reality TV show. At least, Ivak thought he was joking. You never knew when Tante Lulu was involved.

"What reality show? *Idiots Who Get Conned by Morons*?" Rusty snapped.

"Now, now. You have to understand, folks, that Rusty here is a real cowboy. Has his own ranch. Talk about sexy and he knows it."

Some of the ladies in the audience whistled and one of them yelled, "I'm available, cowboy!"

Charmaine pushed her way to the forefront, put an arm around a blushing Rusty's shoulder, and said into the mic, "He's taken, honey. They all are."

There was an exaggerated feminine moan that rippled through the audience.

Tante Lulu went up to the mic, which had to be lowered to accommodate her height. "Hope y'all are havin' fun."

Wild clapping ensued.

"We wanted ta do somethin' special fer our fin-all-lay, an' a little bird gave me an idea."

All the men and some of the women behind her scowled, wondering if one of their feathery brothers had turned them in.

Bird? She probably means St. Jude.

"You could say this person who's gonna lead our fin-all-lay is an angel."

Uh-oh! No way! She wouldn't.

"Didja ever see that John Travolta movie *Michael*?"

She would! Ivak wondered if he could sneak out without anyone noticing.

"Dint you jist love how Michael the Archangel could dance? Betcha he could teach even us LeDeux some moves."

Ivak slunk down in his chair.

"An' the best part is the man with all this same talent is one of yer very own people here in the pokey."

Warden Benton looked right and left to see who it might be.

The band began to play that Aretha Franklin song "Chain of Fools," and Tante Lulu motioned toward him. "C'mon, Ivak."

"You?" the warden asked, clearly shocked.

Ivak was rather offended by the shock. Did the warden think he was a humorless, rhythmless fellow?

Truth to tell, vangels had time on their hands between missions and could practice fighting skills or praying or twiddling their thumbs only so much. They watched a lot of TV and movies. *Michael* was a favorite of some of them. Not him, but others. As a result, he and his brothers knew the "Chains" dance moves very well.

Standing, Ivak went to the stage, like a man on the way to the gallows. Gabrielle caught his eye then, and he could see that this was a surprise to her, too. He pulled her forward to stand beside him. Then, closing his eyes, he let the rhythm of the song seep into his bones. At first he just swayed from side to side. Then two dance steps to the right, followed by two steps to the left, over and over, eventually twirling and moving about the stage. Fortunately, Gabrielle and the others were following him perfectly. Even Rusty and Remy.

In fact, so well was the catchy song-and-dance routine

going over that many in the audience were standing and dancing along with them. Everyone sang along at the catchy "Chains, chains, chains" refrain. The cameraman filming the rodeo and talent show was having a field day with Ivak's contribution. To his everlasting mortification, Ivak got a standing ovation and a call for "More, more, more!"

Hah! Not bloody likely!

The talent show winner was announced then. It was Calvin. The old man was moved to tears and hugged Ivak, thanking him profusely.

As the crowds left the arena, the warden, his friends, and the LeDeuxs stood around talking about what a success the event had been.

Ivak asked Tante Lulu if one of his brothers had blabbed to her.

"You have brothers?' the old lady asked. At his confusion, she told him, "The saints talk to each other, you know."

Was she implying that St. Michael had outed him to St. Jude?

He was about to ask her just that but she was off to the side already, yakking away at Calvin . . . about St. Jude, no doubt.

"Will you be home in New Orleans tonight?" he asked Gabrielle.

She nodded. "Will you come?"

"I'll try, but it might be very late." He didn't want to tell her, but the big assault against the Lucies still remaining in the Angola area had fallen through last night, but would definitely be held tonight. After this, Louisiana would hopefully no longer be a Lucipire enclave. Oh, he had no delusions about wiping them out altogether, but if he and his brothers, who were just waiting for his signal, could destroy the majority, the demons would have to hover close to some other nest.

"I'm off this weekend, so whenever you can get there will be okay." She ran her hand up his bare arm and smiled mischievously when he shivered. "Have you heard from Michael?"

Knowing that she referred to Michael's reaction to their sexual activity, he shook his head. The silence from above was ominous. Maybe the big guy was waiting until the Lucie mission was completed before dealing with Ivak's transgressions.

"One thing," he suggested to Gabrielle, running his hand up her arm now and watching with equal satisfaction as *she* shivered. "Can you be wearing the red dress and high heels?"

He had to give his girl credit for quick thinking because she immediately countered, "As long as you give me a personal demonstration of the *Michael* dance. Naked."

Twenty-Three

They celebrated the way all soldiers do ... with beer ...

The battle between the vangels and Lucies in Louisiana was almost anticlimactic.

Ivak used vangels as bait within Angola and in the surrounding parishes to lure the Lucies into the swamps and thick forests surrounding several sides of the prison property. Mordr was an incredible battle strategist. Always had been, even back in Viking times. Now, with the aid of computers and Harek's expertise, Mordr was able to come up with plans almost instantaneously.

Ivak and four of his brothers—Cnut and Sigurd were busy elsewhere—took battle stances along with their legions at four strategic points to catch those Lucies trying to escape. Rather like a vangel net.

A bloody war ensued. Bloody and slimy.

It was too soon for final accounts, but Ivak guessed that they had sent at least three dozen Lucies to their final slime tonight. There didn't appear to have been any haakai about, but perhaps it was too soon after Dominique's passing for new high commanders to have been sent to the region. There had been mighty mungs, though, and they'd fought hard, wounding many of the vangels.

To their almighty regret, the VIK lost three vangels. They were hopefully in Tranquillity now, licking their wounds and waiting the long years until the Final Judgment. Ivak and his brothers always considered it a success when vangels "died" but were not taken by the Lucies to their torture chambers in hopes of turning them. That was truly a fate worse than death.

As their various karls and ceorls did the cleanup work, Ivak and his four brothers gathered in an all-night roadside tavern that was so seedy the drinkers didn't pay any attention to them, even with their long cloaks. The Vikings were drinking beer, of course.

"Do you think we got them all?" Trond asked.

"I doubt it, but the ones who are left . . . I'm guessing less than a dozen . . . will scatter. Unless Jasper assigns a new commander here right away, they won't linger. And there were wounded Lucies, as well, but they'll sneak off to heal somewhere safe." This was Ivak's opinion, anyway.

They spoke of other aspects of the operation and mused on what Michael might have in mind for them next.

"Will you continue to serve at the prison?" Harek asked.

"For now, I will. Until I hear otherwise from Mike."

"Cnut thinks some of us might be sent to the Middle East. Iran is stoking the terrorist fires these days," Mordr said.

There was always some terrorist hot spot these days.

"Where are you working?" Ivak asked Mordr.

"Pfff! Some cruise boat in the Caribbean."

They all looked at him with disbelief.

"You're complaining about being on a longboat?" Ivak asked. "You're a Viking, Mordr. Have you forgotten?"

"And the Caribbean!" Vikar interjected. "Do you remember how cold it was in the Norselands? Nigh froze my balls off betimes."

"Believe you me, a cruise ship is nothing like a longship," Mordr said with disgust. "There are so many hungry women trolling for husbands, and—"

"Definitely you've lost your Viking genes," Harek concluded, "if you think hungry women are a problem."

Ignoring their teasing remarks, Mordr went on, "—and all that sunlight can be a problem. I've been drinking so much Fake-O and having to search out passengers to save, lest my skin turn into Saran Wrap."

"I should have your problems! I swear the sun never shines inside those walls," Ivak said. "Try living with five thousand men with hunger of a different kind. I always have to be watching my back, and I mean that exactly how it sounds."

His brothers grinned at that picture.

"And your girlfriend . . . how is that going?" Harek asked, having met Gabrielle in her New Orleans apartment.

"Good. Great, actually."

"And Mike?" Trond was grinning, having faced a similar situation not so long ago.

"No word yet."

"Uh-oh!" his brothers said as one.

Ivak stood. "I've got to go back to the prison and meet with Jogeir and Svein. Make sure the prison is clear of Lucies. Take a shower. Then . . ."

Four sets of eyebrows raised in unison.

" . . . then I'm off to get my reward for a battle well fought."

"A medal?" Vikar teased.

"More like red high heels," he said, and walked out before his brothers could question him any more.

Back at Horror, the mood was ... well, horrible ...

Jasper was pacing the great hall in his palace named Horror, fury coming off his demonoid body in scales.

He had not been happy when Dominique's domicile had been demolished in New Orleans, not that he regretted her demise, personally. He was better off without her irritating self. But now that he'd learned that dozens and dozens of Lucipires had been destroyed by the vangels, leaving Louisiana and the southern region almost empty of a demon vampire presence, well, that *was* horrible.

To blame was that damn pain-in-the-arse VIK, of course. Every time Jasper raised his ranks significantly, the vangels swooped in to block his growth. It was unacceptable. He made a sweeping slash with his clawed hand and knocked over a glass-topped table and two chairs. The humans being turned down below in his dungeons would be wondering what all the noise was up above. He would take out his fury on them later. Maybe pluck out an eyeball or two or try out the new anal jackhammer.

Just then, Beltane brought in a battered Lucipire. A hordling with red hair and wounds seeping slime over various parts of his body.

"Sorry to disturb you, master, but this man has news about the Louisiana situation," Beltane said.

The red-haired man bowed low until Jasper gave him permission to stand.

After giving a brief report on the pathetic battle, the man whose tattered name tag read "Roland O'Malley" told Jasper, "I believe one of the VIK is serving at Angola where I was a guard. Ivak Sigurdsson, by name. And I believe there is a woman you could use to lure him out."

Ah! Dominique had mentioned this woman being with Sigurdsson, Jasper recalled.

"Beltane, get me that photograph that Dominique sent to me weeks ago."

When Beltane returned, he showed the picture to O'Malley. "Is this the woman?"

O'Malley nodded vigorously. "If we get her, we get him."

If Jasper had even one of the VIK in his hands, he might be able to redeem himself with Lucifer before the Master of Evil found out about the Louisiana debacle.

"Get the wench and bring her here," Jasper ordered the guard, barely restraining himself from rubbing his clawed hands together with glee. That could be painful. Then to Beltane, he said, "Polish up one of the killing jars. It appears we will soon have a new 'butterfly' to play with."

The worst possible thing happened then . . .

Ivak was unable to get to Gabrielle's apartment until the following morning. It was almost noon; so, he'd brought take-out food from Heavenly Eats, a bottle of wine, and a jar of chocolate body paint he'd seen in a French Quarter window on the way here.

His first clue that something was wrong was his knocking on her door and getting no answer. Well, she might have gone out to do an errand. He berated himself for not having phoned to tell her he was on the way.

His second clue was when he tried the door and it was unlocked. Frowning with concern, he went inside and placed his purchases on the coffee table.

His third clue was Gabrielle's purse hanging from a coatrack.

In her bedroom, he saw the red dress lying on the bed, and the red shoes peeking out from the edge of the coverlet on the floor.

The fine hairs stood out on the back of his neck. He walked into the kitchen, where a strange odor emanated. It was the teakettle on the electric stove; the water had boiled out, and the smell was that of hot metal. He turned the heat off and stood, thinking.

Why would Gabrielle leave without her purse, with a teakettle boiling? That's when he noticed something on the floor. He reached down and swiped up the clear substance with a forefinger. Sniffing, he immediately recognized the smell. Sulfur. A Lucie had been here.

Ivak's brain almost exploded with the images that flickered through it with painful stabs. Gabrielle in the hands of the Lucies. His heart was shattering at the implications that nigh brought him to his knees.

Inhaling and exhaling several times to keep himself from flying off in several directions, he tapped Trond's number into his cell phone.

The minute Trond picked up, Ivak asked, "Do you know how to contact Zeb?"

Zebulan was a double agent . . . a Lucipire who was supposedly working for Michael.

"I don't know. Why?"

"I need to talk to him. Immediately."

"Ivak! I'm on top of the cargo net, in the middle of PT." Trond was in Navy SEAL training at Coronado, California. Ivak assumed he was referring to some type of exercise.

"The Lucies have Gabrielle," Ivak said, his voice rising with panic. "I think it's only been a few hours." He was going by the teakettle. Much longer and the metal would have been melting.

"I'll take care of it right away," Trond said. Ivak could hear him talking to someone, probably a superior, indicating he needed a break. Then, back on the phone, Trond told Ivak, "Sit down and breathe, bro. I can hear your breathing all the way here. We'll get her back. Stay where you are."

"I have to go looking for her. I can't just do nothing."

"Stop it, Ivak. You know very well that'll accomplish nothing. Help is on the way."

Fifteen minutes later, Ivak was sitting on Gabrielle's sofa, bent over at the waist, his face in his hands, when Vikar and Harek arrived.

"I talked to Trond," Vikar said. "He was able to make contact with Zeb."

"And?" Ivak asked.

"Jasper has Gabrielle at Horror."

Ivak roared out his pain and would have teletransported himself immediately to that far, far northern region of the Norselands if his brothers hadn't pinned him to the sofa.

When he calmed down . . . if the loud white noise in his head was being calm . . . Vikar said, "We're going to do this Zeb's way."

Ivak shook his head. "Jasper wants me. That's what this about."

"Think, Ivak," Hared ordered. "Do you honestly think Jasper will just relinquish Gabrielle if you hand yourself over? We must have a plan."

"Time," Ivak groaned. "Every minute she is in his hands means torture. I cannot bear it." He tore at his own hair.

"There's something else," Vikar pointed out. "I was in the same situation when I gave myself up for Armod, and Trond tried to give himself up for Zeb. Michael will not allow it."

"Where is Michael when we need him most?" Ivak was angry with the archangel, and he didn't care how blasphemous he sounded.

It was an hour before they heard from Zeb. In fact, he arrived in person. One minute, the four of them were sitting around, waiting anxiously—Trond had arrived by then—and the next, Zeb was sitting with them.

"Well, well, well," he said. In his humanoid form, Zeb, a two-thousand-year-old Hebrew, wore jeans, a black T-shirt, and a Blue Devils baseball cap. "Looks like someone needs my help."

Ivak raised pleading eyes to the demon, unable to speak over his agony.

"Impressive fangs," Zeb said, observing Ivak's incisors that were elongated with the hunger for violence against the Lucies.

"Fuck you," Ivak replied.

Zeb hissed and flashed an equally impressive set of fangs.

"Are you two dogs done marking your spots?" Harek remarked.

Zeb exhaled loudly, then demanded, "You have to let me handle this."

"But—" Ivak protested.

Zeb raised a halting hand. "There is no way for any of you to enter Jasper's domain and ever leave. Do not think for one minute that he would release the woman in exchange."

"But he released Armod for Vikar that one time," Ivak said.

"That was after days had passed. Vikar had time to plan for an exchange. Do you really want your woman to be in his hands that long?"

"No!"

More gently, Zeb said to Ivak, "I will do whatever I can."

Ivak blacked out then, having been unaware that Harek had come up behind the couch and pinched him on a certain point of his neck. Vikar held him down so that Harek could complete the task. An action of unwelcome mercy.

Ivak did not want mercy. He wanted Gabrielle.

The lone demon to the rescue . . .

Zebulan teletransported immediately to Horror, but he didn't go inside right away. Instead, he stood staring up at the massive "castle" that was coated with ice and dripping icicles. It must be twenty degrees below zero on a good day here in the polar region.

It was important . . . nay, critical . . . that Zebulan succeed with this mission. He hated being a demon vampire. The first few hundred years he hadn't minded so much, having been numbed by the terrible sin he'd committed to earn him this eternal sentence, but then the hundreds and hundreds, then thousands of years after that, he'd come to loathe the atrocities he was forced to perform.

Last year, after doing a favor for Trond Sigurdsson and his woman, he'd earned a meeting with St. Michael, who'd offered him a deal. If Zebulan would remain a Lucipire for fifty more years while secretly doing God's work, Michael would consider releasing him from the horrible fate. Zebulan's quick assent had been a no-brainer.

Zebulan had to find a way of incapacitating Jasper or getting Jasper out of his castle, if only for a short time. And he had to find a way of rescuing Gabrielle that would not be laid at his door so that he could continue with his fifty years as a "secret agent." He only hoped that the woman had not been tortured yet. If she had, she would never be the same again, and not just because of the physical wounds that could be healed. The things she would have seen marked a soul indelibly. Ivak would blame himself throughout eternity.

Zebulan thought a moment and then smiled as a plan occurred to him. Yes, that might work.

First, he teletransported himself to Russia, where he made some purchases. The finest white beluga caviar in the world, worth many thousands of dollars, which he immediately doctored with a powdered sleeping draught. A bottle of Russo-Baltique vodka which could fetch a fortune at auction, also containing a drug. And a gallon of pure virgin's blood. All of which he placed in a fine gift box tied with a black bow. Attached to it was a card reading "With fondness, To my master." Hopefully, Jasper would think it came from Yakov, formerly a Russian Cossack, now one of Jasper's High Command. Yakov lived in a command center in Siberia, aptly named Desolation.

Zebulan placed the box on Horror's front doorstep, rang the bell that sounded like a gong, and stepped back to hide. Soon Jasper's assistant Beltane answered the door, picked up the box, looked around to see who had delivered it, shrugged, then took it inside, closing the door behind him. Zebulan knew that Jasper would be unable to resist the caviar and the makings for a Lucipire version of a Bloody Mary, two of his worldly passions.

Zebulan waited an interminable hour before entering Horror. He figured Gabrielle had been here at least five hours. That meant she would already be down in the dungeons.

Being careful not to be noticed, he snuck into the building. Sure enough, Jasper was fast asleep, slumped in a chair in his main salon, a half glass of the vodka mix sitting on a table beside him, and the caviar container with a spoon in it and a large amount missing.

Also lying there fast asleep was Beltane. Jasper must have offered him a sample, too.

Good! So far, so good!

Making his way stealthily down to the dungeons, he passed with distaste all the humans on various torture apparatuses, some screaming, some with eyes and mouths wide open with terror at their fates. Then there were the tall, clear Plexiglas cylinders known as killing jars that held the humans, similar to butterfly boxes. Jasper used them to bring humans to a state of stasis before beginning his various games.

Gabrielle was in one at the end. Naked and terrified, she pounded on the Plexiglas, screaming for help. To no avail, of course.

Making sure no workers were about, Zebulan rapped on the glass and put his mouth to the speaker hole. "Gabrielle! Gabrielle, do you hear me?" he whispered.

She stared out at him with even more terror in her dark eyes and continued to scream.

He realized that he was in his demonoid form, complete with red eyes, scaly skin, and a tail. Immediately, he transformed himself into human form, as he'd been back in New Orleans . . . denim pants, T-shirt, and baseball cap.

She stopped screaming, tilted her head in question, and asked, "Who the hell are you?"

"Your savior?"

"Get me out of here."

"In due time." Zebulan needed to rescue the woman without Jasper suspecting his involvement. Otherwise, he would be unable to continue working as a Lucipire to complete Michael's work. Not to mention Jasper would make ground Lucipire of him in punishment, or something equally horrific.

"Listen. There isn't much time. This is the plan. You must go along with it." He explained that the red-haired guard from Angola Prison, Roland O'Malley, would be coming here, expecting to have a night of sex with her before Jasper began his tortures in the morning. Zebulan would plant the idea in O'Malley's head. But once out of the glass box and in O'Malley's chamber, Zebulan would rescue her. The blame for her escape would be placed on O'Malley.

She was not happy, to say the least, pointing out all the ways it could go wrong.

"It is the only solution."

She kept shaking her head and saying, "No!"

Meanwhile, time was a-wasting.

"Are you an angel or a demon?"

How to answer that question? I'm a demon, but a good demon? "You really don't want to know." In fact, she'd already seen him in his demon form. She knew. Finally, he pulled out his last bullet of persuasion. "Ivak sent me."

"He did?" she whispered.

He nodded, not about to tell her that Ivak would have shot through the roof if he'd known the details of this plan.

"All right," she said then. "God be with you."

He hoped so!

Twenty-Four

Being home was not so sweet . . .

Gabrielle was in a tropical bungalow somewhere in the Caribbean, a very nice property, but she felt as if she was still living in the middle of a nightmare.

Zebulan had brought her to the place he referred to as his secret hidey-hole and said he had to leave her there for a short time while he went back to Horror, that castle of torture where she had been taken. All the Lucipires were being called to witness the punishment of O'Malley for her escape.

Despite O'Malley's demonic work and the way he had fondled her body when taking her out of the glass cylinder and to his bedroom, Gabrielle had to feel a twinge of sympathy for what the former Angola guard might be now suffering. On the other hand, maybe not so much. O'Malley had been the one to originally fang Hebert, and then Leroy. The start of this whole nightmare.

She was sitting on a sofa, having taken a shower and put on a pair of too-big sweatpants and T-shirt. Zeb had assured her that he had not looked on her nakedness as a man might. She'd thanked him for that . . . and for rescuing her, of course.

Just then, she heard a phone ring. She hadn't even known there was reception here. She found a satellite phone in a kitchen drawer.

"Hello," she said, tentatively. Maybe it was a trick of the demons to find her.

"Gabrielle!"

It was Ivak.

She began to cry.

"Ah, heartling! I am so sorry."

"It wasn't your fault," she said on a sob, wiping her nose on the hem of the long shirt.

"Yes, it was. If it hadn't been for your association with me, they never would have targeted you. I'll never forgive myself."

"Ivak, it was horrible, but nothing happened."

"That's what Zeb said, but . . . nothing?"

"Other than being stripped naked"—and being touched by that slimy O'Malley, which she didn't think Ivak needed to know right now—"and scared to death, nothing." She didn't think she'd ever be able to forget this experience, though.

"Gabrielle, I'm not going to be seeing you when you get back."

"What? What do you mean? You won't be working at Angola anymore?"

"As far as I know, I'll still be at Angola, but I won't be with you anymore."

It felt as if she'd just been sucker-punched. And the tears started again. "Why?"

"This incident has shown me better than anything could that I have no right to get involved with a human. The things that could have happened to you . . . ah, sweetling! I was a selfish bastard."

"So, you're going to cut me off to protect me?"

"Precisely."

"Bullshit!" She hung up on him. She'd been through hell today, literally, and she didn't need this worry, too. She would deal with Ivak later.

Feeling sick in her stomach, she ran for the bathroom. Who wouldn't be nauseous after what she'd witnessed today?

Later that day she was delivered to the driveway of Tante Lulu's cottage. Zeb told her that she would be safe in her apartment, but that she might want to have company for a few days.

"Does Tante Lulu know what happened?" she asked.

He shook his head. "No one knows, except the vangels. As far as anyone else knows, even your brother, you spent the weekend at your apartment, resting after the talent show. Or rather, not resting with Ivak." He waggled his eyebrows at her. He'd been trying to make her smile since he'd returned to the bungalow.

"He's broken off with me, you know."

He shrugged. "He's an idiot."

She did smile then.

"But he loves you."

"That's debatable." She heard the back door opening. Tante Lulu would be coming out here soon. It would be best if she didn't see a demon in her yard. "Good luck, Zeb."

He kissed her on the cheek and said, "Pray for me."

And he was gone.

For a brief moment, Gabrielle wondered if she had dreamed it all, but then Tante Lulu came up to her and asked, "Was that an angel I jist saw out here? They likes ta come and visit with my St. Jude birdbath."

Even angels need help from the saints sometimes . . .

A week later Ivak was miserable.
What else is new?

He was happy that Gabrielle had been rescued. Of course he was. He owed Zeb big-time, and knowing Zeb, he would collect someday in some way. In the meantime, Ivak had been assured Gabrielle would be safe from the Lucies from now on. But he hadn't seen or heard from her himself. That was the crux of his problem.

Oh, it had been Ivak's decision to break off contact with Gabrielle, but that didn't mean he liked it. Doing the right thing shouldn't hurt so much.

Ivak had been working hard with the inmates. In fact, he'd saved five men who had been previously deemed ir-redeemable this past week alone. His skin was a golden tan, as a result. But there was no one to appreciate his appearance, or even pat him on the back.

Of course the warden did enough back patting. He'd been so pleased with Ivak's work on the talent show that Ivak could now do no wrong. Of course, he was butter-ing him up, hoping that Ivak would be doing talent shows every year from now on.

Ivak committed to nothing.

There was a knock on Ivak's office door. Leroy entered after speaking softly to the guard who'd escorted him here.

"Good news?" Ivak asked, seeing the happy expres-sion on Leroy's face.

"The best! I hope! I just talked to Gabrielle, and we have a meeting tomorrow with the St. Francisville DA. The one who prosecuted me in the prison murder."

"That's wonderful," he said, standing to hug Leroy.

"Gabby will meet me there with Luc and Thor. Prison guards will escort me, but . . . will you come with me?"

Ivak would like to, but he didn't think it would be a good idea; Gabrielle wouldn't like the idea, he was sure. If she'd wanted him there, she would have made that fact known. "No, this is your day, Leroy. Besides, I have an-other commitment." A lie. A white lie.

Leroy's shoulders slumped. "I have so much to thank you for."

"No, it's Tante Lulu you need to thank."

Leroy shook his head vigorously. "It was you. Ever since I met you, you've given me something I thought I'd lost." He gulped. "Hope."

After he left, Ivak just sat, miserable, as usual. Then he opened a drawer and took out a small statue of St. Jude that Tante Lulu had given him. He set it on the desk in front of him and stared at the plastic likeness, which was probably not at all what the saint looked like.

Finally, he pressed his palms together in a prayerful fashion. "Is it possible . . . I mean, dare I . . ." He felt silly saying it, but he said the one word. " . . . hope?"

He could swear the statue smiled at him.

Life sometimes throws roadblocks in our paths . . .

Gabrielle sat on one side of a long conference table with Luc and Thor, while the DA and several of his staff sat on the other side. They all had copies of the prosecutor's settlement offer in front of them, waiting for Leroy to arrive to discuss the details.

It broke Gabrielle's heart to see him escorted in wearing handcuffs and leg shackles, with an Angola guard on either side of him. Although she was wary of the staff at Angola after the incident with O'Malley, these two looked kind, and they were gentle with Leroy when they removed the leg chains and motioned for him to sit down beside Gabrielle.

Until this moment, Gabrielle hadn't realized how much she'd been hoping that Ivak would be with him. She hadn't talked to him since that phone conversation the day she was rescued, and he hadn't made any attempt to make contact since then. Just as he'd said on the phone. Well, she'd be damned if she would take the first step. Even if she did still love the louse.

She leaned over and kissed Leroy on the cheek, whispering, "How you doing, sweetie?"

"Nervous."

"Me too."

"You look awful. I mean, your skin is white. Have you been sick?"

"A little bit. Must be a stomach bug." Actually, she'd vomited her guts out this morning. As she had several other times since returning from Horror. It was probably a stress reaction to her experience. In most circumstances like this, the victim would be in counseling for PTSD, but how could she tell a psychologist what had happened to her? They would think she was crazy.

Once Leroy was released, she would probably feel better.

"Okay, folks, now that everyone's here," the DA said. "Mr. Sonnier, in light of the deathbed testimony of Edward Hebert, we are prepared to offer you an out-of-court settlement."

Leroy straightened, and Gabrielle took one of his cuffed hands in hers.

"We agree to your release as time served, providing you enter a guilty plea."

"What? I don't understand." Leroy turned to Gabrielle.

"You'd have to plead guilty if you want to avoid a lengthy retrial," she explained.

"But I didn't do it."

"I know."

"Can we have some time to discuss this in private?" Luc asked the prosecutor.

"Yes, but the offer's only on the table today. After that, we'll ask the judge for a court date."

The prosecutor was posturing, in Gabrielle's opinion, but sometimes that's all the law was about.

Once they were alone, Leroy said angrily, "Hell, no! I won't agree to something I didn't do. It would be on my record for life."

"Leroy, you already have a felony on your record for life. That of manslaughter two for murdering your father," Thor pointed out.

"That's different."

Thor shrugged.

"Why won't they just let me go now that they know Hebert lied?"

"They need to save face," Luc told him.

"And I get thrown under the bus to make them look good?"

"That's about it." Luc shrugged.

"What do you think I should do?" Leroy asked Gabrielle.

"I'm divided," she said. "Like you, I hate your having to make a guilty plea, but it would mean your release within days. Whereas a jury trial could take years, and I'm always fearful about what could happen to you in prison."

Leroy buried his face in his cuffed hands. "I wish Ivak were here to give me advice."

Gabrielle exchanged rueful glances with Luc and Thor. Three experienced lawyers in the room and Leroy would have preferred advice from a prison chaplain. At least that's all Luc would know of Ivak.

Leroy said, "It burns my ass to do it, but I'll accept. Later, I'll worry about the implications. Maybe I'll write a book making them all look like asses."

"That's the spirit," Luc said.

After Leroy and the lawyers signed all the appropriate documents, Leroy was taken back to the prison. It would take days for him to be processed out.

"I'll make space for you in my apartment," she told him before he shuffled out. Later, she would have to look for a bigger place. Tall as Leroy was, she'd have to sleep on the couch, giving up her bed for him. A small sacrifice, considering.

Once Leroy was gone, and Luc and Thor were done discussing details with her, Gabrielle made a mad dash for the ladies' room. Once again, she threw up, though she had almost nothing in her stomach at this point. She decided to stop at the supermarket on the way back to New Orleans and among basic groceries, she was going to pick up some kind of liquid antacid. After all these years of stress, she was getting ulcers now?

She should have been happy on the drive home, but she felt such a weight on her shoulders. Maybe it was the aftereffects of her demon experience. Maybe she wouldn't be able to relax and celebrate until Leroy was actually released. Maybe she was just missing Ivak too much. Maybe she should swallow her pride and call the man.

But she did nothing that night. When she returned to her apartment and put away her groceries, taking a long swig of the pink stuff, she could only think about taking a nap. And to her shock, she slept right through until the following morning. When she was sick again.

Later, she was sitting in her kitchen, having some tea and toast, when she heard her doorbell ring. She glanced at her watch. It was ten a.m. To her surprise, it was Tante Lulu.

Gabrielle opened the door and the old lady came huffing in. "Holy Sac-au-lait! Those steps are a killer. You oughta be in a place with an elevator."

Like I could afford that! She closed the door and followed Tante Lulu into her kitchen, where she placed a paper sack that, from the delicious scent, must hold beignets. Gabrielle watched with confusion while the old lady put a plate on the table and arranged the desserts.

"Tante Lulu, what are you doing here?" *Sorry to be blunt, but sometimes it's the only way.*

"Yer brother gave me a call, and I come ta see what's goin' on."

"Leroy called you?"

"Well, I asked the warden ta have the boy give me a call. I wanted ta know what happened yesterday. You dint let me know," she accused Gabrielle.

"I was so tired when I got home. I fell asleep and didn't wake up until this morning."

Tante Lulu nodded as if she understood. "And you ain't been feelin' good, right?"

Leroy had a big mouth. "That's right. Just a little stomach bug. I feel much better now."

"Jist like I figgered." Tante Lulu reached down into her big purse that she'd set on the floor.

Oh my God! She better not have bought me a gun.

But, no, she handed a small box to Gabrielle.

Confused, Gabrielle glanced at the box, then burst out laughing. "Where did you get this?"

"I had Tee-John run inta the drugstore and buy it fer me."

"Good Lord!"

Tante Lulu chuckled. "He 'bout had a heart attack when I told 'im what I wanted."

"I appreciate your effort, but I'm not pregnant. I can't be."

"Are you sayin' you ain't done the deed with Ivak?"

Gabrielle's face heated up. "Ivak is sterile. He can't have children."

Tante Lulu folded her arms over her chest and raised her chin with stubbornness. She looked surprisingly normal today, with gray hair and a neat pantsuit. "Go take the test."

"But—"

"Go."

Just to appease the old lady, she went into the bathroom and took the test. Stunned, she walked out ten minutes later. Pregnant. She was pregnant. But how could that be? Oooh, Ivak had a lot to answer for.

"Congratulations, honey," Tante Lulu said when she returned, not even waiting for Gabrielle to tell her the test results. "I gotta get that hope chest done right away now."

Later, Gabrielle couldn't recall anything that she or Tante Lulu discussed until Tee-John eventually came to pick her up. At the door, both the nephew and the aunt hugged her warmly, and Gabrielle promised to call Tante Lulu the next day.

It took her an hour to get herself until control.

She was pregnant. Unmarried and pregnant. Well, that didn't matter so much today. But the timing was not good, especially with Leroy about to get out of prison. He would be staying with her, at least in the beginning. Then she would have to think about how she was going to support herself and a baby, how she would be able to work.

On the other hand . . . a baby! Gabrielle put a hand over her stomach and smiled. A miracle, really.

First things first, she got up to get her cell phone and tapped in Ivak's number. She got his voice mail.

"Ivak! This is Gabrielle. I need to talk to you. Right away. It's important." *You stinking liar! You no good charmer. You . . .*

She no sooner ended the call than her phone rang. It was Ivak.

"Gabrielle! I just walked in. What's wrong?"

You stinking liar! You no good charmer. You . . . "Everything. You better get your Viking butt here right away." She hadn't meant to be so shrill. It just came out that way.

"Are you in danger?"

"I'm in danger of killing you if you don't come as soon as possible." *Good thing I don't own a gun.*

"Do you think it's a good idea for us to be together? Oh, I've missed you, of course—"

"Of course!" she said sarcastically. *Then why haven't you called?*

"I don't understand."

"You don't need to understand, dammit!" *I hate you, I hate you, I hate you.* She hung up on him.

And bawled her eyes out.

Twenty-Five

Time to man up . . . or is that Viking up? . . .

Ivak arrived at Gabrielle's apartment an hour later. When he knocked repeatedly on her door and she didn't answer, he teletransported himself inside, through the wall.

She sat on the couch glaring up at him. Her eyes were red and her nose was dripping. She grabbed for a tissue and blew her nose loudly, glaring at him the whole time.

He went down on his haunches beside her. "You're crying."

"He's a genius, too."

She knows I do not like her sarcasm. Why does she persist in that annoying habit? Well, he had more important issues to address with her at the moment. "Can I sit beside you?"

"No."

All right. So that's the way this meeting is going to go. He got up and sat in a chair next to the sofa. "Are you worried about the Lucies? Has something happened with Leroy's case? Are you ill?"

"No, no, and no."

I thought I knew women. Where is my legendary charm? "You look beautiful today."

She stared at him as if he'd grown another head. "Are you really that clueless?"

Apparently. "What's wrong?"

She stood . . . and wrung her hands nervously.

What in bloody hell is going on? He stood, too.

"I'm pregnant."

That was the last thing he'd expected to hear. "How can that be?" *She was with another man.*

"That's what I'd like to know. You told me that I couldn't get pregnant."

"You can't. Not by me." *She was with another man.* His brain was reeling with shock.

"Are you implying—"

"Who was it? Zeb?" *It must be Zeb. There was no time for any other man. Was there? This must be how Serk felt. Now I know. Oh God! I can't think. I can't think.*

She slapped his face, hard, then turned away from him. Her shoulders were shaking with her sobs.

What? What the hell is going on? No one . . . man or woman . . . had ever slapped him before. He fisted his hands and tried to come to some understanding about what had just happened.

The woman he loved was pregnant.

He could not make a woman pregnant.

Therefore she had to have been with another man.

Why would she be angry with him? He was the one with cause to be furious. And he was. "If Zeb weren't already dead, I would kill him. But you can be sure his face won't be so pretty when I'm done with him."

She spun around to face him. Her face was splotched with tears. "Don't you dare touch Zeb. He saved me. And that's all he did."

"But—"

"You are the father," she said tightly.

"Believe me, I am sterile," he tried to make her understand.

"I wouldn't believe anything you said now if your tongue was notarized."

He could be insulted by that . . . if she gave him a chance, but she was off on another tirade.

"You lied to me. I could accept your saying it was a mistake, but, no, you're still playing Mr. Innocent. You must think I'm a dummy who believes everything a man tells her. I was angry with you before. Now I'm just disgusted. Mostly with myself."

She walked over and opened her door. "Out! And never come back!"

Cold fury overtook him as he approached her. "You spread your legs for another man and dare to blame me? Just like a woman!"

She inhaled sharply. "I will never forgive you for that."

Ivak found himself on the other side of the slammed door, stunned.

That night Ivak awakened to a bright presence in his cell living quarters. It was Michael. He was leaning against the bars, shaking his head at Ivak.

"What have you done?" Michael demanded angrily.

"I haven't done anything. Well, if you mean the sex—"

"Of course I mean the sex. What did you think I meant?"

"Well, Gabrielle says that she's pregnant, which is of course impossible. I told her so, but she kicked me out. It is impossible, right?"

Michael sank down to the end of his bed. The anger was coming off his wings in shedding feathers. "What have you done?" Michael repeated.

"I already know that I'll be punished for the sex, but—"

"How could this have happened?" Michael seemed to

be posing the question to himself. "It was not supposed to ever happen. Did you do something unusual?"

"Define unusual."

"Idiot!" Michael got up and paced back and forth in the small cell, muttering to himself:

"Is it something in his makeup? A mistake of nature?

"Could God have intervened?

"Was this destined to happen?"

He turned to Ivak then and said, "Stay here. I'll be right back."

Ivak got up and dressed, figuring he'd never be able to go back to sleep now.

A short time later, Michael returned and told him, "She's pregnant."

Pfff! Tell me something I don't already know.

"And it is yours, Viking."

"No," he protested. "That's impossible. How could that happen?"

Michael arched his brows at him.

"I don't mean that. I mean vangels cannot impregnate women. That's what you always said."

"That's what I thought."

Ivak's heart thundered against his rib cage as he attempted to assimilate what he was being told. He, a vangel, was going to be father to a human child? "Will the child be a human or a vangel?"

"The boy is human."

Boy? Ivak moaned at the intensity of emotion that one word evoked. "What should I do?"

"You're asking me? It's a little late for that."

"You're an archangel. I thought you knew everything."

"Apparently not."

But then Ivak recalled the manner in which he'd denied his child to Gabrielle. She would never forgive him. He took a deep breath. "I love her," he told Michael.

"You have a strange way of showing it."

"I should have listened to Gabrielle before overreacting."

"That is an understatement. Does she love you?"

"She used to before—"

"Before?"

"Before I made an ass of myself."

"Bring her to Transylvania. I wish to speak with her. And whatever you do, don't even breathe on another woman until I understand how this could have happened."

Ivak stiffened with affront, but Michael was already gone.

Even though it was five a.m., he called Gabrielle. And continued calling all day long. No answer. When he went to her apartment, she was not there.

Leroy was released several days later, but Gabrielle did not come to pick him up. A deliberate avoidance of him, Ivak was sure. Instead, she sent a message that Leroy relayed to him. "She doesn't want you to contact her anymore." Seeing the expression on Ivak's face, Leroy laid a hand on his forearm. "Give her time."

Leroy probably wouldn't have been so kind if he'd known his sister was pregnant.

Ivak's emotions reeled from anger, to regret, to shame, to confusion, back to anger. Over and over. He was like a regular popcorn of emotions, and he hated it. He couldn't eat. He couldn't sleep. His hands shook. He talked to himself, mostly berating his thickheadedness. He even found himself teary-eyed on occasion.

When he'd confided to Trond what was happening to him, minus the pregnancy news, Trond suggested, "Seems like you're finding your feminine side."

Ivak had said a foul word and hung up.

Vikar had just laughed and told him to have a beer.

So, Ivak took a leave from the prison to work on the Heaven's End project. Maybe that would occupy his mind.

The landscape people had done a fine job of clearing away the overgrown jungle, and while it was still untamed, he could at least walk around without a machete. He was in the back courtyard after having just consulted with a contractor on the cost of a new roof, and wondered if he shouldn't finance a third world country, instead. That's when he noticed his first guest arriving. Tante Lulu. Carrying a big carryall.

He was afraid to ask what was inside.

"Ain't she a beauty?" the old lady observed, staring up at the mansion.

Maybe she had cataracts.

Now that the kudzu and other vines had been removed, the mansion looked even more run down. Yeah, the building had good bones, but it would be years before it was livable, in Ivak's opinion. Not in Michael's, though; he'd told Ivak he could live here while the work was being done.

Yeah. Right.

"How did you get here?" he asked, taking the carryall out of her hands. It was heavy. Was she carrying bricks to repair one of his walls?

"I drove."

Ivak's eyes must have widened in astonishment.

"I ain't dead yet." Then she chuckled and added, "I drove about ten miles an hour. You shoulda heard all the horns tootin'."

She insisted then on spreading a tablecloth she'd brought with her over a door sitting on two sawhorses. On it she placed a thermos of coffee, two china cups, two china plates, two silver forks, a long knife, and a plastic, lidded box with half of what she called her famous Peachy Praline Cobbler Cake. They ate then, and it was delicious, both the coffee and the cake. Maybe he was getting his appetite back.

That's when she zapped him. "I hear you been some kind of idjit."

He was going to argue, but then he said, "You could say that."

"You doan look so good, boy."

"I've been kind of down in the dumps lately," he admitted. *Vikings throughout Valhalla . . . oops, Heaven . . . must be rolling over with laughter that I would use such words.*

"Well, the good thing about being down is you cain't fall any more."

That is just great advice. I feel so much better now.

"Tell me zackly what happened?"

To his surprise, he did. In detail. It must be that damn feminine side Trond mentioned.

"What you said ta Gabrielle was bad," Tante Lulu said, shaking her head at him.

"I'd take the words back if I could."

"A team of the strongest horses cain't take back a word once spoken."

That is really helpful.

"You daddied that chile."

"I know that." *Now.*

"Do you love her?"

"Yes."

"I'm glad ta hear you admit it. I already knew, of course. Yer eyes were all over her like white on rice from the very beginning."

"She won't talk to me. What should I do?" *How pitiful I am becoming! Since when does a Viking ask an old lady for love advice?*

"A peacock what sits on its tail is jist another turkey."

Is she calling me a turkey? An asshole, I can accept, which is what Trond called me, but a turkey? He gritted his teeth and asked, "Will you set up a meeting for

me? Just one meeting. If that doesn't work, I'll give up."
Gobble, gobble, gobble.

"Some men are born dumb and end up stupid," Tante
Lulu concluded.

*That goes without saying. Now I know what it's like to
eat humble pie. And it's damn bitter.*

"Yer a Viking, You doan need no old lady to act on yer
behalf."

*Huh? Bloody hell, she's right. I need to stop moping
and act like a man. I swear, Gabrielle will listen to me
even if I have to kidnap her and carry her off on my longship, like so many Vikings gained mates in the past.*

Too bad I don't have a longship.

Maybe I could buy one and place it on the Mississippi.

No, a car will have to do. I'm a modern Viking.

He walked Tante Lulu out front to her lavender car and
helped her onto the two cushions in front of the driver's
wheel. The seat had been pushed up as far as it could go
so that her short legs could reach the pedals. "Are you
sure you don't want me to drive you home?"

"You have more important things ta do."

Yes, he did.

"I fergot. I gotcha a present in my truck. You kin put it
in yer new garden."

"What garden?" He went around to the back of the car
where she'd popped the trunk open from inside.

It was a life-size St. Jude statue.

Tante Lulu was chuckling as she drove away.

Ivak saluted St. Jude in his "garden" a short time later.

Give him an inch, and he'd take a Viking mile . . .

He stormed Gabrielle's apartment a short time later.
She was sitting placidly by the front window, having

just washed her hair. It lay long to her T-shirt–clad shoulders, wisps of it curling as it dried. Her bare toes peeked out from under her denim braies. Her face glowed with good health, probably from the pregnancy. To him, she looked so beautiful that his heart ached.

"You could have knocked," she said.

"I did that before and you wouldn't answer." He sank down into a chair facing her. Since she didn't object, he figured it was okay.

"Once. You came here once."

Huh? Does she mean she would have let me in before this? Have I wasted all these weeks moaning and . . . "I'm sorry."

"Big fat hairy deal! Sorry doesn't cut it anymore."

So, she isn't going to make this easy. "I love you."

"You have a strange way of showing it."

She is hurt. Of course, she is hurt. I denied my child. "You haven't been very loving to me, either."

"I had good reason. Your accusation was vile. You didn't trust me."

He said the words then that were so difficult for men to utter. "I was wrong."

"Damn straight you were!"

Do I need to grovel? Of course I do. "Can you forgive me?"

"Why should I?"

"Because I love you. Because I am your baby's father. Because it is the right thing to do."

"So, you believe me now? What convinced you?"

He could feel his face heat with color. "Michael."

"Michael it is now. What happened to Mike?"

"Until I know what my punishment will be, I'm trying to get on his good side." *Do I sense an opening in her anger?*

"You're being punished for my being pregnant?"

Yes! The crack is widening. He willed himself not to

smile. "I'll be punished for the sex. The pregnancy, too. That wasn't supposed to happen."

"Tell me about it!"

"You are being very sarcastic, Gabrielle. It does not suit you." *As if I haven't told her so before!*

"You're pushing it, buster. I'm already rethinking my talking to you. By the way, will I be popping out a vampire or angel baby?"

He shook his head. "It will be a normal human child. No fangs. No wings."

"That's a relief."

"It is a boy."

She gasped, placing a hand over her stomach. Then she reached over and slapped him on the thigh.

"What was that for?"

"For telling me the sex of my child. I wanted to be surprised." She stood and started to walk away.

"Where are you going?"

"To the bathroom."

"In the middle of a conversation, you just up and walk away. Besides, you already went to the bathroom before I got here." He stood to follow her.

"I have to pee. Pregnant women have to pee a lot, idiot." She narrowed her eyes at him. "How did you know I went to pee before you got here?"

"I guessed."

She smacked him again, this time on a forearm.

When she returned in what seemed an excessively long time later—she'd probably been hoping he would be impatient and go away—he told her, "Michael wants to meet with you."

He could see the alarm on her face. "Why?"

He shrugged.

"You're telling me that an archangel . . . a saint, for heaven's sake . . . wants to meet with me?"

He nodded.

"Well, bring him on!" She spread her arms wide in welcome.

Bring him on? Does she think they're going to arm wrestle? That was Jacob, and it was with the devil he wrestled. "Not here. He wants me to bring you to our home in Transylvania."

"The castle in Pennsylvania?"

He nodded again.

"I heard you've been working on Heaven's End. Isn't that your home?"

"It will be eventually, but there is much work to be done first. I could use your help, sweetling."

"Don't call me by that name," she snapped. Then, inhaling sharply for patience as women were wont to do when their men did a lackwit thing or twenty, she said, "I know nothing about historic renovations."

"But you love the house. That counts more than prior experience. We could work on it together. Leroy has already been helping me."

"The traitor! He's supposed to be studying for his graduate college entrance exams."

Ivak knew that. In fact, Leroy was in Tennessee this weekend, where he hoped to get a college scholarship sponsored by some newspaper fund. If that didn't work out, Ivak planned to give him the funds, but he hadn't told Leroy that yet.

"Leroy does study, you know that, but in his spare time he comes out to Heaven's End. Will you meet with Michael?"

"Do I have a choice?"

The crack is widening. "You do. Please. Will you come?"

"I might. I would have to clear my schedule at Second Chances for a day or two. When would you . . . he . . . want me to go?"

"Now." *Thank you, God!* All he'd needed was her consent. He did a mental high five, not daring to do it in actuality.

"Whaaat?" she squealed as he wrapped his arms around her, closed his eyes, and concentrated. "Let me go. Right now. I mean it. Ooooh!"

In the blink of an eye, they stood in the back courtyard of Vikar's run-down castle. As always, it was in the midst of some renovation project or other. Today, there were air-conditioning trucks about the place.

"Honey, we're home," he said, trying for a levity he did not feel.

She blinked with confusion. And hit him.

He still held her tightly to him. "Did I just feel our baby move?" he asked with wonder.

"Babies don't move at two months, you idiot. I'm trying to get my other hand free."

He released her and she stared around her, mouth agape. "A freakin' castle! Oh my God! Oh my God! Oh my God!"

"Shh!" he cautioned. "Michael does not like us to use the Lord's name in vain. *Freakin'* is okay . . . well, not okay, but not as bad as *oh God!*"

"Bullshit!" she said, and shoved him in the chest, glaring when he remained stationary, probably hoping he would land on his arse. "You freakin' moved me from Louisiana to freakin' Pennsylvania in"—she glanced at her wristwatch—"five freakin' minutes."

"I would have teletransported us faster, but I didn't want you to get motion sickness. I have heard that pregnant women have sensitive stomachs. Would you like me to get you a ginger ale? I read on the computer about that beverage settling—"

"I swear, if you weren't already dead, I would kill you."

"Ahem!" he heard behind him.

To his chagrin, not only was Vikar standing there with his wife, Alex, a child in each of their arms, but his other five brothers were there, as well, including Trond and his wife, Nicole, in military camouflage uniforms.

And they were all grinning at him.

Tsking with disgust, Alex handed her child, the one dressed in pink, to Vikar, who now juggled two squirming bodies. Alex stepped forward with both arms spread wide toward Gabrielle. "Welcome, Gabrielle. Ivak has told us so much about you."

That was a lie, but he wasn't about to correct his sister by marriage.

Especially when Gabrielle burst out in tears.

"Shame on you, Ivak," Alex said, wrapping her arms around Gabrielle and leading her toward the castle. Over her shoulder, Alex asked, "What did you do to make her cry?"

"Me? I did nothing."

In the middle of a sob, Gabrielle broke free from Alex's embrace and accused him, "You made me pregnant."

Since he hadn't told anyone but Michael, there was a communal gasp from everyone. Then his brothers burst out laughing.

Trond summed the situation up best. "You are in such trouble, Ivak!"

Twenty-Six

Welcome to Oz ... uh, Transylvania, Dorothy ...

Gabrielle felt like Dorothy, except this was not the Emerald City and she wasn't wearing any ruby slippers. In fact, she was wearing no shoes.

But the Scarecrow was here, as in man with no brain, and she was thinking about doing him some harm. Where was a match when she needed it? In fact, where was the damn Scarecrow? Ivak had been avoiding her ever since they'd arrived an hour ago. Maybe he was the lion instead ... the Cowardly Lion.

No, he was probably off with his brothers smoking congratulatory cigars and preening over his virility. Or maybe he was off on a cloud speaking to an archangel.

Aaarrgh! Her brain was splintering apart.

"Did you say something?" Alex, Ivak's sister-in-law, asked. They were up on the second floor of a bleepin' castle. A run-down, in the process of being renovated, not-so-pretty castle, but a castle nonetheless. Alex had brought her up to her bedroom to talk while her two toddlers were taking a nap in an adjoining room. Another sister-in-law, Nicole, was there, too.

"I was just muttering."

"You'll do a lot of that with the Sigurdsson men," Nicole said.

I'm not sure I'll be "with" Ivak.

"They take arrogance to an art form," Nicole continued.

That was for sure.

"You seem to be in shock." Alex sat down next to her. "Well, we're in shock, too. Pregnant? You're really pregnant?"

Gabrielle nodded.

Alex and Nicole exchanged astonished looks.

"We thought it was impossible," Alex said. "It's never happened before."

"Ivak thought it was impossible, too. In fact, he accused me of being with another man."

Instead of being outraged on her behalf, Nicole nodded and sat down on Gabrielle's other side on the bed. "You have to understand that it's been drummed into us that vangels are sterile."

"You two seem so normal."

Alex and Nicole both laughed.

"I didn't mean to insult you, but do you really believe all this vangel/demon nonsense?"

"How can we not? How can *you* not after everything you've seen, poor girl?" Alex put an arm around her shoulders and squeezed.

Ivak had briefly explained what had happened to Gabrielle and how she'd been rescued to his family and the other fangy people standing about the kitchen, including a woman named Lizzie Borden, of all things, who was cooking dinner.

In the short time she'd been here, she'd learned more astounding facts about the vangels. Apparently, many of them held jobs out in the regular world. Doctor, lawyer, prison chaplain, computer guru, she already knew about, but there were also pilots, artists, landscapers, stone masons, blacksmiths, bus drivers, architects, engineers, chemists, whatever. And all of them were of Norse descent, except Alex, a former magazine writer of some note, and Nicole, who was in Navy WEALS, like her SEAL husband, Trond.

"Did you become vampire angels when you married your husbands?" she asked the two women.

"Good heavens, no. I was the first human ever permitted to marry any of the VIK, and Vikar was the only vangel who'd ever been permitted to marry a human," Alex said.

"I don't understand. What happens when you get old and your husband doesn't?"

"That's the reason why vangels are never supposed to marry humans. But Michael made exceptions for me and Alex," Nicole explained. "We agreed to certain conditions when we married vangels. We live as long as our husbands. When they die, we die."

Gabrielle frowned, still not understanding.

"If Trond should die tomorrow, I would, too," Nicole elaborated. "But if he lives a thousand more years, I would, too.

"And stay the same age," Nicole added. "That is one of the pluses. We . . . Alex and I . . . made the choice because we love our husbands."

"Tell me something, Gabrielle," Alex said, "do you know if your child is mortal?"

"Ivak said it would be. It's a boy, by the way." For some reason, she accepted that Ivak knew what he was talking about in that regard.

"Then he will be like my two 'adopted' children. They will age, but I will not."

It was all too much for Gabrielle to comprehend.

"C'mon, honey, I'll show you to a guest room where you can rest. I can see how tired you are." This from Nicole, who took her to a guest room, one of more than twenty-five bedrooms in this bleepin' castle, while Alex went off to care for her little ones who were waking up. The room was nice, but spare, with only a bed with a heavy coverlet that matched the drapes.

"Have you ever met . . . ?" Gabrielle glanced upward.

"Michael?" Nicole guessed. "Oh yeah!"

"And?"

"I can't describe him. You'll never forget the experience, though."

After Nicole left, Gabrielle lay down on top of the bed. So many thoughts and questions riddled her brain that she never expected to sleep. But she did, and when she awakened abruptly, she at first didn't realize what had disturbed her sleep.

It was dusk outside, so she must have slept for hours, and there was a fur-lined cashmere throw placed carefully over her. *Ivak?* she wondered.

But then she heard the sound that had awakened her. Wings fluttering. Above the castle. And the most delicious scent, like a mixture of cloves and incense. The air around her shimmered. When Gabrielle sat up, she felt the oddest sense of peace.

And she realized, *Michael is here.*

An archangel's work is never done . . .

Ivak was worried.

He'd gone up to check on Gabrielle hours ago, but she was still sleeping. Alex had assured him that pregnant women needed more sleep, but he feared something might be wrong.

For a brief, male-inspired moment of insanity, he'd
contemplated lying down beside her, but then he chose to
cover her with a soft throw instead. But before he covered
her, he stared down at her flat stomach under her denims
and tried to imagine his baby there.

Ivak had had children before. Long ago. Out of wedlock. To his shame, he did not even recall their names,
or how many there had been. That's how unimportant
fatherhood had been to him then. Now, he felt as if his
heart would break if he could not be a father to this child,
which was an impossibility, of course. He was a vangel,
his son was human.

What a mess! And it was all due to Ivak's continuing
sin. Lust.

All too soon, Michael arrived. When Ivak went outside
with his brothers to watch for the archangel, he noticed
they had donned message T-shirts to lighten his spirits.
The lackwits!

Harek's shirt said, "Have You Kissed a Geek Today?"
while the others proclaimed, "Angels Rule," "Kiss My
Wing," "Have Wings, Will Travel," "Do Wings Make My
Butt Look Fat?" and "Fangs for the Memories."

Michael arched a brow on first seeing them, but then
when he walked by them, Ivak noticed a message on the
back of his celestial robe, "Heaven Is Just One Sin Away."

Michael with a sense of humor? It boggled the mind.
He and his brothers exchanged questioning glances.
Almost immediately the archangel's robe message disap-
peared. Maybe they'd imagined it.

Without even turning around, Michael called over his
shoulder, "Ivak! In the library!"

His brothers gave him looks of sympathy. They'd all
been in similar positions.

Instead of sitting behind the desk, Michael sat in one of
the wingback chairs flanking the fireplace and indicated

with a wave of his hand that Ivak should take the other.

"I've investigated the pregnancy issue, and it appears it was my mistake."

Whoa! That was some concession.

"Do you think I am so proud I cannot admit my mistakes?"

Ivak had forgotten that the archangel could read minds. "Am I the only . . . mistake?"

"With regard to sterility, you are. And, Ivak, a baby is never a mistake. Babies are gifts from God, a reminder that He still has faith in mankind."

"Even vangels?" *Even me?*

"Especially vangels."

"Truth to tell, I do consider my son a gift, but I don't see what kind of role I can play in his life. How can I be a father to a child who will grow older than my human form at some point?"

Michael shrugged. "It is exactly what Vikar and Alex face with their children."

Ivak hadn't thought about that. "What can I do?" he asked.

"What do you want to do?"

"I love Gabrielle. If I could be with her and my baby, even if I had to drop out of their lives when the child reached a certain age . . . well, I would consider myself blessed."

Michael shook his head. "There are only two choices. Either you walk away now and have nothing whatsoever to do with Gabrielle and your son, ever, or you marry Gabrielle under the same conditions as Alex and Nicole. You and Gabrielle would both watch your son age." He paused and added, "Thus sayeth the Lord!"

Ivak gasped. He could never ask Gabrielle to do that.

"I will go into the chapel to pray on this problem while you go to fetch your woman."

Like a dog? I don't think so!

"And on your way, try not to impregnate any more women," Michael advised.

Ivak raised an eyebrow. *More archangel humor? Do wonders never cease?*

"The wonder is that you've lived a thousand years and are still dumb as dirt."

Sarcasm, too. He and Gabrielle would get along great.

"Just for the record, and I will chisel it in stone like the Ten Commandments if that's what it takes to get through to you thickheaded Vikings. No More Women! And absolutely, positively, no more babies! Are we clear on that point?"

"Indelibly," Ivak answered, and he wasn't being sarcastic.

Shaking his head with disgust, Michael left.

Ivak was halfway up the wide staircase when he saw Gabrielle coming down. At his urging, they sat down together on one of the steps. He took her hand in both of his and held it on his lap, saying nothing. She leaned against his shoulder, also saying nothing.

It was a perfect moment, which could not last.

"I was given two choices," he said then. He explained what Michael had told him.

Gabrielle nodded. "Alex and Nicole explained some of this to me."

"I love you, Gabrielle." He raised her hand and kissed the fingertips. "I wouldn't ask you to make such a sacrifice."

She turned on the step to face him directly. "Which of those would you consider a sacrifice for me?"

He blinked. It was obvious, wasn't it?

Michael stood before them then and Gabrielle made a small, whimpering sound at first witnessing the archangel's imposing presence. There was a glow about the archangel, like a full-body halo.

"Come," Michael said, taking Gabrielle's hand in his.

Ivak rushed to catch up with the two of them as they walked through the castle and into the back courtyard. There was a hushed atmosphere throughout the castle as they passed by vangels with their heads bowed. When they got to the gazebo, they all sat down. Michael was still holding Gabrielle's hand.

"How is your brother doing?" Michael asked Gabrielle.

Her eyes widened with surprise. "He's all right now."

"Your brother will do great things. He needed this suffering to make him the man he will be."

Gabrielle nodded, drinking in everything Michael said.

"Do you love this sorry soul?" Michael asked her.

There was no doubt which sorry soul he meant, and Gabrielle looked at Ivak with a small smile. "Unfortunately, yes."

Ivak wasn't too happy about the "unfortunately" but he was heartened by the "yes."

"Do you choose to marry him?"

"He never asked me."

Michael gave Ivak a disapproving scowl.

"I never thought I would be rewarded for my sin." And, yes, marriage to Gabrielle would be a reward.

"Ivak! You were punished for lust. Not love," Michael said to Ivak, then turned to Gabrielle. "He is a slow learner."

Ivak couldn't be concerned about that insult at the moment. "Gabrielle, I would like nothing better than to marry you and raise our son together." He got down on one knee before her. "But I could never ask you to outlive what would be your only child."

"Don't you think that should be my choice?" She ran a hand lovingly over his face and hair. "I had time to think while lying on that bed up there." She pointed to the upper region of the castle. "And I decided that the greatest sacrifice would be not having you in my life." She was weeping softly now.

He pulled her to her feet, hugging her warmly.

"You'll marry me?" he murmured against her ear.

"Try and stop me," she sobbed.

A sudden joy filled Ivak, like the blood in his veins had turned molten and was rushing through his body spreading warmth. The bumps on his shoulders felt as if they were unfurling. Looking over Gabrielle's shoulder, he mouthed to Michael, *Thank you.*

Michael nodded and glanced upward, saying, "Well, my work is done," and disappeared.

Epilogue

Even vampires can have happy endings . . .

A Christmas wedding was held in mid-December at Our Lady of the Bayou Church in Houma, Louisiana. The ceremony was conducted by a visiting priest. It was Michael the Archangel, of course, in ministerial garb, his wings out of sight.

No one knew who Michael was, but Tante Lulu suspected. She kept asking him if he knew St. Jude.

Ivak and Gabrielle would have liked to wed at the Transylvania castle, but they wouldn't have been able to invite guests where so many young vangels lived, unable to control their fangs. Besides, Tante Lulu claimed that she deserved to host the festivities. Who could argue with that?

Vikar was Ivak's best man, and his groomsmen were his other five brothers, along with a young vangel named Armod who had a strange obsession with Michael Jackson, and Leroy, who had been accepted to the University of Tennessee, where he intended to get a graduate degree in social work.

Gabrielle's matron of honor was Charmaine, and her bridesmaids were Alex and Nicole. Tante Lulu gave her away.

Among the guests were Warden Benton, who acted like Ivak's best friend, and the huge LeDeux clan.

The Swamp Rats played at the reception held at the Swamp Tavern, which was closed for the day. The highlight of the festivities was when the band launched into "Chain of Fools" and all seven Sigurdsson brothers did the *Michael* dance. Second best was Gabrielle and the LeDeux women teaching Alex and Nicole how to doo-wop.

Gabrielle had refused to marry Ivak until he renovated the kitchen, a bathroom, and one bedroom at Heaven's End where they intended to live while renovations were going on. Ivak would continue as an Angola chaplain for the time being, and Gabrielle had decided to continue with Second Chances.

At a bride and groom shower held weeks ago by Tante Lulu, the old lady had given Ivak a hope chest filled with monogrammed sheets and dish towels, not to mention an exquisite crocheted quilt. Then she had "flocked the bride," an old Cajun tradition where the women of the village gave the bride live chickens so that she could be self-sufficient in the marriage. That meant there were laying hens at Heaven's End. Ivak swore he was going to kill the rooster if it kept crowing at five a.m.

At the end of the evening, in their own bed, Gabrielle nuzzled up against her husband after a lively bout of lovemaking—the first since they'd become engaged, Michael's orders—and said, "I never thought I could be so happy."

And Ivak nuzzled her back before sliding down her body and drawling—he was acquiring a very sexy Southern drawl—"Have I shown you the famous Viking X-spot, dearlin'?"

She laughed. "Just how many Viking spots are there?"

"Hundreds," he said.

Then she was no longer laughing.

Reader Letter

Dear Readers:

So far, I've taken my Viking vampire angels to Transylvania, Pennsylvania (*Kiss of Pride*), Navy SEAL land in Coronado, California (*Kiss of Surrender*), and now down on the bayou with that rowdy Cajun LeDeux family (*Kiss of Temptation*). So, how did you like my blending of the characters from one book into this new one? And the question is: Where will the vangels go next? Any suggestions?

What many people don't realize is that the first of my Cajun books started with Lucien LeDeux's story in *The Love Potion*, a novel that was recently reissued by HarperCollins and continues with seven other Cajun and Jinx novels. It won't be the last of the Cajun contemporary books, but in the meantime, I thought readers would like to know what that outrageous Tante Lulu is up to these days.

There will be more vangel books coming. After all, there are four more Sigurdsson brothers left with stories to tell. Plus, Zebulan, the good demon, intrigues me with his tragic past. Don't you think he would make a good hero?

But before I start a fourth vangel book, I'm back to Viking Series I and a straight historical romance, titled *The Pirate Bride*. In this case, the hero is a Viking (Thork, son of Tykir) and the heroine is the pirate. Medana kidnaps Thork and some of his Norse buddies, but when she sends a ransom note to Thork's father, the old man tells her, "Keep him!" All the books in Viking Series I have been reissued in both print and e-book format by Harper-Collins, including: *The Reluctant Viking*, *The Outlaw Viking*, *The Tarnished Lady*, *The Bewitched Viking*, *The Blue Viking*, *My Fair Viking*, *A Tale of Two Vikings*, leading up to new releases, *Viking in Love*, *The Viking Takes a Knight*, and *The Norse King's Daughter*. All of these books are available new.

And don't forget the reissue coming up soon of *Frankly, My Dear*, a prizewinning favorite book of mine, to be followed by the reissue of its sequel, *Sweeter Savage Love*, featuring Etienne Baptiste, my all-time favorite hero. Who can resist a tortured hero (a former prisoner of war) with a sense of humor?

Some fans have asked why I keep changing genres: contemporary, historical, time travel, Vikings, Navy SEALs, Cajuns, and now vampire angels? Well, even as a reader, I like variety once in a while. And the market tastes change from time to time; in other words, I write what will sell. Keep in mind, though, that there is a common theme in all my books, regardless of the genre, and that is humor. Plus a little sizzle on the side (okay, a lot) . . . lagniappe, as Tante Lulu would say.

If you want to know what it's really like at Angola Prison, read these books, and be prepared, it's not a pretty picture: Wilbert Rideau's *In the Place of Justice: A Story of Punishment and Deliverance*; Daniel Bergner's *God of the Rodeo: The Quest for Redemption in Louisiana's Angola Prison*; or Dennis Shere's *Cain's Redemption*.

Keep a lookout for the novella *Xmas in Transylvania* that will be out at the end of 2013 and please keep checking my website, www.sandrahill.net, or my Facebook page, SandrHillauthor, for more details on all my books and continually changing news. Signed bookplates are available for any or all books by sending an SASE to Sandra Hill, PO Box 604, State College, PA 16804.

As always, I wish you smiles in your reading.

Sandra Hill

Glossary

Adhan—Call to prayer.

Allée—Walkway or road lined with trees or shrubs, especially noted in Old South plantations.

A-Viking—A Norse practice of sailing away to other countries for the purpose of looting, settlement, or mere adventure; could be for a period of several months or for years at a time.

Beignet—A deep-fried donut sprinkled with sugar, a New Orleans favorite.

Berserker—An ancient Norse warrior who fought in a frenzied rage during battle.

Birka—Viking age market town where Sweden is now located.

Boudin—Type of Cajun sausage.

Braies—Slim pants worn by men.

Brynja—Flexible chain mail shirt.

Ceorl (or churl)—Free peasant, person of the lowest classes.

Cher—Cajun male endearment, comparable to friend.

Chère—Cajun female endearment.

Cossack—Russian military warrior during czarist times.

Drukkinn **(various spellings)**—Drunk, in Old Norse.

Etoufée—A popular Cajun or Creole dish that usually features shellfish served over rice.

Eunuch—Castrated male.

Fais do do—A Cajun party down on the bayou.

Fjord—A narrow arm of the sea, often between high cliffs.

Frottir—A washboard-type percussion instrument worn over the shoulders.

Guano—Bat feces.

Haakai—High-level demon.

Hedeby—Viking age market town where Germany now stands.

Hordling—Lower-level demon.

Houri—Beautiful woman, often associated with a harem.

Housecarls—Troops assigned to a king's or lord's household on a longtime, sometimes permanent, basis.

Imps—Lower-level demons, foot soldiers so to speak.

Jarl—High-ranking Norseman similar to an English earl or wealthy landowner, could also be a chieftain or minor king.

Joie de vivre—Joy of life.

Jorvik—Viking age name for York in Britain.

Karl—High-level Norse nobleman, below a jarl or earl.

Keep—House, usually the manor house or main building for housing the owners of the estate.

Kudzu—A trailing vine native to Japan that has gone wild in the Southeastern U.S., now covering roughly seven million acres, it grows about one foot per day.

Lagniappe—A small gift given by merchants at the time of purchase, like a thirteenth donut when ordering a dozen.

Longships—Narrow, open water-going vessels with oars and square sails, perfected by Viking shipbuilders, noted for their speed and ability to ride in both shallow waters and deep oceans.

Lucifer/Satan—The fallen angel Lucifer became known as the demon Satan.

Lucipires/Lucies—Demon vampires.

Mais oui—But yes.

Mead—Fermented honey and water.

Muezzin—Person at the mosque who leads the call to prayer.

Mungs—Type of demon, below the haakai in status, often very large and oozing slime or mung.

Patois—Nonstandard language, can refer to pidgins, Creoles, dialects, or other forms of native or local speech.

Pirogue (pronounced *pee-row*)—Type of bayou canoe.

Po' boy—A New Orleans favorite type of submarine made on a baguette-type loaf, featuring meat or fried fish, often topped with an olive spread.

Praline—A sweet Creole candy.

PT—Physical training.

SEAL—Sea, Air, and Land.

Sennight—One week.

Seraphim—High-ranking angel.

Skald—Poet or storyteller.

Stasis—State of inactivity, rather like being frozen in place.

Taliban—Islamic military and political organization that rules large parts of Afghanistan.

Tangos—Bad guys, terrorists.

Teletransport—Transfer of matter from one point to another without traversing physical space.

Thor—God of war.

Thrall—Slave.

Traiteur—A folk healer, often Cajun or Creole.

Trusty/trusties (various spelling)—Inmates who are given special privileges.

Valhalla—Hall of the slain, Odin's magnificent hall in Asgard.

Vangels—Viking vampire angels.

Varangian—Viking guardsmen who served the Byzantine emperor from the tenth to the fourteenth century.

VIK—The seven brothers who head the vangels.

WEALS—Acronym for Women on Earth, Air, Land, and Sea.

Zydeco—Type of Cajun music.

Keep reading for
an excerpt from

THE PIRATE BRIDE

The newest sexy and hilarious
historical romance from
Sandra Hill

Available Fall 2013
from Avon Books

When he was bad, he was very bad. When he was good, he was still bad ...

Thork Tykirsson sat in a bustling tavern in the trading town of Hedeby, brooding.

He'd tupped the ale barrel. A mere once.

He'd done another type of tupping. Once.

He'd engaged in an alehouse brawl. Once.

He'd told a ribald joke. Once.

He'd tossed dice for a vast amount of coins. Once.

Ho-hum.

His virtuous behavior—*Bloody hell! Who ever heard of a virtuous Viking?*—followed on his having quit pirating a year ago when that evil Saxon king Edgar had finally gone to his eternal reward. Everyone knew that Vikings were pirates of a sort. Not him anymore.

He could go a-Viking, he supposed. A respectable occupation that he enjoyed on occasion. He freely admitted to having plundered a monastery or two for gold chalices or silver-chased crucifixes. How many chalices does one church need anyhow? You could say Vikings did the priests a favor, helping them avoid the sin of greed. And the hated Saxons deserved everything a Viking Norsemen sent their way. Same went for those arrogant Scots and the foppish men of Frankland. But, truth to tell, he had more than enough treasure.

The most appalling thing was that Thork was actually considering marriage, something he'd avoided with distaste for years. In fact, he had already made a preliminary offer to Jarl Ingolf Bersson for his daughter Berla. He planned to set sail in the morning for the Norselands and his father's estate at Dragonstead, where he had not been nigh onto five years now. Barring unforeseen circumstances, he would return before winter, when a final betrothal agreement could be made. That should please his father.

But married? Me? I will become just like every other man I know who succumbs to marital pressure. Wed locked and land locked. No doubt I will soon have baby drool on my best tunic, doing my wife's bidding like a giant lapdog.

"Bor-ing . . . I've become bor-ing," Thork exclaimed aloud with horror. "I was once deemed the wildest Viking to ride a longship, a wordfame I worked good and well to earn, and now . . ." He shuddered. " . . . I am becoming a weak-sapped, sorry excuse for a Norseman, and I haven't even wed yet. What will become of me?"

"Methinks you are being too hard on yourself," said Bolthor, once a fierce warrior, now an aging skald noted for his big heart and bad poems. "Your father will be proud of you, and that counts for more than a bit of boredom."

And that was the heart of the problem: his estrangement from his sire, Tykir Thorksson, and his determination to restore himself in the old man's good favor. At just the thought of his father, Thork instinctively tugged on the silver thunderbolt earring that hung from one of his ears. It had belonged to his father, and his father's father before him. There had been many a time in the past ten years when his father would have liked to take it back . . . if he could catch him.

Just then, there was a commotion at the door.

"The crew is missing," Alrek, the clumsiest Viking alive, said breathlessly as he rushed into the alehouse and tripped on some object hidden in the rushes, almost landing in Thork's lap.

"What crew?" Thork asked.

"Your crew."

Thork crossed his eyes with impatience. "The crew of *which* ship?" He'd brought three longships here to the trading town of Hedeby to sell the amber he'd harvested in the Baltics these many months. And wasn't that respectable occupation yet another sign of dullness growing in him like a blister on a Saxon's arse?

"Oh." Alrek blushed. "*Swift Serpent.*"

Thork's smallest, but one of his favorite vessels. "Are you saying all of the *Serpent*'s seamen are missing?" That would mean about sixty rowers.

"Good gods, nay!" Alrek was momentarily distracted by the serving maid who smiled at him as she poured ale into the horn he lifted off the loop on his belt, making sure Alrek got a good look at her mostly exposed bosoms. Alrek blinked several times . . . with amazement, no doubt. It *was* a voluptuous view, although the maid's hand shook nervously as she refilled his and Bolthor's horns, as well. Odd that a tavern maid, dressed to entice, would be so nervous.

But that was neither here nor there.

Alrek shook his head to clear it and turned his attention back to Thork. "Only a half dozen."

"Only a half dozen," Thork repeated. "Alrek, the men

are no doubt off somewhere wenching, or they are too *drukkinn* to walk back yet."

"But you told everyone to be on board by midnight so that we could set sail at dawn," Alrek persisted.

Bolthor jerked with surprise as the serving maid trailed a fingertip over his shoulders as she walked away. Not many women approached the old man, who had seen more than fifty winters, when there were younger, more comely men about. Not to mention the black eye patch over his one eyeless socket, due to an injury in the Battle of Ripon many years past. But then Bolthor said, "Alrek, Alrek, Alrek. When will you learn? A Viking man does not take well to orders, especially when bedsport is available."

Thork agreed. "The men will be there in good time, or left behind to find their own way home."

Alrek shook his head vigorously, causing ale to slosh over the lip of his horn. "Nay. Something is amiss, I tell you. There are strange people about Hedeby this night."

"There are always strange people in Hedeby," Bolthor remarked. "Why, I recall the time there was an archer from Ireland who could shoot three arrows at one time. Or the man who could touch his eyebrows with his tongue. And then there was—"

"Not that kind of strange. These men I see skulking about . . . they are small in stature and curved in the wrong places. Like those two over there staring at us."

Thork and Bolthor both turned to see the two men leaning against the wall, wooden cups in their hands. They were, indeed, shorter than average, and they had hips like a woman, if the tunics that covered them down to their knees over tight braies were any indication.

"By the runes! They must be sodomites," Bolthor declared.

"Sodomites?" Thork exclaimed.

"Yea. Sodomites are men who prefer men to women."

"I know what a sodomite is. One of my best friends was . . . never mind!" Thork said, waving a hand dismissively. "Alrek, surely you are not saying there are vast numbers of man-lovers about this night, waiting to prey on innocent seamen. As far as I know, they seek like-minded males."

"They are not all like those two. Some are taller. Some wider. But they are shifty-eyed and move in a sly manner. And there were a goodly number near *Swift Serpent*."

Alrek ever was fanciful, and a worrier, besides. But Thork did not want to offend the man. "Well, best we get back to the ship ourselves. In truth, I am beginning to feel a bit shaky," Thork confessed, downing the rest of his ale, and attaching the horn to his belt.

Bolthor did likewise, swaying on his feet as he stood. Being the giant he was, no one wanted to be near when he fell, so Thork took him by the elbow and steered him toward the door. He noticed with seeming irrelevance that the two "sodomites" were gone.

Alrek followed behind them, muttering something about the bitter aftertaste in his mouth from the ale.

Most of the stalls were closed for the night as they made their way slowly along the raised board walkways that crisscrossed the well-ordered market town. Thork had erected his own stall earlier that day and sold all the amber he'd brought to market, saving one large, pale yellow stone with a tiny bumblebee inside to gift his mother, Lady Alinor.

Ahead he could see the palisaded harbor with the earthen ramparts that rose over Hedeby in a half circle. They approached one of two gates in the wall that regulated traffic in and out of the city. Hedeby was situated at the crossroads of Slien Fjord and the Baltic Sea, from whence they'd come after harvesting the amber. In the daytime, it was a bustling center for commerce because of its strategic position linking trade routes of eastern empires with the west . . . the Norselands, Frankland, and Britain.

As they turned a corner, Bolthor lurched for a hitching post outside a stable, bent over, and began to heave the contents of his stomach over the side into a muddy trench. Thork leaned against the railing for support, his knees suddenly feeling weak as butter. Alrek had both hands on his stomach and was groaning at the pain.

Suddenly, Thork felt a hard blow to the back of his head. Even as he fell, he saw that Bolthor and Alrek were following his path to the ground, Bolthor with a loud thud that broke a few planks.

It was then that Thork gazed up woozily to see that they were surrounded by a *hird* of little men led by the two from the tavern.

They seemed to be discussing him, Bolthor, and Alrek, as if they were goods.

"How are we ever going to get them back to the ship?"
Ship? What ship?

"I forgot. *Pirate Lady* is at the far, far end of the wharf."

Pirate Lady? *What kind of name is that for a ship? Ah, she must mean* Pirate's Lady. *Still, pirate? I do not like the sound of that.*

"Drag them, I suppose."
Do not dare!

"Where's a horse when you need one? Ha, ha, ha!"
I'll give you a horse, you misbegotten dwarf of a man! Pirate or not, pirate's whore or not, when I get up, you will regret your sorry jests.

"Wrap them in ells of sailcloth and lift them up onto yon wagon. If anyone asks, we can say that they are graybeards who died of old age, and we are carrying them to the funeral pyres."

I am not a graybeard. I am only twenty and eight.

"I get the big one. Think of the bairns I could have with his seed."

Bairns? How do they expect to carry babes in their wombs if they have no wombs?

"The clumsy one is adorable. Did you notice his dimple?"

What about me? Thork thought, then immediately chastised himself for caring.

"We'll draw lots when we get back to the island."

Island? Uh-oh!

Just before he blacked out, totally, Thork realized something important. The men's voices sounded female. Very female.

Oh good gods! They were being taken captive. *By women!*

The women went a-Viking . . . a different kind of a-Viking . . .

Medana Elsadottir, best known as the Sea Scourge, had never intended to become a pirate. In fact, when she'd left . . . rather, *escaped* . . . her home in Rognvald, land of the Danes, ten years ago, she'd never even heard of female pirates.

And she'd certainly never intended to take other women with her, nor continue to gather recruits to her unlikely *hird* of sea soldiers. Her followers now numbered an amazing one hundred and ninety-three, including nineteen children ranging from ages one to eight. They lived—women only, except for the six boys—on a hidden, mountainous island named Thrudr, or Strength, appropriately named because that's exactly what each and every one of them had gained with their independence.

Their stronghold was accessible by a narrow landmass that connected a smaller, visible island to the hidden caves in Thrudr, but only when the tide was down once a day.

"I could scarce recognize you in that disguise, Medana," Agnis the Weaver said. "'Tis much better than the last visit when you pretended to be a leper."

They both laughed at the memory. It had taken Medana days to soak off the false pustules made of mud and sand and tree sap.

On this trip to Hedeby, Medana was dressed as a nun, complete with a simple brown homespun gown and veil over a tightly bound white wimple. The only thing showing that might identify her as the sister of three powerful, greedy Norse chieftains were her thick blond brows, violet eyes, and bruised-looking, overly lush mouth, a trait of men and women alike in the line of Skjold, the legendary first king of all the Danes. But it had been ten years since she was sixteen years old and had last seen her evil siblings; they would scarce recognize the woman she'd become, even without a disguise. "It's hotter than the depths of Muspell, though. Being a nun in July was not my best idea, but I'll be back on the ship soon and change into my tunic and braies," Medana remarked as they sat at a table in Agnis's small house behind the permanent merchant stall they maintained in the market town. The walls were adorned with the products of Agnis's gift for colored patterns in the cloth she wove on the large loom in the back corner. The room was perfumed with the sweet scent of dried herbs hanging from the ceiling rafters . . . lavender, verbena, and such.

"We should make a good profit on all the goods you brought this time," Agnis remarked as she removed the wooden platters from the table. They'd just finished a simple meal of cold slices of roast venison, hard cheese, manchet bread, and weak wine. On the way to the low chest that held a wooden pail of dishwater, she patted the head of her nine-year-old son, Egil, who was carding wool in the corner.

Even though Agnis resided here in Hedeby and did in fact weave and sell fine wool cloth, she was also Thrudr's agent, offering all the products produced or harvested on the rough, mountainous island . . . furs, honey, leather shoes and belts, soapstone pots and candles, wooden bowls and spoons, bone combs and such. A pregnant Agnis had been among the five women with Medana when first she'd fled Stormgard all those years ago. They'd barely survived that first winter. And the next two years hadn't been very easy, either, as more and more women somehow found their way to their hidden sanctuary. Now, they were independent and self-sufficient, but there were things they needed that they could not grow, catch, or make. Like grains, spices, metal weapons and implements, rope, needles, a bull to serve their milch cows, and vegetables they were unable to grow in their northern region.

"Your visit is short this time," Agnis said, topping off Medana's cup of wine.

"Yea, a necessity. Our old bull Magnus died, and two of our cows are about to go into heat. We needed to buy a young bull, which I did, and get it back home to do . . . his duty."

Agnis laughed. "The things a woman must do!"

"As for the short visit, believe you me, my women are full of complaints. This is their time for"—she arched her brows meaningfully at Agnis—"you know."

"Same as the cows," Agnis jested, laughing, then glanced toward her son to make sure he wasn't listening. Egil had put aside his carding tools and was playing with a pet cat.

"Exactly!"

"Why are you not out there enjoying yourself?" Agnis asked, waving her hand to indicate the town.

"That is not my idea of enjoyment," Medana said, not after the experience that led to her departure from Stormgard. "But I do not begrudge my women their bedsport, even if their time is limited."

"Hopefully, some of the man seed will take root," Agnis said.

"Pray Frigg it does." While they did not have men at Thrudr since they were not willing to trust their lives to the brutish actions of the male species, they still yearned for one thing that only men could provide. And that one thing wasn't just sex. It was children. After any trip a-Viking, or a-trading, there was always at least one woman who found herself breeding. Once, an amazing three got with child on a trip to Kauptang, no doubt due to their extended stay when their longship took on water and had to be dry-docked for repairs.

Medana and her crew had gone a-pirating on their way to Hedeby, and their plunder had been exceptionally tradeable. That on top of the goods they'd produced at home and brought to market should mean a good year for the women back at Thrudr. No gnawing on roots and moldy bread as they had the first winter in exile when there had been no meat or stored vegetables for the cook fire.

Medana and Agnis talked long into the evening, dividing the profits of this latest endeavor, discussing plans for the future, and relating news of the people they both knew.

"Is Gregor still pursuing you?" Medana teased.

"Always. The man does not give up." Agnis grinned. 'Twas clear to one and all that Agnis had a fondness for the Russian goldsmith who visited the trading center several times a year.

"Mayhap you will give in one of these days?" Medana suggested.

Agnis shrugged. "Mayhap, but then I am enjoying the gifts he brings me." She lifted the neckline of her gown to show Medana a fine gold chain. "How is Olga doing?"

"She rules the kitchens like a hardened warrior." Olga was Agnis's aunt, who'd come to them two years past when her husband died.

Agnis shared some stories about her aunt that had them both laughing, but then she turned serious. "Your brother Sigurd was here two sennights ago." At the look of concern on Medana's face, Agnis immediately added, "I had Bessie take over the stall for me." Bessie was the shortened name for Beatrix, a Saxon holder of a nearby pottery shed. "I am certain he did not see me."

Medana let out a breath she hadn't realized she was holding in. She had reason to fear her brothers, even after all these years and what she had done to thwart their plans, but Agnis also had cause to be wary. Sigurd was Egil's father. If the child of his loins had been a daughter, Sigurd would not care, but a son, now that would be a different matter. Furthermore, he would be angered at Agnis, a thrall, leaving without his permission.

It was late when Medana returned to *Pirate Lady*, the longship anchored at the far end of the wharf. A guardswoman standing at the rail greeted her with a hearty "Who goes there?" It was Elida, Thrudr's mistress of threads, who was in charge of all sheep shearing, spinning, weaving, and clothes making. Everyone on the island had a title for the numerous jobs needed for them to subsist: Mistress of hunt, fish, and fowl. Mistress of farming. Mistress of animal care. Mistress of cooking. Mistress of laundry. In fact, there were so many titles these days, it had become a matter of jest, especially when someone had to be called mistress of the privy.

With a smile, Medana replied, " 'Tis me. Chieftain-ess Medana." She smiled even wider at the title, which had been assigned to her as a sign of deference.

After the first few years on the island, the women felt the need for some order of authority, so they'd modeled themselves on the male-dominated Norse society. High king or chieftain; jarl, which was comparable to an English earl; karl; ceorls; and thralls. Thus, jarl-ess, karl-ess, and ceorl-ess. The five members of Medana's council were considered jarl-esses. There were no thralls; slavery being forbidden, even for captives. Not that they'd ever taken captives. "Has everyone returned?" Medana asked.

Elida nodded, but she shifted her eyes hither and yon, never quite meeting Medana's gaze. She was nervous for some reason. Must be because this was the first time she'd been given such responsibility. A talented weaver, Elida had requested a chance to prove her worth as an archer in Medana's personal guard. Already Elida's small hands were calloused and scratched, and, even with practice, the slim woman couldn't hit a Saxon boar from three paces. It would take sennights for the ointments of her healer, Liv, to restore Elida's skin to the point where she could once again handle fine wool. Medana doubted that Elida would be going a-Viking again.

Moving on toward her small quarters, Medana inquired politely of Bergdis, one of her rowers, "Did you find a man to mate with this eve?"

Bergdis, who was Mistress of buildings and woodworking back home, rolled her wide shoulders—all of the rowers were well-muscled on their upper bodies to handle the hard exercise required to pull oars—before replying, "Yea, I did. But only once. There was no time for more."

It must have been an energetic mating because Bergdis's tunic was lopsided, half on and half off one shoulder, and the two braids that she normally wore to keep her frizzy red hair off her face had come undone. Her thick eyebrows were more grizzly than usual. Pity the man she'd set her eyes on this night.

That was unkind, Medana immediately chastised herself. Bergdis was a good woman who'd overcome huge tragedy in her former life. She deserved every reward that came her way, especially if it was a child, please gods.

Medana shrugged. Her crew knew ahead of time that this visit to Hedeby was destined to be short. If they made good speed, they might go a-Viking on the way home, but they must be careful not to visit those places they'd plundered on the way here. Stealth was an important tactic for female pirates, not having the strength and manpower of their male counterparts.

She noticed that Bergdis seemed nervous, too, rubbing the palms of her hands together. "Is something amiss?" Medana asked.

"Nay. Why would you ask me that? I've done nothing wrong."

Bergdis's defensive response startled Medana. "It was only a question. I wasn't accusing you of anything."

Just then, there was a pounding noise coming from below in the hold of the longship. Bang, bang, bang! Like a booted foot kicking wood. "What is that?"

"Must be the bull," both women said.

"I hope it does no damage. Mayhap I should go down and make sure the creature is tied securely. I wouldn't want him hurt. After all, his services are sorely needed. I swear Helga is in as much need of a man as many of you." Helga was one of their most fertile cows.

Neither of the women smiled at Medana's jest.

Her rudder master, Solveig, stepped up from behind her and said, "Not to worry. I will take care of the matter. You know I have a way with animals."

That was the first time Medana had ever heard Solveig

had a way with animals, seeing as how she was Mistress of shipwrighting, but Medana was not about to argue the point now.

Her chief housecarl, Mistress of military, Gudron, a huge warrior of a woman who could heft a heavy broadsword with the best of men, handed her a wooden goblet. "Have a drink of ale to toast our voyage home." Medana noticed that Gudron had crystals twisted in the blonde war braids that framed her square face. No doubt she'd been man hunting this evening, like many of the others.

That was nice of Gudron, even if the ale did taste a bit sour. After taking a few sips, Medana handed the cup back to her. She yawned widely then. The two cups of wine, watered down at that, plus these new sips of ale, shouldn't be affecting her so. "I am off to bed for a few hours' sleep. We set sail at daybreak."

Whether it was the wine and ale or the sway of the ship or just exhaustion, Medana slept soundly and did not awaken until the ship was already under way. Which was odd. Her crew had always waited for her orders before setting sail in the past.

It was later, when they were already too far out to sea to turn around, that Medana learned what the noisy cargo was that they carried below. And it was no bull.

Next month, don't miss these exciting
new love stories only from
Avon Books

Lord of Wicked Intentions by Lorraine Heath

Lord Rafe Easton never thought he'd want a companion,
but when he sees Miss Evelyn Chambers—an earl's
illegitimate daughter—he's determined to have her, if
only as his mistress. For Evelyn, circumstance gives her
little choice but to accept the lord's indecent proposal. But
when dark discoveries threaten to destroy them both,
what they find in one another may be enough to save
them both . . .

Half Moon Hill by Toni Blake

A rugged loner and ex-biker-gang member, Duke Dawson
is looking for some peace and quiet in the little town of
Destiny, Ohio. But when Anna Romo comes wandering
through his woods and into his cabin, she completely
shakes his world. Their passion is palpable—but can she
convince a man who has turned his back on life to take the
biggest leap of faith of all and fall in love?

One for the Wicked by Karina Cooper

Dr. Kayleigh Lauderdale possesses the only cure for what's
killing the city's witches. Desperate to acquire it, the
resistance sends Shawn Lowe to retrieve it. He never
planned on saving or *wanting* anyone—least of all, the
daughter of his sworn enemy. But when the world turns
upside down, it will take everything Kayleigh and Shawn
have to hold on . . . to life, to hope, and to each other.

Give in to your Impulses!

These unforgettable stories only take a second to buy and give you hours of reading pleasure!

Go to *www.AvonImpulse.com* and see what we
have to offer.

Available wherever e-books are sold.

AVONIMPULSE